DEADLY AIM

Boyd calculated that they were about a half mile off when he squeezed off the first shot. The booming echo had barely begun to reverberate when the burly man in the center of the pack went flipping out of the saddle, rising higher than the head of his horse with the impact of the bullet. In an instant, Boyd had thrown back the breech and rammed in another shell. . . .

Boyd already had his second target dead in his sights. He pulled the trigger, squeezing the rifle lovingly as he did. As the gun thundered in his hands, he saw his target suddenly go out of his saddle as if plucked by a giant hand, but he had no time to savor the kill. He could hear splashing in the water behind him. . . .

McMASTERS

LEE MORGAN

JOVE BOOKS, NEW YORK

MCMASTERS

A Jove Book / published by arrangement with
the author

PRINTING HISTORY
Jove edition / June 1995

ISBN: 0-515-11632-7

A JOVE BOOK®
Jove Books are published by The Berkley Publishing Group,
200 Madison Avenue, New York, New York 10016.
JOVE and the "J" design are trademarks
belonging to Jove Publications, Inc.

PRINTED IN THE UNITED STATES OF AMERICA

10 9 8 7 6 5 4 3 2 1

One

It was maybe the saving of him that he went to his brother in Oklahoma City, but it had to be recognized that he didn't so much go to his brother as he found himself in Oklahoma City and then dimly realized that his brother Warren lived there. He wasn't in very good shape. He'd been wandering in a drunken haze and a daze of despair for so long that he wasn't certain of anything. All he could ever see clearly were those dancing flames and the screams that came every night in his ears. He could dull them a little with whiskey, but not enough to shut them out completely.

He guessed he'd been wandering for three months or better. Not that he cared. It could have been a year for all it mattered to him. He didn't care about anything or anyone, and certainly not himself. All he could remember was a succession of saloons and an occasional whorehouse and a fight now and then and a dim memory of lots of gunfire.

His name was Boyd McMasters, and in that year of 1889, he was twenty-eight years old, an ex-sheriff, a widower, and a man who didn't consider himself as having a dime's worth of reasons for living.

It was almost on a whim that he went to see his brother.

He knew where Warren's office was because he'd been there before. His brother was the vice president of the Cattleman's Association and their home office was in Oklahoma City, where it occupied all floors of a grand, three-story brick building on the Enid Road, close to the railroad depot toward the edge of town.

He was conscious of the stares he drew as he opened the door and stepped into the outer office. He could see the clerks and men wearing green visors looking up and staring, but he didn't much care. He knew he looked trail-worn and haggard. His hair was shaggy, his clothes were wrinkled and dirty, and he hadn't shaved in several days. He'd lost enough weight that his clothes kind of hung on him, but when you drink whiskey all day and night, you don't have much of an appetite and you tend to lose weight.

He started down an aisle toward the back, where he knew Warren's private office was located. He had his eyes fixed on the door, and was making his way with deliberation when his path was suddenly blocked by a lady with bluish-white hair and a pencil in her hand. She asked politely, but firmly, if she could help him.

He frowned at her for a moment. "What did you have in mind? I could use a drink; that would be a help."

She got a very stern look on her prim face and said, "I mean, do you have any business in here? This is the Cattleman's Association as it says clearly on the sign outside. We don't sell ardent spirits here."

He said, "Here to see my brother, Warren McMasters. He in?"

She looked at him disbelievingly. "You are Mr. McMasters' brother?"

"My name's Boyd," he said. "Warren will remember."

She looked him up and down for a moment, still not certain. She pointed to the floor with her pencil. "You wait right here. I'll go and see if he can see you."

"Oh, he'll see me. We were raised together. Know each other pretty good."

Which was not exactly the truth, but then he didn't think the lady would be all that interested, even if she had stayed to listen. The truth was that Warren had had a large hand in raising Boyd. When their father had been hooked to death by a Jersey milk cow, Warren, who was twelve years Boyd's senior, had taken over as man of the house and had seen over Boyd and his two sisters. They hadn't exactly been raised together but more in sequence, like a straight with Warren being the high card.

Boyd stood there patiently, aware of the interest he was drawing from the clerks and office workers who had overheard his claim to be Warren's brother. He reckoned he might be doing Warren's reputation a disservice, but he figured his brother could manage it. Warren had always been able to manage everything, all the way from keeping their mother going, to finding a way to see that everyone not only got fed, but also got the occasional treat or sweet. Warren was a good man, Boyd thought, and it was a damn shame the world was not made up of more of his kind. Unhappily, it wasn't.

Warren came bursting out of his office, shoving the prim-faced lady in front of him out of the way, his eyes searching. When they lit on Boyd, his expression changed to one of distress and sadness, but that didn't stop him from coming quickly to his brother and grasping his hand and putting an arm around Boyd's shoulder. Warren said, "Boyd, where the hell have you been? You've nearly worried me to death."

Warren stepped back and looked at Boyd. He said in his brusque, matter-of-fact way, "Hell, you look like they just dug you up and not a minute too soon. When did you last have a bath? Or a meal, for that matter?''

Boyd stood there, trying to smile. He was glad to see his brother, but not like he would have been in other years. At six-one, Boyd was a couple of inches taller than his brother, but Warren, even in Boyd's good times, had always been heavier, burlier. Now, with Boyd almost twenty pounds under his usual weight of 180 pounds, the difference was very marked. Worse was the drawn, haggard look on Boyd's face that seemed to draw them closer together in age. Boyd had light, sandy hair and light brown eyes, but now his hair was dark with dirt and his eyes were simply dead.

Warren suddenly seemed to become aware of the clerks who had stopped working and were staring at them. He swept his eyes around the outer office and the clerks hastily returned to their business. He clapped Boyd on the back and said, ''Come on, boy; let's go in my office. I've got a bottle of good corn whiskey. We'll have a drink.''

Boyd smiled slightly with his dead eyes. ''Or two, or three.''

They sat in Warren's office. Warren was wearing a tweed business suit with a foulard tie and a soft collar and a big gold watch chain stretched across his vest. Boyd was slumped in a chair across from him, his hat in one hand, his other full with a glass of whiskey. Warren waited until his younger brother had downed half the glass before he said softly, ''Boyd, I can't say as I know how you feel because I don't. But I can't stand by and let you go down a hole in the ground either. There hasn't been a day that has passed since the news reached me that I haven't had men hunting you. Where in hell have you been?''

Boyd looked down at the floor and shook his head. ''I don't know, Warren. I honest to God don't know.'' He lifted his half-full glass. ''Part of it is due to this, I reckon, but part of it is just because my brain don't want to think. When it does, I start to think about . . ." He stopped and shook his head as if to rid himself of an unwanted attachment.

Warren sat quietly waiting. When it appeared that Boyd was not going to speak further, he said, "It seemed like you just fell off the face of the earth. Your mayor got word to me as quick as folks realized what had happened. I got to Pecos as fast as I could, but you were long gone. Boyd, you never even took your money out of the bank. What the hell have you been living on?"

Boyd shook his head again. "I don't know. I had a string of horses with me. I guess I sold a few."

"There's been men looking for you all over the country. Once it was all figured out, we could pretty well put together what had happened. I know it's no consolation, but you done the country a service when you wiped out the Winslows. You left tracks when you ran them down in the Davis Mountains. I guess you know that you killed them all."

Boyd lifted his head and held out his glass. Without a word, Warren again poured it full. He looked into Boyd's eyes. There was nothing there.

Warren said, "There was a raft of reward money for the Winslows, over five thousand dollars all rounded up. All you have to do is collect it."

Boyd gave his head that same quick shake as if something was buzzing around him. He said softly, "Warren, I don't want to talk about it. I just came to see you for an hour or so and then I'll be moving on."

Warren leaned forward and stretched a hand across his desk. He said softly, "Little brother, I know that, right now, you don't think you'll ever care again about anything, and maybe you won't. But Boyd, you at least got to give it a chance. Hannah would want that."

At the mention of his dead wife's name, Boyd flinched as

if he'd been struck in the face. He said sharply, "Don't! Don't ever!"

"Listen, Boyd. I ain't going to let you give up. You're my brother, my blood. I had a hand in your upbringing. I can't watch you crawl off and die. I've got to try and help you, even if you don't want me to. Nothing like that has ever happened to me, so I can't say that I know how you feel. You've been tried about as hard as a body can be tested. I ain't even going to pretend to know how you hurt inside, but letting go and falling apart is not the answer. You can't end up this way, Boyd. I know you don't want me to, but I've got to say it again. You can't do this to Hannah's memory!"

The only response from Boyd was a sharp intake of his breath as if he'd been punched in the stomach. After a moment, he raised his full glass and almost drained it.

Looking at his brother with worried eyes, Warren said, "First thing we have to do is to get out to my house and get you cleaned up and let Muriel get some groceries in you."

Boyd shook his head quickly. For a second, he almost looked frightened. "I can't do that, Warren. I can't be around you and Muriel and your children."

"What not? For God's sake, we're your family."

Boyd looked at something far away. "Because you're happy and I can't be around happy folks. I can't be around a family like yours. The only company I can stand right now is those that are as miserable as me."

Warren was a long time in replying. He heaved a sigh and said, "Maybe I understand it and maybe I don't. I know I can't force you to do anything you ain't a mind of, never could, but I can't let you walk out of here wasting away. I'll have you thrown in jail first, Boyd."

Boyd looked up and half smiled. It changed his face. His

brother could almost see the happy, handsome young man who'd once lived there.

Warren asked, "That strike you as funny?"

"No, I just thought it was the kindest thing anybody has said to me for a while. But I still can't go to your house. I need to move on, Warren; I have to keep moving. Somehow it keeps me from thinking too much."

There was frustration in his voice when Warren said, "Goddammit, Boyd. Don't you want to get back on your feet?"

A flicker of a smile passed over Boyd's face. "How do you know I ain't the way I want to be, Warren? How do you know I ain't satisfied as I am now?"

"Well, goddammit, because you look like a scarecrow and you drag around like you're half dead and you are about one clod of dirt short of filthy. If nothing else, will you let me try and get you healthy again? Get you eating and built back up? Get that whiskey out of your system?"

Boyd raised his glass. "I can't get along without this, Warren. You can't cut me off from this; I couldn't take it."

His brother said with some exasperation, "Hell, I didn't mean for you to go bone dry. I just meant for you to occasionally have something in your hand besides a glass or a bottle, like a fork and a knife. Boyd, I can't stand to see you like this. Goddammit, if you won't do it for yourself or anyone else, do it for me. I'm begging you, get yourself back up the ladder a little and see how you feel. If you don't like it, fine. I'll give you some money and a case of whiskey and send you on your way. But hell, boy, I've got to have my try. Give me that, Boyd. I feel responsible for you."

Boyd studied his brother's agonized face for a moment. Surprisingly, he was touched. It amazed him that he could feel even that much. He said, "If that's what you want, Warren. Hell, I owe you more than I can ever pay back. But I still won't go to your house. I could stay at some hotel, some out-of-the-way place." He gave a fleeting smile again. "There ought to be some run-down joint full of out-of-luck bums like me."

Warren grimaced. "That's no good; you'd just be going to hell in one place instead of on the move. You need somebody to help you get over the hump. If you won't come out to us . . ." Warren thought for a moment, leaned back in his chair, put his hands to his face, and then came forward to lean his elbows on his desk. He said hesitantly, "There's a lady here, a widow lady, the wife of a man who used to work for me." He hesitated for a second as if looking for the right words. "I know her. She's a mighty fine person, but I wouldn't want it getting back to Muriel how well I know her. I think she'd take you in and take care of you. She makes her living how she can now."

Boyd said evenly, "You're not sending me to a whore, are you, Warren?"

His brother looked up sharply. "I said she was a lady, Boyd. Don't ever say anything like that about Martha again."

"I don't know too many ladies that take men in off the street."

"You're not just off the street; you're my brother. I think she'd do it if I ask her. Besides, it'll give me a chance to give her some money that I know damn good and well she can use." He reached in a drawer, took out a piece of blank paper, and then dipped a pen in an inkwell. For a moment he sat poised, trying to think what to write.

Boyd said gently, "Warren, I know you want to help, but you can't seem to get it through your head that I'm content the way I am. I don't want to get what you call back on my feet." He stopped and his voice almost broke. "Since . . . since what happened . . . I ain't got no will no more. It don't count, nothing does, and you've got to understand, Warren, I . . . I seen what happened to her. I . . ." He tried to go on but he couldn't. He quickly drained the whiskey in his glass.

His brother said, "Boyd, I told you I could not know how you feel. I don't reckon anybody could that didn't go through it. All I'm asking is that you pull yourself back together physically and then see what you think. I'm not asking for much of your time. A week will do. Hell, two or three days is enough if that's all you can take. Just give yourself a chance, Boyd."

Boyd shrugged. "If it'll please you," he said. He pointed with his chin at the note his brother was trying to write. "What in hell do you propose to write that lady so that one sight of me won't scare her off? How you going to describe me?"

Warren thought a second and then wadded up the sheet of paper. "You're right. Besides, you'd never find her house even if I could trust you to go looking for it. I keep a buggy here. I'll have it brought around and I'll take you to her."

"I got a horse."

"He look as bad as you?"

Boyd smiled slightly. "No, he don't drink."

Warren left the room for a moment to send for his buggy. It was still a pretty spring day, although dark clouds were building up in the west. When Warren returned, he and Boyd had one more drink.

Warren said, "I can't be around you much longer. I'm not used to drinking this much this early in the afternoon. I don't reckon there's much point in asking if you ate any lunch."

Boyd gave him a look.

Warren asked, "You still carrying that special revolver you rigged up?"

Boyd barely turned his head. "Feels like it's still there.

Haven't had an excuse to use it lately. The cartridges have probably turned green.''

A boy stuck his head in the door to tell Warren that his buggy was outside. They left the office, Boyd thoughtfully taking the half-full bottle of corn whiskey with him. They walked through the outer office. All of the clerks and other staff kept their heads down studiously over their work.

Warren tied Boyd's horse on the back of the buggy. The animal clearly had good bloodlines, but his coat was shaggy and his mane and tail were tangled and matted. His ribs weren't showing but, like Boyd, he could have done with some extra feed. Warren looked at the horse and shook his head. "Hell, Boyd, I can't believe you'd let a horse get in that shape. That the only one you got left?"

Boyd climbed up on the driving seat. "Yeah," he said listlessly. "You sure this ain't a cheerful woman?"

"Not so you would notice," Warren said. He joined his brother on the seat and took up the reins.

As they drove, Warren said, "Her name is Martha Blair. I figure she's a couple of years older than you, somewhere around thirty. She's not exactly what you'd call comely, but she's got a nice figure and a pleasant face and—"

Boyd interrupted quickly. "I don't care about that, Warren. In fact, I'm wondering if it's a very good idea for me to be around a woman. I mean, I ain't got no interest."

Warren said softly, "There won't be the slightest resemblance, Boyd. Martha Blair is a tall lady with brown hair. She's not going to remind you of anyone you don't want to think about."

"I still don't understand why she would take me in. Are you going to pay her that much money? I know I ain't no prize."

"She won't be doing it for the money. Martha is . . ." Warren stopped, searching for words. "Well, she's an uncommon sort of person. She's got a ton of heart and she doesn't just practice her religion during church hours on Sunday. But more than that, she knows suffering; she knows hurt. She knows what it feels like to lose somebody you figure you can't live without.'' He turned his head toward Boyd. ''You won't have to explain a thing to her. She'll never ask you a question. I know you think nobody has ever gone through what you have, but she's one that did. And she lived through it.''

''You said her husband used to work for you. Did she lose him?''

''Yes, and also her one-year-old son, both at the same time.''

Boyd didn't speak. He didn't want to know any details. He looked around as they drove. They were heading into the residential district of Oklahoma City. They passed through an area of fine, large houses near the center of town. As they drove farther along, the houses began to diminish in size and splendor. Finally, Warren wheeled the buggy horse around a corner and they were into a division of modest cottages set on bare, unadorned lots.

Warren said, ''She's got a nice comfortable house just up ahead. Got some cottonwoods that give shade in the afternoon. She's got a good well. Keeps a milk cow and a buggy horse so there will be a place to pen up your animal. I'll see about getting some grain and hay out here later on this afternoon.''

Boyd said dryly, ''Just be damned sure you see to sending me a good supply of whiskey. '' He held up the bottle he'd been sipping on. ''This is nearly dry and I'd reckon Mrs. Blair ain't going be keeping none around the house.''

''I'm also going to send out a supply of groceries as quick as I get back to town. I'll make sure they send out enough whiskey for you to wash in if you're a mind, but don't be too sure Martha doesn't have a pretty good supply already on hand. I'm not trying to halter you, Boyd. I know better.''

Without warning, he suddenly turned the buggy up a drive that led to a small house set off the road about a hundred yards. It was a neat, frame, whitewashed affair with a front porch that ran the length of the house. The look of it alarmed Boyd. It looked very similar to the house he'd built for Hannah before they married. He said with panic in his voice, ''I can't go in there, Warren! I can't! Turn around!''

But Warren kept steadily on. He said, as if he were reading Boyd's mind, ''It doesn't look a thing like your house, Boyd, any more than a hundred thousand others in this part of the country and Texas do. Look around here. Most of the houses look like this. This doesn't remind you of anything. Once you get inside you'll see how different it is. I've been to your house, Boyd, and I've been in this house. They ain't nothing alike. Take a drink.''

Boyd put the bottle to his lips and finished off the last of the liquor as Warren pulled the buggy up in front of the house, which was guarded by a dozen tall, leafy cottonwoods. He tied the reins to the whipstock and jumped down, saying, ''Let me go in and prepare Martha. Hell, maybe you've got nothing to worry about. Maybe she'll turn you away. Even a good woman has her limits, and you are damn near outside any circle I've ever seen drawn.''

His brother was gone what seemed to be an uncommonly long time to Boyd. Once, he was almost certain, he saw the curtains twitch at the windows of a front room, as if the lady of the house was giving him a good looking over.

Then Warren was back. While he was getting Boyd's saddlebags out of the back of the buggy, he said, ''She'll take you. You can stay an hour or a month; that's up to you.'' He untied Boyd's horse from the back of the buggy and stopped for a moment. ''Boyd, I didn't tell her much, mainly because I don't know much. I just gave her a general feel for the situation.''

Boyd said softly, looking down, ''I wish you hadn't done that.''

''Goddammit, Boyd, I had to give her some kind of explanation. People don't go around looking like walking corpses for no good reason. Hell, man, you've got to get over this. You've either got to face what has happened and try and make yourself another life or give up completely. If you're determined to die, why in hell don't you put a bullet through your brain and save us all a lot of bother watching you do it the slow way?''

Boyd raised his head. ''I've thought about it more than once. I can tell you what cold steel and gun oil tastes like.''

''But the point is you haven't done it, so somewhere down deep inside you, there's a part that doesn't want to give up.''

Boyd shrugged and shook his head. ''I don't know,'' he said.

''Well, go ahead and get down and go in the house.'' Warren eyed Boyd critically as he stepped off the buggy. ''Martha took a look at you from the window and she reckons it's better to buy you some new clothes than wash what you've got. That's if what's in here''—he patted the saddlebags—''is in the same shape as what you're wearing. I'm damned if I know what size to get you. You got an idea what you weigh?''

Boyd shook his head and turned to look at the house. The door had opened and a woman had come out to stand on the porch. She was tall, he could see that, and appeared to be wearing some kind of wraparound day dress. He couldn't make out her features, but he thought she looked kind.

Warren said, ''Well, I'll let the clerk at the mercantile figure it out. I'll take a set of jeans and a shirt with me and tell him to subtract about twenty pounds. You go on ahead and meet Martha and she'll get you settled. I'll put your horse up and then go on into town and get sent out what you'll need in the way of vittles and such.''

"Don't forget the whiskey."

"Hell, she's already got the bottle open. I don't reckon you can drink up her supply in the few hours it'll take to get the stuff sent out."

"Don't bet on it."

"Go on now, Boyd. Listen, she wants you to herself for a couple of days, so I won't be coming back until she sends for me."

Boyd's head whipped around. It was the quickest he had moved since Warren had laid eyes on him. "I don't much like the sound of that."

Warren grimaced. "She's got her reasons. She doesn't think you ought to be around anything or anyone that will remind you of, well, remind you of anything. At least not until you get settled down."

"Sounds like a load of bullshit to me."

"Well, whatever it is, you might give it a try. She isn't going to hurt you, Boyd, and God knows, anything at this point could only be a help. Now you go on up there. She's waiting for you. I'll see you soon."

Boyd glanced at the woman and then at his brother. He said, "This seems like a damn fool thing to do. I'm not a baby on a sugar tit."

"Give it a try, Boyd," Warren said wearily. "If nothing else, you might get a bath and a shave out of it and maybe a fresh set of clothes that will come nearer to fitting you. Now go on."

As he stepped up on the porch, he could see that she was not homely at all, even though Warren had made her sound so. She was wearing a thin, cotton wraparound housedress that tied at the waist with a sash of the same material. He noted vaguely that the pattern of the dress was some kind of flowers, but it had faded so that he couldn't tell what the flowers had been. Some kind of bluebells, he guessed.

The door was open. She put out a hand, took him by the shoulder, and steered him into the dimness of the front room. Her hand felt soft and gentle on his shoulder, and he was aware that the thin dress showed off some appealing curves and a voluptuous bosom. She said, "I'm heating water on the stove for your bath right now. The tub is in the kitchen. Walk toward that door in the back corner of the room."

He didn't know what he felt: a sort of relief, a kind of restful acceptance. He was so tired and so weary, it seemed all right to rest, even if just for a while. He didn't think that would be a slight to Hannah's memory. He knew he couldn't ever let himself feel good again, could never avoid the pain, but it didn't seem so much if he gathered his strength enough to be able to really punish himself. It took a surprising amount of strength to go on beating yourself and he knew he was about played out. He figured Hannah would not feel slighted if he allowed himself some doctoring.

Martha was still guiding him. She didn't need to, he could easily see the lighted door to the kitchen, but he vaguely liked the feel of her hand on his shoulder.

They went into the kitchen and she had him sit down in a wood chair at the table that was in one corner. The middle of the kitchen was taken up by a galvanized tub that was going to be about two feet too short for him. He reckoned it was too small for her too. He was an inch over six feet and he'd been conscious that she came up to his chin, which was tall for a woman. She was at the sink, pumping cold water into a five-gallon bucket. He could see under the hem of her dress that she was barefoot. Her dress was short-sleeved and he could see she had strong, firm, suntanned arms. He watched the muscles working in her arm as she levered the handle of the pump. Hannah had been a little bit of a thing, bright and blond and bursting with vibrant energy. She could have worked the pump, but not as easily as this Martha was doing it.

He could feel the heat from the wood stove. There were two big kettles of water heating on its top. Steam was starting to come out of the spout of one of them. Martha turned around and poured the full bucket into the bathtub. She looked at him and said, "You'd better start taking off your clothes now. This is going to be ready in just a moment. Start with your boots, then your gunbelt, and then your jeans."

He stared at her. He said, "I need a drink of whiskey."

"After you're in the tub, I'll give you a drink."

"I need one now."

She looked at him a second. "All right, but the water is starting to boil on the stove. You'll have to take it down fast."

He nodded. "Lady, I said I needed a drink, not wanted one. Damn right, I'll take it down fast. It ain't doing me no good in the bottle."

With a swift move, she left the sink, opened the cupboard, and set a bottle of whiskey in front of him, pulling the cork as she did. He didn't bother to look for a glass, just grasped the bottle with his two shaking hands and had a hard long pull. He set the bottle down, gasping a little, waiting for the whiskey to work.

She looked at him. "Feel better?"

He stared at her. "Whiskey ain't like love, lady. It takes a little longer to work."

She said softly, "I know."

He picked the bottle up and had another drink, wondering just what she really knew. Out of regard for Warren, he didn't ask.

Boyd wondered if she was planning on being in the room when he took his clothes off. For some reason, it seemed like it would be all right, that it wouldn't be betraying Hannah. He had lain with a few whores since he'd left Pecos, but he'd been drunk and he'd called them all Hannah, so that had been all right. Whores didn't count, and he had been careful to not see anyone in his mind except Hannah.

But Martha wasn't a whore, or at least Warren had said she wasn't.

She poured him another drink of whiskey in a glass and handed it to him. He nodded gratefully and put the glass to his mouth and swigged down half of the fiery stuff before he gagged. He bent over, coughing. He felt her take the glass out of his hand.

"It can't be rushed," she said. "Nothing can."

He glanced up at her, trying to pinpoint the quality in her voice. It was soft and tender, but there was something else that he couldn't place. It wasn't just concern and it wasn't pity. What was it? He wrinkled his brow, trying to think. He glanced up to her face and found the answer in her soft blue eyes. It was experience. She understood because what was in him was in her too.

When he'd stopped coughing, she handed him the glass again and he finished the whiskey.

She said, "I'm going to start pouring in the hot water. You'd better shuck out of your clothes."

When he made not a move, she folded her arms under her breasts and said, "Are you feeling shy about being naked in front of me? Well, don't be. It doesn't make any difference, and besides, I think I'm going to have to wash you. You don't look as if you've got the will to do anything. Do you want me to help you undress?"

What she said made some sense. He shook his head slowly. "No, I can do it, but don't make that water too hot.

It's like an August day in this kitchen with that stove roaring.''

"Hot water will relax you. It's the whiskey making you hot. The back door is open and there's a good breeze blowing through here."

Boyd started pulling off his boots, surprised at how much effort it took. It seemed to him that his body had gotten him to the kitchen chair in Oklahoma City and then it had up and quit. He could feel the layers and layers of exhaustion weighing him down.

She took the first of the big kettles off the stove, holding its handle with a big rag to keep from burning herself. She poured the hot water into the cold already in the tub and steam began to rise.

He had managed to get his boots, his socks, and his gun-belt off, and was fumbling with the buckle of his belt when she came to help. With a few deft moves, she had his jeans down around his ankles and he was stepping out of them.

She said, "You don't wear underwear?"

He shook his head. Hannah had been surprised about that too. He said, "Never took to it. Always galled me."

Then she had his shirt off and was leading him to the edge of the tub. She said, "Step in and sit down and tell me how hot it is. I can't tell with just my hand."

He got in the tub and awkwardly lowered himself into a sitting position. He said, "It's pretty damn hot!"

Without a word, she pumped the five-gallon bucket full and poured half of it in the tub, distributing it around. She looked at him questioningly. "How's that?"

He let his body sink into the warm water. By working himself down, he could get a good part of his upper body under the water, even though his knees and a lot of his legs stuck up. He said, "That's middling better, but it's still on the hot side."

"You need to sweat that poison out of your system."

Boyd said, "I'd just drink more."

"I'm not talking about whiskey."

In surprise, he glanced up at her face, but she was turning away to put the bucket on the countertop. He knew what she meant; he was just surprised that she had put it into words. He knew he was full of poison: the poison of hate, of anger, of despair, of bitterness, of a loneliness so deep he could feel it in his bones.

She turned back with a large bar of coarse lye soap in her hand. He'd expected a gentle touch, but she started on his back with the rough soap as if she meant to take the skin off. She scrubbed his whole upper body and hair, and then had him immerse himself completely, head and all, into the water. When he came up, the soapy water was several shades darker.

She said, "I don't think we're going to get it all off on the first try."

She washed him all over, being gentle only with his penis and his testicles. Strangely, there was nothing sexual about it. He felt not the slightest bit aroused. He didn't know if that was because he was so tired or because he felt a kinship with the woman.

At the end, she had him stand up in the bathtub while she poured a bucket of warm water over him to rinse off all the soap and what she claimed was loose skin. After that, she had him step out and stand on the floor while she went and got him a bedsheet to wrap himself in. She said, "You'll have to wear that until your brother sends you out some new clothes. I've looked in your saddlebags, and the rags you've got in there are worse than what you were wearing. I'm going to burn everything. Now, you sit down. I've got some stew made and I'm going to heat it and you're going to eat some. I've got some bread, baked fresh this morning."

He protested immediately. "Hell, Mrs. Blair, I can't eat. It ain't in me."

She was firm. "I'm not asking you to eat a lot; just a little start will do. You're not hungry because of the whiskey and your stomach has shrunk because you haven't been eating. If you can get a little down, it will be a help. Besides, you can make the whiskey work better if you don't drink it on an empty stomach. You can feel better for longer."

He pulled his head back. "How the hell do you know about that?"

She was folding him into the sheet. "Does it matter?"

He sat down, watching her at the stove. She had gotten quite wet giving him a bath, and her thin, wet dress clung to her body, clearly showing its outline. He said, "I reckon not." He glanced at his gunbelt. She'd laid it on the top of the table. His dirty, ragged clothes were piled at the back door.

Boyd looked at his revolver, thinking about the last time he had fired it. It was the only pleasant memory he had, though he doubted other people would describe it as pleasant. He pushed the rig farther away, doubting if he'd ever use it again. He'd been so proud of it at one time. He'd always been something of a tinkerer, good at most things that took good hands and ingenuity. He'd made a new cylinder for his two revolvers, rechambering them to accommodate seven cartridges. In a time when most men carried six-shooters, it had given him an edge, especially with troublemakers who could count.

But all that was done. He was through with guns, through with the law, through with everything.

Martha set a plate of stew in front of him. He looked at it dubiously. It looked like an awful lot to eat. There were chunks of beef and potatoes and onions in a thick gravy. She'd added a big slice of bread to his plate.

Martha said, "Eat what you can; start with one bite." She set a cup of coffee in front of him and then sat down facing him, a cup in her own hand.

He nodded at the coffee. "I need some whiskey in it."

"It's already in."

"How would you know?"

She said, "It may surprise you, Mr. McMasters, but you are not the first person who's had a tragedy in their life that they didn't think they could live over."

It suddenly angered him. He said evenly, "Lady, I didn't ask to come here and I can leave just as quick."

She held her coffee cup with both hands. "I didn't mean to make it sound like I thought you were feeling sorry for yourself. I was just telling you that there will be plenty of times when I'll know what you want before you say it. For a long time, I didn't think I could drink anything without whiskey in it."

It cooled him down. He looked at her curiously. "You still take a drink?"

She made a motion with her cup. "What the hell do you think is in this? But no, I don't put it away like you do, or like I used to. I'm over that now."

He dimly remembered that Warren had told him something about her loss, but he hadn't really been listening. That was another thing he didn't do much of anymore—listen to other people. He wasn't being rude; he just didn't care.

"Give that stew a try."

She'd given him a big spoon and he picked it up, took some gravy, and put it in his mouth. It was good, thick and rich-tasting. He swallowed it and then tried a small chunk of beef. That was harder going, but he managed it. He took a sip of the coffee, noting with approval that Martha hadn't spared the whiskey.

Martha said, "Your brother brought your saddle in and

left it on the floor in the front room. There's some kind of rifle sticking out of the boot. At least, I think it's a rifle, though it looks more like a cannon. Where'd you get a rifle that big?"

He was eating another spoonful of gravy. He said, "Made it."

"You're a gunsmith? I thought your brother said you were a sheriff."

He looked up at her. "I'm not anything now."

"What caliber is that rifle?"

"What do you know about rifles?"

"Enough. The barrel is octagonal."

That surprised him. To know that, she'd had to have taken the gun out of its boot. He said, "It's a .70-caliber. The revolver is a .40-caliber on a .42-caliber frame. That one has a six-inch barrel. The one in my saddlebags has a nine-inch barrel. Anything else about guns you want to know?" He said it harshly, showing more emotion than he thought was in him.

She smiled lightly. "You're not as dead as you think you are."

He ignored her and went on eating, taking up the thick piece of bread to mop it around in the gravy. She got up and went to the stove to get the coffeepot. He said, "I don't know why you're doing this, taking me in. I hope it's for money because it don't make me no never mind."

She said dryly, "I made too much stew. I needed another belly." Martha came back to the table carrying the coffeepot in one hand and the bottle of whiskey in the other. She poured her cup full of coffee and put a little in his. Before she sat down, she uncorked the whiskey and poured his cup full.

He looked up at her. "That's a hell of a way to get a man to stop drinking."

She shrugged. "You don't know it, but you are so soaked with it now that what you are drinking is not even bothering to stop on its way through you. You could drink this bottle and not get drunk. You've drunk yourself sober."

He looked at her, chewing thoughtfully on a piece of bread. "So you are an expert on guns and drunks. Anything else?"

She gave him a steady look. "Forgetting. And surviving."

He felt another flash of anger toward her. She couldn't have lost much if she was up and around and content with one drink. A remark was coming to his mouth, but he left it unsaid. The woman was a friend of Warren's and he didn't want to do any more damage to others than he already had. He said, however, with badly hidden sarcasm, "I reckon the preacher came out and fixed things up for you."

She smiled faintly. "Is that what you think?"

"I'm expecting you to trot out the religious tracts at any time now."

"I take it your faith needs support by such things as preachers and church pamphlets."

He flushed. He didn't at all care for the way matters were going. For answer, he bent his head and finished his plate of stew. His appetite had grown amazingly after the first few bites. He pushed his plate toward her. "Do you have any more of that?"

She shook her head. "You don't need any more right now. Let your stomach get over the shock."

That surprised him. "One minute you are spurring me to eat, and then when I'm ready, you tell me I've had plenty. Hell, Mrs. Blair, I wish you'd make up your mind."

She got up, taking his plate with her, and put it in the sink. "I'm going to shave you now and try and give you some kind of haircut."

He ran his hand over the heavy beard stubble on his face.

"I hope you got a sharp razor. You ever shaved a man before?"

"Well, I certainly have never shaved a woman."

"You've got a mouth on you, don't you?" he said.

She came back to the table carrying a steaming basin of water and a cup full of shaving soap. She set them down, and then went to the cabinet and came back with a leather case and a long honing strap. She hung the strap on a hook on the door, took a straight razor out of the case, and began honing the razor.

He watched her, still wrapped in the sheet. He said, "I wish somebody would get here with some clothes. I ain't used to sitting around in a sheet. It's damn warm in this kitchen with that stove still hot."

"Take it off."

"I'll wait on the clothes."

When the razor was sharp, she laid it down and began working a lather up in the cup. With his head tilted back, she laid on a thick layer of lather and let it sit for a moment. After that, she dipped a small towel in the hot water in the basin, wrung it out, and put it around his face. He flinched a little from the heat.

She said, "It's not that hot. I just handled it."

His voice came out muffled from the towel. "My face ain't all that used to hot water."

"Neither is the rest of you, judging by the color of the water in that tub."

"How about if we switch places and let me have at you with that hot towel, Mrs. Blair?"

She took the towel off, applied a fresh coat of lather, and began shaving him. She said, "Do we need to be so formal, Boyd?"

He couldn't speak because she was shaving him around his mouth. The razor was pulling hard through his heavy beard. Every now and then, he could feel the razor take a slight nick out of his skin, but he never flinched. When he could speak, he said, "I don't plan to stay long, Mrs. Blair. You have to understand, this is all kind of strange to me."

"I'm not exactly experienced along this line myself, Boyd."

He cut his eyes upward at her face. She was intent on her work. He said, "That surprises me. You seem mighty practiced. You seem to know what you're doing and you do it with ease."

"Confident? I'm not confident about anything. I'm resigned. There is a difference, Mr. McMasters, if you insist on being formal. I have simply been doing what obviously needed doing."

"You gave a strange man a bath."

She shrugged. "You didn't appear as if you could handle the chore. It seemed to be the only way to get you clean."

They both heard a knock on the front door. She put the razor down and said, "Don't move." She went out of the room, wiping her hands on her apron. He took the opportunity to take a drink straight out of the bottle. She might think he was soaked, but he was starting to feel some shakes inside.

When she came back, she said, "Warren sent out half the town. I'm having the man unload it in the front room. Will you be strong enough to help me get some of the heavy boxes in the kitchen?"

"I hope so," he said. "But we better do it before you cut my hair."

She picked up the razor and started back to her shaving. "I didn't know you were a Biblical scholar, Mr. McMasters. You made a joke. Did you know that?"

"Yeah," he said bitterly. "Thanks for reminding me."

She was shaving his neck. "I know the feeling. You're

not supposed to let yourself enjoy anything. It's treachery. Isn't that right?

He pushed her hand away and his eyes blazed at her. "Listen, what did my brother tell you about me?"

She said, "Your brother didn't tell me anything to speak of, but he didn't have to. All I had to do was look at you. That was enough."

He suddenly sighed. "Lady, if you are trying to stir me up, you're wasting your time. I don't really care about anything."

She put the razor away and then wiped his face with the warm, moist towel. She said, "No, you're confused. You've finally run up against something you can't settle with your guns or your fists. What you're down with is going to take time. There is no other way."

He said harshly, "What the hell is it to you anyway?"

"Not a thing," she said. "I'll get my scissors and try and get some of that mane off you."

He watched her walking away, uncomfortably conscious of the way her hips and buttocks moved as she walked. The woman was bothering him and he was damned if he could figure out why. She was nothing to him. He was incapable of caring, and yet she was bothering him.

After she had cut his hair the best that she could, she brought him a set of new clothes Warren had sent out. The shirts were fine and nearly fit. They were cotton and linen and felt good next to his skin, but the jeans were new and stiff and uncomfortable. Martha said for him to suffer the new denim as best as he could, and she'd boil the other two pair and he could switch the next day.

It had been a trick Hannah had known about, breaking in new jeans, and hearing her say it was like a blow. He said, "How'd you know about boiling jeans to get them fit to wear?"

She didn't answer him. They were in the front room and she just gave him a look and went into the kitchen. She said, "I think I'm going to take a bath myself if I can get this bathtub cleaned out."

"You want me to help you?"

"No, thank you. It's too heavy. I'll just dip it out with this bucket. I guess then I'll need a shovel."

He pulled on his socks and his well-worn boots and walked over to one of the front windows and looked out on the street. There wasn't much to see, just a few scattered houses and some landscape. He'd seen a lot of that lately.

There were two other rooms in the house; one was a sort of catch-all storage room and the other was the bedroom. He stood in the doorway of the bedroom looking thoughtfully at the bed. There wasn't but the one. He expected she'd make him a pallet of some kind. He'd had a sleeping roll tied behind his saddle, but it appeared to have gotten lost.

In the dimness of the gathering twilight, he walked out to the shed to see about his horse. The animal was standing next to a hay sack that hung from the roof, contently munching grass. Martha's buggy horse was standing in the small corral, looking bored. Boyd made sure both horses had plenty of water before going back into the house. He reckoned he'd stay the night and then take off in the morning. He didn't much care for the woman's rather offhanded treatment of him and he didn't like the way she seemed to look right through him and know his mind better than she ought to.

He decided he needed a stiff drink.

Two

She said, "You can sleep any place you damn well please, but I think a bed beats the floor. And I ain't got no extra blankets or ticking to make a pallet. So it would be the wood floor."

She was standing in the doorway of the bedroom with a kerosene lamp in her hand. He said awkwardly, "I don't sleep with no clothes on. I mean, I sleep with no clothes on."

"So do I," she said. "Warm as it is, I wouldn't expect you to wear a coat. But you suit yourself. But if you are staying out there you had better light another lamp."

He could see a faint glow from the kitchen. Martha had put a big copper pot on the stove, filled it with water, and then put his other two pairs of new jeans on to boil. She'd put in some lye soap which she had claimed would soften them in one washing. He supposed she knew about such things from the husband she'd lost. But he didn't want to ask her any questions. He didn't want to tell her about himself and he didn't want to hear her story. All he wanted to do was get a little stronger, get a little money, and get back on the road. He'd eaten another plate of the stew and some bread and he could already tell it was having an effect. Physically he could tell he had gained a little strength from the food and the rest. His mind even seemed more at peace. He reckoned that was because the woman had forced him to look outward instead of staying inward with those few horrifying hours that he carried around like a mental anchor, one that kept his thoughts from straying very far in any other direction.

But he still didn't know about sleeping with her. That seemed somehow wrong, though the stove being on most of the night was going to make the rest of the house warmer than the bedroom. He couldn't decide in his mind if he would be being unfaithful to Hannah's memory. It almost made his head hurt trying to think about it. But what the hell, she had bathed him and looked at him standing around naked. Of course those matters seemed more in the nursing line. That could be understood. But you didn't sleep with your nurse.

She made up his mind for him. She called from inside the bedroom, "You better come or not. I'm getting undressed and then I'm going to put this lamp out. You're liable to break your neck in the dark if you get tired of the floor in the middle of the night."

He said, "I'm coming," and started for the bedroom door.

She called back. "You'd better bring yourself a bottle of whiskey in case you get the night shakes."

It puzzled him. She even knew that. But he rather suspected she knew it of herself rather than her dead husband. He fetched the bottle from the kitchen table, hearing the water in the copper pot already beginning to bubble, and made his way toward the light coming through the bedroom door.

She was lying on the far side of the bed with her back to him. She said, "When you get in bed I'll turn the lamp off.

Or does the dark bother you? I could leave it on low.''

He sat down on the side of the bed and pulled off his
boots and stockings and then his stiff jeans. He said, ''No,
I ain't that bad off. Not yet at least. Ain't no bats or snakes
been coming after me in the dark.''

He shucked off his shirt and then rolled in between the
coarse sheets. There was no blanket on the bed and not likely
to be a need for one. Both windows were open, and the
curtains fluttered limply with what breeze there was.

''Are you in?''

''Yeah.'' He punched the pillow up beneath his head and
turned on his side so that his back was to hers. Still, it was
a small bed and he was very conscious of how close she
was. He could smell the woman odor of her, a smell he
hadn't been aware of in a long time. The whores had been
so doused in perfume to hide the fact that they never bathed
that they didn't count. It cut him like a knife as he remembered when he'd last smelled that wonderful musk.

The room went dark as she turned off the lamp. He shut
his eyes determinedly, willing himself to go to sleep. But he
knew it was going to be a chore. The day had been very
unusual and there'd been many new thoughts and matters to
mull over. But the biggest problem was he hadn't had
enough to drink. Usually he sat up until one or two in the
morning and drank until he passed out. He doubted that it
was much after ten o'clock. The whiskey was on the floor
right next to him, but he resisted, hoping he could sleep
without drugging himself. For some reason he didn't want
to give the woman the satisfaction of seeing him have to do
it.

Sleep wouldn't come. He lay tensely, conscious of every
shift the woman made, every creak of the house, every night
sound. After about a half an hour he felt himself starting to
sweat. He knew what that was a sign of, but he fought off

taking a drink. In a little while he started shaking inside. The shakes began slowly, just in his chest, but they soon spread throughout his body so that sometimes he felt like an arm or leg was going to fly off. He knew what was happening; he'd gone through it before when he hadn't been able to have whiskey on hand. And he knew it was only going to get worse. He was getting badly behind, and if he didn't take a drink soon he'd start having what he'd heard old drunks refer to as the "horrors."

Within another half an hour he began to shake on the outside and his teeth began to chatter. He was burning up and freezing by turns. He tried to draw himself up into a ball, a tight ball, trying to hold himself together. He was panting and there was a searing pain in his guts.

All of a sudden he felt a sharp movement from the woman's side of the bed and felt her hand on his chest. She said, "You poor fool. What are you trying to do, kill yourself? Where is that whiskey?"

He couldn't answer; his teeth were chattering too hard.

There was the sound of a match being struck, and then the lamp began to glow and chase the dark out of the room. She came around the bed and was suddenly in his sight. He was vaguely aware that she looked pink and white and soft and had lovely rose-tipped breasts. But he had only a second or two for examination. She sat down beside him and lifted his shoulders with her right arm. She had the bottle in her left. She held it near his mouth and said, "You can't just play around with this poison. It'll kill you if you try and stop sudden like that. Haven't you ever seen an old drunk have a convulsion? Now take a good pull."

Almost as if she were nursing him, she fed him small amounts of the whiskey at steady intervals. After the first hard pull she'd waited five minutes to let the whiskey go to work before she'd given him a second, shorter dose. After that she gave him smaller and smaller drinks until she could see the shaking begin to subside. She put the whiskey on the floor and said, "No use ruining the start you made. Just enough to keep you halfway yourself. I'll handle it from now on. Shove over."

She pushed her way into the bed, moving him toward the side she'd been lying on. She said, "We'll leave the lantern burning. Not much kerosene left in it anyway."

Then she put her arms around him and drew him close to her naked body. She said, "I'll hold you close and you won't shake so bad. It's better if someone's holding you. It's not so frightening."

He was grateful for the warmth of her body. The room was warm, but he felt as if he were freezing. His back was to her, and after a few moments, he turned over and buried his face in her soft breasts. With her free hand she softly stroked his back. She said, "It's hell to get off that stuff. You don't do it right and it can kill you quicker than if you keep on drinking it."

After a while he felt himself begin to relax. He knew he was in the arms of another woman, not a whore, but it didn't seem to matter so much. He thought Hannah would understand. He burrowed himself deeper into her soft, smooth flesh as she tightened her arms around him.

He awoke alone and confused. Enough daylight was streaming in through the windows for it to already be well up in the morning. He didn't have a watch anymore. He'd sold it. For a moment he didn't recognize his surroundings, and then, as he sat up, the previous night began to come back to him. His head was heavy and his stomach was queasy, but that was nothing unusual. He inched his way to the edge of the bed and swung his feet to the floor, shucking off the sheet as he did. He wondered where the woman was and what she thought of him. His bare foot touched the bottle of whiskey, and he reached down and picked it up and held it against the light. It was still at least a third full, which was pretty good going for him, he reckoned. Mostly he was never able to save more than two drinks for the next morning, and here was nearly enough whiskey to carry him until noon, depending on what time it was.

He set the bottle back on the floor and listened. He could hear sounds coming from somewhere in the house—where, he wasn't exactly sure. He sat and studied. To his misfortune he could remember every detail of the night before, including the sweats and the shakes and having to be held in her arms like some mighty large baby. He sat there, his cheeks burning slightly, and tried to decide how he was going to handle the matter. If he had any sense, he decided, he'd pull on his clothes, slip out the front door, and ride off. The only problem with that was that his revolver and rifle were in the kitchen.

But what the hell, he thought; he was through with them. Why not just leave them?

Because, he answered himself, they were worth money and he could sell them to buy whiskey. So he wasn't going to be able to slip off after all.

He sat there, letting his stomach keep turning over faster and faster. The bottle was there. Help was sitting right beside his foot. He didn't understand why he didn't avail himself of it. Maybe because that was what she would expect him to do.

He made it another ten minutes before he put out an unsteady hand, grabbed the bottle by the neck, and upped with it for a short pull. Then he sat there, the bottle cradled in his lap, and panted, waiting for the whiskey to go to work. It took another ten minutes for it to have an effect. When he could feel improvement he took a hard, long drink and then set the bottle back on the floor with at least two inches of whiskey left in it. After that he began to dress, starting with the stiff jeans and then putting on a soft linen shirt that had what he took to be ivory buttons. His brother had never been stingy, that was for sure.

He got his feet into his boots and then got up, leaving the whiskey where it was. He passed through the front room and found Martha in the kitchen, sitting at the table with a cup of coffee in front of her. The copper pot was gone off the stove, but there was a fresh bottle of whiskey on the table. It hadn't been opened.

She looked up as he entered and smiled. She said, "You look some better. I was glad to see you sleep this morning."

He slumped into a chair. "What time is it?"

"Not quite nine. I've got your jeans drying on the line. They ought to be just about ready if you want to take those off. I can boil those today."

"No rush," he said. He watched as she got up to get him a cup of coffee. She was wearing a little yellow frock with a V neck and a gathered bosom that held her ripe breasts. He could tell it was old, not because it was faded, but because he could see where some of the seams were straining. She'd bought it when she'd been slimmer.

She set a half-full cup of coffee in front of him and started to open the whiskey. He put out his hand. "No," he said.

She gave him a look. "Do you know what you're doing?"

"I had a starter in the bedroom."

She shrugged and sat down. "I'll fix you some breakfast when you're ready. I've got eggs, and your brother sent out a cured ham big enough to last a year."

He grimaced. "I'm not exactly up to it right now."

"Take your time," she said. "We've got plenty."

He sipped at his coffee, blowing on it between sips. "Martha, I got to be getting on down the road. I don't feel right staying in one place too long.''

She ignored the remark. ''Tell me how come you tried that damn fool stunt last night? As long as you've been soaking it up you know what can happen if you try to get on the wagon too fast.''

He was quiet for a moment, staring down at the tabletop. She'd covered it with a checkered tablecloth. He said, ''Maybe I thought you were getting just a little too much fun out of watching me lap it up.''

''So right after supper you cut yourself off. Was going to make it until the next day.''

''Something like that.''

''Well, if it matters to you, I was not having much fun watching you lap it up as you called it. And I wasn't feeling sorry for you. But I did give you credit for knowing how to handle it. I reckon your pride got in the way of your better judgment.''

''I reckon it did. But listen, unless it gets into personal matters, I'd be obliged if you'd tell me how you know so much about handling drunks.''

She smiled slightly. ''The correct medical term is dipso-maniacs. It sounds better. For ten years almost I was a nurse, a trained nurse. I worked at the hospital here, one of the biggest in this part of the country. I've seen plenty in worse shape than you were. And I've seen a few die when some well-meaning friend or family locked them in a room to dry out. Wasn't a pretty sight.'' She sighed and shook her hair out. The day before she'd had it pulled back into some sort of a bun; now it was hanging loose. It framed her face and made her look younger. She said, ''But the best way I know about it is from my own personal experience. But that's not something I want to talk about.''

''You won't get asked,'' he said. He finished the coffee in his cup and got up and poured himself another cup, full this time. His hand was still a little unsteady, but he made it back to the table without spilling any.

She said, "Don't you want me to soften up those jeans before you go?"

"They'll wear in," he said.

She was silent for a moment. "Are you leaving because of what happened last night, that you let yourself be comforted?"

His face went red under his heavy tan and his dark eyes snapped. He said harshly, "That ain't very damn friendly for you to bring that up like that. And I don't consider I was getting myself comforted. I was drunk. Drunks do a lot of stupid things. I'm leaving because you seem to think you know what's good for me. Well, take it from me, you don't. I don't want your help nor anyone else's."

She heard him out and waited a few moments more before she spoke. She said, "Boyd, I think you do want some help. Or I think you want to try and help yourself. I don't think you're as hellbent on destruction as you'd have us all believe."

His eyes were still hard, but his anger was spent. He didn't have a lot left in him to lose. He said, "And what makes you say that?"

"Because I think you really were trying to put the cork in the bottle. You just went at it the wrong way. If you really want to whip it I can help you."

He looked into her eyes for a moment. They were startlingly blue. He hadn't noticed before. After a moment he looked down. "Who am I kidding." He reached out and picked up the bottle of whiskey. "This is the only thing that makes drawing a breath bearable. I get off this I'd have to think, and I couldn't stand that."

She didn't say anything. She got up and went to the stove. She said, "I baked some biscuits fresh this morning. This batch ought to just be browning.'' Using her apron for a hot pad, she opened the oven door of the big wood range and took out a sheet of big, golden brown soda biscuits. She set the sheet quickly on the cabinet and deftly flipped two off onto a plate. She split them, put a dollop of butter on the hot halves, and then dipped honey out of a bowl and spread it over the biscuits and the melting butter. She brought the plate, along with a knife and fork, and set it in front of Boyd. She said, ''Ain't nobody knows why, but they say sweetening takes away some of the shakes. I know it did for me. One time I ate a whole jar of preserves. Just ate them right out of the jar with a spoon. Strawberry they were.'' She gave him a little smile as she went back around the table. ''Besides, a couple of biscuits ain't as scary as a platter of ham and eggs. Start small.''

He flicked a finger at the bottle of whiskey. ''How long does it take to get that stuff out of your system? I mean, so's you don't feel like you are going to fly apart if you don't get a drink?'' The need for one right then was already beginning in him. He could sense its coming by the slight flutter inside his chest.

She shrugged. ''Depends on how long you been putting it away heavy. A year, ten years, a month.''

He didn't say anything, just looked down at the biscuits and picked up his fork. He took a tentative bite, liking the taste of the honey.

She said, ''If you do it hard it can be done in three or four days. Go at it easy . . .'' She shrugged. ''Ten days or two weeks.''

''Two weeks is a long time.'' He ate another bite of biscuit, swabbing it around in the butter and honey.

''Not if you're not in a hurry.'' She studied him. ''How long you been pouring it down?''

Without looking up he said, ''Maybe three months.''

"And you didn't drink heavy before?"

He looked annoyed. "Hell, no. Who the hell you think I am? One of your dipso . . . diso-whatever-you-call-its?"

"Don't get on your high horse. There are plenty of folks that don't need a reason. You keep forgetting I don't know much about you except you're Warren's brother and you've had some kind of trouble. You've got it in your mind that I see more than I do. I don't. That's just you looking in, not me."

He put his fork down. He said flatly, "This feels damn strange. I never saw you before yesterday and here we are talking about my business."

"And if I was still at the hospital and they brought you in with a bullet in you, more than likely I'd be looking inside you for real. Nurses help doctors now. We don't just change bandages. Though I don't think you need bandaging so much as sewing back together."

"You say it can be done hard in three days?"

"That's a hard three days. And you can't do it by yourself."

He looked up at her. "Why not?"

"Nobody's that tough. And besides, it won't be you doing the thinking. It will be the whiskey, or the lack of it. But something put you in the bottle, some trouble. Until you get that settled and tended to, there's no point in trying to dry out because you'll just pour out another one at the first reminder."

He suddenly squeezed his eyes with his thumb and forefinger. Through tight lips he said, "Don't talk about that!"

She didn't answer right away, just sipped her coffee and watched the anguish on his face until it began to dissipate. She said, "Your business is your business. Warren just asked me to get you cleaned up and get some food down you. He didn't say anything about easing up on the bottle. I don't care how much you drink.''

He was still squeezing his eyes. "I got to stop. Somehow." He gave a little gasp. "I got to stop long enough to find out if I want to go on. I can't think fuddled up like I am." He was panting and starting to sweat. He hadn't taken a big enough drink.

She got up quickly, brought a glass, opened the whiskey, and poured the glass half full. She said, "You better take some of that down right now. You are about to fall off the hill."

"No," he said stubbornly. "Warren said I had to pull myself together long enough to figure matters out. He's right. I got to get my eyes cleared up enough I can see. I don't like what I see, I'll use a bullet." He took his hand away from his eyes and looked at the glass of whiskey. "Not that stuff. It's too damn slow."

"I agree with you," she said. "But I'm telling you that you can't just go bone dry. You'll never make it. Take that drink. Then wait awhile before the next. You don't have to kill yourself doing this. It doesn't have to hurt."

He gave her a fierce look. "Lady, you don't know shit! I *want* to hurt!"

She sat back and folded her arms. "Then hurt."

He said, "You'll get your money either way. I'll see that Warren pays you."

She got up deliberately. "You go to hell. There's not enough money in the world will buy a sonofabitch like you into my house." She walked past him and out of the kitchen.

He was sorry immediately, but it was a long five minutes before he could get himself up out of the chair to go find her and apologize. He used the time to finish the biscuits. The glass of whiskey was still sitting there as he got up, a little shaky, and went to find her. He could feel the sweat on his face and his mouth starting to go dry.

She was in the bedroom, sitting in front of a little dressing table brushing her hair. He'd expected to find her angry, but she looked calm enough. She glanced around as he filled the door frame. "How you feel?"

The words fumbled around awkwardly in his mouth until he could get them straightened out. He said, "Look here, Martha, I'm damn sorry for what I said. I apologize. I ain't got no call to talk to you like that."

She immediately put the brush down and got up and came toward him. She said, "I understand you're not yourself. And I shouldn't have said what I did, but sometimes my temper gets away from me. Let's go and I'll cook you some ham and eggs."

"I ate the biscuits."

She put her arm around his shoulders. "Yes, but you need more." She frowned. "You're trembling. Boyd, you're being a damn fool."

"I can't help it," he said. "I'm in a hurry."

They went into the kitchen and he sat down at the table. "For what?" she asked. "In a hurry for what?" She looked at him keenly. "To find out if it's worth it?"

"Living? Yes."

She put the glass of whiskey in front of him. "Sip at that or you might not get a chance to live to find out."

Against his wishes, but taking her advice, he took small drinks of the corn whiskey while she fixed his ham and eggs. She said, "You don't drink a little, you'll never be able to hold this food down."

He drank part of the glass of whiskey before his breakfast came. With some effort he forced the ham and eggs down along with a piece of bread, and then put the rest of the whiskey in a cup of coffee and sipped at it.

She sat, leaning her elbows on the table, watching him.

"You want to do it hard. Because that's the fastest."

He nodded, still shivering a little.

"You've got to understand you are shocking the hell out of your system. It's got used to that half gallon of whiskey a day. You cut it off and it will rebel. You've got to cut down like I tell you. Will you do that?"

He sipped at his coffee and nodded.

"You'll think you're going to die and then you'll wish that you would."

He nodded again. "I'll stand it."

She gave him a look and said dryly, "You say that today. Wait until tomorrow night and tell me that. Once you start you can't turn back because the ground you'll have won will have cost too much to throw away."

"I said I could stand it."

She got up. "I'm going to get you a pair of jeans off the line. Take off those ones you've got on and I'll boil them."

He was a good deal more sober than he'd been the day before when she'd bathed him. He flushed slightly. "Martha, I can't just sit here with no britches on."

She got the copper pot out of the corner, put it under the spout of the water pump, and began filling it. She said, "Don't be so damn silly, Boyd. Won't be many secrets between you and me before this is over. Now pull off your boots."

Reluctantly, he complied while she set the copper pot on the stove and stoked up the fire. But he still hadn't taken off his jeans when she went out the back door to the clothesline.

When she came back in she was carrying his other two pairs of jeans. They looked considerably less blue and a lot more wearable. When she saw he hadn't undressed, she just stood in front of him waiting. Reluctantly, he stood up and got out of his pants as fast as he could, and then grabbed a pair out of her arms and started pulling them on. But she'd already turned away to drop his stiff jeans in the copper pot and add half a cake of lye soap.

When she turned back around he was already dressed, with his boots on and sipping at his coffee. He said, "Martha, I am much obliged. These things is soft as squirrel fur."

"It's the lye soap. Denim has some kind of stiffener in it. I don't know why. Maybe they expect you want to stand your pants in the corner when you ain't wearing them."

"Anyway, I'm much obliged."

"How you feel?"

"Not too bad. Little jumpy."

She said, "Maybe you'll have an easy time of it. I've heard of it happening." She paused and gave him a long, thoughtful look. "I know you ain't going to listen, but I'm going to tell you again that you'll just get back in the bottle if you don't stand up to what's troubling you."

He stared at her. "Troubling me? My God, is that what you call it? Hell, I thought it was something serious."

She said, "Your hands. Where did you get those scars in the palms? They look like they are not very old."

He quickly put his hands in his lap. "They're nothing. Rope burns. I got tied on to something I couldn't hold."

"I believe that, but I don't believe they are rope burns." She sighed and said, "Boyd, you're going to have to talk about it someday. I hate to see you go through all the suffering for nothing."

"Talk about it?" He put his fingers to his eyes again and squeezed as if trying to force something out of his head. "Talk? Hell, I cannot stand to think. Why do you reckon I've stayed sodden drunk?"

She shrugged. "Find out the hard way. I did." She stood up and held out her hand. "I might as well wash that shirt. You've got it pretty well sweated up. Expect to go through three or four a day. Or just don't bother wearing one."

• • •

It was not so bad the rest of the day. He was allowing Martha to tell him when to take a drink, even though he often didn't want one when she said it was time. To him, it seemed a strange way to quit something. The only bad time came in the evening when she said she'd bake him a big pie. She said, "I've got some dried apples and some raisins. I'll make you a syrupy cobbler." He almost shouted out, "No!" and jumped to his feet. It startled her so that she took a step backward. When she wanted to know what the matter was, he could tell her. He'd always had a sweet tooth that Hannah had catered to. Since that night he'd never been able to even think of cake or pie or cookies without feeling a deep, stabbing pain. He apologized to Martha and told her he just didn't care for sweets and not to go to the trouble. She nodded uncertainly and let it go.

The night was not so bad, mainly because they stayed up late and he took a big drink before they went to bed. He was self-conscious about sleeping naked with her, but there seemed to be no choice. He was careful, however, not to look at her. He thought he was going to have an easy night, but sometime toward morning he woke up shaking, and she got a drink down him and held him until the worst went away.

Next morning he sat on the side of the bed half dressed and said, "Lord, I don't reckon I was ever so glad to see the sun in my life."

"Think how it would have been if you'd been alone."

He reached his hand backward to her and she took it. She said, "I hate to tell you, but the worst is far from over."

By mid-morning his stomach was churning on him and he was sweating and trembling. Martha said, "We can cheat a little. Not cut down today, just hold it like it was yesterday."

He shook his head and gritted his teeth. "No."

"I could give you some laudanum. That would help some,

but to my mind it's worse than whiskey. It won't stop the shakes, but it will help your stomach.''

''No.''

He couldn't do much with the midday meal except pick at it. Finally Martha just buttered him some cold biscuits and watched while he shakily tried to eat, holding the biscuits with both hands. He said, trying to laugh grimly, ''Be hard to believe I'm a damn good shot right now, wouldn't it?''

''Boyd, you're pushing it too hard. Take a drink now.''

''When is it due?''

''Not for an hour. Four o'clock.''

''Then I'll hang on.''

By four o'clock he'd sweated through the new shirt Martha had given him. He took it off and she added it to the one soaking in a bucket of cold water. He didn't bother putting another on.

When four o'clock came he resisted the drink, but Martha insisted. She gave him two inches in a water glass and had him drink it over a fifteen-minute period. After that they went out into the backyard. The bright sunlight hurt his eyes, but he wanted Martha to pour some cold water over him. She soaked him down with three buckets. It felt good for a moment, but the sensation didn't last. In the process she got her dress soaked. It was another of the thin, worn, wraparound kind that she'd had on the first day, except this one was a very light tan. It clung to her and he couldn't help, even in his discomfort, being aware of her body. It made him feel ashamed, but there was nothing he could do about it. He figured it out by telling himself he'd looked at other women when Hannah had been alive, but the excuse sounded weak even to himself.

With his shirt off, she touched a scar welt on his shoulder. She said, ''You get that from a rope burn also?''

He didn't answer. His mind was too full of the new sensations going through his body.

By five-thirty the four o'clock drink had worn completely off and he was having a bad time. He wasn't due another drink until half past seven. Martha had scheduled what she called his doses to be heavier at night so he could get some rest. She'd said she called them doses because that was what they were. "It's not whiskey anymore, Boyd. Now it's medicine and you got to take it like that."

By six-thirty it was good and dark and he was holding himself together by wrapping himself tightly in his own arms. They were in the front room. She sat in a chair watching him pace back and forth. He said, "How come you ain't nursing now? Don't you work at the hospital no more?"

Pain showed in her face. She said simply, "I can't. They have too many babies there."

He wanted to ask her then, but he knew better. You ask and hear, you've got to tell and be told.

He stood before her gasping, racking with tremors. He said, "For God's sake, what makes this so damn bad? What causes it?"

She shook her head slowly. "Nobody knows." She paused. "I guess it's like losing an old friend. Or somebody you love. It hurts when they're gone. Why don't you take a drink? I hate to see you like this."

He shook his head resolutely. "I've come too far. No. But God, when I think of how I used to laugh at the old drunks in the saloon that would have to bend over and lap that first drink out of the shot glass because their hands was shaking so bad they couldn't get it to their mouth."

She suddenly stood up. She said, "Come into the bedroom and I'll hold you. It will help."

He followed her. In the bedroom she circled around the far side of the bed and quickly undid the sash that held her wraparound dress together. It fell open and she shrugged it off her shoulders.

He was just coming in the door as her dress hit the floor and she stood there naked. He was trying to kick off his boots, but the sight of her arrested him in the very act. He stood there with one boot off and the other half on. His eyes were drawn to her bush, the forested mound that lay where her legs met. It was a deep, golden blond. Her hair tended toward the blondish, but it was nothing like the crown of her public area. He was instantly aroused. As she was lying down on the bed on her back, her legs up and open, he was struggling with his jeans. His member had come to a full erection and he was tingling all over. She was staring at him. As he finally kicked his jeans off, she raised her arms toward him and he lunged onto the bed and then toward her. She seemed almost a blur. All he could see were her large breasts tipped with the big, cherry nipples and her soft mounded stomach that ran into the golden forest.

He buried himself in her and she pulled him in even deeper. Without guidance his member slid into the sleek, wet, waiting openness of her, and a warmth came over him like that of a man suddenly bursting in out of a snowstorm into a well-warmed cabin.

After that he was dimly conscious of her breath in his ear and the wetness of her mouth and the rhythm of their togetherness. She had her legs locked around his waist and her arms across his back, chaining him to her.

The trembling was gone; the cold was gone; the panic was gone; the fear was gone; the uncertainty was gone. All of it had fallen, like him, into the deep, moist, smooth softness of her. There was her breath in his ear and some words he couldn't hear because of the roaring inside his head. He felt himself climbing a mountain. Climbing higher and higher and higher, his excitement mounting as he did. Dimly he was aware that there was something growing inside him that was about to burst. He didn't know what it was and he was too caught up in the sensations of his body to care. He was aware of nothing except the warmth and the feel of her and the feel of them together.

When he exploded it was as if the whole earth was torn to bits. The sheets shattered and the bed fell apart. The roof of the house was blown away and the walls went whipping away with the force of the explosion. He heard a high screaming yell, felt himself rising higher and higher, and then realized he was doing the screaming. He was suddenly at the top of the mountain, and then he skidded and began to fall back to earth.

He collapsed into her and lay there panting while she talked softly in his ear and smoothed his back and his buttocks with her gentle hands. Finally, when he could, he rolled gently off her and lay on his back on the bed for a second. He was slowly coming to consciousness, and with it came the realization of what he'd done. Martha was no whore. She was a real woman. He waited for the guilt to come, knew it would come, expected it.

On her side of the bed she just lay quietly, watching him, being still as if she knew what was happening to him.

He waited a long two or three minutes and there was no guilt. There was nothing except a great feeling of peace and satisfaction. He turned his head slightly so he could see her face. She smiled slightly but didn't speak. He said, "I didn't mean for that to happen. I didn't want to take advantage of you because I was having a rough time."

"I didn't do it out of pity. You needed it." She paused. "So did I. Maybe more than you did. It's been a very long time. I didn't know it would be you."

He stared at her. He guessed he was hearing what he thought he'd heard. He didn't want to ask.

She said, "How do you feel?"

"Some better."

"It won't last. It's time for that drink. Isn't there a bottle by the side of your bed?"

"Yes."

"Hold it up so I can see it."

He rolled over and found the bottle and lifted it up. "How much?"

"An inch."

He sat up, looking at the bottle that was about three quarters full. An inch, he calculated, would be down to the top of the label. He carefully took a pull, feeling the burning fuel hit his stomach. He took his lips away and held the bottle up to the light again. There was about one more good pull left. He waited a moment and then had that. After that he sat quietly for a few moments, and then he turned on the bed and put his feet on the floor. He set the bottle down. He had come to a decision. He said, "I want to talk. I may not be able to do it, but I think you are right. I got to at least try."

"Are you sure you're ready?"

He shrugged. "Who can say. But I better do it now before this last drink wears off."

"Be careful."

Three

For a long moment, Boyd sat there trying to think how to begin, trying to decide what needed to be said and what he was afraid to say. They seemed to both be a part of each other. Finally, he began, hesitantly at first, and then, as he forced his mind to unfold, saying the words quicker and with finality. He talked in a low monotone, staring down at the floor. He said, "I was nothing like you see me now. I used to be a very confident man. I was also about as happy as a man could be. My life couldn't have been any better. I was good at nearly everything I turned my hands to. I didn't know what loss or failure was."

He stopped and grimaced. It was hard to believe that the words he was speaking were completely true. He continued, "Up until about three months ago, I was the sheriff in Reeves County out in far west Texas. I lived in the pretty little town of Pecos. Everybody in town was a friend of mine. I'd grown up in that country in my later years after I left home at fifteen and went to cowboying, leaving the home that Warren and my mother had made for us kids. That was after our daddy was killed."

Boyd raised his eyes and stared at the wall opposite him.

It appeared to be some kind of flowered pattern. He could see where it was starting to peel in a few places. "I was a good sheriff," he said. "There was never much trouble around Reeves County to begin with, and I made sure none ever got a chance to get started. If neighbors had a falling out, I got them to talking before they could begin fighting. You didn't break the law in Reeves County because people knew I wouldn't stand for it."

Boyd stopped again, thinking. "I drew wages of seventy-five dollars a month as sheriff, but I made nearly that much trading horses and raising cattle and even playing poker. I'd take a drink with someone or smoke an occasional cigar. Hell, it was fine. I just thought that was the way of it, the ordinary way, the way most folks had it. I'd built a house about five miles out of town, had me some good cattle land. I had a little seed herd. Hell, I'd even fixed up running water into that house off an artesian spring that I had on the place. I knew every board and nail in that house because I had put them in myself." He paused. "I guess I had too much."

He stopped talking for a long moment and stared at the floor, swallowing hard. The difficult part was coming. He said hoarsely, "But all of that was nothing next to her. All of that and a million dollars wasn't a drop in the bucket to what I had in Hannah Anderson. The day she agreed to marry me was the happiest day of my life, and I'll never know why she chose me when she had her choice of every available man in half the state." He had to stop for a moment. He went on. "That she was beautiful wasn't but a part of it. She was like being around a ray of sunshine. There never was a rainy day around Hannah. Hell, I used to like to go off just so I could look forward to coming home to her."

Behind him, Martha said softly, "Boyd, take it slow. Don't push yourself."

He cleared his throat, his voice getting stronger. "Lord, it was perfect. We fit together like that." He held up his two fists together with his fingers entwined. "A man never wanted a better wife. She'd tease me for being a big kid with a sweet tooth, and then she'd go and make me a plate of fudge."

Behind him, Martha made a sound as she drew in her breath. She now understood about the cobbler.

Staring at the wall, his gaze blank, Boyd went on. "We'd been married a little over six months when the trouble happened. It hadn't been more than a week that Hannah had told me she was going to have a baby. I was walking on air. I remember going into the saloon and buying a round for the house. I remember coming home a little tight, something I almost never did, and the fun Hannah made of me. She teased me about our baby having a drunk for a father." He looked around at Martha. "Not such a joke now, is it?"

Martha looked at him silently. She knew there was nothing she or anyone else could say. She just waited quietly.

Boyd turned back around and picked up the whiskey bottle and looked at it. He took a tentative sip and set it back on the floor. It wasn't a drink so much as an acknowledgment of what he'd just said. It was a while before he could pick up the thread again. He started speaking so low that Martha could barely hear him.

"There was an outlaw bunch loose in the country west of us, the Winslow gang. There was the old man, Rip Winslow, and his four sons. They had other members of the gang that came and went, but it was the Winslows themselves that was the heart and soul of the bunch. There was never a meaner bunch of cutthroat villainous bastards ever come down the pike. They wouldn't stop at anything from murder to cattle theft to bank robbery to holdups. They were already well known by the time I was elected sheriff some three years ago. Lucky for me, they weren't wont to operate in my county. They done their evil deeds a good deal to the west of me, more toward the New Mexico border. I knew about them, and once in a while I gave the idea of them coming my way a moment's worry, but for the most part they didn't have much to do with my life.''

Boyd continued. ''They had been operating pretty much at will for nearly five years. You'd think that they'd have been brought to justice long before, but it wasn't that easy. They had a hideout in the Davis Mountains and rougher country you don't ever want to see. It's so cut up and criss-crossed by ravines and draws and box canyons that you can get yourself hemmed up without even trying. There is so many bushwhacker's nests in there, natural ones, that ten men could hold off an army. Several times, large groups of armed law officers had chased them back to their hideout and followed them into those mountains. They got cut to ribbons. Wasn't nobody ever able that got close to their lair.''

Boyd coughed. It seemed like either a lot of time had passed or the whiskey was not working right. Little trembles were starting in his stomach. He said, ''So the Winslows were just more or less free to dash out at a time of their choosing, commit their depredations, and go back to ground. Oh, the law caught a few men that rode with them, but none of the Winslows. The old man and his sons lived back in those mountains, it was said, with their wives and women, and lived pretty high on the hog. Took trips down into old Mexico when they wanted a vacation. Had it pretty good.'' A bitter look passed over his face. ''Just like me. I thought I had it pretty good.''

Boyd stopped speaking and stared for a moment, thinking of the words that were to come. Behind him, Martha said,

"Boyd, maybe you better not. This is no time to get yourself upset."

He cleared his throat. "There's not much more. It gets pretty simple after this." He coughed again and picked up the whiskey bottle to look at it. Still holding the bottle but staring at the wall, he said, "One day some sheriff business happened to take me and my deputy to the town of Saragosa, which is a town about fifteen miles south of Pecos. Our route took us by the Fort Stockton to El Paso road that runs east and west. Now, that is desolate country. But then, it all is. Wide-open and empty. That was one of the reasons the Winslows could go and come so freely, not many to see them. And of course, them as did know about them carefully kept their mouths shut out of fear.

"But on that day, me and my deputy came over a hill and around a sheer bluff and caught the Winslows in the act of robbing the Fort Stockton to El Paso stage. There were about nine of them, but we had cover and they didn't. They'd stopped the stage right on the bald prairie. Me and my deputy dismounted and hid in some rocks without them being any the wiser. I didn't have that big rifle with me, but both of us had our saddle carbines and the stage was no more than a hundred yards away. I fired a warning shot and called on them to surrender, but they immediately returned fire and started milling around on their horses. We opened up on them with our carbines, moving around in the rocks. We done it so as to give them the impression we were a bigger party than we were. They set in to charge us, but I shot one man out of the saddle and my deputy got one and they gave that idea up and wheeled off and started toward the southwest. I got off a few more shots and one of them fell out of his saddle. A couple of the others turned back like they were going to pick him up, but my deputy and I were both reloaded and we made it so warm for them, they cut and run and caught up with the others.''

Boyd stopped to catch his breath. It was not hard talking about this part. In fact, there was a certain satisfaction to it. He said, ''The upshot was that we'd killed the biggest fish of them all, old man Rip Winslow. He'd been killed when they charged us. I'd rode off to see about the man I'd dropped as they were fleeing, and sent my deputy to see to the stage. It turned out I'd wounded one of the brothers; Rafe his name was. He was a young one, not much over twenty years old but already as mean as a snake. I don't know how the bullet come to knock him off his horse because I'd just hit him in the side and it wasn't serious at all. I collected his horse and got him on it, him cussing me a mile a minute until I slapped him across the mouth and tied him on his horse. After that, I took him back to the stage. The driver had been badly wounded along with the shotgun guard, so there was nothing to do but put my deputy up on the seat and let him take the stage on to El Paso, since none of the passengers could handle the team and the driver and the guard needed to get to a doctor in a big hurry. I . . .'' Boyd suddenly shuddered and gasped.

Martha said quickly, ''Take a drink, Boyd. You're getting behind. I haven't been watching the time. Take a good one now.''

He took a hard pull off the bottle and then waited for it to settle. He said, ''I thought of a funny thing last night when I couldn't sleep.''

''I didn't think you found anything funny about last night.''

''I just remembered that I used to smoke those little Mexican cigarillos. Smoked about fifteen or twenty of them a day, and now and then a cigar. Well, sometime in the last couple of months, I not only forgot to eat, I forgot to smoke.''

"Just the whiskey on your mind, huh?"

"Just the whiskey."

"Do you think you should be telling all this now? You're going to have a bad night as it is."

Boyd looked around at her. "You said it was something I had to do unless I wanted to fall right back in the whiskey bucket. I don't understand it, but you sound like you know the why of the thing."

"Just please don't push yourself." Martha moved across the bed to where she could put her hand on his back and massaged it lightly.

"I didn't mention that it was none of our business, the stage robbery. That grinds on me to this good day. I was over the Reeves County line, out of my jurisdiction. If we'd just kept riding, none of this would have happened." He looked down and heaved his chest in a sharp intake of breath.

"Would you do it different, knowing what you do now? Would you have ridden past that robbery?"

Boyd looked around at her and there was agony in his eyes. "I don't want to think about that question, Martha. I keep looking for an answer different than the one that keeps coming up. I don't want to think about it."

"What happened after your deputy pulled out with the stage?"

It took Boyd a moment to come back. He said, "I've got to tell you, I was pretty excited. For a young man like me, a young law officer, to have killed the leader of the gang and taken one of the main members prisoner . . ." Boyd shook his head slowly from side to side. "Hell, that was pretty high cotton. I couldn't wait to get him to town and in jail and get home and tell . . ." He suddenly stopped.

"I know," Martha said, then suddenly got up. "Boyd, as important as this is, it's also important that you eat. That roast I put on ought to be done. We'll go in the kitchen. You can leave that bottle here because there's one on the table.''

He looked up at her as she came around the bed putting on her dress. He said, ''I got to get it out while I can, Martha. I may not can get the cork out another time and it is liable to stay bottled up.''

''You'll be all right,'' she said. Martha put out her hand and helped him up. ''There's no need for you to get dressed unless you want to. I'm just going to put some potatoes on to boil and then you can go on. I know how hard this is for you. That's why I want you to take little breaks.'' She squeezed his hand and there was tenderness in her face. ''Please don't hurt yourself any more than you already are. I know what that kind of wound feels like. I almost know what's coming.''

Martha went in the kitchen and Boyd sat for a moment more. Finally, he put on the soft jeans and padded after her in his bare feet.

He sat down at the table and, after a few seconds, began talking again. She was at the stove and he talked to her back. Somehow it made it easier. He said, ''I was about halfway back to Pecos when I became aware that I was being followed. It wasn't the whole gang, just three or four. They never tried to catch me, figuring, I guess, that it would cost them the life of their brother if they tried to rush me, which was true enough. They kept following, holding about a mile back, all the way into town. It worried me considerably until I got to the jail and got my prisoner inside and under lock and key. I could see right off that I wouldn't be going home that night, not with my deputy off and no one but me to guard the jailhouse. Meanwhile, this Rafe was cutting up and carrying on something about this hole in his side. Well, I wasn't going to go for the doctor, not with three or four of them murdering bastards outside. I wasn't too much concerned about them being able to break in because the jail was made out of rock and had only one heavy wood door and there were bars on the windows. But we'd got there just after dark and I'd brought him in the back way so as to not attract attention, so none of the townspeople even knew I was there with a prisoner, much less such a one as a Winslow.

"I was careful not to make a light in the outer office in case they were lurking around the windows. I got some whiskey and some clean rags and struck a light back in the cell area where I couldn't be seen from outside and did what I could to bandage my prisoner, not that he was hurt that bad. In fact, he got it in his head that, when I untied him, he could give me a scuffle. I knocked that thought out of his mind right quick. After that, he was a good deal easier to handle, although he didn't ease up much on the cussing he was giving me."

Martha came over from the stove with a cup of coffee and put it in front of Boyd. She sat down, her eyes fixed intently on his face, and waited.

"I felt like I was in a tight fix, but I just didn't know how bad. There was some help in town, men that were handy with guns, but I had no way of getting to them without leaving the jail. The jailhouse and the sheriff's office are set off a little way from the center of town, kind of by themselves behind the courthouse."

Boyd took a sip of coffee and looked again at the bottle of whiskey. Then he turned his head toward the pot where steam was rising out of the boiling potatoes. He said, "I was expecting anything. I had plenty of ammunition out and my guns laid handy. I figured they'd try something, but I calculated they'd leave it until the town was good and asleep. Some time passed. I don't know how much because I was never sure what time I got my prisoner to the jail. But some-time around midnight, there came a knock on the door. I yelled out from the back where I was in a safe spot to find out who it was. They never answered. The next thing I knew, I heard a window breaking up front. I got ready. I figured they'd pry the bars off and then come swarming through, which wouldn't have done much except get them killed. But that wasn't it. A voice sung out for me, called me by name, called me Sheriff McMasters. They must have hung around town and asked questions in the saloon because I found out quick that they knew quite a bit about me. They said . . . they said . . .''

Boyd stopped to clear his throat and to let the wave of emotion pass that had suddenly hit him. Martha reached out and put her hand over his. ''Boyd, you'd better stop now. Don't go so far that you can't get back.''

He said with pain in his voice, ''I just want to get this part out. Just this . . .'' He swallowed and took a breath. ''They told me they had my wife, Hannah . . . they told me they had Hannah out at my ranch. They told me exactly where it was and what my house was like. They described Hannah to me so I'd be sure they had her. They said I was to bring Rafe out to my ranch and surrender him to them or they'd kill Hannah. They set in to tell me exactly how they would kill her. They said . . .''

Martha got up. She said, ''That's enough right now, Boyd. I want you to take a drink while I fix you a plate and then I want you to eat. You can have a hard drink after supper and then see if you want to go on.''

They ate together, mashed potatoes with butter and slices of roast beef in its own gravy. There were sliced tomatoes and onions on the side. Boyd surveyed his plate and shook his head. ''Lord, this is an awful lot of food, Martha.''

''Just eat it a bite at a time. Eat what you can.''

He was without a shirt and she ran a critical eye over him. "I believe I can see some improvement. You may not be feeling better, but you are looking less like a corpse. You need another shave, though."

He cut his meat up and began eating small pieces. "Is tonight going to be bad?"

She shrugged. "We'll get through it. You're already way down. I ought to give you another bath, much as you're sweated."

"Hell, it's late. What time is it anyway?"

"A little after nine."

He looked past her toward the night outside the opened kitchen door. He could see far-off flashes of lightning. "Looks like a storm coming up." As if to echo his words the faint sound of thunder came into the kitchen.

"Maybe it will cool things off. Eat, Boyd. Do you feel any stronger?"

He nodded slowly and smiled. "Yeah, I think I could almost bathe *you* now."

She gave him a slow smile. "Maybe I'll let you."

A thought flickered across his mind but he dismissed it. His brother had acted like he didn't want his wife knowing of his friendship with Martha. Boyd wondered what he'd meant by that, but he wasn't going to ask Martha. It was none of his business. Instead, he said, "Does the day ever come when you tell me about you?"

She shrugged. "There's nothing to tell, Boyd. Life is life. Sometimes it's good, sometimes you think it's not so good. But it can be anything you want to make it."

"You don't want to talk about it?"

She put her fork down. "I didn't say that. I just don't think I have anything to say that would interest you."

He gave her a look from his warm, brown eyes. "I think there's a great deal about you that would interest me, Martha, but I'll wait until you feel like telling me. You've the same as told me you were knee-deep in the whiskey barrel. What put you there?''

''Knee-deep? Hell, I had my head under and was going down for the third time.''

''Who pulled you out?''

She thought carefully for a moment. ''Nobody can pull you out. You got to do that for yourself, but you can have help that makes it easier. No, makes it possible. Your brother was the main one to give me a hand.''

He felt he was on dangerous ground and he didn't want to pursue it. The thunder was sounding louder as the storm approached. He determinedly took up his knife and fork and attacked the roast beef and potatoes.

She had found him a cigar, forgotten by some past visitor. With the dishes cleared away he sat there smoking and thinking. She sat across from him, watching, waiting for him to start talking again. He said, ''This cigar is kind of dry. Reckon how long it's been here?''

She pulled a face. ''I don't have any idea. Haven't been that many men through this house. My brother has visited and he smokes cigars, but so does Warren. I can go and get you some fresh ones tomorrow. It's ten o'clock. You can have a drink any time you're ready.''

He gave her a careful look. ''I'm kind of saving it for when I really need it. Like your last cartridge.''

She said, ''I'm not at all sure you should go on. I have a bad feeling about where you're going. It might hurt too bad.''

''Sometimes I think I'm beyond pain, Martha. Then something will strike me with such force that I will think I never knew what hurting was.''

She waited, her hands on top of the kitchen table. The thunder was still rumbling outside and they could feel the disturbance in the air. A light rain, like the advance scouts for an army, was pattering on the tin roof of the house. Martha said, ''I guess I should shut that back door but that cool breeze feels so good. Someday I have to get a screen door for there.''

After a few more minutes Boyd continued his story. ''So after what they told me at the jailhouse,'' he said, ''I didn't see where I had any choice. If they had my wife, I was more than willing to swap their brother for her, but I had to make sure they couldn't just shoot me out of the saddle when I stepped outside with my prisoner. There was some baling wire there in the office, and I got a length of it and wired it tight around the barrel end of my carbine. I got my prisoner and run the wire around his neck, drawing it up so that the muzzle of my carbine was pressed right up against the lower part of his head. Then I ran the balance of the wire down to the trigger and I wired my finger and the trigger together. Of course, that made the man nervous as hell, having the muzzle of a rifle jammed up against his head with a wire to the trigger. I showed it to him and explained that, if I was shot or if I even stumbled and fell, the weight of my body would pull the trigger, my finger and it being wired together, and the gun would fire. Since the rifle was wired to his head, there was no way it wasn't going to blow his brains out when it went off. I told him he'd better explain it mighty carefully to his relatives outside in case one of them took it in his head to interfere with me. I said I was willing to make the swap, but I was going to be damn certain they lived up to their end of the bargain.''

She stared at him oddly. ''Can you think like that all the time? Warren said you were very smart, but I didn't know how he meant. Can you invent something for every situation?''

Boyd smiled sadly. ''Do I look like I'm very smart?''

"This has nothing to do with that. Go on. Did your prisoner call out to the others?"

Boyd smiled. "Oh, yes. You never heard a man give such careful instruction in all your life. I can't blame him. I was walking a rifle length behind him, holding on to the good end of the rifle, and he was wired up to the bad. He even called out for his brothers to make sure the rigging on our horses was properly done so my saddle didn't slip because of a loose cinch.

"Anyway, we walked out like that, him at the end of the rifle. Just as we went through the door, I cocked the hammer back with my thumb. I thought the man was going to faint. I'd actually cocked it only halfway back on safety but he didn't know that. He was scared that the slightest mischance could set that gun off. You never saw a man move so careful in your life. We did have to take it slow. I called out for his friends to keep good and clear of me, that we would meet them at my ranch."

He stopped and glanced at the bottle of whiskey. Without a word, she got a glass and poured a healthy two inches in it. He looked at it, but just shook his head. Even though the night was cool, his upper body was soaked with sweat. He could feel it running down his back. His left hand suddenly jerked convulsively and he started to tremble all over. He gritted his teeth and twisted his face, gasping slightly. Martha got up and came swiftly around the table and held the glass to his mouth. She tilted it up and he sucked down a little less than half of it, then pulled back with a gasp. He said breathlessly, "Just give me a minute. My cigar has gone out."

He sat there, letting the whiskey work while she relit his cigar and passed it across to him. After a moment, he said, still speaking in short bursts, "Boy! That stuff has its own timetable. Regular as a train."

"And hits about as hard."

Boyd leaned back and drew in several breaths. "It's about over. I'll be quick. We both got mounted, kind of awkwardly, but we managed, then we rode out of town toward my ranch. Naturally, we had to take it slow, so I reckon the ride took a good hour at the pace we were going. I still hadn't put the carbine on full cock because I didn't want to kill the man by accident. If he died, I had no doubt what would happen.

"We rode on and finally came to the wagon track that went back to my place. I remember there was a good moon that night and a clear sky. My house was built up on a little rise and I could see a faint glow from the kitchen, as if they had one lamp burning. The bunch that had been ahead of us had held their distance on the ride out, but as we got closer and closer to my house, they let the distance drop until they were no more than a hundred yards away. When we were less than a quarter mile from my house, they stopped and motioned for me to pull up. I was close enough I could see the rails of my corral. I could see the loft door in my barn was open. They said it was time for me to release their brother. I said I wanted to see that my wife was all right before I turned him loose. They said there just wasn't any way that was going to happen. They said they weren't about to let me get near my house while I still had their brother. They said I could try and play hard if I wanted, but they had other brothers and they were going to have it their way. They said I could go ahead and kill Rafe if I wanted, but they had a man in my house with a gun on my wife and he had orders to kill her if there was any kind of commotion."

Boyd stopped to puff on his cigar for a moment. He could see the scene as clearly as if it were no more than five minutes old. The four men facing him on their horses, his house and barns beyond, the little glow in the back of the house. He could even smell the early spring grass and the faint odor of cattle. He shuddered inside, but not from the lack of whiskey. The pain that racked him was a memory that was so vivid, it seemed as if it were happening at that second.

But when he went on, his voice sounded almost normal. He said, "Well, I could see I didn't have a very good hand. All I could do was hope they'd keep their end of the bargain. I called out to them that I would unwire their brother from the rifle and let him go to them, but I wanted the other man out of my house. They said for me to send Rafe over and they'd ride off and their man would follow. They said they didn't want no more truck with me, but I kept thinking about their father, about how me and my deputy had killed old Rip Winslow. I put that up to them and asked them their feelings. It seemed to make them laugh. They said I'd done them a favor, that the old man was starting to get in the way. I had no other choice but to believe them. I stalled as long as I could, trying to think of some way to bargain myself closer to Hannah, but they wouldn't have it. Finally, I gave in and released Rafe, but when I had done it, I immediately turned my horse and spurred him off to one side, taking myself out of rifle range. I might as well have saved myself the trouble. As soon as Rafe came up to them, they let out a big whoop and went riding off toward the southwest. I started toward my house, but then one of them broke off and rode back a little way toward me. I still had the wire dangling off my rifle, but I could use it. He never came close enough. He pulled up and yelled some things about what they had done to Hannah and what a lucky man I was. Then he said she was a hot piece, but she was fixing to get even hotter. After that, he wheeled his horse and rode to catch up with the others."

Boyd had said it, his face showing no expression, but the

telltale of how it had affected him came when he reached for the glass of whiskey and drained it. Martha knew he wasn't taking the drink because of the shakes. She made a helpless motion with her hand, moving it closer to his.

He ran his tongue over his lips. His gaze was fixed out beyond the back door as if he were seeing something a long way off. He said, "I started toward my house. What the man had said enraged me, but I didn't fire for fear there really was a man in the house who might kill Hannah. Not that I believed there was a man in the house because there had never been more than four of them following me and the same four who rode off with Rafe. But I still took my time, being careful on account of Hannah." Boyd paused, as if searching for words. "I guess I was about four hundred yards away from the house when I began to realize that something wasn't quite right. The house commenced to grow brighter and it made my heart leap. I thought it was a good sign that Hannah was going around lighting lamps now that she was free. She never did much like it dim. She liked it bright and cheerful. Then, after a minute or two more, I thought it was getting just a little too bright inside the house. That's when I realized the house was on fire, burning good. I put the spurs to my horse, but I knew I was going to be too late if Hannah was caught in that house. I could only hope they were burning my house out of revenge. I told myself that they surely wouldn't hurt Hannah. No man, no man with the slightest hint of decency in him, could harm a woman, much less a fragile little thing like Hannah. I . . ."

Boyd stopped and mechanically picked up a match, scratched it under the tabletop, and then relit his cigar. For a moment, he looked at the flame of the match, turning it in his fingers. He said, "It was a frame house, all wood. I'd bought it from the owner of a store that was tearing down his place and putting up another one. I got it at a good price.

Lumber is dear out in west Texas and this was good seasoned lumber that had already got all the warping and twisting out of its system. I thought I'd made a good buy and I had." Boyd nodded his head thoughtfully, as if he were considering it from a business standpoint strictly. "Of course," he said offhandedly, "it was about as dry as tinder. I don't reckon gunpowder could have burned much faster. By the time I came skidding up on my horse, the place was blazing like an inferno. I could feel the heat from fifty yards away, and by the time I got closer, my horse wouldn't go. He started to buck and turn away. There wasn't nothing to do but jump off and run as fast as I could. The outer walls weren't quite a solid mass of flames, but they were close. I jumped up on the side porch that ran alongside our bedroom. I got to a window and I could see inside. Through the flames, I could see the room, I could see Hannah."

From outside there came a sudden clap of thunder that made Martha jump. Boyd seemed not to notice it. The storm was upon them and the rain beat down in sheets as the thunder rolled and boomed. Martha hurried to shut the back door and then went running around the house, closing windows. When she came back into the kitchen, she started to make some remark about the storm, but the look on Boyd's face stopped her. She sat down quietly across from him. She could see that he had gone far away.

Boyd had been able to catch sight of Hannah through the flames. She was on the bed, on her back, and he could see her writhing around. He could not see clearly, but it appeared that she was tied. He became frantic. With his boot, he kicked out the window only to be driven back by a blast of heat and flame. He grabbed up a burning plank and tried to knock in the frame of the window, to enlarge it, but every time he made the hole bigger, it seemed to increase the flames. In his anguish, Boyd was almost mad with frustration and helplessness. He could see that the fire had started in the kitchen and was burning toward the front of the house. The bedroom was almost in the middle and he thought he might have a better chance to reach Hannah from the front.

The porch and roof were on fire as he ran around to the front of the house and kicked in the door. The knob was too hot to touch. Tongues of flame licked out at him, but the fire was not as bad as in the back of the house. He began blundering forward, but the smoke was so thick, he could barely see where he was going. A burning piece of the ceiling fell and hit him on the shoulder, knocking him to his knees. He got up and struggled on, blundering into the wrong door in the dense smoke. He could barely breathe and he was aware that his shirt was smoldering.

It seemed to Boyd that he could hear Hannah's screams over the roar of the fire. Not caring about the fire or his own pain, Boyd managed to reach the bedroom door. He pulled it open, the knob searing the skin off his palm, and he reeled back before a plume of flames. It knocked him down and he struggled back up. For just a second, he saw the sight that would stay with him forever. He clearly saw Hannah tied to the bed, screaming as the roof crashed down. Then, there was nothing but fire to see.

But still, Boyd tried to reach her. In his pain, he ran back down the hall and into the kitchen, which was now a smoldering wreck. He was trying to work his way through a charred wall when gusts of heavy smoke overcame him. He remembered staggering out of a hole in the kitchen wall and falling to the ground in the cool night.

The thunder boomed again, louder, and Boyd could see the lightning flashing in sheets across the sky. Wistfully, he thought of how miraculous it would have been if such a rain would have been there at just that time. Two lives would have been saved.

Martha asked, "Do you want some coffee?"

Boyd looked up. "What?"

"Nothing."

He picked up the stub of the cigar and looked at it. As if he'd told her about the fire, he said, "Next morning, at dawn, there was nothing left. The house had burned to the ground. There was nothing left of Hannah, nothing to remember her by, not even her wedding ring. I sifted the ashes all around the bed for anything, but the fire had been so fierce, it had burned her all up, bones and all."

Martha watched him carefully, saying nothing.

"I was able to figure out what they had done. There was a small mound of tallow in a tin pan in the kitchen and there was a kerosene can, almost empty, near there. They had filled that pan with kerosene and then set a tall candle in it and lit it. The candle would have been sitting right below the curtains that Hannah had on her kitchen window. That's the little glow I saw that I thought was a lamp. It was a lamp, all right. A lamp of hell. When that candle burned down, it set the kerosene on fire, and the kerosene set the curtains on fire and that was that. They calculated it. They stood off from the house and held me off until they knew the fire was about to start. They wanted me there in time to see it, but not in time to do anything about it. Tied a sweet little girl to a bed and burned her up and there wasn't a damned thing I could do about it."

Martha reached out and took his big hand and opened it and rubbed the burn scars. She said, "Boyd, it's almost midnight. I want you to take a good drink and we'll go to bed. I don't want you to talk anymore. I don't want you to think anymore. I know that's hard, but you've got to try. Will you do that?"

"Yeah," he said. He stood up. "I'm kind of tired. Do I drink now?"

"Yes. This is going to be the roughest night yet. Take a hard one, a good pull. Then we'll go to bed and listen to the rain."

As he got up from the table, he said, "I never found anything of her. Nothing." He stood there staring at Martha with a puzzled frown on his face. "Maybe if I had gotten to bury her, it would have made it easier to take somehow. If I hadn't seen her through those flames I could almost believe she'd vanished somehow."

Martha put her hand up to his cheek. She handed him the bottle. "Don't think about it, Boyd. Take the drink, please."

Boyd started up with the bottle and then lowered it. He said, "Sometimes, I think I just dreamed that I saw her, that I was out of my head with the smoke. When I went after the Winslows, I kept thinking that maybe they had spirited her off, that when I caught up with them, they'd have her safe and sound."

Martha took his arm and pushed the bottle up toward his mouth. He drank, hard and deep. When he lowered the bottle he said, "It's funny about a thing like that. It seems so real and yet it seems like a dream, the way she looked dancing through those flames." Boyd's eyes suddenly went dead. "But those screams weren't in no dream. I'll hear those for the rest of my life."

"You've got to come to bed, Boyd. You've got to get to sleep while you're at rest from that last drink."

It was a bad night, worse than she had warned him it would be. He went to sleep almost straightaway, but then he awoke around three o'clock, shaking and sweating and feeling like he was flying apart. Martha held him tight and tried to talk him through it. She said, "Just hang on, Boyd. Hang on. This is the worst of it. Do you know you only drank about a third of the bottle today? Think of that. Coming down from two quarts a day this fast."

Boyd was hurting too bad to speak, but he wanted to tell Martha that he had drunk just two quarts on the good days. Most times he couldn't remember how many unless he happened to save the empties.

The storm had passed over and the air seemed even hotter. The breeze flowing through the windows seemed like a blast furnace. He tried not to think of Hannah in the midst of the fire, but he couldn't shake the image. He bit the side of his hand until he tasted blood, trying to burrow his way into Martha like an animal hunting a hole.

The bad time began to lessen with the coming of the dawn. He stopped shaking uncontrollably and his nerves felt like they were back in his body. He began to relax. Some time later, he was partially conscious that Martha was getting up, but he thought vaguely, as the expression went, that she was going to pick a flower and would be back in a few moments. He slipped into sleep.

Boyd came awake with Martha shaking him and calling his name. It seemed like only a moment had passed. He sat up in a reflex action. "Wha . . . What?"

"Boyd, honey, you've got to get up and eat breakfast and you've got to take a small drink."

Boyd stared at her blankly. "I want to sleep." He slumped on the bed, but she shook him again.

"Boyd, you've got to do this thing right or it won't work. Come on, you're almost home. You've got to eat. You don't have to bother dressing."

Drowsily, he followed her into the kitchen. She was wearing a loose cotton robe that she hadn't bothered to tie together. He could see the bathtub in the middle of the room. He said, "I don't want a bath."

"I just took one. Sit down and take a drink, a medium one, and I'll make you some scrambled eggs and biscuits."

Boyd took the drink, not wanting it, but he was too worn

out to argue with her. There was a stub of the cigar from the night before, and he lit it and was able to take a few puffs before she dished his breakfast up. While he ate, he watched Martha take the big bucket and empty the bathtub of enough water so she could push it out the back door and drain it completely. She brought it back into the middle of the kitchen and began filling it with cold water.

He was awake enough to appreciate what he was seeing through her open robe. He particularly liked it when she leaned over and her oval breasts drooped just the slightest. There was the bright yellow patch, outlined against the white skin of her stomach. He could feel his member stirring, even though he was drinking coffee and eating honey-covered biscuits.

When he noticed that one of the kettles on the stove was starting to steam, he said, "Wait a minute. I said I didn't want a bath and you said you already had one. What's that for? Company coming?"

Martha looked at him, her hands on her hips. "Boyd, you've got enough dried sweat coated on you that you smell worse than a goat. You've got to bathe, then you can take a nap. A warm bath will help you relax."

"I'm relaxed now," he said with ill humor. "If you'd just let me sleep."

"I've got to change those sheets and I can't do it until you take a bath. Come on, Boyd, the worst is almost over. Hurry up and eat. The water is almost ready."

Boyd got in the tub, half snarling, but the warm water felt soothing. At first he insisted he could bathe himself, but she said she could do a much better job. She said she didn't believe he'd use the rough lye soap the way he should.

Martha lathered him down, taking off, he claimed, about two layers of skin. She laid the soap down and began washing him off. She slipped the robe off her shoulders and put her hand under the water and began massaging him gently. An instant erection occurred. She knelt by the tub, kissing him on the ear and in the mouth while she stroked him faster and faster. His emotion rose with the rhythm of her caress. Her tongue explored his mouth. He could feel himself rising almost straight up in the water. The back of the tub was hard against his spine and his feet were flat against the other end, straining with the climb of his excitement. Her breasts were only inches from his face. He put up his left hand, lifting the plump, rose-tipped pear in his hand. He tore his mouth loose from hers and was about to cram it full of the big nipple when he suddenly rose half out of the tub and exploded.

It seemed to go on and on under the lightness of her touch. But then he reached the top and fell back into the warm water. He sagged against the sides of the tub, his head back, panting. She kissed him and smoothed his hair, smiling. She said, ''My, my. What a good boy.''

Boyd still couldn't get his breath. ''Good . . . good . . . good heavens. Oh, me, oh, my.'' He caught his breath and shuddered as the last of the feeling passed.

Martha gave him a last kiss. ''Now, you've got to stand up so I can rinse you off. This water is too soapy.''

''Whew!'' he said, sagging down. ''You're sure right. There's nothing as relaxing as a warm bath.''

Martha pumped the big bucket almost full and then added some warm water. As she was struggling to lift it off the stove, he suddenly put out his big left hand and took the bucket by the handle, lifting it out of her hands. As if he were handling a bucket of feathers, he turned the big pail upside down over his head and let the water sluice down his body, washing away the suds and grime.

She stood there, startled. ''Look at you!''

He blushed slightly. "I was always kind of strong. It just comes natural."

"Do you think you could have done that four days ago?"

He stepped out of the tub while she picked up a towel and started drying him off. "Four days ago? Four days ago, I couldn't have lifted my hopes."

"Have you now?"

He gave her a frank gaze with his brown eyes. "I don't know, I haven't been sober long enough. But if you're talking about what I said about tasting a bullet rather than whiskey, I don't think it's going to be either one. Other than being awful grateful to you, I don't know what I think."

She pitched the towel aside. "Why don't you drink another cup of coffee while I change the sheets. It won't take me but a minute and then you can have a nap." She paused. "The worst is over, Boyd. You can take another little drink now. It would make you sleep better."

He shook his head. "I don't want one. I'm going to pass on this one."

When Martha left the room, Boyd didn't bother with the coffee. Instead he wrestled the heavy tub over to the door, tipped it up, and poured the water down the back steps. The air smelled fresh from the night's rain. The sun was bright in the sky but it wasn't overly hot. He stood a moment in the open door, looking out, seeing the world as if it were a place he hadn't visited in a long time. Then he turned back, filled the bucket, washed out the tub, emptied it again, and then set it upside down on the bottom step to drain.

When he went into the bedroom, Martha was just finishing with the bed. He lay down, feeling tired and drained. He said, "What are you going to do while I sleep?"

"I've got to go out," she said. She was turning to a chiffonier. She opened it and took out a starched white dress.

He asked with a little alarm, "You going to be long?"

She came over to the bed and smoothed his hair back. "No, don't be afraid. Your bad time is over."

"Where are you going?"

She held up the dress. It had a blue collar and hem. She said, "I have to do some home nursing. That's how I make my living. I wouldn't go except that I have this elderly couple that needs looking in on about now. I won't be gone long."

He raised up and started to swing his legs around. "I'll go hitch up your buggy horse."

She pushed him back down. "I have hitched that horse so many times, I can do it in the dark. It's a simple rig. I want you to get some rest. You know, I am really starting to see the difference. Especially when you lifted that bucket." She hesitated. "It won't be long before you will be in condition to do some deciding."

"If you go anywhere near town, will you try and find me a brand of little Mexico cigarillos called Primeros? They might not have them. If not, just any kind of little cigars, the cheaper the better."

She smiled. "You've remembered you smoke."

"And eat." He paused, giving her a significant look. "And other things."

He lay down with his head on the pillow, watching her while she dressed, enjoying it when she pulled on some sheer, long white stockings. She had a little cape that went with the uniform and white shoes. His eyes were starting to close as she leaned down to kiss him. "You rest. I won't be gone long."

He was hard asleep before she ever got out of the house. Since before a time that he could remember, his sleep wasn't interrupted by dreams harder to bear than the reality he woke to. He slept without the alcohol working in him. He slept without memory churning in him. His body and mind finally gave in to his needs and let him have four hours of peace.

Four

They were sitting at the table after lunch, and Boyd was smoking one of the strong Mexican cigarillos that came in a cardboard box that fit in a man's shirt pocket. You could get ten of them for a nickel, and Boyd had always considered them over-extended, even at that price. Martha hadn't bought them, hadn't been able to find the brand, but instead, she'd brought him some tame Virginia tobacco that might take years to kill a person. Warren had come by while Boyd slept, and it had been Warren who had hunted out the Primeros and brought him several boxes. He'd also brought a couple of bottles of fine cognac, which puzzled Boyd. "He brings whiskey to a drunk who he hopes will stop drinking?"

Martha answered, "Warren brought the cognac to me. He was almost flabbergasted at how far you had come. I wanted to wake you, but he wouldn't hear of it. I wish I'd have shaved you before I left. He still said he couldn't believe the change in you. He was very proud."

Boyd gave her a look. "That I didn't commit suicide? That's kind of a backhanded compliment."

Martha got up and fetched the pot and poured them another cup of coffee. The bottle of whiskey sat untouched. She sat down.

He said without preamble, "I guess the ashes weren't even cool when I realized my life in that place was over. I caught six or seven of my saddle horses, took them on a long lead, and headed for town. I figured the Winslows had about a seven- or eight-hour start on me that would be more like twelve by the time I set in to run them down. I remember how cold it was, even if it was early spring. It had just come full dawn and I was shivering."

Boyd took a sip of his coffee. "Maybe I wasn't shivering from the cold." He looked out the back door. "I wasn't thinking much of anything. I reckon matters hadn't soaked in and I just had one thing on my mind and that was going after the Winslows. Didn't do a lot of thinking, just what was necessary. I got into the jailhouse without anybody noticing me; the town wasn't good up. I wasn't looking for much, just a few supplies and my big rifle, the one you have propped in the corner of the bedroom. That's not a regular-caliber gun, so I've had to cast my own brass cartridges and my own bullet heads. Fortunately, I'd just loaded up a hell of a mess of them, about three hundred. I loaded them in a pack along with some canned goods that were around, and filled up some of those canvas sacks that hold water. I wasn't too concerned about what I was taking because I didn't plan to stop much. We had some horse feed and I took a couple of fifty-pound sacks of those. I expected to be using the horses pretty hard."

He stopped and got out another of the Primero cigarillos and lit it. He shook the match out. Martha was watching him intently, although he wasn't talking to her so much as describing aloud something he remembered in detail.

"I didn't have much trouble picking up their trail. I knew where they were headed. They had more than enough of a start, but I thought I could get close enough so that their signs nearest to their hideout wouldn't be blown away. That's what made them so hard to find. They always got back in that rough country well enough in advance of any catch party that they just seemed to melt into the ground. I figured if I hurried, I'd about come up to them as they were heading for their hole.''

She said, ''You didn't think of trying to get some help to go with you? You said there were capable men in Pecos.''

He gave her a look of surprise. ''What would they have to do with it? It was between me and the men that had done what they'd done. It wasn't anyone else's business.''

''But you were the sheriff.''

He shook his head. ''Last thing I did before I walked out of the office and mounted up was to leave my badge on the desk. I never expected to see the place again and I haven't. So far as I know, I've still got money in the bank there.''

''So you took this personal.''

He gave her an astonished look. ''How the hell else would I take it?''

''I see.'' She nodded. ''That explains some things. I didn't mean to interrupt you. I want to hear this part.''

''There's not much else to it.'' He stopped and put up a finger. ''There is this one thing, though. Oddly enough, Hannah had asked me the day before to get her some carpet tacks for a new carpet her parents had given her. The bag of them was on my desk, two pounds of carpet tacks, the big ones, and for some reason, I guess because I was thinking of her, I put them in my saddlebags.''

''Carpet tacks?''

''I'll explain them in a minute. Anyway, I picked up their trail about ten miles out of town and cut toward it by heading south. Then I set in to catch them. I was better than three days and three nights on the trail and I hardly stopped except to change horses. Finally, about the second night, I did pull up for six hours or so, but that was to let the horses sleep, not me. That evening, I got to thinking about how it had all happened, and it came to me that if I'd killed the man Rafe instead of wounding him and taking him to jail, none of this would have happened. And then, strangely enough, the carpet tacks came into my mind, and I got them out of my saddlebags and spread out a saddle blanket and dumped out a bunch of my revolver cartridges. The carpet tacks were brass, a third of an inch across with the nail, or the spike end, about half an inch long. Hell, you've seen carpet tacks. You know what they look like, how they are rounded at the top. Well, I took one of those tacks and found I could shove it easily into the lead slug of my cartridges.'' His gunbelt was still on the table. He reached out and withdrew the big Colt revolver. He released the catch and let the cylinder fall out. He dumped the cartridges out on the table for her to see. He had been right. The brass of his shells was turning green, but it was easy to see the dark brass of the carpet tacks jacketed on top of the gray lead slugs. He held one up to her. ''If I'd hit Rafe with one of these, he would have never lived. When this cartridge hits flesh or bone or anything, that carpet tack causes the lead slug to fly apart and pieces of lead to go flying all through a man's body, spreading on impact. When that slug hits, it gets to be about the diameter of a half dollar and would knock a man down if he was to be hit in the arm. The flying lead would make so many holes in him, he'd bleed to death before he could ever get help.''

He slowly loaded the cartridges back into his revolver and shoved it back into the holster. ''The cartridges for my big rifle are the same.'' He looked at her. ''That night, I resolved I had wounded my last man. If it comes to guns, it's past the time for wounding. If you draw a gun, you had better be ready to kill or be killed. I was young then, a hell of a lot younger than I am now.''

"Do you think you will ever draw a gun again?" Martha asked.

He shrugged. "I don't know what I'm going to do, Martha. Hell, today is the first day that my brains haven't been addled by the whiskey or the lack of it. I've got to get used to this new situation."

"Did you ever catch your men?"

He nodded slowly. "I had them in sight by the time they reached the foothills of the Davis Mountains. I've got a telescopic sight that goes on my big gun. I could see them when they couldn't see me. I followed them straight into their hiding spot. They left a lookout behind them, but I killed him during the night. I also killed two of my saddle horses, just rode them to death. The rest of the horses were nearly dead from lack of sleep and water and hard usage, but I had run my quarry to the ground. I followed them right to their doorstep, a cavern so deep in a tangle of ravines and cuts and draws and switchbacks, you'd have to stumble on it if you didn't have a guide. I got in a secure place about three hundred yards from the mouth of their hole and then I called for them to come out."

He paused and lit another cigarillo. He said, "You know, I get to feeling bad that I might be taking up too much of your time. Warren never mentioned that you were a visiting nurse."

If the change of subject surprised her, she made no sign. She shook her head. "No, you were the patient who needed me the most. I don't have many patients this time of the year, mostly in the winter with the flu and ague, and sometimes folks with broken legs."

Boyd asked, "How do you avoid the babies?"

She gave him a direct look. "I don't work with them. What happened next?"

"Once they realized who it was and that I was alone, they thought it was funny. They commenced to whoop and holler and ask why I didn't just come in for breakfast. They asked me how my wife was, and a few of them told me what they'd done to her while they were waiting on me to get there." His jaw tightened. "I believed them; it didn't bother me. I still believed they might have her, might have taken her along. I yelled that if they'd let her go, I'd leave them in peace. I could tell it puzzled them at first, but once they got on to it, they made their women call out to me like they were Hannah. Except they didn't know what to say. Pretty soon, I reckoned they didn't have her and I gave them one more warning to surrender. They started laughing again, only they didn't laugh too much after I started lobbing in those big shells that shattered and slung pieces of lead everywhere." He paused thoughtfully. "Have you ever heard a cavern full of men and women screaming?" He smiled maliciously. "They screamed much louder than Hannah ever did. I really liked hearing that sound. I could even imagine them running around in there, looking for a place to hide from all that lead bounding every which way, but I knew they couldn't hide, not unless they had some deep holes. I was hearing first one and then another get hit. Their screams had a special quality to it, a pain in it, a lot of pain. They weren't getting stunned by one slug taking them out; they were getting chewed up."

Boyd paused and drew on his cigarillo. "I don't know how many shells I threw in there, maybe fifty or seventy-five. At some point, they began to hollering they wanted to give up. There wasn't near as many of them screaming now. I just kept lobbing those big shells in there. I wanted to make sure they had their minds made up."

Martha watched Boyd carefully, noting that his hands were rock steady, his eyes almost unblinking. She knew that he was back in that killing place. She could sense his almost deadly calm even in her sunlit kitchen.

"Finally, I quit firing. I about had to because the barrel of my rifle was so hot it would have taken the skin off of you."

"How did you make that ride with all your burns?" Martha reached out and opened his hand that was on the table, running her finger over the pink thick scars. "They must have been a bloody mess."

He said steadily, "I never noticed."

Martha got up and said, "I am going to have some cognac with my coffee. Do you want some?"

Boyd shook his head. "Not yet. It's a little early in the day for me." He gave her a smile and she returned it.

When she was seated again with a fresh cup of coffee and a small glass of cognac, he said, "After I quit firing, four of them appeared in the door of the cave waving some kind of white flag. Two men and what appeared to be two women." He paused, his eyes going reflective as he remembered the scene. "I took a good long moment to look them over, making sure they weren't carrying weapons. One of the men was bleeding from the arm. When I was satisfied that they didn't have any weapons ready to hand, I called to them to come forward fifteen or twenty paces down the little defile that led to their cavern. I started climbing down from the rocks where I had taken up my station. I left my rifle and descended with a revolver in both hands. I was careful not to make myself a target, in case someone was lurking back in the cave trying to lure me out for a shot. I had the four come so far forward that the angle was in my favor, not that I was taking many chances. I kept a shelf of rock between me and the opening of the cave while I came upon the four of them. I guess I was worrying too much about the cave because when I got about ten feet away, the woman on the far end suddenly stuck her hand in her apron pocket and came out with a snub-nosed bulldog pistol. She . . . *he* . . . it turned out to be a young man in a woman's dress. He got off one shot, which missed. After that, I shot the four of them down as fast as I could.''

''Just like that?'' Martha asked.

He twirled the cigarillo in his mouth and said, ''There wasn't no other way.'' He cocked his eye at her. ''I was disappointed that the one in the dress turned out to be a man, but at least one of them was a woman. I hoped that one of the dead men loved her very much. I hoped that it was one of the two that had come out to surrender. I hope he had at least a second before I killed him to know how it felt.''

She turned her head at him. ''Were you a hard man before, Boyd? Your brother said you were just the opposite.''

''I was capable, and I could hold my own, but I wasn't cold and I wasn't hard.''

''Do you think this made you so?''

He studied her face for a second. ''How do I seem to you?''

''You're changing, of course, every day. I saw you when you were so whipped down, you could barely hold your head up. You're still changing. I'm wondering who will come out at the end of the tunnel.''

''If it explains it, I'll tell you that I took my satisfaction out by killing the Winslows and their gang and their women.''

Boyd looked away, his mind going back to when he'd carefully entered the cavern. It had been surprisingly light with a number of lamps still burning. There had been furniture, lots of it, and he had wondered how they had managed to get some of the bigger pieces into such a remote and tortured place.

There had been bodies all around, a few of them still groaning. Boyd had walked among them, shooting the wounded in such a way that they wouldn't die right away but would have plenty of time to enjoy their suffering with no chance of helping themselves. He'd found Rafe in a corner, nursing a belly wound. Rafe had looked up, his eyes terrified. Boyd had shot him in both kneecaps.

There had been a wealth of supplies in their hideout, and he had spent time carrying out some foodstuff and a case of whiskey and a sack of grain for his horses. He had needed to get them to water.

Lastly, he'd found several five-gallon drums of kerosene. He'd doused the place down liberally and then, after pouring the last on Rafe, Boyd had casually lit the wounded man's sleeve. Rafe had caught fire immediately, and Boyd had walked out of the cavern without looking back.

He had made his way out of the torturous country, finally finding prairie. He'd pushed ahead, looking for water for his spent horses. Once, he had stopped and looked back. Against the light blue sky, he had seen a rope of black, thick smoke rising from somewhere in the mountain fastness. He'd turned and ridden on, suddenly tired, spent, and numb. The edge that had pushed him so relentlessly in his pursuit and revenge had gone. There hadn't seemed to be anything left to do. He had become a dry leaf in the wind, drifting and blowing aimlessly. Almost blindly, he had turned his horses north with no clear objective in mind. He'd had no plans, no thoughts, no interests, no concerns. For almost three months, he had simply drifted.

He said, "And now you know just about as much as I can tell you. You said it would help to talk about it, but I'm not so sure."

Martha said, "I said there was no way you would stop drinking if you did not face your troubles. What are your plans now?"

Boyd shrugged his shoulders. "I don't really have any. About the only thing I can feel any enthusiasm for is killing bad people."

She was startled by the baldness of his statement. She said, "Boyd, you've got to realize something. You can kill a thousand men and you can lay with a thousand women, but you are never again going to have what you had. The past is gone. Go on from here."

He looked at her for a long moment. "What happened to you, Martha? What are you carrying around?"

For a second, she stared past him, fighting the feeling that was coming inside her, but she couldn't. Her eyes teared up but tears didn't run down her cheeks. She dabbed at her eyes with the back of her hand. After a moment she said, "I suppose you have the right to ask that. The answer is that I'm alive. I feel very guilty about that. I have to fight with it every day."

"I don't understand."

"We were on a train." Her voice became soft and distant, as if she were talking about someone else. "My husband and me and our baby. We were going to Wichita Falls, Texas, which is where I was raised. Our car and another passenger car had been placed on a siding while they hooked us up to another train. A freight train missed a signal and came on to the siding and plowed into our car. My husband and baby and most of the people on the car were killed. I was hardly bruised."

"How long ago was that?"

"A little over two years ago."

He reached across and took her hand. "You're a hell of

a woman, Martha. I don't know where you got the kindness to worry with me.''

''No,'' she said. ''It has helped. Knowing what you had to do reminded me of what I had to do. You can't just give up, you owe it to the ones that went on ahead. I'll never love another man the way I loved my husband, but I might love again. It'll be different, but it may be as strong in its own way.''

Boyd said, ''Thank you for getting the mud out of my brain. You did me a great service.''

She gripped his hand with both of hers and smiled shyly. She said, ''And you did me a service. You were the first man since my husband. I had forgotten how good it could be. You're a wonderful lover.''

Boyd was speechless. All he could do was stare at her.

The next afternoon, Boyd and his brother Warren were sitting in Martha's front room drinking coffee and talking. Martha had gone out, either on business or to give them some privacy, Boyd was not sure which.

Warren had been there half an hour, most of which he'd spent commenting on how well Boyd looked and how proud he was of him, before he finally got down to what he'd come for. He said, ''Well, now that you've got your head back on your shoulders, have you decided what you want to do?''

Boyd looked at him steadily. ''What do you mean, do? *Do* as in work, *do* as in live somewhere, *do* as in run for political office? What the hell do you mean, Warren?''

Warren had a slightly disgusted look on his face. He said, ''Don't come with that on me, Boyd. You know damn good and well what I mean. You were a sheriff; do you want to be a sheriff again? You were headed into the cattle business; do you still want to go into the cattle business? Do as in *do* something. Is that exact enough for you?''

Boyd sipped at his coffee and took a moment to light one of the Primero cigarillos. He said, "Ain't you kind of rushing me a little, Warren? I've just now got my head out of the jug. What makes you so sure that I'm ready to go out into civilized society?"

Warren said, "I'm not planning on you setting on your life's work this afternoon, but I am expecting you to start giving it some sort of thought. I have some ideas on that line, but I want to hear what you have to say first."

Boyd drew on his cigarillo thinking about exactly what he wanted to say and how to say it. He was hesitant with the words because he wasn't sure himself. If there had ever been a time in his life when he had been more uncertain, he couldn't remember it, so for the sake of argument and to give his brother an answer, he said, "I don't want to do a damn thing, Warren. I just want to drift whichever way the wind blows, whichever way the current carries me. That and kill anybody that I think doesn't happen to be living right. Is that clear enough?"

Warren suppressed a slight smile. In another man, he might have thought the talk was all josh and fun, but in Boyd's case you could never be too sure. He said, "As I understand it then, you plan to go back to drifting and drinking and you plan to shoot folks you identify as bad people, like the Winslows? You've already killed all of them, Boyd, isn't that enough? Do you need some more?"

"Yeah."

Warren shook his head. "I don't think that you can do that, Boyd. In the first place, if you go to drifting and drinking again, I don't think that you'll be in any shape to do it. I think the one that'll be killed will be you."

Boyd looked at his brother. "What makes you think I am headed back into the bottle?"

"What makes me think that you would stay out of it?"

"That's something that you would have to take up with Martha."

Warren asked, "What do you intend to do for money on this drifting-without-drinking-but-killing plan that you have laid out?"

"You told me that there was money due me for rewards on the Winslows, somewhere around five thousand dollars."

Warren nodded. "That's correct, but it'll take some effort on your part to collect it. You'll have to go where the various outfits are that are presenting them, prove who you are, and collect the money. Everybody knows that it was you that wiped out the Winslows, but they aren't going to send it to you in the mail. However, I can tell you that the Cattleman's Protective Association was part of that reward package. We had two thousand dollars up, and I can tell you that part won't be too hard to get. Two thousand dollars isn't going to last you very long, Boyd, drifting and damning the evil."

"You got two thousand dollars ready to hand over to me?"

Warren nodded again slowly. "I do. You've also got one hundred forty-six dollars that you left in the Pecos bank which I drew out and held for you. Yes, I can get you the two thousand within twenty-four hours."

Boyd said, "I want you to give a thousand dollars of it to Martha."

Warren looked up and smiled. "She's quite a lady, isn't she?"

Boyd nodded. "She'll do."

"You remember you asked me what was I sending you to?"

Boyd said, "Let's not mention that anymore, what do you say?"

"But you want to give her a whole thousand dollars? That's a pretty nice piece of change."

"What would you think putting up with me for five days was worth, Warren, especially in the condition I was in?"

Warren snorted and said, "Well, if you bring it down to that, I'd probably say the whole two thousand dollars. But you could use half of it yourself." Warren paused. "I've got a plan that I would like to put to you and see if you think that it fits in with what you want to do, only it's more in line with the way the law looks at such activities as you have planned."

"What would that be?"

"Do you know anything about the Cattleman's Protective Association, Boyd?"

"I know a little. You've got agents out in the field that try to protect your members' cattle and property and such. Can't say that I've ever met one, but I know that it's a pretty big operation."

Warren said, "We're in every state and every territory that's in any way doing much business in cattle. I'd say that the cattle business wouldn't be at the prosperous point it is today if it hadn't been for both the Cattleman's Association and the Cattleman's Protective Association. The Cattleman's Association is made up of ranchers, stockmen, breeders, and auction houses and other folks involved in the cattle industry. The Cattleman's Protective Association is the enforcement arm of the Cattleman's Association. We put agents out in the field to make sure that your cattle and property are safe."

Boyd asked, "And just how do you do that?"

Warren said, "The same way any other law enforcement agency makes sure that your lives and property are safe. With a gun, Boyd, several guns, a force of arms."

Boyd looked at his brother for a moment. "Warren, I don't quite get that. The Cattleman's Association is a private business. Your agents can't go around carrying guns and enforcing the law.''

"Yes, and the Pinkerton Detective Agency was a private business in the Civil War. Now they are the United States Secret Service with Allan Pinkerton at the head of a federal bureau, right where U.S. Grant put him. Boyd, we've got lots of good friends in the Congress and law enforcement all over the country. They welcome and need our help. Take your own situation, for example. You were a sheriff in Reeves County. When you jumped the Winslows, you were out of your jurisdiction. That's the situation in every state and territory. You have a sheriff who is confined to his own county and a town marshal who is confined to his town only. Texas has the Texas Rangers, but there's only about a hundred of them, the only state law that you have. The federal marshals are spread thin, and the problem is that these cattle rustlers and other people that interfere with the cattle business cross state and territorial lines. We are the only organization that is widespread enough to cross those lines and we can go after the problem, wherever it is, and we are welcomed by the local law in most cases. We have very few instances where this sheriff or that sheriff or that ranger or whoever doesn't want us taking a hand in their business. But more than that, as private citizens, we have the right to protect the rights of the men that we are working for. That's just natural law.''

"Are you telling me that your agents can go out and catch a cattle rustler or a brand changer or even shoot them or string them up?''

Warren smiled slightly. "Well, we haven't hung anybody lately, but there have been many cases where our agents have had to use force to protect the lives and property of the people we work for, which is the Cattleman's Association.''

"You didn't get any problems from the local law?''

"We cooperate with the locals in every way that we can. Like I said, they're glad to see us, we make their job easier. Boyd, you know that country you lived in was enormous. You can't tell me that there is enough law to cover that much territory, even if you had ten times as many sheriffs, can you?"

"No, I reckon not. It's a big country and it's a big job. That is how the Winslows were able to get away with their depredations for so long." His face set in a hard line as he said the name of the men he had so hated. "But what has all this got to do with me?"

Warren said, "I am proposing that you become a member of the Cattleman's Protective Association and that you become an agent in the field. Strap on a gun for us. I know how capable you are, Boyd. You've been a sheriff with an impeccable record. The fact that you're my brother isn't getting you the job; the fact that you are a very worthwhile man is what will."

Boyd smiled. "Naturally, it doesn't hurt any that my brother is the vice president of the organization, does it?"

Warren smiled. "You have to get cute, don't you? Yes, I am the vice president and I do have some say in it, but if I thought you were sorry, I wouldn't hire you even if I was the president. I have an obligation to the people I work for, the cattlemen. Boyd, these are rough times out on the range and out in the far-flung territories. They have trouble with the nesters, they have trouble with the farmers, they have trouble with drifting bands of marauders, they have trouble with the straight out-and-out thieves, they have trouble, in some areas, with bandits coming up from Mexico. These are good, honest men trying to make a living and improve the cattle business. They need all the help that they can get. It's work that needs doing."

"I have no doubt, Warren, but I'm not in a joining mood.

I really don't think that I am what you are looking for. There could come a day when all I feel like doing is laying around, getting drunk. I'm going to drift.''

Warren said, "I knew that was exactly what you were going to say and I am ready for you. I am going to make you a captain. Our agents have ranks, normally two to three men to a station, and the captain is the head of the station. I am going to give you a rank that is equivalent to any of our men that you'll run into. All I want you to do is drift from place to place and look for trouble. You say you're looking for some bad guys? I've got plenty of bad hats that I can point you to; there's no shortage of them. If it's your desire to kill people who are doing harm to others, this is the perfect job for you. All you have to do is drift because no matter where you go, there are agents of the Cattleman's Protective Association nearby. The pay is one hundred dollars per month plus your mount, plus a per diem of five dollars per day to feed you and your horse and put a roof over your head.''

"That's two hundred and fifty dollars a month, pretty fair wages for a non-lawman lawman. That's more than I was making as a sheriff.''

Warren answered dryly. "We're bigger than Reeves County.''

Boyd looked thoughtful for a moment, twirling the cigarillo in his mouth, then said, "No, I don't think so, Warren. You said that you would hire me or not hire me even if you were the president. Well, that's the job I want.''

Warren looked bemused. "President? Well, Boyd, that job ain't open.''

Boyd said, "Well, that's the only one I would take; otherwise I would have to answer to somebody, and that's it in a nutshell. I don't want to have to answer to anyone, not even you, my own brother.''

Warren said, "But you answered to someone when you were sheriff."

"That was then. This is now."

"Boyd, this is the best chance that you'll get." Warren slapped his knee in exasperation. "You've got to realize that there is not going to come along a better opportunity than this, not for you. You have to pull yourself back together, Boyd. This is exactly what you want."

"No. It ain't written down anywhere that I have to pull myself back together. It ain't written down anywhere that I have to do anything. I don't want to be beholden to anybody, to answer to anybody, or even to explain anything to anybody."

"Son, the only way that you will get that way is to be dead. No matter what you are doing, even as a bum in an alley, you'll have to answer to somebody because some sheriff's deputy will come along and kick you in the ribs and tell you get up and move along. Life don't work that way, Boyd. You've got responsibilities, maybe not to anyone else, maybe not even to yourself, but you'll find that certain circumstances force responsibilities upon you that you can't get away from, try as you might."

Boyd looked troubled. "I don't want to talk about this anymore. Why don't we have a drink of that cognac and talk about something else?"

Warren raised his eyebrows and said, "You're going to take a drink? Does Martha know that?"

Boyd smiled slightly. "Martha says that I ain't no dipso . . . dipso something."

"A dipsomaniac?"

"Yeah, that's it. That's a drunk that has to have it, that has an excuse. She says I ain't one, that I can take it or leave it alone now that I've gotten rid of my troubles. You see, Martha helps you on those kind of things."

There had been such a bitter tone in Boyd's voice in the last few words that Warren looked at him gently. He said, "Have you gotten rid of your troubles, Boyd?"

"You know damn good and well that I haven't, that I won't ever get over them, or get rid of them, or get above them, or beside them, or under them. They'll be in me the rest of my life."

Warren sighed and heaved a great breath. He said, "Boyd, there ain't no real good time to talk about this, but there ain't no other time, so I am going to bring it up now because it has to be talked about. Son, your old life is over with. I know what you mean by drifting; what you really mean is that you are going to go looking in hopes of finding that old life. You're not going to find it, Boyd. It's gone. Hannah is gone, your baby is gone, your ranch is gone. The ground is still there but the house that you built is gone. Pecos is going to go on, but you couldn't go back there to live, you couldn't stand it. You've got to understand that you have to find a way to make a new life. You're a different man now, Boyd, this has changed you.

"You know, for most of your life, you had things easier than anyone I've ever seen. Everything came natural to you. You were always the best-looking kid; you could ride better, you could shoot better than anyone else. You were always a hell of a hand with the ladies and no one could ever say no to you. You're one of the best-natured men that I have ever met in my life. You needed a job to help you get started, so you mentioned to a few friends in Pecos that you'd like to be their sheriff and bam . . . you were their sheriff. You married the prettiest girl in six states. You had a pretty easy life, but that's all over now, and you have scars, not just on your face, but inside of you as well, that won't ever go away. You're going to have to replace that life with a new one that fits the person that you are now. I see a hardness in you that

I never thought I would see and that I have seen in very few others. Boyd, I have to tell you that even sitting here across from you, you scare me a little bit. No, don't stop me, don't put up your hand. You do. You've got a menace about you now; you're frightening. There is a cold something burning inside of you now. I don't know if it's hate or revenge, but it's steel, cold steel. I don't know who you are now, but you'll have to change your life because you can never go back to that carefree man who was alive on this earth three months ago. This sounds harsh, but you are a different man." He sat back on the divan.

Across from him, Boyd shifted uncomfortably in his chair. "What you say may be true, Warren, I don't know. I don't think I hate, and I don't know what you mean about this business of looking dangerous. I don't feel different except that I feel very sad and I feel that I don't care much about anything except you, my sisters, Muriel, your kids, and Martha. Seems like the rest of the world is a very hostile place. I guess maybe that is where you get the impression that I kind of look mean, because right now I see the rest of the world as a hostile place and I don't ever plan to be caught off my guard again. Let the man who comes up against me be careful. I was lying in bed the other night, shaking, wondering out loud about things, and for some reason I said, when you starve with a bear, the bear starves last. That's the way that I am going to be from now on, Warren. I am going to be the bear."

Warren nodded. "That's exactly what I just got through saying. You give the impression that you consider the rest of the world hostile, that everyone else is the enemy. You also give the impression that you're the bear and that you're going to starve last. Like I said, I wouldn't want to be the man to go up against you. That's why I think you should take this job. You're going to kill someone illegally, but if you take this job, it'll keep you at least between the fences. It's your only chance." Warren sat back on the divan and folded his arms, looking at his brother and waiting.

Boyd sat there, not speaking, looking at the cigarillo in his right hand. He took a deep draw on the cigar and blew a long puff of smoke toward the ceiling. His eyes slowly swiveled to Warren's. When he spoke, his voice was quiet and flat and resigned. He said, "Warren, you apparently are going to force me to say it. I don't want anyone to know this about me. I don't want to even know it myself. I'm going to state it as simply as I can. I don't ever want the responsibility for anyone else, ever again. I had it once. Hannah was my responsibility; the unborn baby was my responsibility. Where are they now, Warren?" Boyd's voice almost broke, but he recovered himself. "They're gone, Warren, that's where they are. Whose fault is it? It's mine. I don't trust myself to take care of others. Do you understand me now, why I can't take your job? Have I made myself plain?"

Warren looked at him a long moment. His own voice was husky. "Son, you can't look at it like that. If you did . . . well, you just can't."

Boyd said, "You were going to say that I wouldn't have any reason left for living, but you don't want to say that. Right?"

Warren nodded. "Yes, that's about what I was going to say. You made that mistake once, but I can't let you think like that again. You're back to almost normal, you're thinking again, you're not sodden with whiskey. My God, man, Martha is happier than I have seen her in years just from taking care of you. You can't withdraw from people, Boyd. You have to live with people and there is a responsibility to that. You're not made to run off and hide. Maybe you don't see that now, maybe you won't see that for a month, but you will see it. Don't lose all that time, Boyd. As your blood kin, I am begging you, don't lose all that time."

Boyd looked away. He stood up and said, "I'll get the cognac." His throat was tighter than it had been in weeks. He didn't want to hear any more of what his brother had to say. The coffeepot was empty and he put some fresh on to boil. While he waited, he took the decanter and two glasses and set them on the table between where Warren was sitting and the place he had been occupying. He said, "I'm making some fresh coffee, won't be but a minute."

Warren asked, "What time is Martha due back?"

"She didn't say."

"I've got an idea that we ought to take that little lady out for some supper tonight. What do you think of that?"

"Out to supper? Hell, I haven't been out to supper in I can't remember when. I can't go out to supper, I haven't got a hat. Martha threw my hat away with the rest of my clothes."

Warren suddenly jumped to his feet. He said, "By golly, I knew I forgot something. I bought you a new one. Let me run out to the buggy and get it."

With that, Warren hurried out the front door and Boyd headed back for the kitchen. Boyd watched the coffee slowly come to a boil, wondering if he had really told his brother the truth. Was he afraid of responsibility or was he simply afraid of being hurt again? He honestly didn't know. He did believe, however, that he wasn't ready or fit for anything of any importance, especially if it involved other lives. He didn't trust himself anymore. All he wanted was to be in a position that if anyone lost in the game, it could only be him.

Five

He and Warren sat drinking coffee and cognac. Warren had given him his new hat, a pearl gray beauty with a four-and-a-half-inch brim, a 10x beaver with a horseshoe crown. It was the model he had worn ever since he had been old enough to wear a man's hat.

Warren said, "Of course, we've always had the same size head, at least since you've been grown. I didn't know if all that whiskey that you've been swilling had changed the shape of it."

Boyd smiled slightly. "Warren, I thought you knew that whiskey doesn't change the outside of your head, it's the inside that it changes. Don't let on that you haven't drunk enough to know that."

Warren said, "Would you believe this is the first drink that I've ever had in my life?"

Boyd laughed. "Well, you're my big brother, so I'm obliged to believe you. However, those red veins in your nose kind of give a lie to that."

Warren chuckled, taking a sip of coffee and leaning back on the divan. He said, "Well, would I be stepping on your toes if I asked you what your immediate plans are? You've the same as told me that you have no long-range ones, but you seem fit enough now, you look decent, at least halfway. I just wondered what you might be thinking of doing here soon.''

Boyd said, ''Well, Martha has indicated that she would like for me to stay around here at least another couple of days.'' He glanced up at his brother slyly. ''She seems to think I'm good company, even if other people don't. In fact, I don't even think she thinks I'm dangerous, so I was figuring on sticking on around here and letting my old pony get some more rest. I thought I would try to collect what money I could and then sort of amble on.''

''And leave Martha just like that?''

''What's that supposed to mean?''

Warren put up his hand quickly. ''Nothing, nothing. Hell, I didn't mean anything by it. I thought we were just joshing.''

Boyd gave his brother a long look. He said, ''I'm very grateful to Mrs. Blair. She is a nurse and I am her patient. I am going to miss her. She's a nice lady, but there will be another patient along after I'm gone.''

Warren said, ''You're jumping to conclusions, my young brother. I didn't mean anything more about it than that. I think it is a fine damn thing you are going to do by giving Martha that money. She doesn't work that often and she can use it. I don't think she is going to take it very easily. Be careful how you offer it.''

Boyd said, ''I kind of have the mind that you'd give it to her in payment of taking care of me, make it seem like it came from you.''

Warren shook his head rapidly. ''Oh, no. You're not putting that off on me. If you're going to give the lady a thousand dollars, then you're going to take the credit for it. You talked about your lack of responsibility to people. Well, this is one that you can't duck. If you want that lady to have a thousand dollars, then you're going to have to give it to her yourself. By the way, you owe me seventy-five dollars for the clothes. The hat is a gift.''

Boyd smiled slowly. ''What about the groceries that you sent out, and the whiskey, and the feed for my horse? What do I owe you for that?''

Warren thought a moment. ''Well, I guess that comes within family business. If you had stayed with me, I would have been out the same amount on groceries and feed for the horse, but I would have had to put up with your company in the bargain, so I think we'll just let that ride. We'll call it square on the seventy-five dollars for the clothes of yours.''

Boyd said, ''Well, if I had known that I was going to have to pay for them, I could have done without them linen shirts. I reckon that you had to pay five dollars apiece for them.''

''You're way low, my son. You ain't bought a linen shirt in a good while, I take it. Those shirts cost seven dollars apiece.''

Boyd laughed. ''Warren, if you weren't my brother, I would ask to see the receipt. You wouldn't be trying to get in my pocket, would you?''

''Anyone tries to get in your pocket right now, they would come up dead empty. I've got your money, so I'd be damned careful how you talk to me.''

Martha came in a little after five. She took a moment to admire Boyd's new hat, and then was flustered at Warren's suggestion that they go out for supper.

Warren said, ''I suggest that we go out to the Palomino Club and make a fine night of it.''

Martha said, ''Oh, my goodness. The Palomino Club. Oh, Warren, that's far too grand. I don't have a thing to wear there.''

Warren said gently, "Martha, you could wear your oldest housedress and you would still look better than any lady in the place. Now you go along and get ready, we'll be leaving here about six-thirty."

Martha glanced at Boyd. She said, "I need to shave Boyd first."

Warren interrupted her. "That boy got you trained to that? He can shave himself. I've been watching his hands and they are steady enough to stack a deck. He didn't tell you that he used to be a fair hand with the cards in his day?"

Boyd said, "You ought to know. I learned it all from you and almost got myself killed as a result. By the way, what is this Palomino Club?"

"It's a roadhouse about five miles out of town on the way to Elk City. It is a right nice place and has as good of food as you will find in this part of the country. They also have a casino where you can do a little gambling, faro, shoot some dice."

Boyd said, "Well, I ain't exactly dressed for that kind of sociability myself."

Warren laughed. "Son, they're not interested in how you look, they're interested in your money. They know I've got money, so we'll all be welcome." He turned around to Martha and asked, "How does that sound? A night out on the town?"

She was almost blushing. She stammered, "Well, I . . . I just don't know. It's been a long time."

"Well, missy, you just run along and start getting ready, and I'll see that Boyd gets himself shaved and straightened up."

Boyd said, "What about Muriel? Do you want to go get her?"

Warren said, "Muriel is down with a cold and she has a sister visiting her. I don't like the sister and if Muriel comes, then the sister will have to come and that would ruin the whole party. No, let's just make it the three of us. We ought to get away from here no later than six-thirty, get out there, eat a good meal, and we can be back early to get a good night's sleep."

Martha said, delight fighting with concern on her face, "I just hope that I can find some old rag to wear. I hope I don't embarrass you two gentlemen."

Boyd said, "Martha, I reckon it would be the other way around."

She hurried out of the room toward the bedroom. Boyd smiled, watching her go. He said, "She's like a little kid."

Warren said, "I doubt that she's had much fun in her life these past few years. Did you know that she used to be a blonde?"

Boyd almost blurted out his confusion about the different color of her hair, but he contained himself in time. He said, "No, how could she have been a blonde?"

Warren said matter-of-factly, "Right after the train wreck when her husband and her baby were killed, her hair went snow white. I reckon that she lost thirty, forty pounds in sight of three months. I guess you know, she tried to drink every bottle of whiskey in the county. When her hair finally started growing in again, it grew in that light brown. I am beginning to see light streaks of blond in it again, so maybe it will come back in blond one of these days."

Boyd nodded. It explained a great deal.

They set out a little before seven, just as dusk was beginning to fall. Martha had outdone herself. Somewhere, she had found a flowered green and yellow, long, velvet dress that went well with her coloring. She had done something fancy with her hair so that it was up, and Boyd could see she was wearing slippers with silver buckles. Around her neck, she had some sort of jewelry that completed her ensemble.

When she had come into the living room after dressing, both Boyd and Warren had swept off their hats and given her a low bow. It had made her giggle, but Boyd had been sincere when he'd said, "Martha, you look plumb larruping. I mean, downright larruping."

Warren had said, "Very elegant, Martha. You'll knock their hats off."

Now they drove through the gathering evening. Warren had a smart little buggy horse that stepped along at a good clip. It happened that they were on the right side of town to shorten the trip, but it was still five or six miles to where they were going. Warren said, "I think you'll enjoy it. Folks need a little night life once in a while."

Warren was driving, Martha sitting in the middle, and Boyd was on the outside. Boyd was wearing his gunbelt. He had almost not brought it, but Warren had said, "For heaven's sake, Boyd, you look undressed without your gunbelt. I haven't seen you without it since you were fifteen years old. Put it on." Boyd had protested that he wasn't sure he even knew how to use the gun anymore, but in the end he had added it to his otherwise plain dress.

As they drove, Warren said to Martha, "Boyd tells me that it's your belief that he can take a drink every now and then without falling back again."

Martha said, "Well, you're sitting next to living proof of it. I don't think that Boyd will ever drink that way again." She turned her head to the right and glanced at Boyd. "But that will be up to him. Only Boyd can decide how to run his life. He didn't drink that way before his troubles. I think he is going to handle his troubles now, but I don't know." In an almost proprietary gesture, she reached out and touched Boyd on the knee. "That's all I know."

Deliberately changing the subject, Boyd asked, "Warren, how come they stuck this high-class place out here in the middle of nowhere? Looks like, if you were going to put in a fancy cafe and a casino, you would want to do it downtown."

Warren chuckled. "There's two reasons. One, it is close enough to town where the Baptists and the others can get to it and it is far enough for the Baptist preachers to preach against it. That's not the real reason, though, that it's out here on this road. It's on the quality side of Oklahoma City and there is a slew of rich ranchers that live out this way, them folks that are carrying the cash. The Italian fellow that built it, I can't recall his name . . . I keep wanting to say Ravioli, but I know that ain't right. That's some kind of dish, isn't it, Martha? Anyway, he knew what he was doing when he put it where he did. He gets a crowd in there about every night. Of course, he has the good sense to close it on Sunday. Martha, have you ever eaten Italian food?"

Martha shook her head. "Just spaghetti, not any really fancy Italian food."

Boyd said, "I wouldn't even know what it looks like."

Warren said, "Well, then you're in for a treat. I'll do the ordering. We'll get some of that veal *parmesan* and some of that *scallopini*. I don't know what all those names mean. I generally let the waiter pick it out." He laughed. "We're going to have a good time. Martha, do you still know how to dance?"

The Palomino Club was a rambling, one-story, lit-up establishment with horses and buggies hitched all around. It was set off from the main road at least a quarter of a mile. Warren pulled up and a young Negro boy came out to take the reins. They stepped down, Boyd helping Martha to the ground.

Inside, they were greeted by a man in a swallow-tailed

coat and with a huge drooping mustache. He said in an accent that Boyd hadn't heard very often, "Ahhh . . . Meester McMasters. So wonderful that you should come tonight. We will have a table for you immediately. There are three? No Meesus McMasters? Ah, but this lovely lady. Yes, this is wonderful."

They walked into a large dining room, well lit with low-hanging chandeliers, and were shown to a table in a corner with a white starched tablecloth and gleaming silverware and crystal. Boyd felt almost shabby in the surroundings. Through several sets of double doors he could see into the gaming part of the establishment. He could hear the low murmur of the gamblers, hear the noise at the dice table, hear the sound of the croupier at the roulette table.

They were seated, and a waiter wearing a white shirt with a black bow tie immediately appeared. He asked, "Mr. McMasters, should I bring the wine now?"

Boyd looked across at his brother. "Warren, have you started drinking wine?"

Warren said good-naturedly, "Boyd, try not to embarrass me in here any more than you have to. We're not in the Square Meal Cafe." Warren turned to the waiter. "Yes, why don't you bring us a bottle of red wine, the one I like so much, while we look at the menu."

In another corner of the big room, a small string orchestra was playing. On the dance floor, Boyd could see several couples swaying with the music. He guessed there were thirty, maybe forty, tables in the room with most of them occupied. The men were dressed in suits with foulard ties and the ladies were dressed in elegant gowns. He still thought that Martha was the match of any of them.

When the wine came, the waiter poured out all around and then Warren lifted his glass. Martha and Boyd followed suit. Boyd said, "Luck." He took a big swallow. He had meant to knock it straight back as befits the toast, but he almost gagged. Across the table, he could see his brother smiling at him.

Warren said, "Boyd, that ain't whiskey; you're not supposed to hustle it down so it can get to work. You're supposed to enjoy it. Sip it slow."

Boyd set his glass down and looked at it. "Well, Warren, if you have come to enjoy this wine, then our trails have split a long way back."

"You mean to tell me that you don't like it?"

"Well, if it was just plain grape juice, then, yeah, I'd like it. But it is mighty thin for alcohol."

Martha said to Boyd, "It is an acquired taste, though I don't know why anyone would go to the trouble to acquire a taste for something they didn't like." She looked around the room. "Isn't this grand? This is so exciting!" She reached over and patted Warren's hand. "I can't tell you how much I am enjoying being out like this. It's been forever."

The orchestra struck up a waltz and Warren stood. "I believe this is our dance, Martha. If you sit here waiting for Boyd to ask you, you'll be here forever."

Boyd watched them walk off, smiling to himself. He was delighted to see Martha having a good time. Maybe it would take some of the sadness out of her eyes. He took a sip of the red wine, which wasn't so bad when it was sipped, he found. He kept sipping until his glass was empty, and was about to congratulate himself on a job well done when the waiter hovering nearby filled it again without saying a word.

When they returned from the dance floor, Warren sent for the menu and then ordered for all of them. Boyd didn't recognize his meal as anything he had seen before, but it tasted good enough. It was some kind of meat in a white sauce with what he took to be noodles and then one thing and then another.

Martha had something that Warren said was chicken *cacciatore*. Boyd had never heard of it, but it seemed to him like a pretty handy way of doubling the price on plain old chicken and gravy. He liked the bread. It was crusty but soft inside and warm. He put on lots of butter. When the meal was finished, they had some kind of ice cream concoction that Warren called *spumoni*. Boyd didn't much care for it, and he had a hard time eating the sweet dessert. It was the first time his mind had flashed back to Hannah. For a while, it brought his mood down, but then he pulled himself back together with an effort and took Martha to dance.

As they were waltzing, she said, "Well, what a liar your brother is. You are a marvelous dancer, Boyd."

"No, Martha, like most of the things this past week, you make me look good doing it, just like you make me look good dancing." She smiled at him and briefly put her cheek on his chest.

They made a quick foray into the casino. Warren and Boyd shot dice while Martha watched. Warren had given Boyd fifty dollars to bet with, and Boyd managed to turn it into twenty in very short order. Dice was not his game. He liked poker, where you played the man, not the odds. He liked the games where you could face the opponent and read his eyes, where luck didn't really enter into it.

They talked Martha into trying her hand at roulette. Surprisingly, she quickly won fifty or sixty dollars. Warren insisted that she keep the money, even though he had staked her.

It was finally time to go home as it was past eleven. As they left, the man in the swallow-tailed coat bowed Warren and his party out and then yelled for the boy out front to fetch the buggy. They waited in the cool of the evening, and then climbed onto the seat. As they drove down the circular driveway that led to the road, Martha sighed. "I haven't had that good a time in ages," she said. "I can't ever remember having a better time." She took Warren and Boyd's hands and squeezed them. "Thank you both, very much."

Soon, they were on the road heading back to town. It was a dark, cloudy, almost moonless night. The road was difficult to see and Warren was driving slowly and carefully. Without warning, three dark shapes suddenly appeared on the road before them. The buggy horse snorted and reared up. Warren pulled back on the reins and gentled him. He said, "Whoa, whoa, whoa."

They could distinctly see the shapes of three men on horses blocking their way. Warren asked, "What the hell is this?"

The man closest to Boyd said, snarling, "This is a holdup. What the hell did you think it was? We'll just have your money and your valuables."

Warren said, "Are you crazy? You can't hold us up on the road this close to town."

The three horsemen had moved in front of the buggy, lining up to the side of the buggy horse. The one nearest to Warren said, "Damn your eyes, mister. You had better hand over your valuables and your cash or we'll be taking this lady off your hands."

Boyd could feel his heart thumping, could feel the cold calm coming over him. Everything suddenly appeared to slow down. He could see the three horses arrayed out to his right. He was aware of Martha out of the corner of his eye, her hand to her mouth. He could see the pistols in the three men's hands. He had not heard the sound of a revolver being cocked.

Warren said, "If you're smart, you'll leave us alone. I'm head of the Cattleman's Protective Association, and I can assure you that I will have fifty men after you tomorrow.''

The man said, ''But that'll be tomorrow, won't it, mister? I'm tired of fooling with you. I think we'll just take the lady anyway.''

Boyd could suddenly see the men clearly. They were no longer dark shadows. He could even see the color of their shirts, and he could see some of their faces beneath the shadow of their hats and the revolvers in their hands. Only the one at the far end had his revolver cocked.

Warren was blustering. He was about to make a protest, but it never left his lips. With a high-pitched sound, Boyd suddenly launched himself in a sideways leap from the buggy. Even as his feet drove him up and sideways into the air, he had drawn his revolver. Still in the air, still laid out horizontal to the ground, he cocked his revolver and shot the man at the far end in the side of the chest. Everything was moving very slow, so slow that he could see the power of the bullet explode inside the man, killing him before he could even fall out of the saddle. By the time Boyd hit the ground on his side, he cocked his revolver again and fired at the second man in line. It was a more difficult shot because of the angle from the ground, but he saw the bullet take the man under the jawline and almost lift him before it flung him over the back of his horse. The man nearest was suddenly confused. He was backing his horse away and trying to turn it, the roar of the gunfire still echoing in the stillness of the night. He had half turned, still backing his horse, the robbery forgotten, when Boyd raised himself on an elbow and shot him in the side. The man's arms went straight up flinging his gun away, and then he fell over the side of his horse.

As the echoes of the gunfire faded away, Boyd slowly rose to his knees and then his feet. The road agents' horses were milling around nervously. Boyd picked his way through them, going from man to man, making sure they were dead. He kicked the middle man in the side to make certain of it. He holstered his revolver.

Only then did Boyd become aware of the screaming. For a terrifying second, it sounded like that long-ago horror that he could still hear, Hannah screaming as the flames had taken her. He began to tremble, then sweat broke out across his forehead. It took him a moment to realize that the sound was from behind him and that it didn't sound like Hannah at all. He turned and saw Martha with her hands to her face, her face slightly tilted up. She was screaming and yelling, ''No!'' Warren had his arms around her trying to reassure and comfort her.

As quickly as he could, Boyd stepped up into the buggy and gathered Martha to him, pulling her away from Warren. Cradling her cheek on his chest and with his arms around her, he talked softly into her ear. ''Martha, honey, it's all right. We just had to take care of some bad men. It's all over with; it's done. Please, please, don't cry.''

He could feel her trembling in his arms, but little by little she gained control of herself. With a sigh and a shudder, she was still. Boyd hugged her gently. After a moment, she drew back and said, ''I'm sorry. I don't know what happened.''

Warren, from the other side, quickly said, ''It's all right, Martha. We understand.''

Boyd put his cheek to hers and smoothed her hair and said, ''We're right here, don't worry.''

The road agents' horses were starting to mill around. Boyd handed Martha back to the comforting arms of Warren and then climbed out of the buggy. Almost as if they weren't even there, Boyd walked among the bodies of the slain robbers and casually gathered up their horses. As if it were an everyday chore, he led them to the back of the buggy and tied them to a snubbing ring. He walked back to where the bodies were and almost contemptuously rolled them off to the side of the road. He collected their guns and threw them onto the floorboard of the buggy, then climbed aboard.

He said to Warren, "I guess we had better go in and notify the sheriff."

Warren was staring at him with wide eyes. "Yes, I guess that's what we will have to do."

Boyd said, "Those bodies will just have to lay there. We ain't got room for them in the buggy, and I'll be damned if I'm going to tie them on their horses."

Warren was still staring at him. He said, "Yes, you're right. I guess we can let the sheriff worry about that."

They started down the still, dark road. As they drove, Warren asked Martha if she wanted them to let her off at home before they went into the sheriff's office. She said, "Oh, no! Please, don't. I don't want to be alone right now."

"It might be some time, you understand?"

Boyd said, "We'll keep her with us, Warren. She doesn't care how long it takes."

Warren looked at him curiously. "Whatever you say. You're the doctor."

During the rest of the ride into town, Martha leaned against Boyd, both of her arms entwined around his left arm, and held his hand. Every so often, she would tremble. Boyd himself was icily calm. He felt nothing, not even surprise that he had reacted. He knew there were questions that he wanted to ask himself, but it just didn't seem like the right time. Even with the pistol still warm against his side, he resolutely shut himself off to what had just happened. He didn't want to examine it. That would come soon enough.

They were seated in the sheriff's office in the courthouse in downtown Oklahoma City. The sheriff was a tall lean man in his late fifties named Clarence Frank. Warren said he had been sheriff for as long as he could remember. It was a big office with room for a lot of deputies. When they had given him their news, the sheriff had dispatched three deputies to bring back the bodies. They were back now, laid out in the jail part of the courthouse.

Boyd and Warren were sitting across from Sheriff Frank. One of the deputies who had gone out to recover the bodies was lounged against the far wall. Martha was sitting across the big room, away from what was being said. She was still shaking. The sheriff had understood and had been careful in talking with her. He knew about what had happened to Martha two years ago.

The sheriff came back to Warren and Boyd, looking at Boyd but talking to Warren. In a tone somewhere between awe and disbelief, he said, "Warren, are you to have me believe that this young man, this brother of yours, launched himself out of the buggy and killed those three road agents damned near by the time he hit the ground, and them no more than five or six feet away? Is that what you would have me to believe?"

Warren said, "Clarence, I know how you feel. If I hadn't been there myself, I wouldn't believe it either."

The sheriff said, still talking to Warren, "That was Jack Pike. We've been looking for him for a long spell for just such foolishness that he tried to pull on ya'll. You know, that isn't the first robbery—in your case, a robbery attempt—that we have had on that road out to the Palomino place."

Warren said, "I would imagine that a robber would figure that folks would be coming out of the casino with a good bit of cash on them and that it is a dark road."

"Well, we think that Pike was in on more than one of those robberies. In fact"—now the sheriff spoke to Boyd—"there is a five-hundred-dollar reward on Pike's head, dead or alive. We're pretty certain that he is dead. I don't know what caliber that revolver of yours is, but you blowed a hole in him where the bullet came out that you could stick your foot in. What caliber is it?''

Boyd said softly, ''It's just a .40-caliber.''

The sheriff shook his head. ''It's the damnedest .40-caliber that I've ever seen.'' He turned to Warren. ''Did you get a look at the hole where the bullets came out? It looks like the lead slug just went to pieces. The one Boyd shot in the side had holes coming out all over him. Damn, never saw anything like it.'' The sheriff turned back to Boyd. ''You used to be the sheriff over in Pecos? In Reeves County?''

Boyd nodded and then cut his eyes toward Warren. Warren stepped in quickly. He said, ''Clarence, my brother had some unfortunately personal problems in Pecos. He lost his wife and he's not anxious to talk about that time.''

The sheriff said, ''Well, if he wants a job as a deputy, I'd swear him in tonight.''

Boyd said even more softly, ''No, thank you, sir. I'm planning on moving on in the next few days.''

Sheriff Frank said, ''Well, you have to stick around long enough to collect that reward.''

Warren spoke up and said, ''I'll collect it for him, Clarence, don't worry. He has so much reward money stacked up now, it'll take him a long time to spend it. Do you have any more questions for us tonight? We'd like to get Mrs. Blair to bed. All of that shooting upset her.''

The sheriff stood up. ''I can more than understand.'' He put his hand out toward Boyd. ''Boyd, I'd like to shake your hand again. You've done this part of the country some good work tonight. I don't know how you can shoot so fast, but I sure wish to hell *I* could.''

They shook hands all around, and then Boyd and Warren

collected Martha. They stepped out onto the boardwalk. Their buggy was waiting. Warren stayed on the boardwalk in front of the jail while Boyd helped Martha into the buggy. Boyd glanced back and saw Warren waiting. Boyd said to him, "What is holding you up?"

Warren said, "It's not that far to my house from here. I think I'll just hoof it. I need some of this night air to clear my head, so why don't you take the buggy and yourself and Martha to her house?"

Boyd said, "You sure?"

Warren said, "Positive. It would be quicker for me to walk from here rather than drive you all the way out there and then back. By the way, I want to congratulate you on your under-use of the demon rum tonight. It was me who managed to do the biggest part of the drinking. I guess Martha's right, you can drink some and then leave the rest alone."

Boyd said, "What about your buggy?"

Warren said, "You'll be bringing that in to me around ten o'clock in the morning. I want to see you in my office."

Boyd asked, "What for?"

"You know damn good and well what for. I don't want to hear any more of this talk out of you that you don't want to be responsible for anyone else but yourself. You disproved that tonight in a mighty big way. Who were you being responsible for when you shot those three sonofabitches on the road? You were being responsible for me, for Martha, and maybe for yourself, I don't know. You can say what you want, but I know what I saw."

Boyd started to protest. "Now wait a minute, Warren. Let's don't get carried away with this. I haven't thought it out yet. It was an impulse. It just happened."

"It happened because it was in you to happen, for no other reason. You can't stop those instincts; you can't stop the quickness. It is a part of you, and it is still a part of you to feel a responsibility toward yourself and others. You are not going to throw your life away anymore. There's an important job for you to do and I am going to see that you do it.''

Boyd said, "Don't be so damned sure about that.''

"Get in the buggy and go on. Good night.''

Boyd and Martha drove slowly away. Martha sat close to him on the drive to her house, neither one of them speaking a word. She went in quickly while Boyd saw to Warren's buggy horse, turning him into the corral with Martha's stock. After he had made sure of the feed and water, he went slowly back into the house.

Martha had put on a pot of coffee and had lit two lamps. She was sitting at the table with a glass of cognac in front of her. Boyd went around the table to the far side, where he usually sat. He took a moment to unbuckle his gunbelt and place it on the table.

Martha reached out for a glass, poured him an inch of cognac, and put it in front of him. He made no move other than to get out a cigarillo and light it, striking the match on the underside of the table. He could see that Martha was still pale. He asked, "Reckon you're going to be all right?''

She half smiled. "I feel mighty silly. I acted like a hysterical girl, I'm sorry, it's just that it was . . .''

Boyd reached out and put his hand on hers and said, "You don't have to explain. I guess that it was loud and it must have brought back some memories for you. I feel terrible that it had to happen.''

She looked across at him with serious eyes. "I started screaming when I first heard the guns because I thought it was them shooting you. I saw you go out of the buggy and then I saw you on the ground. I was screaming because I thought they had shot you, and when I got started, I couldn't stop.''

Boyd didn't know what to say. He patted her hand and then took a sip of the cognac. He said, "I know it was very confusing. I didn't intend to do what I did, I just reacted." It disturbed him that she had started screaming because she thought it had been him that had been shot. He didn't want her to feel that way, but, he thought, maybe she would have felt the same way if it had been Warren or anyone else. He said, "I guess it takes a while to get over all of this, or do you ever get over it?"

She sighed. "I don't know, Boyd. We're all different. I thought that I was safely beyond the edge, but I'm not real sure that it had to do with the train wreck. I think it had to do with the fact that I thought you were being shot at."

He tried to make a joke out of it. "Hell, if they had caught me about five days ago, they would have done me a favor shooting me dead."

She looked at him in wonder. "I still can't believe it. I saw it, but I still can't believe it. Are you really that quick? Are you so deadly? In one instant, those men were there, and the next, they were gone. I don't think my heart beat more than four or five times. I couldn't see where the gunshots were coming from, I was just aware of the sudden glare. Boyd, you are very well, you're not sick at all anymore. My God, how steady your hand must have been, how quick your mind was."

He took another sip of cognac. "Don't make it more than it was, Martha. I've always been a pretty fair hand with a gun; let's not let it get out of hand. It was just reflex. Unfortunately, it gave my damn brother the ammunition to get me to take that job."

"With the Cattleman's Protective Association?"

"Yes. He says I can just drift and take care of trouble wherever I find it. He says it would be just perfect for me."

She said timidly, "But that would take you away from here."

He didn't like the way the conversation was going. He said, "I would have been going away from here anyway, Martha. I am looking for new country."

Martha looked down. "Yes, you said that at the very first. I understand, I guess, that you want to get as far away as you can."

"I like to keep on the move. Warren claims this job will allow me to do that and also keep me from supporting half of the saloons in the state."

"Maybe you should take the job. We all have to have something in our lives to hold on to, be it a person, a place, a job. Maybe that job can be your something."

He said, "What's yours?"

Her eyes got wistful and she looked off past him. She said, "Hope."

"Hope for what?"

She shrugged. "I don't know. Hope that I will find something to replace what I lost. It's hard to say. I just go from day to day. The nursing is important to me, but it is not the only thing."

"The hope, is that it?"

"Yes, that's very important."

He wanted to ask her if by that she meant another home, another husband, another child, but he knew better. You can't replace that once-in-a-lifetime thing that you had and lost. He said, "Well, I don't know. Warren thinks he can buffalo me into taking this job, just like he used to buffalo me when I was a kid, but it's not the same anymore. Right now, I don't know how I feel."

She asked softly, "How did you feel tonight? Afterwards?"

"After I killed those men?"

"Yes."

"I felt nothing at all. I didn't feel victorious, I didn't feel guilty, I didn't feel sad, I didn't feel happy. I felt no more than if there had been a rock blocking our way on the road and I had shoved it aside. That's all they were to me, they were just blocking our way of progress."

She said with awe in her voice, "I didn't know people could feel that way."

"I didn't before. Now I know that I do." He paused for a moment. He tried to work his face into a smile. "You know, you really are something when you get yourself all gussied up like that. What do you mean, you didn't have a thing to wear? That dress looked like it had just come out of a shop."

She laughed. "You'd be surprised what you can do with a needle and a few pins here and there. Which reminds me that I need to go take it off before one of the pins stick me."

They went to bed in the early morning hours. They didn't make love but they slept very close together. They clung together like two people lost in the midst of a tornado, clinging hard, afraid of being torn apart and blown away.

Six

Boyd said, "Warren, we've got to get one thing straight if I am going to take this job. I have no intentions of taking any orders from anybody. Is that clear?"

His brother said, "Boyd, there won't be anybody out in the field that outranks you. Now, there are a few superiors back here at headquarters that we like to think have the right to direct the men in the field. I don't know if I can convince them to make an exception of you or not."

Boyd smiled slightly. "Well, you know my attitude is that I have no superiors and damn few equals. What do you mean, these men are my superiors?"

Warren laughed ruefully, "Well, I am supposed to be one of your superiors, but I know damn good and well not to take advantage of that because you will resign immediately. I am just trying to convince you that if you will stay somewhere close to the guidelines of the organization, you won't get any problems from anyone here."

They were sitting in Warren's office in the big red brick building. Boyd could see out through the windows behind Warren. There was a little traffic passing back and forth as the railroad depot was very close to the headquarters of the

Cattleman's Association. He said, "Warren, I hope you really know what you are doing with me. I'm not the man I used to be."

"I know that, Boyd, and I am fully aware that you're not the carefree young man you were. I'm telling you that I think this job could be the saving of you. I think you're worth saving whether you think so or not. I know that you are walking around here thinking that if you had just done something, anything, what happened would not have happened. The past is the past, Boyd. Now, I've got a contract drawn up here for two years."

Boyd shook his head. "I ain't signing no damn contract. If I am going to leave, I am going to leave, contract or no contract."

"There you go, starting before the gun. You know, Boyd, if you are going to ride in a horse race, you've got to run by the rules. At least let the race get started before you go to complaining about it. Now this contract is all to your advantage. It can't make you keep on working. There is no way in the world to have an agent out in the field and force him to work. All this contract does is guarantee you two years of employment at a set figure, sets out the terms of your employment, such as we'll represent you in any legal matters, that we are going to furnish you, as I told you, with your mounts and with five dollars per diem, which is five dollars a day when you are out in the field for food and lodging. It merely states the responsibilities that the Association is willing to bear on your behalf. It also has a thousand-dollar insurance premium payable to the person of your choice in case you get killed. Nowhere does it say that you can't pack it in the day after tomorrow."

Boyd said, "Well, all right, but I still don't like signing things."

"Well, I can't put you on the payroll until you sign."

"Who the hell says I want to be on your payroll? Sounds to me like I've got plenty of money. Maybe I can do that, just go looking for the Jack Pikes of the world and shoot them for the money."

Warren said, "I hear that bounty hunting isn't what it's cracked up to be. There's a lot of those rewards that are harder to collect than you think; some are harder to collect than the people that you are hunting. Yes, you have quite a bit of money right now, but you can go through it in six months if you set your mind to it. But it's not the money that's important here, Boyd, it's having a purpose. That's what this job is all about. Now sign this contract, and let's get on with the other business."

With a touch of ill humor Boyd said, "Give me a pen."

Warren swiveled the document around in front of Boyd, dipped the pen into the ink, and handed it to him. Boyd signed his name in the place indicated.

Warren said, "There, that's wasn't hard, was it. You're now a captain in the Cattleman's Protective Association."

Boyd gave his brother a sour look. "Hooray," he said.

Warren said, "Now, you mentioned that money. Some of it has come in and some of it is still due in. What do you want to do with it?"

Boyd said, "Put it in the bank. Send me out of here with a couple hundred dollars and put a thousand dollars in an account for Martha."

"Oh, no, Boyd. I said that you'd have to give her that money."

"I'm going to give her the money. I said for you to put the money into an account for her and I would take her a deposit slip. How does that sound?"

"Fine. They'll be paying that five hundred dollars on Jack Pike within the week because it was put up by local people. In fact, I think the Palomino Club put up the biggest part of it. There's going to be some mighty relieved people around here with Pike laying over in the morgue with his toes pointing up.'' Warren was silent for a moment looking at his brother. ''Sheriff Frank figures that Pike has killed four, maybe five, men around here, but he never got off a shot against you. How do you account for that?''

''I don't know. I wasn't thinking about it at the time.''

Warren asked, ''How come you didn't shoot Pike first? He was the one that was doing the most talking. And he was the closest.''

Boyd said, ''Because he didn't have his revolver cocked and the man on the far end did. Figured I would have plenty of time to get him.''

Warren asked, ''You saw all that? In those conditions, with very little light, in that very little time we had?''

Boyd said, ''No, I made it all up. Warren, why would you want to ask me a question like that?''

Warren shook his head. ''Don't get touchy, I'm just still trying to figure it all out. That was the damnedest stunt that I've ever seen. I don't expect that I'll ever see the equal of it. I believe you now when you say the bear starves last.''

''Well, now that I'm a duly authorized captain, agent, whatever you call it, what do I do now? Do you swear me in? Do I take a secret oath?''

Warren heaved himself up and said, ''Well, right now, we're going to step across the street to Elite Cafe and have a bite of lunch. After that, we'll come back here and they'll have your identification papers made up and some credentials that will stand you in good stead with any law official, local, county, state, or federal. Then we'll talk about the first job that I would like for you to go on.'' He threw his hands up as if to avoid a blow. ''That's not an order, Boyd, it's only a job that I hope that you'll do. But if not, start drifting and tend to the Association's business.''

Boyd said, "Let's go eat. All this talk has made me plenty hungry, especially watching you work me around like you did when I was a kid."

His brother smiled. "I think I did a pretty good job."

Boyd put on his hat. "Well, you're good for a free hat every once in a while. Other than that, I can't see much advantage of having you for a brother."

They didn't try to talk much business over lunch. Instead, they reminisced about their family, Boyd's childhood troubles that he had managed to get himself in and out of, and the trial he had been to Warren—to hear Warren tell it. It was a pleasant lunch. They had fried chicken and mashed potatoes and spring peas. Boyd commented that it was a good deal easier to eat when you were familiar with what you were eating. Warren told Boyd that he just didn't have the feelings for the finer things in life. Boyd replied that if that meant laying down ten dollars a head for some stuff on a plate that you couldn't recognize, let along pronounce, then he could do without the finer things in life. He added that he was very glad to see Martha have such a good time.

Warren said, "It was a shame that it was spoiled for her by the holdup. I thought she was further along than that, Boyd."

Boyd almost replied by telling his brother that Martha had screamed because she thought the men were shooting at him, but instead he said, "It was noise of the guns. She didn't really know who was shooting. Hell, Warren, she's a woman. What did you expect? Even if she hadn't had the experience that she had, she would have still screamed."

Back in Warren's office, they got to the matters at hand. Warren gave Boyd his credentials and a copy of his contract in an oilskin pouch. He said, "Carry that with you everywhere. Here is an identification card to carry in your wallet. That contract pretty well spells out the do's and the don'ts of the Association. I wish you would follow them when you feel like you can. Technically, I guess you're not supposed to kill anybody unless your life is in direct threat, or I guess the lives of our other agents, or members of our Association. I don't know, and I'm not going to try and tell you, Boyd. You just do what's right. You always have, so I'm not going to worry about that. The job I have for you is a real mess, going on now for about six months, maybe even longer than that. The two agents that I have handling the affair haven't been able to make much headway. I've even sent in two reinforcements and still the trouble is going on."

Boyd interrupted to ask how many agents the Association had.

His brother shrugged. "A little over three hundred. It fluctuates somewhere between three and four hundred, depending on the troubles, and sometimes we take on temporary people. By the way, that's something that you can do. You can take on a man for five dollars a day for as long as you need him. We don't like to see temporaries hired on for more than thirty days, though. You pay him yourself and send in the vouchers. You're supposed to stay in constant telegraphic touch with us"—he sighed—"but I will leave that up to you. I would like to know from time to time where you are."

Boyd sat back impatiently. "Tell me about the job. Stop playing big brother for a little while."

Warren leaned back in his chair, hooked his hands behind his head, and looked up at the ceiling. He said, "It's damn complicated. It involves a big area, about three hundred square miles of eastern Colorado and western Kansas. We've got several Association members up there that are trying to upgrade their stock by importing Aberdeen Angus cattle from Scotland. I don't know if you're familiar with the Angus, but that is a small, black, square-built cow that is prime beef. If you cross the Angus with a range cow, even if it is

part Longhorn, you'll double the price of your beef. In order
to run an upgraded breeding program, you have to be able
to protect the stock that you are trying to upgrade—in other
words, fence them off. The problem with that is that both
Kansas and Colorado are open-range states. I don't know
how familiar you are with open-range laws. I think parts of
Texas are open-range.''

Boyd said, ''It goes county by county.''

''That ought to make a nice hash. Anyway, the law says
that you can't fence your neighbor off from common water,
can't fence him off from the right to move his cattle from
one grazing area to another, and you can't fence him off of
state land. But by law, you can protect your assets with fencing so long as you don't break any of those rules.''

Boyd said, ''And you have some rich Association members that are having some trouble with those rules?''

Warren gave his brother a sharp look. ''Don't get the idea
that all Association members are rich cattlemen. We've got
members with as few as one hundred head and members with
one hundred thousand head and they all pay the same
amount of dues.''

Boyd said, ''Go on.''

''It's pretty simple. Our clients have been trying to fence
off breeding pastures where they can selectively keep their
Angus purebreds separated from the range stock except those
they want to breed. Their neighbors don't seem intent on
allowing them to go on about their business peaceably. So
far, they've torn down about ten miles of fencing and have
managed to get their cattle mixed in with those high-priced
Anguses. That ain't right, Boyd. You may not be stealing a
man's bull, but if you mount him on your cow, and he's got
a hell of a lot better bull than you've got a cow and the calf
is going to be superior, then you are stealing. The other side
to it is that the natural law says that an unbranded calf, a

dogie, belongs to the man who owns the mother cow, because the dogie will follow its mother. Well, up there we've got dogie calves that look as black as the heart of the devil, following old slipshod range cows that never saw the day they were worth over fifty dollars a head, and that calf's worth about three hundred. Of course, there is no way to prove anything on the man that owns the cow. He'll usually say he doesn't know how that Angus bull got out and got to his cow. He'll make a big squawk about why didn't his neighbor keep his damned old sorry bulls put up and not be ruining his purebred American stock. It's a hell of a mess and our clients are losing a lot of money. The problem is that there is no clear means to go to the law about it, because they can't catch them tearing down the fence and they can't prove that they are deliberately getting their cattle together with that Angus stock.''

Boyd said, ''Well, you say you've got several ranchers that are Association members? How many are around them that aren't? In other words, how many enemies?''

Warren shrugged. ''The hell of it is that they will come and go with one bunch coming in there, setting up shop and getting their cattle mixed in with the Angus, and then they disappear. At any one time, I'd say that we have ten to twelve other ranchers, some with families, some without. There are about three or four permanent that we believe are involved with making all the mess.''

Boyd asked, ''Are you telling me that your four agents can't catch anybody tearing down fences?''

''Not so far. We know they're doing it, according to the chief of the agency down there, a man named Jake Mangus, but we've never been able to put our hands on them or run them to the ground or even get an identification on them.'' Warren threw his hands in the air. ''That's the frustrating part of this. We don't have anything to really go to the law about—no clear case of rustling, no nothing. What they are doing is stealing what it takes to make calves, either that which comes out of the bull, or that which goes into the cow. That's what it comes down to, but it means real money, Boyd. The difference between the get from those old range cattle and the Angus is anywhere from two to three hundred dollars and it is ruining the breeding programs. It's gone on far too long.''

Boyd said, ''I don't see where you think I can do anything that your other men haven't been able to do.''

Warren leaned forward. ''You've got one advantage and that is that you're smart, and it is going to take some brains to figure this one out and how to handle it.''

''I thought you understood that it was something other than brain work that I was looking for.''

''I have no doubt that you will get a chance at some of the other kind as well. But right now, I need you to go up there and straighten out a mess.''

''Who is this Jake Mangus, your chief there? What's the situation on him?''

Warren pulled a face. ''He's a vinegary sonofabitch, pushing forty. He's been with the agency about fifteen years and he is a bully type. He's more or less worked himself up by more or less being around. He's about as smart as my boot heel. He'll probably try and give you some trouble. He is not going to like the idea of some captain, especially my brother, coming in and taking over matters. In your credentials, I've included a letter to him, in as strong of words as possible, that if he wants to keep his job, he will cooperate with you, he will give you every assistance, and he will follow your orders.''

''What if he don't care? What if he throws his hands up and quits?''

''So much the better.''

"What if he's with the crowd that is doing the stealing?"

Warren said, "The thought has crossed my mind more than once. In that case, you're to treat him no different than the others that are actually tearing the fences down."

"What about the other men you got there?"

Warren looked over a piece of paper as if to refresh his memory. "Mangus's assistant is named Gates Hood. He's a young—well, I can't call him a recruit because he's been with us about three years. I've never met the man myself, but I understand that he's capable and likeable and also from Texas near the border of Mexico. I think you can expect him to be noncommittal. I don't think he will take sides between you and Mangus."

"Gates Hood? That's a hell of a name. You don't know where along the border?"

"I think around Del Rio."

"Well, I've got some friends down there. Maybe we'll have some in common."

"The other two men are named Bob Sweeney and Earl White. I sent them up as reinforcements. Nothing much to say about them. You can look at their records before you leave."

"When *am* I supposed to leave?"

Warren said, "If I had my way, you'd be on that train that's pulling out right now, but I guess you'll want a couple of days to say your good-byes to Martha and get yourself ready. We've got to get your banking business tended to and we have to get your horse business settled. Would you want to buy them here—we've got a good horse business here—or would you rather wait and pick them up in Kansas or Colorado?"

"I don't know yet."

"Well, why don't you and Martha come over for supper tonight?"

Boyd asked, "Is Muriel's sister still there?"

"She's leaving today."

"Won't it look kind of strange, me and Martha coming over there like a couple?"

"Muriel's a big girl."

"I'll ask Martha."

Warren said, "Well, get on up and get the hell out of here. Did you bring your horse?"

"Yeah, I tied him behind your buggy and brought him in with me."

"Is he worth taking to Kansas with you?"

Boyd said, "He's still a pretty good piece of horseflesh, got a lot of territory left in him. I'm not in any rush to get shut of him."

"How will I know if you are coming tonight?"

Boyd walked toward the door and turned around. "I guess when we show up. Muriel always cooks enough for ten or twelve anyway. Will it make much difference?"

"I guess not."

On the way back to Martha's house, he decided to put his horse through the paces. With a shock, he realized that he hadn't ridden the animal since they had both staggered into Oklahoma City almost a week ago. The horse looked considerably better than Boyd remembered, and he seemed light and lively as Boyd stepped aboard him from the back of Warren's buggy. The horse was a six-year-old roan gelding and it had always been one of his favorites. It was half quarter horse and half Morgan cross with quick speed, and was a good stayer over the long haul. He wasn't a particularly big horse, being only about sixteen-and-half hands high and weighing about a thousand pounds, but he was nimble and quick and could get you out of a bad spot in a hurry if you needed some help. He'd been a good friend during the long drunken haul that had finally ended in Oklahoma City. To his distress, Boyd could remember more than one night when the horse had chosen the time and place to stop. Many a night, Boyd had tumbled out of the saddle and slept where he fell, and the next morning, the roan would still be standing there, stomping his feet, impatient to have his bridle bits taken out so that he could graze. Boyd remembered with shame the way he had treated the animal.

Now, on the road leaving the more populated part of Oklahoma City, he began riding the horse in a tight circle and slapping the spurs to him for a short burst of speed. After that, he loped him for a while, walked him, and listened to his breathing, which sounded as fit as a dollar to Boyd's ears. With about a mile to go, he put the horse into a gallop and let him breeze along for a full half mile before pulling him into a lope and then a canter and then a walk. The horse was still breathing easy. Boyd patted him on the neck. He said, "Well, old son, I reckon that you might as well come along with me. Do you think you'll like working for the Cattleman's Protective Association, catching rustlers and such?"

The horse pricked his ears backward as he always did when Boyd talked to him. Boyd said, "You're probably wondering if I've gone crazy, going to work for Warren and the Cattleman's Protective Association. What we ought to do is get all the money that we can and spend it and have a fine old time. I'd get me about six whores and get you a couple of mares. No, I forgot, mares wouldn't do you much good."

When he was at Martha's, he turned the horse in and put him in the shed. He unbridled him and put him out with Martha's buggy horse.

He entered the house through the back kitchen door. Martha was sitting at the kitchen table with a cup of coffee in front of her, wearing one of her wraparound dresses, only it was loose and he could see the fullness of her breasts, almost down to the nipples. It had come open and he could see the inside of one of her thighs. Boyd could feel the heat suddenly rise in him, but instead of doing anything about it, he poured himself a cup of coffee and then went around the table to sit down facing her.

She asked, "Well, did you and Warren get your future worked out?"

Boyd said, "Oh, we always get my future worked out whenever Warren and I talk. Sometime, just for the hell of it, I'd like to work out Warren's future." He got out a cigarillo out and lit it, drawing in the blue smoke and then blowing it out in a great puff.

"I never tried that, smoking. Is it pleasurable?"

He shrugged. "It's like any other habit when you get into it. It becomes a part of you and you don't think of it as being pleasurable or not pleasurable, it's just something that you do or not do."

She said, "Like living. One day after the next. Did you take the job?"

He nodded. "I reckon. I signed the papers and I am supposed to go to Kansas."

She hesitated for a second and then said, "When will you be leaving? Soon?"

He said, "I'm afraid so, Martha. I've got some affairs to tend to, either today or the day after. Warren wants me there as quick as I can get there." He paused for a moment, looking at her softly. "I'm going to miss you." Then, because it sounded so personal, he rolled his eyes around the kitchen and then added, "And all of this. It's been a good hospital for me and you've been a good doctor."

"Nurse. I'm a nurse."

"You've been much more than that, Martha. You've been doctor, nurse, friend, a great many things."

She said, "You left out lover."

He looked down at the tabletop. "I wasn't sure you wanted me to mention that. I'm not sure that's what you would call it. Were we being lovers, Martha?"

She shrugged. "I don't know, Boyd. Maybe it was just another way of comforting each other." She smiled. "Whatever it was, it felt good and made me feel alive." She looked away. "I haven't felt like a woman for a long time."

He reached over and took her hands in his. "Martha, I wish there was something that I could do or say right now to let you know how grateful I am to you."

Her head came back around to him. She said, with a glint of amusement in her eyes, "Don't be so sure that I helped you, Boyd. Now you'll start to feel again, and you may prefer the way it was when you didn't feel anything. Sometimes I wonder if I wouldn't be better off not feeling anything."

"You had a good time last night. Didn't that feel good?"

"Yes, oh, yes."

Boyd said, "Martha, I am going to ask you something. You and I have both stepped around each other's business with mighty light feet, and I think that's been wise, but I still want to ask you this, but that doesn't mean you have to answer it."

"I know that, Boyd."

The words felt awkward to him. He said, "Martha, I'm only a little over three months into this thing and you've had over two years. Are you content to be alone? Surely there are a lot of good men in this town who would want a woman like you. Obviously, he'd have to be a man who was ready for the kind of person you are. . . . "

She said, "What kind of person is that, Boyd? Crippled emotionally?"

He gave her a soft look and shook his head. "You know

I don't mean it like that, Martha. Last night still has you shaken up, or you would not have said that. What I mean is the warm, caring person you are. Men aren't used to a woman like you. They're used to some silly bit of fluff who they keep barefoot and pregnant. They're not used to a woman who can talk on their level, who is as caring and giving, or one that has as much sense as you do. You know that's what I meant. You're not crippled emotionally. If there is a cripple around here, it's me.''

"Yeah, you really looked crippled leaping out of that buggy last night."

"That bothers you, doesn't it?"

"Of course it bothers me. Those men could have done us great harm and I am eternally grateful that you were there. I had no idea that you could do something like that. It took me by surprise.''

"Well, the way you have been looking at me lately, I've been about half convinced that you're scared of me."

She laughed and shook her head. "No, not of you and your gun. I'm just thinking about how I am going to miss you being around here, that's all. Do you think you'll ever be coming back?"

Boyd laughed. "Hell, Martha. Let me get gone before I have to start worrying about coming back. I don't know what this job is going to involve. It's brand-new to me and I've only had about two hours on it, no experience." He looked around the kitchen. "By the way, I noticed that when I came in, I didn't see any cooking or eating utensils out. Did you eat lunch?"

She shook her head. "I wasn't hungry. Actually, I'm about a couple of pounds overweight, well, more like ten, judging from the trouble that I had getting into that velvet dress last night."

"Are you sure that's the reason?"

"Look who's playing nurse. Did you eat lunch? I think that's the better question."

"Yeah, Warren took me over to some cafe that he eats at regularly, the Elite. Contrary to last night, I knew what I was eating today."

"You didn't like that Italian food?"

Boyd said, "I like steak and potatoes a good deal better. When you find something that you like, I don't see any point in going around trying a bunch of other slop, do you?"

She shook her head and said, "No."

Later that afternoon, they were sitting in the front room playing a game of rummy, at which Martha was quite the expert. As she was putting the cards away, he said, "You know, I was asking you earlier about other men in this town. I can't imagine that there isn't a flock of suitors lined up outside your door."

She put the cards in the drawer of the desk and then sat down on the divan. Boyd was still sitting at the table in the corner near the door to the bedroom. She said, "Oh, there were for a time, but I was carrying so much extra baggage that I wasn't really fit company for anyone."

"What about now?"

She shook her head. "They seem to have forgotten about me."

"Why don't you have Warren put the word around?"

She laughed without much humor. "I'm not really that interested, Boyd. When did you turn matchmaker? Would you like it better if there was a man around here?"

He shook his head. "No, of course not. Why would you ask that?"

"Oh, I thought you might feel more comfortable rather than being alone with me all the time."

He was becoming decidedly uneasy. "Martha, I don't mean anything by what I said. Of course I'm not uncomfortable being alone with you. I wouldn't like another man being around here.''

She smiled. ''Then it's your good fortune that I haven't taken a man, isn't it?''

He decided to let the subject drop.

Still later that afternoon, Boyd rode into town and hunted up the gunsmith's shop. With some difficulty, he explained to the gunsmith that he wanted a mold that would cast a slug for a .70-caliber rifle. He still had a number of the brass casings; he always kept those, replacing only the percussion caps and reloading them. He had left his bullet mold for his big rifle back in his office in Pecos. He had never expected to use it again.

Boyd worked out a plan with the gunsmith to take a mold that cast the slug of a .58-caliber Springfield, enlarge it, and adapt it to a .70. The only part that had to be exact was where the lead slug fit into the opening of the brass casing. The gunsmith was reluctant to promise that he could have the mold made by the next day, but agreed to undertake the task when Boyd offered to pay him double. The gunsmith said, ''It's going to cost you forty dollars. I'll have to work all night adapting this mold.''

Boyd said, ''That's fine as long as I can get it soon, and I'm going to need about two pounds of smokeless powder and some firing caps. I'm also going to need some cleaning equipment for both a .44-caliber carbine and for that .70 gun.''

He paid the man what little money he had for the cleaning equipment and fluids and gun oil, and then left, promising to be back the next afternoon to pick up the gun mold as well as the powder and the lead.

After that, he hunted up the tobacco shop, where he was able to buy a couple more boxes of Primero cigarillos.

As he rode back to Martha's, he decided the roan was nearly as fit as he had ever been. There was no question about taking the good horse, but he did want to pick up a second animal, a traveling horse. He knew that western Kansas and eastern Colorado were flat plains country with a lot of distance between places. He would need a good traveling horse, and he decided that the next morning he would go over and get Warren to go down to the horse market and try to pick up a second mount.

As Boyd approached the house, his mind went back to Martha. He was troubled about her, but there wasn't anything he could see to do about it. The situation was such that it was best left alone.

That evening, after supper, he set up shop at the kitchen table and began to clean and oil his three guns and to assess the ammunition that he had on hand. Cartridges for the two .40-caliber revolvers would be no problem, nor would rounds for his saddle carbine, but it was going to take him some time to cast enough slugs to reload for the .70-caliber. He only had about twenty shells left, and he was suspicious of them. They had been out in every kind of weather and the powder could have very easily gotten damp and lost its power. He knew that using bad cartridges was an easy way to make bad things happen.

Martha sat across from him while he was cleaning and oiling his guns. She said, "You do that as if you really enjoy it. You handle those weapons as tenderly and as nicely as you ever handled me."

He laughed lightly and said, "Yeah, Martha, but you go off a hell of a lot easier and faster. I've got to baby these."

She smiled. "I suppose I had that coming."

Later, they went to bed early and made love with rising and falling degrees of voracity. They started by exploring each other's bodies with their fingers, their mouths, their tongues. Then as he lay on his back, Martha got over him on all fours, letting her breasts dangle in front of his face. He took her nipples, alternately, in his mouth one at a time. Each time he switched, she shuddered and convulsed. Finally, she guided Boyd into her as she lowered herself down to cover him. She began pumping with a steady pace, slowly at first and then faster and faster. As his back arched and his arms clutched her to him, their mouths locked together, arms trying to squeeze the flesh of each into one fused union.

They exploded almost simultaneously, Martha throwing her head back in a high-pitched wail of pleasure and Boyd burying his face into her breasts, kissing her frantically.

They clung together for a long moment after they were both spent. Slowly, she rolled off the top of him. She asked, her voice coming out of the dark, "Do you think that will be the last time, Boyd?"

Boyd sat up and fumbled for a match to light the lamp. He reached for a cigarillo and lit it off the same match. He said, "Martha, I thought you were the original one-day-at-a-time girl."

She sighed. "Sometimes that is easier to say than to do, but it sounds good, doesn't it?"

"Yeah, I don't know if that was the last time, and neither do you. I am not leaving forever, Martha, but by the time I do get back, there might be someone else in your life a good deal more important than I am."

She didn't say anything for a moment, just lay there letting her breathing come under control. She said, "Why don't we try and get some sleep?"

Seven

Boyd left right after breakfast the next morning and headed up to Warren's office. Together, they went over to the Cattleman's National Bank, and Warren helped Boyd establish an account in his own name with the reward money that had come in and the money that Boyd had left in his bank in Pecos. It amounted to some twenty-four hundred dollars. Because he planned to buy a horse that day, and also to have some money in his pocket, he took six hundred dollars in cash. He also took a thousand dollars out of his money and opened an account for Martha, putting it in her name. Because he thought she might want to have some money around the house, he held out fifty dollars for her and tucked that and the deposit slip into his shirt pocket.

Warren said, "That's mighty generous of you, Boyd."

"I don't reckon that you'd have done any less."

"You understand that the Association is going to give you traveling money?"

"What I understand right now is that we better go find me another horse. What I need is something with pretty good legs. That's a lot of flat country up there, and I would imagine that it is a long way between waterholes, both for man or beast.''

The horse auction barn was only six or seven blocks away, so they walked over. As they did, Boyd asked Warren different questions about what he should expect to run into.

Warren said, ''Well, Jake Mangus is headquartered in Garden City, Kansas, which is at the extreme eastern end of the trouble. The main problems are occurring around some towns and villages named Syracuse and Towner and Tribune in Kansas, and Sheridan Lake and Bristol and Coolridge in Colorado.''

Boyd said, ''Is it?''

''Is what?''

''Is Garden City a garden?''

His brother laughed ruefully. ''I doubt it. I've seen that country. Gardens are damn few and far between.''

''How come you've allowed Mangus to headquarter so far from where the trouble is?''

''Well, for all I know, he may have moved more into the middle of things. I haven't heard from him. That will be your job, to move headquarters. Looking at the map, my suggestion would be to move somewhere close to Syracuse, but that's up to you.''

''What kind of water is around there?''

''The water through Kansas is the Arkansas River. I believe that's the name of it. In Colorado, the main water supply is Sheridan Lake, but there are all kinds of streams and ponds and stock tanks around there. Boyd, your trouble isn't over water; it's over fences; it's over stealing cattle. I don't care how you call it, it's still stealing cattle.''

''Yeah, but when you're dealing with cattle out on the range, sooner or later the trouble is going to collect where the water is.''

Warren shrugged. ''You may have something there; I

don't know. You'll have to play it by ear once you get on the scene and see what it's like. When do you expect to leave?''

"If I can buy a horse today and I can get some cartridges made for my big rifle, then I'll try and get out of here on a train tomorrow. Do you have any idea what time the train into Kansas will leave?''

"I know there is a northwest-bound train that leaves out of here at eleven in the morning that heads on to Liberal across the line there on the strip, and then heads on up to Colorado City and Colorado Springs. How you get from Liberal to Garden City is anybody's guess. I doubt if there is any train between Garden City and Towner or Syracuse or any of those other villages. I expect that you will have to go overland.''

"You going to telegraph this Jake Mangus that I am coming?''

"Oh, hell, yes. The minute I'm certain that you're on that train, the telegram will go off.''

Boyd suddenly stopped and looked around at his brother. He said, "Send the telegram today. I told you that I'd go and I don't want him meeting me. Let me find him.''

By that time, they were at the big horse barn. They held auctions there on Mondays and Saturdays, but during the other days of the week people kept other stock in stalls for sale.

For the next hour, Boyd and his brother looked over the horses by having them brought from the stalls to the large center ring. Boyd found a big, rangy chestnut mare that he liked. He mounted her and believed, as her owner claimed, that she was a solid four-year-old.

Warren said, "Yeah. She's a four-year-old maybe, but she's a hard four-year-old.''

Boyd agreed. "I'd say she's a coming five years, but that's better."

He walked around the mare, slapped her flanks, and dropped his hat in front of her, making sudden loud noises. The mare was calm enough to suit Boyd.

Warren said, "After she hears a few shots, she'll get used to the gunfire. She's not skittish at all, it doesn't appear, at least not any more than she needs to be."

"I don't mind a horse being a little skittish. Just don't want one that's dead."

Boyd paid three hundred dollars for the mare. He left the mare there to get freshly shod. He wanted lighter shoes put on her than the big, heavy, deep-caulked shoes that she was wearing. Those were good for the rough and rocky country around Oklahoma City, but the horse didn't need it on the soft plains he'd be heading for. All heavy shoes did was slow an animal down, and a bit of speed at the right time could turn out to be mighty important.

With their horse business finished, the two brothers went back to the office. Warren was anxious that Boyd meet the president and several of their directors, but Boyd chose not to. He said, "Either I'll make them a good hand or I won't. If I do them a good job, then there will be plenty of time to meet them. If I don't make them a good hand, they won't have anything to throw back in your face."

Warren commented that was the most lopsided set of thinking that he had ever heard, but he gave in on the matter.

Warren had a list of the names of the Association members ready for Boyd, and it went in with his other documents. Warren said, "Now, do you want me to get you a chair ticket for the train tomorrow? Do you want me to have your travel arranged?"

"Yeah, get me half a stock car."

"You need half a stock car for just two horses?"

"Yeah, and for me."

"You're not going to ride in the chair cars? Are you going to ride back there with the horses and all that blowing dust and straw?"

"Yeah, the company's better. Go ahead and get all of that arranged. I'll be going through to Garden City. Will you know by tonight how they'll ride me?"

Warren said, "I'm sure I will, so I'll stop by Martha's and give you final instructions. I guess it'll be the last time I'll see you until you get back."

"I just hope that gunsmith can make me some slugs. It may turn out that I need that rifle awful bad."

The gunsmith had finished reshaping and enlarging the .58-caliber mold, and he had cast two slugs by the time Boyd walked into his shop with a brass cartridge case in his pocket from his .70-caliber rifle. Together, they tested the first lead slug. It was just slightly too large, but that didn't matter to Boyd. He said, "That's no trouble at all; this will do just fine." He was well pleased with the results and told the gunsmith so. "Can you do me another favor? I usually load the cartridges myself, but where I'm staying, I don't have the room and I don't have the tools. I'd like to get you to load me a hundred cartridges. I've got the brass outside in my saddlebags. Do you reckon you could get that done for me by late this afternoon?"

The gunsmith looked doubtful. Boyd pulled out two fifty-dollar bills and laid them out on the workbench. He said, "There ought to be a little bonus in this hundred dollars to cover the mold and the lead and the powder and your time and trouble in loading those cartridges for me."

The gunsmith said, "Well, I will say this: You sure know how to talk to a man. Bring your cartridges on in and I'll try to have them done for you by six this evening. Will you be wanting any extra ammunition?"

Boyd said, "Yeah, but we'll talk about that when I get back."

His business done, he headed back to Martha's house and put his horse away. He figured he would go pick up the chestnut mare later on that afternoon, then circle back and get what he needed and what was ready at the gunsmith's place.

Martha fixed them a lunch of fried ham and grits with sliced tomatoes. They didn't talk much as they ate. There seemed already to be a feeling of sadness about the place. Boyd, for the life of him, could not understand why he felt as he did about leaving Martha. He supposed it was more sympathy than anything else, for surely he could not be feeling anything for her as a woman. He could not imagine himself ever feeling anything toward any other woman after Hannah. He would not allow himself to because of the betrayal it would represent to even entertain the thought of Martha as someone who could replace Hannah. No one could replace Hannah, ever, for the rest of his life. Still, he felt a certain loneliness. Already, he missed Martha and he didn't know why.

Something was bothering her too. She talked little, ate even less, and didn't seem to have much energy. She asked when he was leaving, and he told her what the plans were. She nodded, accepting it, and said she would have his clothes washed and ready for him by the next morning. She said, "Take off that shirt you're wearing and those jeans, they might as well go in the pot too. I can have something washed and dried for you by the time you leave this afternoon."

He did as he was told, no longer bothered by walking around the house naked in front of Martha. She got a big kettle of water and started heating it on the stove, and put his dirty clothes in the heating water. However, she insisted on hand-washing his linen shirts, something he couldn't quite understand. But then, as she told him, he wasn't supposed to understand.

He said, "I reckon I'll go take a nap while you tend to that washing. I probably need to get as much sleep as I can, either to get caught up on it or try to get ahead."

Martha said, "I'll call you about three o'clock."

He went in and tried to get comfortable on the bed, but he was restless. Something was bothering him and he could not figure out what. He tried to make his mind a blank, tried to not think about the job, tried to not think about the past, tried to not think about leaving, tried not to think about anything. It didn't work. His mind kept coming back to the images of the first bath Martha had given him, the way she'd shaved him, and the way she'd gentled him through the hard four days of getting dried out from three months of solid booze. He thought of the way she'd taken in a whiskey-sodden, desperate derelict and put him back on his feet. He could never repay her for that. Not with money, certainly not with that thousand dollars. He knew what she wanted; at least he thought he knew. He just wasn't prepared to give it.

The thought of the money suddenly made him sit up quickly on the bed. The shirt she'd taken off him had the fifty dollars and the deposit slip for $950 with her name on it in the pocket. He didn't want her to find it like that. He suddenly spun around on the bed and got up and started for the kitchen. As he got to the door, she was turning to come toward him. He could see she was holding the money and the slip in her hand. She said, her voice even, "Boyd, what is this?"

He suddenly felt very uncomfortable. He hadn't known how he was going to give it to her, but he would have picked a better way than this. He said, "It's nothing, Martha, it's really nothing. It's thanks to you for saving my life.''

She said, her voice calm, too calm, "Is this what your life is worth?''

"You know what I mean, Martha. Look, I've come into that reward money and I know you're not exactly flush. You've become someone very special to me and I wanted you to have a little security, that's all.''

She was giving him a look with hard eyes. "Boyd, do you know what this makes me feel like?''

He sighed. "Oh, hell, Martha. For God's sake, please don't take that attitude. I beg you, don't take it like that.''

Her voice was growing colder by the moment. She said, "Well, I suggest you tell me another way. I mean, after what we've done and then you offer me this amount of money. Just how am I supposed to take it?''

He said, a touch of desperation in his voice, "As what it is. As payment for nursing me.''

She cut him off before he could go any further. "I thought it was understood that I was already being paid,'' she said. "Warren arranged for payment of my nursing services. If you pay me anything else on top of that, we can only see it as for another service, one that I don't get paid for.''

He felt silly standing there naked talking to her. He went over and sat down on a chair opposite the divan. "Martha, you've got to quit taking it like this,'' he said. "You're acting insulted.''

"I am insulted, Boyd, very insulted.''

"Martha, I was not trying to insult you, I was trying to share my good fortune with a friend. Can't you believe that?''

"I believe that it is one of two things. It's either charity, which I certainly don't want, or it's payment for making love. I don't think I have to tell you what my opinion of that would be.''

He said grimly, a slight touch of anger rising in him at her hardheadedness, "Now listen, Martha, you and I both know the money is for neither of those things. It's out of gratitude and it's out of the willingness—no, the desire—to share with a friend, a very close friend, someone who has gone through . . . well, I'm not going to go on with that. Now is that so bad?"

She walked toward him and dropped the deposit slip and the money in his lap. She said, "I wish you would please take this back."

"Martha, do you want it to end like this? Do you want us to end our friendship with a misunderstanding between us? Ain't either one of us the strongest person in the world right now—emotionally, as you call it. We don't need another hurt in our lives."

She had turned to go into the kitchen, but she stopped at the door and swiveled her head around to him. She said, "Maybe it's just as well that it does end this way, Boyd. I was slipping past the point that I never thought I would reach again. I know that there can never be anything more between us than what we've had so far. Unfortunately, I was beginning to want more."

He stood up slowly. The deposit slip and the fifty-dollar bill fluttered to the floor. He said, "Martha, I've known how you felt. I felt a little of it myself. I don't think I have to explain to you that it doesn't have anything to do with either you or me and why I can't take it no further."

Martha said, "I understand."

"I want to make sure you do. It's still too fresh. I'd feel like I was betraying someone. I'd feel like a traitor. I can use this"—he touched his member—"but I can't use this." He put his hand over his heart. "Not yet. And you, you deserve all of it and I just don't have that to give. I wish you would please take this money. I would at least like to make your life a little easier any way I could. If you don't want to spend it on yourself, spend it on your patients. Do whatever you want to with it."

She shook her head. "I can't take anything from you, Boyd, especially you. I certainly can't take any money. As far as saving anyone's life, you saved mine. Those men the other night wanted more than just our money, they wanted me too. You stopped them."

He took two steps toward her and said, "That's just my point. A week ago, I wouldn't have been able to stop them. I would have been too weak, too addled, too soaked in whiskey to have done anything except sit there with slobber running down my chin. You put me back on my feet. For God's sake, please, let me show you some appreciation. Let me leave you in a situation where I won't worry about you while I'm gone."

Her face suddenly softened. "Will you do that, Boyd? Will you worry about me?"

He crossed quickly to her and put his hands on her shoulders. "Are you crazy? Of course I will worry about you and I'll miss you like the living daylights. I had thought about asking you to go with me, but then I was afraid to do that, afraid of what it would signify. Can you understand that?"

She nodded slowly and sighed. "Yes, unfortunately I can, Boyd. I wish it didn't have to be this way, though, because I am ready to go with you but I do understand that you're not ready to take me. Perhaps that day will come."

He said, "Yes, perhaps the day may come and it may not be too far off. Who knows? But I will be back, I promise you. I'd feel better if I knew you were solvent, that you had something to fall back on."

She gave him a half smile. "Oh, I'll get by, Boyd. I don't want much so I don't need for much."

He said, "Well, there's the deposit slip. I'm not going to

pick it up. There's fifty dollars on the floor. I'm not going to pick that up. If you want to sweep it on out the back door, you can, but it will be your doing. That money is going to stay in that account. What you do about it is up to you.''

She kissed him lightly on the lips. ''It will be there when you get back. You may well need it. Don't be sure that all the hard times are over with, Boyd. You have no idea of the number of times I've had to bite my lip to keep from calling you some name like honey or sweetheart. The last few days it wanted to come so naturally to my lips.''

He looked down and nodded. ''I know it, and it doesn't get any easier. Tomorrow is going to be a very hard day for me when I have to get on that train and pull out.''

She said, ''Yes, but you have to do it, and maybe you'll find yourself somewhere out there, and then maybe you'll come back to see me.''

She suddenly turned. ''I've got to see to your clothes. The water in the kettle is boiling.''

It was not long after supper when Warren arrived with Boyd's tickets and his documents and a letter of credit drawn on the Cattleman's Association that would be good at any bank he was likely to run into, plus some cash and other paraphernalia of his office as an agent of the Cattleman's Protective Association.

Boyd insisted that Martha sit with him while they talked. He had gotten the chestnut mare that afternoon and picked up his cartridges. For all intents and purposes, he was ready to go. Warren had brought him one of his leather valises to pack his clothes in because it was going to take up most of the room in his saddlebags to hold his ammunition and his spare revolver.

Warren said, ''As you can see from your ticket, you leave here at eleven o'clock tomorrow and you'll end up in Liberal, Kansas, tomorrow night around ten. There's a local train, the Kansas-Missouri line, I believe, that will take you into Garden City. I've got Jake Mangus's address written down for you. He and his assistant, Gates Hood, live in a boardinghouse. I reckon you'll put up at the hotel. Are you planning on moving the headquarters closer to the action?''

"I can't see why not, but I can't say until I get on the ground and see what's going on."

"I think the first thing you should do is go visit the three main Association members and let them know that you've taken over the job."

Boyd said, "You want me to get Mr. Mangus mad as hell right off, is that it?"

Warren smiled. "I don't imagine that he'll be getting much madder than he will be after he reads that letter I gave you. I also sent him a telegram today telling him when you will be arriving and when he can expect you and for him to be there, along with the other three agents. You might as well get ready for the fact that they're going to take the attitude that you got the job because you're my brother. It'll be up to you to prove them wrong."

Boyd said, "Look, Warren. I want you to understand that if I see I can't handle this job, I'm not going to embarrass myself or embarrass you. You'll get a wire from me saying that I quit and that's all. It won't be for the lack of trying, however, because I will give it my best effort."

Warren said, "That's all I ask, Boyd. Just give it a try, that's all I ask."

Martha said hesitantly, "Any idea how long this could take?"

Warren chuckled. "Afraid of having this woebegone scoundrel back on your doorstep too quick?"

Martha flushed slightly. "No, not exactly."

Warren glanced quickly from her face to Boyd's. He said

hurriedly, "Martha, there's just no good way to tell how long it'll take something like this to work out. It could be a few weeks, but it's more than likely going to be months. It's a very complicated situation. There's a lot of people and some big money involved. It's not going to get settled overnight."

Boyd said to Martha, "I wonder if we could get another cup of coffee and maybe just a little more of that cognac?"

She got up immediately, took their cups, and went into the kitchen. Boyd gave his brother a fierce look. He said softly, "You watch your goddamn mouth. Can't you see . . ." He stopped.

"Can't I see what?"

"Nothing, just watch your damned mouth."

When she brought the coffee and the liquor back, they sat and talked a while longer before Warren had to go. Boyd said, "I'll walk you out to your buggy, big brother. Guess I'll be saying adios to you tonight. There's no point in you coming down to the train station."

Warren looked around at Martha. He said, "You know, this idiot's going to ride in a stock car all the way to the middle of Kansas instead of riding in a chair car like a proper person. He prefers to ride back there with his animals."

"Like I said, the company's better and you get a better view of the landscape."

They went out through the front door, walking across Martha's patchy yard to where Warren's buggy was tied. Warren stepped up into the seat as Boyd untied his reins and handed them to him.

Boyd said, "Well, you know I'm obliged to you. I guess if it hadn't been for you and Martha, I'd've fallen off the edge of the world."

Warren gazed off toward the house. "I'd say Martha did most of the fixing."

"Yeah, but you were the one that got me to her and got her to take me in. I expect that you paid her pretty well."

"I paid her the same wages that we pay all part-time Association help, five dollars a day."

"Hell, Warren, that don't come to more than forty or forty-five dollars, not counting the groceries and such."

Warren gave him a wink. "Don't worry. I saw that she done a little better than that. Besides, you gave her a thousand dollars."

Boyd started to tell his brother that she wouldn't take it, but he stopped himself. That business was between him and Martha. He put out his hand and they shook. He said, "I guess I'll see you when I see you."

Warren kept hold of Boyd's hand. He looked at his brother and said, "Son, there is just one thing I want to make sure of, that you're over your suicide ways."

Boyd wrinkled his brow. "What suicide ways?"

"That stunt you pulled the other night, taking on three men with drawn guns. That's the nearest thing to suicide I have ever seen."

Boyd regarded him coolly. "You see any marks on me?"

"It still looked pretty reckless. All I am asking you is to not try and get yourself killed. You'll have plenty of chances to get killed on the other fellow's hook. Don't try it on yours."

"Warren, I know that for many years I was required to listen to you and you were never wrong, but I am going to tell you that you are wrong now. I don't plan to put myself in situations where I'll try to get myself killed. I can assure you that's not anywhere in my mind. I will try to win any gunfight I get involved in. I don't want to stop any bullets. I want the other fellow to stop them. You understand me?"

Warren let go of his hand and nodded. "All right, I believe you. Now go up there to Kansas and make me proud of you.''

Boyd said, ''The hell with you. I want to make myself proud of me.''

Warren smiled, gave his little brother a quick wave, then slapped the horse with the reins and the buggy moved off, disappearing into the darkness. Boyd watched him for a moment, and then turned and headed back into the house for his last night with Martha before he left for Kansas.

They were stiff and almost formal with each other. Boyd was afraid to say anything. It seemed that every thought that came to his mind pointed toward the fact that he was leaving and that there wasn't anything lasting between them, and that there might never be anything lasting between them.

On her part, Martha seemed busy about the house, doing and redoing chores that weren't even necessary. Several times, she asked Boyd how long he expected to be on the train. She wanted to make sure she packed him enough food to last the entire trip.

He said, ''Martha, there is no call for you to go to that trouble. I ought to be able to jump off the train at a stop somewhere and load up on groceries.''

Of course that in itself—asking her not to do something for him—was another form of denying her. It seemed he couldn't say anything right, so in the end, he simply said nothing.

They did not sit around the kitchen table and talk as they normally did. Boyd sat in the front room on the divan and Martha busied herself around the kitchen. At an early hour, somewhere before ten o'clock, she pleaded fatigue and a headache and said she was going to bed. Boyd nodded and said he would be along shortly.

After she was gone, he sat thinking and wondering about this sudden new turn his life had taken in little more than a week. He hoped he would be up to it, not because he was afraid of letting Warren down, but because he really hoped he could find some way to replace the life he'd once had. He either wanted to be alive or dead. He didn't want any more of that half-life he had led for three months. That was over.

He couldn't help but notice that the deposit slip and the fifty dollars in cash still lay on the small table at the end of the couch. He'd put a book over them when Warren had come in, but the corner of one of the bills was still sticking out. He shrugged. It was all the same to him whether she used the money or not. It could just stay there.

He got up, went into the kitchen, and began to pack his saddlebags, loading each pouch with ammunition for all three of his guns. He put a bottle of whiskey in each one, and then took the time to wrap his spare revolver in the shirt he was wearing and stuck it in on top of the rest of the load. He buckled the flaps and set it all by the back door. There was still the matter of packing his clothes in the valise Warren had brought him, but he would do that in the morning. He went into the kitchen with the intent of drinking one last cup of coffee, but the stove was cold and the pot barely warm. He poured himself out an inch or so of cognac in a glass and sipped it slowly as he smoked one final cigarillo.

He was in no rush to go to bed. He didn't know what he would find waiting for him there. Finally, he could stall no longer. He put out the lamp and went quietly through the front room and into the bedroom. Martha had left the lamp on his side of the bed on low. She was on her side, turned away from him. She didn't stir as he sat on the edge of the bed and took off his boots, stripped off his jeans, and got under the sheet. He glanced over at her, expecting some sort of good night, but she just lay there, very still. He turned the lamp off, punched up his pillow, and then turned on his side with his back toward her, waiting for sleep to come. He hated to see them part in such a way, but there seemed no help for it.

He came awake the next morning with the sun streaming through the window, aware that she was already out of bed. He got up slowly and dressed and took a drink of water from the pitcher by his bedside. He got his boar-bristle toothbrush and went into the kitchen, where she was fixing breakfast. He took a small amount of baking soda, put it in the palm of his hand, worked it around, and then stood at the sink, brushing his teeth. She'd deliberately turned away as he had come into the room, even though he'd mumbled a good morning to her. He could see that it was going to be no better.

When he finished brushing his teeth and shaving, she had his breakfast on the table. He sat down to eat and she disappeared, saying, "I'll get your clothes packed."

He said, "Thank you." He turned to watch her leave. She was wearing the yellow frock, only this time she had it buttoned all the way up to her neck. He wondered if she had slept in it. It made him angry, but he forced himself to cool off and tend to his breakfast.

He was at the point of lighting a cigarillo and drinking his second cup of coffee when she appeared, wondering where his fourth shirt was. He explained that he had used it to wrap his second gun in so that it wouldn't get nicked and that it was in his saddlebags. She made a face and opened the flap of his saddlebags, took out the gun, unwrapped it, laid it on the table, and then disappeared with his shirt. She came back with some old rags, rewrapped his gun, put it back in the pouch of his saddlebags, and buckled the flap. She said, "Now, you have gone and gotten gun oil on your shirt. I'll have to set it to soak, and it will have to be packed wet. It's going on to eight o'clock and I don't think it will have time to dry."

Boyd said, "Martha, why don't you sit down and let's talk for a bit?"

She said, "There is too much to do." She disappeared again.

By the time he saw her next, he had been out to the privy out behind the shed and had come back in. She was busy at the sink counter, filling a large cloth sack with slices of ham and biscuits and chunks of cheese and cans of peaches. She said, "This ought to hold you on your trip without you having to get out and go to some cafe."

He nodded. "Thank you. I'm much obliged."

She said, "You know, I do wish you would take that money and that deposit slip with you. I honestly don't want it, Boyd."

He said evenly, "Martha, it is there and it is going to stay there, unless you move it. You can do what you want to do with it, it's up to you."

She said, "Well, if or when you ever come back, it will still be there."

He said, "Suit yourself."

A few minutes before ten, he went outside and saddled his roan, tying his saddlebags behind. Then he put a halter on the chestnut and a lead rope and tied the lead rope to the horn of his saddle. Both horses were calm and disinterested in the proceedings.

He went back into the house. Martha was sitting at the table. He said, "I reckon that I better go. It'll take time to get my horses loaded. I don't guess there's any way I could tell you how much I appreciate what you have done."

She got up and said, "I'll walk out with you."

They got to his roan and he stopped to turn and face her. He said, "Martha, I hate that something has come between us. I wish there was something that I could do about it."

"I know you do, Boyd, and I know there is nothing you can do. It will just have to be. I know that you are searching for something that you're not going to find. As I told you once before, you can kill a thousand men and sleep with a thousand women, but you still are not going to recreate that life you had before."

"How come you haven't tried to start a new one?"

"Maybe I did but it just didn't work."

He said, "Martha, I am asking you to give this a little time, give me a little time. I don't know who I am yet. I only woke up about three days ago. This is a brand-new world and I don't know what's out there."

She put her hands to his face in a sudden surprising gesture. She said, "Don't get yourself killed, Boyd. Don't take any unnecessary chances and don't be reckless. You don't have anything to prove. I know. I tried for a long time to prove that I needed to be miserable, but it doesn't help anything."

"You are the second one to be worried about me being intentionally reckless. I have no intention of it, Martha. I have intentions of standing right here someday again. I don't know if you'll still be here like you are, but I intend to be back."

"I hope you are, Boyd, but I have learned not to count on anything."

"Am I now supposed to be the one to talk to you about hope, like you did me?"

She laughed. "I guess the shoe is on the other foot, in a way. You'd better get mounted up. You don't want to miss your train."

He said, "Will you kiss me good-bye? I want to leave with some hope that I haven't completely ruined my welcome here."

She said huskily, "You could never do that." Her arms went around his neck as she pulled his mouth to hers. He held her tightly and they kissed and rekissed and then finally stepped apart.

He said, "I'll bring you a present when I come back."

She took two steps backward as he put his foot into the stirrup and mounted up. She said, "Promise?"

He was turning the roan around, the lead rope swinging the chestnut along with him. He said, "Yeah, what would you like?"

She laughed. "I'd like to see you with a proper haircut."

"All right." He lifted his hat. As he touched his spurs to the roan, he said, "Will you give me a present?"

"Yes, what?"

"I'd like to see you blond all over."

She let out a surprised shriek, but it faded from his ears as he put the roan into a lope and rode up the lane that led from her house to the main road. He turned left, heading for the train depot.

It took less time to get his horses loaded than he had expected. Two railroad crewmen pointed out his car, and then set a ramp in place so he could lead his animals up into the stock car, half of which he had bought for the trip to Garden City, Kansas. The car was partitioned off with a fence across from the side he wasn't using. That part was empty.

Boyd said to one of the crewmen, "I hope to hell that you're not going to fill that other half with smelly cattle."

The crewman said, "Well, not before you get to Liberal. Of course once you get there, this car will be getting switched to . . . I believe it is the Kansas-Missouri that you pick up out of there, according to your ticket. God knows what they'll put in there then. Mules, most likely."

Boyd was in the process of unsaddling his roan. The crewmen were eyeing the unusual way his saddle was rigged out. He had a gun boot on his right for his saddle carbine and a specially made boot on the left side for the big .70-caliber rifle.

One of the crewmen said, "That's some kind of cannon you have there. What do you shoot with that? Bears?"

Boyd said, "Yes, whenever bears require my serious attention, then I use this serious rifle. It looks like this water trough is low. Where can I get some more water for it?"

The crewman said, "Never mind, sir. We'll see that you get more water and more hay. I might could wrangle you up a chair if you've a mind and don't want to sit on a hay bale."

"I would take that appreciatively."

The man looked at his watch. "It's about twenty minutes until the train pulls out so we had better get to rushing around."

After they left, Boyd untied his valise and the sack of food that Martha had prepared for him. He had them slung across the back of the chestnut and tied to the horse's overly abundant mane. In due course, he would get his hands on a pair of scissors and cut that mane down. The chestnut's tail also needed tending to. He was all for a horse having enough tail to defend itself against flies, but he didn't like for it to get caught up in the brush. He reckoned he would run into a bunch of that on the prairies of Kansas and Colorado.

The crewman returned with a couple bales of hay and some water for the horses. They hadn't been able to find a chair, but they had managed to find an old, rickety stool. He was sitting on that stool when the train began to jerk and jolt its way out of the station. He was thinking of the job that lay ahead. He had an idea that more than a quick gun would be called for to right the situation as Warren had described it.

The horses fidgeted and looked nervous at the rocking and

banging of the train as it slowly picked up speed. The chestnut neighed in concern and looked around wall-eyed. Boyd got up, patted and soothed her, and got her settled down as the train picked up enough speed to run smoothly. Through the slats, he could see the last of Oklahoma City begin to disappear, the houses getting further and further apart, and within five or ten minutes they were in the country. Soon enough, the wind came whistling through the slatted car and began blowing hay and sand around. Boyd didn't much care. It was his preference when he had to take his horse with him on a trip to ride in the stock car. To him, it was much freer and easier than sitting in the chair cars with a load of other people jammed in around him.

The train passed a little farmhouse set among the rolling hills in that part of Oklahoma. He saw a woman standing out in the front yard, shading her eyes as she watched the train go by. There was something about her that reminded Boyd of Martha, something in the way the woman was standing, the gesture of her hand, something in her face that made him think that she was yearning to be gone from her lonesome farm, pulling away on the steel rails toward some excitement and adventure that would lay ahead. It made him feel sad about Martha. She deserved better than having to sit and wait for some happiness to come to her.

He wondered, though, if he was any smarter. He was going off, but whether or not there was happiness, he had no idea. He yawned; he hadn't slept very well the night before. Lately he had grown accustomed to sleeping next to Martha, feeling her cool smooth skin next to his, but last night there had been a wall between them.

Boyd immediately put those thoughts out of his mind. For the next hour or so he stared out through the slats of the stock car, watching the landscape slowly change from hilly and wooded to flatland where the trees were growing sparser and sparser. Now and again, the train rumbled across a bridge that crossed over a small creek or a river, but the landscape had now definitely established itself as rolling prairies, spotted with farmhouses and now and then a place he could identify as a cattle operation.

In the early afternoon, he began to feel hungry, so he opened the cloth sack and began to make himself biscuit sandwiches stuffed with ham, taking one drink of whiskey and then washing the rest down with water. He was reaching down to make himself another sandwich when he noticed a folded piece of white paper. He opened it. In her neat, careful script, she simply said that she apologized for the way she had acted his last day there and that she would be there, waiting, if and when he chose to come back. It wasn't signed. He took the note, carefully folded it into a small square, and slid it into a safe place in his billfold. He replaced his billfold in his back pocket and then stared out the slats, the food forgotten.

Eight

The trip was long, boring, and dusty. Boyd arrived in Kansas late that night after several delays. His car and several others were switched off to a siding. According to one of the train-men in the switching yard, the Kansas-Missouri train would pick him up sometime early the next morning. Boyd simply went to sleep, expecting to wake up already rolling toward Garden City. Instead, he came awake at daylight, still sitting in the freight yards of Liberal, Kansas. It wasn't until a little after noon that he was finally hooked onto the Kansas-Missouri train and headed toward Garden City. It would have been all right if he had known there would be such a wait. He could have gone into Liberal to get something to eat, a shave, or perhaps even a bath, but he couldn't leave the train because no one could tell him for certain when the little teapot engine, as one freight yard hired hand had re-ferred to the Kansas-Missouri engine, would hook him up.

As it was, Boyd finally got into Garden City around five that afternoon. He was tired and filthy and restless. Once he got his horses on the ground, he inquired as to the best hotel in town and was assured that it was the Morgan House, which was downtown and couldn't be missed. He had not expected Jake Mangus or the other agents to meet him, and they were not there. He didn't even know if they were in Garden City, but the agency was there, at least the office. That could wait until the next day.

He rode directly to the hotel, finding it in the middle of a broad main street. Garden City was a clean town with nearly, he calculated, as many churches as there were saloons. It wasn't bad for a state that had been a railhead for many a Texas cattle drive. The place looked to him to have somewhere between three and five thousand inhabitants. He hoped that the hotel had a good dining room and that he could get a bath straight off. He pulled up in front of the hotel and dismounted, took his big rifle out of the boot, slung his saddlebags over his shoulder, untied his valise from the saddlehorn, and then mounted the boardwalk and went into the hotel.

The clerk gave him a glance, being uncertain and none too impressed by his appearance; Boyd was certain of that. Boyd ordered the best room that the man had, and told him that he had two horses outside that needed to be attended to and that he wanted a bath immediately. To emphasize his point, he put down a ten-dollar bill and never asked the price of the room. That got the clerk's attention.

The clerk asked, "How long will you be staying, sir?"

"I don't know, but you'll have money every day that I am here, if that's what's worrying you. Just see to my horses, my bath, and show me to that room because I am damn tired. I've been on the train for two days. Oh, can I get a shave around here?"

"Yes, sir. There's a barbershop right here in the hotel and you can go in there or I can have him sent to your room."

"Send him to my room. Do I bathe in my room or do you have a community bathroom?"

The clerk said, "No, sir. This is a modern hotel. You've

got a bathroom right there in your room. I'll have some boys bring in some hot water. The cold water is already running."

Boyd said, "Give me the key then and point the way."

"Yes, sir." The clerk turned and hollered for a boy, who came bounding immediately from around the corner. He took Boyd's valise and his big rifle and hurried down the hall to the end room.

With the key, the boy let Boyd into a spacious corner room with a connecting bath, which impressed him. He didn't normally throw money around, but then, why not? He'd never had five dollars per diem before either.

He gave the boy fifty cents and asked him to make sure about his horses. Then Boyd sat down on the bed, opened his saddlebag, got out the bottle of whiskey, and poured himself a drink. He sat there relaxing, trying to adjust himself to where he was. He sipped at the whiskey for a moment, and then got out a cigarillo and lit it.

Boyd was not looking forward to encountering Jake Mangus or Gates Hood. He really didn't want to encounter anyone, but he especially didn't want to face the resentment that he knew would be plain in their actions. He didn't actually much blame them. He was the brother of their boss coming in to be their boss, totally untrained, totally uneducated about the situation, and now he was going to give them orders. He could imagine how delighted they would be with that. There were two other agents but he had forgotten their names. Warren had written them down, but he had forgotten to look.

Yes, it was shaping up to be one hell of a swell party. The main battle he was facing first off was not with the fence busters and the rustlers, but his own people. Even in his best days, when he could make a friend out of nearly anyone, he would have dreaded the coming confrontation. In his present mood, Boyd would have almost rather had an arm jerked out of its socket than bring four men into line and break them to the lead, break them to the saddle. But that was what he was going to have to do if he was to accomplish anything.

He sighed and poured out another drink. He felt surprisingly lonely in the hotel room, even as nicely furnished as it was. He wondered why he always sat down on the bed when he came into a hotel room. He couldn't ever remember sitting in a chair. He wondered if it was his way of making himself at home. He had no earthly idea, no more than he had an idea what the first meeting with the agents was going to be like.

There was time to worry about that later. Boyd kicked off his boots and stood up to take off his shirt. His bath would be coming soon, and hopefully the barber too. There would be time to worry about the other stuff later after he had a good meal and a night's rest.

Boyd went out that evening, after having a bath and shaving. He had a new haircut that he thought even Martha would have been proud of. He stopped in the dining room and had a meal of roast beef, mashed potatoes, and green beans. After he ate, he wandered down the streets until he found a saloon. He had a couple of drinks and played poker for a few hours before going back to his hotel and going to bed. The poker was almost funny; he couldn't lose. He won almost eighty dollars in a small-stakes game, and he calculated if he had been playing in a pot-limit game, he would have won thirty or forty times that much. He thought that was the way of it. A man on five dollars per diem, drawing a hundred dollars a month, and with several thousand dollars in the bank, couldn't lose. He wondered how the rest of his luck would hold up.

Boyd had breakfast early the next morning in the hotel dining room, eating a half-dozen eggs, along with bacon and biscuits that weren't near as good as Martha's, and drinking a cup of coffee. After he finished, he went to the front desk and asked for directions to the sheriff's office. He found out that he was within walking distance of the place.

It was still early, not quite eight o'clock, so he went back to his room and sat down. Thoughtfully, he poured himself a drink, and then watered it down from the pitcher on his bedside table. That was a new twist for him; he couldn't recall ever drinking watered-down whiskey, but as it turned out, it went down smooth. He had been surprised the night before that he had actually paid very little attention to the whiskey. As a matter of fact, once he started playing poker, he hadn't drunk at all. As he left the table he'd bought a round for the losers, but he'd left without joining them.

Boyd was nervous and he knew it, but it was in a different way than usual. It was an uncertain ground, this business of walking in and being someone's boss. He had been a boss before, but the men who had worked for him had been of his choosing. Now, he was a boss who was being thrust upon some other men, and he either had to win their cooperation, force their cooperation, or fire them. There were no other alternatives.

That wasn't the real cause of his nervousness. The flat fact of the matter was that he didn't want to be anyone's boss. He wanted to play a lone hand. He felt like he could handle the trouble; he just wasn't sure he could handle the trouble *and* put up with the constant association of four hired hands. He was aware, as he got ready to leave the hotel, that he was not the same man that he had once been. So much had changed, and he had no experience in facing these kinds of situations. He would just have to see which way his stick floated and which way his luck ran, and if it came to it, how tough he still was.

A little after nine, he took the leather envelope containing

his credentials that Warren had given him and set out to the
sheriff's office to present himself. The sheriff, a man named
Bill Black, could not have been any less interested. He said,
"As I understand it, your trouble is not around here. It's
about thirty or forty miles west of here, out of my county
and out of my jurisdiction. I appreciate you letting me know
that you are in town, but all I ask you to do is not to break
any laws and don't make any trouble, either for me or for
yourself."

The sheriff had been kind enough to give him directions
to the Cattleman's Association office. As he stepped out on
to the boardwalk, he noted that the Garden City was a clean
and quiet town on the surface. Boyd wondered if it really
was that way.

As he walked, he thought about whether Jake Mangus and
the other agents would be jealous and rebellious enough not
to be awaiting his arrival. They could always plead that they
hadn't received the telegram, that no word had gotten
through and no messages had arrived, and force him to go
and search them out in strange country. That would put him
at a distinct disadvantage, and it would also tell him what
kind of men he would have to deal with.

But they had not done that. Jake Mangus and Gates Hood
were waiting for him at the storefront office which had at
one time, obviously, been a men's haberdashery. Jake Mangus was a short, stocky man, on the wrong side of thirty-
five. He had a bullying look and swagger about him, and
Boyd immediately expected a rebellious bluster. Instead,
Mangus went overboard with his welcome and his vows to
cooperate and how glad they were to have Boyd there. He
had, Boyd thought, all the earmarks of an apple polisher or
a politician.

Mangus started to ask about Boyd's brother, Warren, but
Boyd immediately stopped him and set both of the men

straight. He said, "Yes, I've got a brother named Warren McMasters, but I work for the vice president of the Cattleman's Association. So do you, and the two are not the same as far as I'm concerned, and they shouldn't be to you either. Let's get that settled right here and now and let's have nothing else said about it. I'm here to do a job. If I can't do that job, Warren McMasters will fire me just as fast as he would either one of you."

It was Gates Hood that had him puzzled. According to his records, Boyd and Gates were the same age, twenty-eight, but Gates was a tall, thin, stringbean kind of man who looked like he still had peach fuzz on his cheeks. He was sandy-haired and lanky and slow-spoken, with freckles that showed through his tan. He didn't look to be any more dangerous than a pencil. Boyd had read his record and knew that he had handled several tough situations around the Texas border.

To add to matters, Gates had a high-pitched voice that almost went off into a screech when he was excited. Gates also had a habit of ending most of his sentences with the phrase "if you take my meaning."

There were only two desks in the small office, but Gates went into the back where Boyd supposed the stock for the haberdashery store had been located and came back with a couple of chairs. Gates cleared his stuff off one desk, put it over on the one occupied by Jake Mangus, and got Boyd set up at the desk where he had been working.

Boyd's first question was where were the other two agents that Warren had sent to help. Jake Mangus said, "Well, they be in Lakin."

"Where's that?"

Mangus said, "That be a town about thirty miles west of here, right near Lake McKinney. That's closer to the trouble than we is here."

Boyd asked, "What are you two doing here?"

Mangus answered, "Well, this is where we were told to meet you."

Boyd sat down at the desk. "Let me see a map of the area where we have the trouble."

Mangus and Gates Hood looked at each other. Gates said, "Well, sir, we ain't got no map. We never taken it into our heads that you'd be wanting a map, if you take my meaning."

Boyd asked, "How do you expect me to understand the situation if I can't see it down on paper? Do you plan to describe some country to me and some people that I've never met and some troubles that I know nothing about? Was that your idea?"

Gates said, "Well, Mr. McMasters, I don't think we gave it that much thought, if you take my meaning."

"So you don't have a map?"

"Yes, sir, that's correct. We ain't got no map."

Boyd asked, "Is there a courthouse here?"

Gates nodded his head. "Yes, sir."

Boyd turned to Mangus and said, "Jake, I want you to go over to the courthouse and get me any kind of a map that you can of the area that we are talking about."

Mangus scratched his head. "Well, Mr. McMasters, I ain't real sure they'd have something like that. You see, the trouble ain't just in Kansas. It goes on into Colorado."

"Have you ever heard of a United States Geological Survey?"

They looked at each other and then at Boyd. They both shook their heads.

Boyd said, "They make sectional maps of every part of the United States that show topography, show the water, how much rain each area gets. It shows it all. Mangus, go over to the courthouse and find me a map, or maps, of the country that we are talking about, and then both of you had better get ready to take me to dead center of where the trouble is because that is going to be our next move.''

Mangus nodded and got up. ''Yes, sir, Mr. McMasters, but you've got to understand, this ain't right up my alley. But I will do my best.''

Boyd watched Mangus as he went out the door. There was still a bell, like most retail shops had, that rang as he opened and shut the door. Boyd had sent the chief of the agency on purpose, specifically to let him know there was a new boss. He turned back to Gates, who was sitting there regarding him.

Gates said, ''Are you going to be an iron ass, Mr. McMasters?''

Boyd blinked. ''What?''

''I just asked if you are going to be an iron ass, Mr. McMasters. I like to get the feel of the man that I work for.'' Gates had such an innocent, sincere expression on his face that Boyd laughed.

''No, Gates, I don't plan on being an iron ass, but if the situation calls for it, I guess I could be an iron ass if I need to be one.''

''I wasn't being no smart aleck, Mr. McMasters. I was just trying to get the lay of the land, if you take my meaning.''

''Yes, I take your meaning.''

Gates said thoughtfully, ''Jake ain't as dumb or as easy as he looks.''

''I didn't think he was, Gates, but then neither am I.''

Gates chuckled in a high pitch and said, ''You ain't got a good look at yourself in the mirror lately, have you? You don't look easy and you don't look simple, if you take my meaning.''

Boyd said, ''Let's me and you make a deal, Gates. Let's

just assume that I take your meaning and if I don't, I'll speak up. All right?''

Gates looked confused for a moment. ''I don't take your meaning, sir.''

''I'm telling you that it ain't necessary to say 'if you take my meaning' every time you say something.''

The confusion cleared from the brow of the young man. He said, ''Oh, yeah, I understand you now. Folks have been telling me that now for quite a while. I reckon it is kind of a bad habit. I chew tobacco and I spit too.''

Boyd resisted the urge to laugh. He said, ''Tell me about the water, Gates.''

''What water?''

''The water where people take their stock to drink. What do you mean, what water? Water is generally the cause of any trouble in any place where there is cattle and horses.''

Gates said, ''Well, this be open-range country, Mr. McMasters. People can't fence their neighbors off from common water.''

Boyd said, ''I know that, Gates. I want to know where the main water supply is in the part of the country where our clients are having the trouble.''

''Oh.'' Gates took off his hat and scratched his head. Boyd could see his sandy hair. ''Well, that would be Lake McKinney, which spills out and makes the Arkansas River, which it is called until it runs to the Colorado border, and then it splits and gets called the South Fork and the Twin Buttes River. There are several creeks around here, but you're talking about the principal water as I take your meaning.''

Boyd said, ''I'll wait until Jake gets back with the map.''

Mangus was not as long in returning as Boyd had expected. He came through the door with two rolled-up blue maps in his hand. He said, ''Well, I am the one with the surprised egg on my face, Mr. McMasters. They had them, but I would have never thought to have asked. They cost five dollars for the pair of them. I just charged them to the company. Reckon that was all right?''

Boyd took the maps, but before he spread them out, he said, ''You two settle down. I'm going to tell you the situation as I understand it from the vice president in Oklahoma City. Correct me as best as you can.'' He detailed his understanding as best as he could, although he was woefully short of names, dates, and places. ''Tell me this, who is our biggest client with the biggest complaint?''

Mangus said with a look of slight distaste on his face, ''That would be Del Cameron. He's got a big outfit, with at least ten thousand acres that he owns, and he is grazing about twenty thousand more acres that he is leasing from the federal government. He is running at least four thousand head of cattle all total. At least five hundred of them are those little black woolly things, those Black Anguses. To tell you the truth, Mr. McMasters, as big of an outfit as he is and as many hired hands as he's got, it looks to me like he ought to be able to tend to his own troubles, but he is the main one that has been squawking in my ears.''

Boyd looked at Mangus. ''Jake, you say he's got a lot of hired hands?''

''Yes, sir, that be a fact.''

''But he joined our Association to protect his property and his rights.''

''Yes, sir.''

Boyd said, ''Well, it sounds like to me that you want his cowhands to do our job of protecting his cattle and property. Is that right?''

Mangus looked confused. ''Well, no, that wasn't exactly what I meant, Mr. McMasters. I just thought that he had done so much complaining about the job that we were doing that it kind of got next to me.''

''What about it, Gates?''

The lanky young man shook his head. ''I don't do the talking with the customers. That's Jake's job. I've been try-ing to figure out who has been tearing down the fences and getting their cattle mixed in with Mr. Cameron's bulls and getting their bulls mixed in with his cows so they are drop-ping them part-black calves that are following their range-stock mamma. We've got some stealing going on around here, and I'll be damned if we can catch them. But no, sir, I take your meaning . . .'' He stopped suddenly, and then hesitantly asked, ''Is it all right if I say I take your mean-ing?''

Boyd said, ''Tell me what you're thinking, Gates.''

''Well, of course I know that it's our job to catch them that is up to no good, but that is mighty big country and there is a bunch of folks that could be in the wrong. I can't come along and just because a man who ain't in the Asso-ciation has a range cow with one of them part-black calves following it, I can't claim he tore down fence and got his cow in with Mr. Cameron's bull, or Mr. Harris's bull, or Mr. Cap Wiley's bull, or vice versa. But no, sir. I understand that the cowhands' job is to tend to the cattle.''

''Good. I'm glad that we got that straightened out. Now, where are those other two men? Are they in Lincoln County? Is that the center of the trouble?''

Jake Mangus looked over at Gates. Gates looked over and scratched his head. He said, ''Well, no, sir, Mr. McMasters, that ain't altogether the problem. We got several spots.''

Boyd wheeled around to the desk and took one of the maps and started unrolling it. He said, ''Okay, let's figure out where the trouble spots are.''

Jake Mangus and Gates came over from the other desk and crowded in behind him. The map included most of a section of Kansas with just a little strip of Colorado on the side. The maps didn't go by state lines or county lines but by lines predetermined by the surveyors. The water, the elevation, high ground, and low ground were easily identifiable, along with notes about the average rainfall. Boyd located Garden City almost in the center of his first map. About thirty miles to left he could see the little town of Lincoln next to Lake McKinney. Then running on further west were the villages of Kendall and Syracuse and Coolridge, and then, crossing the border into Colorado, the town of Holly. He could see the winding route of the Arkansas River as it came out of Lake McKinney, which was very near Lincoln. There were other small lines for little springs and creeks, but he was concentrating on the main watering holes.

Boyd got a stubbed pencil out of his pocket and held it over the map. He said, "I want you to show me where our main customers are."

It was Gates who stubbed a finger down almost in the boundaries of Hamilton County, which was in the extreme southwest corner of Kansas. He said, "Right just about here, Mr. McMasters, about six miles west of Syracuse and about three of four miles up from the river there. That's the biggest part of Cameron's ranch."

Boyd made an X on the map and added the initials D.C. He then got Gates and Jake Mangus to help him sketch out the general area that Cameron controlled. His land ran across the Colorado border and into the other state a little south of the town of Holly, and ran south about seven or eight miles, then turned back to the east and then to the northeast of Syracuse.

Boyd said, "That's a whole lot of territory that man takes in."

Gates said, "Yes, sir, he's got considerable cattle. Did we ever get a good count on them, Jake?"

Jake Mangus said, "Varies anywhere from fifteen hundred to thirty-five hundred head depending on his breeding operations."

Boyd said, "I was told this trouble had been going on for about six months, but you all are talking about dropping calves. How could there have been any calf crop in six months?"

Jake said slowly, "Well, it's been only about six months since the trouble has heated up, but it's been going on for about two years. They sent me out here two years ago to headquarter for this very reason."

"Two years!" Boyd looked around him in surprise. "Well, hell, that's too long for a situation like this to last. What's the biggest pasture that Cameron has fenced?"

Gates put his finger down on the map. "He's got a thousand acres trapped right about here which he uses for his main breeding grounds."

Boyd said, "I thought that you couldn't fence more than five hundred acres of free range area."

Jake said, "Yeah, but that's where he beats the law. He's got five hundred of it in Kansas and five hundred in Colorado. It might even be a little bigger than a thousand acres."

Boyd said, "I see." He studied the map for a moment more and then said, "What do you mean six months ago things started heating up?" He looked around at Jake. "What do you mean by heating up?"

Jake said, "Why, that's when they started shooting one another."

Boyd was startled in spite of himself. He said, "I didn't hear any word about gunplay. Who's been shot?"

Gates answered. He said slowly, "Well, Mr. Cameron had four of his riders killed, and Jim Harris had one or two of his killed, and then Asa Hale had one of his riders shot and one of his sons wounded. So all in all, that's about five or six that's been killed or wounded.''

Boyd looked at him trying to conceal his amazement. ''And you've let this continue? You haven't raised a general alarm to Mr. McMasters in Oklahoma City? What has the sheriff been doing about these things? Hasn't there been an investigation?''

Jake looked affronted. ''Well, of course there's been an investigation and the sheriffs have been involved. There's Jack Morris over in Lincoln and the sheriff of Hamilton County, Howard Duffy. We've been involved; we haven't been just sitting here. We've gone out and taken a look. That's why we have these two other hands in here, Bob Sweeney and Earl White. The two your brother sent us. No, sir, we haven't just been sitting here waiting. But Mr. McMasters, that's a whole lot of country out there. That's a lot of ground to cover and we can't be in more than one place at a time.''

Boyd said dryly, ''Seems like that one place has been Garden City, where nobody is shooting nobody.''

Jake's face flushed. ''Mr. McMasters, I was sent here to headquarter in Garden City and that was my orders. I've got two men in Lakin. Ain't nobody told me to move my headquarters.''

Boyd stared at him wondering if he was just lazy or just stupid. ''You didn't just take it upon yourself to get a little closer to the action?''

Jake shook his head slowly. ''Mr. McMasters, if you ain't noticed, the Cattleman's Protective Association is a big outfit and they have rules and regulations. Now my instructions when they sent me out here two years ago were to settle in and set up an office in Garden City and sign up anybody who wants to join the Association. Tend to business, and that's what I've done. Quite a number of folks is in this area. Ain't all in the western part where there's been trouble.''

"I see," said Boyd slowly. He saw the futility of trying to talk to Jake Mangus. He said "All right. By the way, you said Asa Hale. He's not on my list of our clients, people who do business with the Association."

Gates said, "No, sir, and he ain't likely to be either."

"Who the hell is he?"

Gates said with contempt in his voice, "A bunch of white trash, that's what the whole Hale family is. They're a bunch of squatters. They're sitting on a whole bunch of land out there in Kerney County squatting. I don't know how many hundred-and-sixty-acre tracts they proved up, but it's considerable. I wouldn't be surprised if in the last five years he hasn't been able to get his hand on better than two thousand acres of government land. In deed, fee simple."

Boyd understood proving up land. Any man could file on a 160 acres of land, and if he could prove it up either with a crop or livestock within a year, prove that he could live on it and make a living, it became his in fee simple. Which meant at no monetary cost to him. Apparently what Asa Hale had been doing was proving up one piece after another. The law did say that you had to be eighteen years or older. He said to Jake Mangus, "How many kids has this Asa Hale got?"

Gates Hood laughed. "We ain't never got a count on them, Mr. McMasters, but there's a bunch of them. And some big large boys that I reckon would be easy over eighteen. Old Asa has got to be pushing fifty himself, and he's got more kids than he could name."

Jake said, "Yeah, and he's got every one of them squatting on another hundred and sixty acres. The way his wife is throwing out kids and he's setting them up on the prairie in little dugout cabins, he's going to own most of the country before he's through."

Boyd said, "Where is he mainly located?"

Gates leaned over and stubbed his finger onto the map. "He's down here in the southeast corner of Hamilton County and spreads on over into the western part of Kerney County. He's all along the river. He's also a thorn in Mr. Cameron's side along the north and east borders. He's also got a number of calves and yearlings that sure have a lot of Black Angus in them. I guess you could say that it was a coincidence that many of Mr. Cameron's breeding stock could have gotten out and gotten next to Asa Hale's cattle, but that's one hell of a coincidence."

Trying to get a picture of exactly what he was facing, Boyd asked where the other two main clients were. Gates pointed out where Cap Wiley had better than two thousand acres. He was north of Cameron's spread. Gates said, "One thing he don't like about it—Cap Wiley, that is—kind of makes it hard for him to get at some serious water on the Arkansas River. He's got some spring creeks that run across his land, but they dry up on him in the hottest part of the summer."

"What about Jim Harris?" Jake Mangus pointed to the northern part of Kerney County. "He's over here due east of Syracuse and to the north of where Asa Hale's place is. He's a young man with a nice wife trying to make the best job of breeding that any of them are doing. The closest spread to Lake Buchanan, and I'd say he has the best grass. If there was anybody that Asa Hale is nipping at, it's Mr. Jim Harris."

Boyd slumped his shoulders in a slight gesture of despair. They were right. There was so much territory. He was looking at a distance of at least fifty or sixty miles square. How in hell the five of them could patrol that was beyond his wildest imagination. He said, "And we have other Association members scattered around in there?"

Gates said, "Yes, sir, but they don't amount to much and

they ain't trying to get involved in this breeding program like Mr. Harris and Mr. Cameron and Cap Wiley are.''

"How about more squatters? Any more like Asa Hale?''

Gates Hood laughed. "Thank the Lord, no, not any of his size. We got some, but they are mostly sodbusters trying to raise a corn crop or maybe some oats or wheat. The ranchers welcome them because they buy feed off of them. No, we ain't got any problems except those with Asa Hale.''

Boyd sat back in his chair. "So am I to conclude that Asa Hale is our problem? That he is the one who is tearing down our fences and letting those blooded cattle loose on the prairie?''

Jake walked around to the front of the desk and stood looking down at Boyd. "Well, you can figure that all you want to, Mr. McMasters. If you want to ride up there to that ranch where old Asa Hale and his boys are, you had better be able to make it stick. That's a pretty rough bunch of folks. I don't like them, but I am not fixing to challenge them anytime soon. They got some hired hands also that are mostly kinfolks. It's like a rat's nest up there.''

Boyd sighed. He said, "Well, hell!'' with feeling, then stared at the plate-glass windows onto the busy street of Garden City. He heaved a sigh and stood up. "Well, you all better get saddled up. We're going to leave this afternoon. I don't expect there's a train that goes out west, is there?''

Gates shook his head. "It's horseback in that direction, at least from here.''

Boyd said, "One thing. This Asa Hale, where does he get his range cattle?''

Gates and Jake looked at each other and shrugged. Jake said, "Beats the hell out of me, Mr. McMasters. Has them shipped in, I reckon. I know that Mr. Cameron has some cattle shipped in from Texas, and even some wet cattle from Mexico. The one you can say is doing the most to stay with the breed of Angus is Jim Harris. But Mr. Cameron and even old Cap Wiley are bringing in cattle that they winter here and send to the markets in Kansas City and Wichita. You could say they are running a beef operation as well as a breeding operation. But Mr. Harris is primarily into breeding.''

"I see," Boyd said. Though in reality he didn't see a damn thing except a much bigger job than Warren had indicated. To him it looked hopeless. He could see no way to narrow the problem down to one group of men, much less one man. How can you catch someone in the active business of tearing down fences if you're on a flat plain and the man you're after can see you as far as you can see him? If he can see you, then he won't tear the fence down. And if you can't see him tear the fence down, then you can't take action against him. Boyd shook his head. It just looked like one hell of a mess. He said, "I'm going to the hotel. Meet me over there right after lunch and we'll leave for Lakin. We'll try to be there by this evening and set up a headquarters there, although I may want to push on further. It just depends.''

Gates said in his high-pitched voice, "There's a right fine boardinghouse over at Lakin run by a right nice lady. You'll enjoy meeting her.''

Boyd just gave him a look. "Gates, never mind.''

But before he could get out the door and head out to the hotel, Jake Mangus planted his short bulk in front of Boyd and said, "Mr. McMasters, there is one thing I'd like to get straight with you.''

Boyd said, "Go ahead.''

His voice just tinged with sullenness, Jake Mangus said, "I want you to know I've done you a good turn whether you realize it or not. I know from what you said that you don't think much of the way I'm handling matters down here.'' He looked away and got a little more of the hurt, pouty sound in his voice. ''I reckon you figured that I should have this figured out by now, but you just wait till you get a look at this country.''

Boyd said, ''Fine, Jake. But what's the favor you've done me?''

''Well, I want you to know that Mr. Del Cameron has been just about as upset as a wet setting hen and he has been near to rebellion. I mean near to leaving the organization. Disassociating himself from the Cattleman's Protective Association. I want you to know that I have stopped him several times myself from writing a letter to the headquarters in Oklahoma City, and when I got word that you was coming I assured him that headquarters was sending a top hand down here to get this whole mess straightened out. I want you to know that I have kept Del Cameron ready and waiting for you to get here.''

Boyd looked at the man as if he had lost his mind. ''You call that a favor?''

''Sure do.''

Boyd pushed by him and went out the door. He said, ''I'll see both of you at the hotel at one-thirty rigged out and ready to travel.''

He went down the boardwalk to his hotel, the heels of his boots thudding against the planks of the walk, his spurs making an angry jingle. He silently cursed Warren and the day he'd been dumb enough to ride into Oklahoma City and listen to his brother. How, he wondered, was being put in an impossible situation supposed to help him get back on his feet? It was impossible to win a fight when he couldn't find the enemy or identify or even guess at it. Out loud he said, ''Damn you, Warren, damn you.'' A woman turned her head as she passed him on the boardwalk. He lifted his hat and said, ''I stubbed my toe.'' As he walked on he thought, ''In more ways than one.''

Nine

By two o'clock that afternoon they were five miles along the road to Lakin with about twenty to go. Boyd was riding the chestnut and leading the roan. Gates was on a fine-looking young dun stallion that Boyd judged to not be quite four years old but that had a nice way of going and appeared to have good manners. Neither Gates nor Jake Mangus was leading a second horse, as they had remounts stationed in Lakin. They both claimed that they had been in Lakin and Syracuse up until the time they got notification to come into Garden City to meet Boyd.

Boyd asked Gates, "Ain't that stud horse of yours a little young? He appears to me to be a mite prancy."

Gates said in that boyish voice of his, "No, sir, Captain McMasters. This here is not a horse I'm planning on using in what you might call extreme circumstances, if you take my meaning. Oh, excuse me, sir, I didn't mean to say that. This here ain't a horse I intend to be riding if there's trouble. I'm just breaking him in and I figured the road work would help him along."

Boyd was amused by Gates's addressing him as "Captain," something he'd been doing since they'd left Garden

City. Even Jake Mangus had thrown it in once or twice. He supposed that was his rank, though he'd never had rank before and he wasn't used to the formality of the thing.

The way Jake Mangus rode a horse did nothing to improve him in Boyd's eyes. He was riding a big-shouldered, big-hocked gelding quarter horse with a big neck, and was constantly sawing at the bit. The horse didn't know whether to go or stop.

Boyd said, "Jake, that horse is Association property."

Jake Mangus looked over at him, his horse almost trotting sideways. "Well, yeah, I reckon you could say that. We are allowed mounts and remounts. That's what my contract says anyway."

Boyd said, "Well, then, if that's an Association horse, get the hell out of his mouth. You are about to ruin his neck."

Jake looked sullen, but he relaxed the pressure on the reins. He looked as if he expected the horse to suddenly dart forward, but the horse just settled down to the pace of the other two.

So as not to appear to be singling Jake out, Boyd said to Gates, "And how come you are riding that young of a stud, Gates, or is that not an Association horse?"

Gates said seriously, "This horse happens to be my personal property, but even if he was an Association horse, I wouldn't want to cut him until he got his neck made full. You can see he still needs to grow a little in the forequarters and the neck. I don't want to cut him until he gets some."

Boyd said, "Well, that's quite all right. If he's your horse you can do anything you want with him."

"Well, he's my horse, all right. I bought him with my own money. I kind of like to raise a few on the side and sell them to make a little profit, if you take my meaning."

They kept on riding and Boyd marveled at the country. He was not a well-traveled man, having spent much of his time in south and central and west Texas, and he'd never seen anything like the Kansas prairies. He'd heard the term flat as a billiard table to describe land, but he'd never seen it until he'd got to Kansas. There was flatland in west Texas, even down in south Texas to the border. But it was such poor country that it was mostly rocks and cactus and sand and greasewood and mesquite trees, and he just naturally associated flat country with poor country.

Here it was flat but lush. He'd never seen such grass. It stood eight to ten inches high, sometimes a foot high, with cattle grazing it. It was very easy to spot where the meandering creeks went across the prairie. They were lined with pussy willow, cottonwood, and sycamore trees. He did notice there were very few hardwood trees, oaks and hickories and such that he was most used to.

Boyd said as they rode, "If I ever saw a country that was designed for raising cattle, this has got to be it."

Jake Mangus made a snort. "You oughta see it in wet weather. It'll bog up worse than a two-ton bull. The damn place turns into a marsh and a man needs a damn good horse to get across it."

Gates said, "Hell, Jake, it ain't all that bad. It's pretty good country, I think. Of course, I might be prejudiced since I'm from country somewhat like it."

Jake gave him a sneering look. "Northern Oklahoma ain't like nothing but New Mexico on a bad day."

Boyd asked evenly, trying to keep the dislike out of his voice, "Where are you from, Jake?"

Mangus swelled up a bit. "I'm from real cattle country. I'm from Montana."

Gates said, "Captain, don't get him started on it. My God, he never shuts up about that place. I've been to Montana, though, Captain. I can tell you that you may get knee-deep in mud once in a while down here, but you'll get knee-deep in snow nearly all of the time up there."

Jake said, "What do you know about it, boy? We raise the best beef in the country right there in Montana. Only place that can touch it is Wyoming."

Boyd said, "Well, for the time being, we're in Kansas and Colorado, so let's keep our concern about the cattle business right here. As soon as I get to Montana, Jake, I'll tell them you said hello."

He wished he could feel better about Jake Mangus, especially on such short acquaintance. It was not his general rule to judge a man so quickly and so harshly, but the truth of the matter was he didn't like the man. He was obsequious and he was an apple polisher. He didn't appear overly bright, he acted lazy, he hadn't done his job, and he mistreated his horse. Still, Boyd wanted a chance to like him, or at least to judge him fairly.

Gates was a different proposition. He didn't know how the young man would do in a tight place, but he was good company, friendly, and from what Boyd had heard, he could do his job better than his boss.

Boyd didn't know a great deal about the other two men supposedly waiting for him in Lakin, Bob Sweeney and Earl White, other than what their records had indicated. Sweeney had been with the Association for five years, mostly stationed in Louisiana and Tennessee, where they had very little trouble. White had a year in with the Association. He was a former deputy sheriff, and he had apparently distinguished himself in some trouble that had occurred in Arizona and New Mexico. Boyd could only assume that his brother had picked the two, one based on experience and the other on ability. He would find out how right his brother had been in a very short time.

They pushed on at a good clip, and by five o'clock that afternoon they were in Lakin, a small town with somewhere around a thousand souls. It was a typical cattle center with a depot and holding pens for shipping stock.

There were two boardinghouses and a small hotel in Lakin. Jake and Gates were rooming together in one of the boardinghouses, and the other two men were in the other. Boyd decided to take the best room he could find in the small hotel, which turned out to be a suite of two rooms on the ground floor. It didn't have its own bathroom, but there was one a few steps down the hall. He didn't know much about being a boss, but he had deliberately decided to hold himself somewhat aloof from the men who were under his command. It had occurred to him, not as a conscious thought, but as an idea that kept intruding into his mind, that some of the depredations that were being practiced against the Association members might have been made easier by collusion with an Association agent.

He established himself in the hotel and then directed Jake Mangus and Gates to look out for themselves at supper. He said he wanted to see them and Bob Sweeney and Earl White in his room at the hotel at eight o'clock that night. "I figure to get a look at the situation and I want to hear what everyone has to say. I have to figure out some way to get this matter settled, but first, I have to get an overall picture of what is going on."

Gates said, "But Captain, you don't want to eat anywhere else but our boardinghouse. That lady there sets the best table in town."

Boyd said, "I wasn't sent down here to eat. I was sent down here to do a job, Gates, and then get the hell out of here. Y'all enjoy the table at the boardinghouse, but see to it that you and the rest of them are here at eight o'clock."

Gates looked uncertainly at Boyd. "Yes, sir, whatever you say. You're the boss."

"Fine. Now go along and let me get settled in."

He got his horses taken care of in the hotel's livery, and then he made certain he could get a decent meal at the hotel. After that, he went to his room, broke out the whiskey, and sat down with the maps and a pencil and a smoke and a drink to try and get some idea of how to solve the trouble.

By the time he went into the dining room at supper, he didn't have any better ideas than he'd had before. He had no approach, no plan, no suspicions. All he had was a lot of territory with a lot of people that could be involved, and how to narrow it down to the ones that were actually involved was a job that he couldn't even begin to fathom.

In spite of his confusion, he made a meal out of a large T-bone steak with some fried potatoes and sliced tomatoes and onions. One thing he was pleased with was how well his strength was returning. He was getting stronger and stronger every day. He wasn't at one hundred percent yet, but he was much closer than he ever thought he would be. For that, he would have to give thanks to Martha. He tried not to give thought to her. It didn't seem right that he should give thought to anyone other than Hannah.

When the four agents showed up, Boyd had decided on one course of action. He didn't know if it was right or wrong, but at least it was something to do. First of all, there was the business of meeting Bob Sweeney and Earl White.

Bob Sweeney was no surprise. He was a man in his late thirties who appeared content to get by and draw his paycheck. He'd never make you any trouble and he'd never get you out of any.

Earl White, on the other hand, was a different breed of horse. He was a tall, muscular-looking man just under thirty. He was also the only one of the agents besides Boyd who wore a cutaway holster, the kind of holster that a man wore when he wanted to get at his weapon in a hurry. White seemed to wear a perpetual slight sneer on his face, but there was intelligence in his deep-set eyes. There was a scar on his cheek, and a piece was missing from the crown of one of his ears. It went with the record that he had established in Arizona and New Mexico. He obviously wasn't a man who was afraid when the bullets started flying.

Boyd said, "All right, I'm going to make this short and sweet and then you can get on about your business. Jake, I want you to take Bob and Earl and go ahead and man the office here in Lakin and patrol around just like you have been doing."

Jake said, "That's fine with me, Captain. What do you plan on doing?"

Boyd said, "Well, I can't get much of a line on these people so I'm going to take Gates and . . . Gates, you do know all these people around here, don't you?"

Gates said quickly, "Yes, sir. I know them all pretty damn well."

"Fine. You and I will take off in the morning and go see Cameron and Harris and Cap Wiley. Then I guess we'll go over and see Mr. Asa Hale and his sons."

Earl White suddenly laughed.

Boyd switched his eyes to where Earl was sitting in the corner. "Something strike you as funny, Earl?"

White said, "Yeah. The idea of you riding up to old Asa Hale's place and asking him a bunch of questions. I hope to hell you get out of there with your hide."

Boyd said, "Well, why don't I just send you out there to tell him to come and see me?"

White took out a cigarette and lit it. He said, " 'Cause my mamma didn't raise no fools. I don't care for the odds."

"You just completely convinced that there will be trouble?"

"I ain't convinced about nothing, Captain McMasters, but I am convinced that Asa Hale is not a man you push too hard. You're the boss. You do what you're of a mind to.''

"That's what I intend to do, Mr. White. If I get any more objections from you, you'll be heading up the road looking for another job. You just do what you are of a mind to, remembering the instructions I gave you.''

White gave him an insolent look. "Yes, sir, Captain McMasters.''

Boyd looked around the room. "You all can take off. Except for you.'' He looked at Gates.

They all got up and, looking first at each other and then at Boyd, all except Gates slowly filed out of the room. Just before he went through the door, Jake Mangus stopped and said, "Now I understand, Captain McMasters, that you want me to go on like we've been going on?''

"That's what I said, Jake. Just carry on business as usual.''

The door shut and Boyd sat down in an overstuffed wing-back chair. Gates stood uncertainly in the middle of the room. Boyd motioned him towards the divan in the middle of the sitting room that joined his bedroom. After he was seated, Gates said, "Captain, you done took me by surprise.''

"How's that?''

"Well I just never reckoned you to be a real iron ass. If you take my meaning.''

Boyd wanted to laugh. "What do you mean you never took me to be an iron ass? Am I acting like an iron ass?''

"Yes, sir. You are coming in giving orders and there ain't no doubt about it that you mean them. Most of the time everybody makes suggestions and we all get together on how to do it. But you just give the orders and that's it. Enough said.''

"That's being an iron ass?''

Gates looked uncertain. "Yes, sir, I reckon that's what you would call it."

"Well, Gates, I need to tell you my theory. It is that there can only be one boss and that happens to be me. I don't have time for nor do I want a lot of discussion, and if something goes wrong I know who to blame. So if that makes me an iron ass, so be it. But I am running this operation until such time as somebody with authority tells me different."

"Yes, sir, don't bother me none. I think it took a couple of the other boys up short."

"You mean Earl White?"

Gates said, "No, I mean Jake."

Boyd got out a cigarillo and lit it. He said, "Jake don't much like me, does he?"

Gates shrugged. "He thinks you're powerful sure of yourself."

Boyd laughed. "Well, I'm glad he does. That makes him a majority of one. But don't you reckon he thinks I'm sure of myself because of my brother? Isn't that the fact of the business?"

Gates looked uncomfortable. "Well I wouldn't want to make a comment on that, Captain. I'm just one of the hired hands around here."

"It doesn't make any difference. I don't give a holy hopping hell what Jake Mangus, or anyone else for that matter, thinks. I know what's what and what's not what. Anything Jake thinks he can keep to himself, or find another job. Now what do you think of riding out to Asa Hale's with me? Earl White seemed to think we'd be taking our lives in our own hands. What do you think?"

Gates looked slightly unhappy. "Well, those ain't the most welcoming folks you ever met. In fact, they get downright surly when you go asking them questions that they don't think is any of your business."

Boyd yawned. "Well, that's why I want you along with me, Gates, to handle the heavy work and keep the flies off me while Mr. Asa Hale and I have a discussion."

Gates looked more and more uncomfortable, but just nodded his head. "I reckon I hired on to take orders, and if they are the orders, then I guess I have to follow them, Captain."

Boyd said, "Why don't you go over to the boardinghouse and be here a little before dawn. Bring a change of clothes with some staying power because we'll be out more than a few hours."

Gates walked to the door. "Yes, sir, I'll be going along now." He twisted the knob and looked back at Boyd. "I don't reckon you're an iron ass, Captain McMasters; I reckon you just intend to get the job done."

Boyd pointed his finger at him. "You're on to it, if you get my meaning."

They both laughed, and Gates went out the door. Boyd turned back to the maps that he'd spread out on the bed, hoping to find some answers there.

They rode out early the next morning not too long after dawn. Boyd had no special plan in mind other than to work his way down the line. Jim Harris was the closest ranch to them. His brand was a rocking J, and both Jake and Gates had pronounced him the most sincere of the Association members intent on upgrading their cattle. He did not have a large operation, but he did have a selective breeding process. As they rode, Gates told him a little about the man. "I ain't met him but two or three times. He is kind of a standoffish fellow. He ain't unfriendly if you take my meaning. He just doesn't go out of his way to make you feel welcome. He's been here about four or five years. I'd say he was in his early thirties. He's got the prettiest little wife you ever saw in your life."

Boyd said, "They got any kids?"

"I ain't never seen none around there."

"How many hired hands does he have?"

Gates said, "I wouldn't reckon more than six or seven, if that many. He keeps his operation close to home. He keeps breeding traps close to home. I don't think he has more than four full-time hands."

"You know how many riders Asa has?"

"Well, again it's hard to say. You can't tell if it's one of his grown boys or a hired hand."

They were riding northeast on a road that would eventually lead to Syracuse. A little ways out of Lakin they left it and started drifting toward the Harris ranch. A few miles short of where they were headed, Boyd had an idea. He said, "Split up with me here, and I want you to ride over to Syracuse and to Mr. Del Cameron's place and tell him that I am on my way and that I will be there this afternoon. I want to make sure he is there when I arrive."

Gates Hood gave him a quizzical expression. "You wouldn't be trying to play the high muckety-muck by arriving with word sent on ahead, would you?"

"That would be the general idea, Gates. I'm glad that you're a man who understands these things. That way Mr. Cameron, who I've heard likes to kick up a commotion, can at least know that he is being taken seriously and that a special agent from the home office is coming to see him personally. I want you to go and tell him that in just so many words. Meanwhile, I'm going to ride on over here and see Mr. Harris. It appears to me that most of our business will be with Mr. Cameron and Asa Hale."

Gates shook his head. "I hope to hell it's not Asa Hale. I'll go to see Mr. Cameron. Do you reckon you'll be there sometime after the noon meal?''

"I'd figure on it, Gates. I'll turn off here and you head east.'' They parted, with Boyd bending toward the north to the Harris ranch while Gates headed off to tell Del Cameron that Boyd was on his way. Boyd rode over the pleasantly rolling plains conscious of the swish-swish his horse's hooves made in the tall grass. Even the sounds of his horse's movements were muffled by the denseness of the soft earth. It was lush country, all right. He figured he was five or six miles from the Harris ranch, the Rocking J. He topped a rise and ahead he could see, about a mile or so off, a line of trees following the meandering curve of a creek. He was passing more cattle now, the Angus breed predominant in their characteristics. As he rode he thought that any man who couldn't make a living here without stealing didn't know the first thing about the cattle business. Unfortunately, that thought brought to mind the remembrance of what he had been going through when all his troubles began. The problem was that such thoughts stayed with him. The result was a blackness over his mind and his humor. He shook his head and readjusted his hat to the smooth lope of the chestnut mare. He had to quit thinking in such ways.

As he rode toward the creek the distant sound of a horse's neigh reached his ears. He saw his mare's ears prick up as she answered with a call back. There was a lone rider or a loose horse somewhere inside the tree line. Boyd was a lone rider out on the bald prairie. He had best make it clear his intentions were purely peaceful, especially in a country where there was so much trouble.

As he neared the tree line he thought of calling out. Then he decided there was no point. He was riding across open range, his horse pulled down to a walk. He was obviously a threat to no one. For that matter, it could just be a loose range horse stopping at the creek for a drink of water. He went on toward the little line of willow and cottonwood. They appeared to grow back from the creek about ten or fifteen yards. He decided, if nothing else, he would take the opportunity to taste country water and to take a pull from the jug of whiskey in one of his saddlebags.

His horse walked quietly in on a bed of grass into the shade of the trees and small bushes. Just as he got near the edge of the creek, he was aware of a horse with a figure sitting next to it on the other side of the water just slightly to his right. He would aim his horse exactly at the person as he crossed the creek. The creek was only about five yards wide at the place where he struck it, and only about knee-deep to his horse. He was well into the water when the figure raised its head. It was a girl, a woman. She looked up startled, her eyes wide. She got quickly to her feet, but by that time he was almost to her. He said, "Howdy, ma'am. My name is Boyd McMasters. I'm an agent for the Cattleman's Protective Association."

She was still looking up at him, her eyes wide and staring. She turned her head left and right, almost like a wild animal looking for an escape. He suddenly realized why.

Someone had hit her in the face, someone or something. He could see the crusted blood that had come out of her nostril, and the left side of her face was already swelling and starting to discolor. He quickly swung down from his saddle and went to her, whipping off his hat as he did, repeating his introduction. He then said, "Ma'am, is something wrong?"

She backed away from him. "No, no, no," she said. "I'm fine."

She was a very comely-looking young woman whom he took to be in her mid-twenties. She had black hair and deep green eyes that were set wide apart, a heart-shaped face, and big, generous lips. She was wearing riding breeches and jodhpurs with a short-sleeved silk shirt that did justice to the well-shaped breasts it hid.

He took a step or two toward her. "Ma'am or miss, whichever it is, if I can be of some help. You look like you've hurt your face. You've got a little blood on your nose, and the off side, well, I guess the left side of your face . . . ma'am, you've got a pretty bad bruise there."

She put her hand quickly to her cheek and said, "No, I'm all right. I hit a limb. Yes, my horse rode into a limb."

He said, "Well, did it knock you out of the saddle?"

She said, "No, no, no. Please, mister . . . I didn't get your name. Please, I just need a little time to compose myself."

"Well, can I see you home? You might be hurt worse than you think you are."

She said, "No, I'm fine, please." Her voice became imploring. "If you will please go on your way, sir, please. I would like to be in peace."

Reluctantly, he retreated to his horse and swung aboard. He said, "Are you sure? Are you far from home?"

She said, "No, I'm fine."

She had retreated some five yards down the creek from her horse. She truly was frightened, but he didn't know what of or why. He wanted to help her, but she obviously didn't want any help. What she was was embarrassed, and she didn't want anyone else seeing her. He didn't think she had hit a limb at all. He had seen a lot of faces that had been struck by a fist and he knew what they looked like. Hers looked like one, but all he could do was tip his hat and nod at her. He said, "Well, all right. I'll be going now."

He turned his horse back toward the north and picked his way through the trees until he was out on the prairie again. He glanced back, but there was no sign of the woman. He put the spurs to his horse and kicked the chestnut into a lope. The mare responded easily, taking the rolling hills in her ground-eating gait. A mile farther on he topped a rise, and he could see the ranch house and the outbuildings of the Rocking J, home of resident and proprietor Mr. James Harris, also a client in good standing of the Cattleman's Protective Association. As he rode he tried to remember how many cattle and how many acres Mr. Harris had. He knew he had to get in the habit of remembering such things, but hell, he hadn't had the job that long.

On the road toward the ranch headquarters, Boyd could see several men working around the place. As late in the spring as it was, there wasn't much calf work to be done. About the only maintenance job that had to be done, with grass aplenty and water aplenty, was worming and doctoring sick cattle and perhaps putting out salt blocks. They said salt made cows gain weight and become a better grade of beef. He didn't know about that, but in his short career as a cattleman, he had read up as much on the subject as he could. The men he saw were working in a small corral off one of the barns and appeared to be shoeing horses.

As he entered the ranch grounds proper, passing under an entryway that announced that it was the Rocking J, he saw that a man standing by the fence watching the work going on within was dressed better than an ordinary cowhand would be. He had on denim jeans and a denim work shirt, but his were starched and pressed, and his boots were shined and his hat was also, unmistakably, of a high quality. The man turned as Boyd pulled his horse up.

Boyd said, "Howdy, I'm Boyd McMasters. I'm from the Cattleman's Protective Association."

The man walked toward him. He said, "Get down, Mr. McMasters. I'm Jim Harris. This is my place."

Boyd dismounted and stepped forward to shake hands with Mr. Harris. "Glad to make your acquaintance, sir. I'm new here. I've taken over the agency, and hopefully I can do something about the trouble y'all have been having. At least that's what I've been sent to do. So if we don't get it fixed, you'll know who to complain to, or about, I should say."

Mr. Harris shook his head. "If you are talking about tearing up fences and losing cattle, or at least having your cattle used by other people's cows and bulls, I haven't had any, Mr. McMasters, so I'm not the man you should be seeing. I think perhaps Del Cameron and Cap Wiley are the gentlemen that you want to talk to."

Mr. Harris was a bland, ordinary-looking man just beyond thirty. He was well built, and Boyd could see the curly blond hair coming out from beneath his hat. Boyd asked, "Well, would you have a minute or two so we could talk about it?"

Harris said, "Well, I guess those men could shoe those horses without my immediate supervision. Come on in the back and we'll go in the kitchen and have a cup of coffee. I think the cook has just put on a fresh pot."

When they were seated in the large, airy kitchen full of sunshine and the good smells of food and coffee, Harris said, "Now, how can I help you, Mr. McMasters?"

"Well, I'm sort of new to this type of breeding business, Mr. Harris. I have a basic understanding that you are trying to introduce this Angus breed to upgrade your beef cattle. Is that correct?"

Harris nodded. "In point of fact, Mr. McMasters, the idea of doing this was mine. I was the original settler who came into this part of the country for that express purpose. Prior to that, most of the cattle that had been raised around here were feeder cattle that went to the market the following year. I brought in breeder cattle and started making calf crops and raising steers and heifers."

"In terms of dollars and cents, Mr. Harris, what is the difference between one of those range cows crossed with an

Angus and a straight range calf on the beef market?''

Harris thought for a moment. "At least two hundred dollars, perhaps more. You can buy any of these range cattle, a yearling on up, for about thirty to fifty dollars. A registered Angus heifer is going to cost you about two to three hundred dollars and a yearling bull, five hundred. A proven bull will cost you anywhere from a thousand to two thousand. The breeder cows that you keep are worth anywhere from three hundred fifty to five hundred dollars, so you are talking about a lot of money.''

Boyd said, "I didn't understand that this was originally your idea.''

"Yes, I came here about four years—well, maybe it's closer to five.''

"Would it be a fair question to ask you what this land is worth?''

Harris smiled. "Then or now?''

"Anywhere in the last few years.''

"You've got two kinds of land on this ground; you've got grass that is immediate to water and you have grass that you have to go around or through other people's natural grazing area to get to common water.''

Boyd asked, "What is the difference in the price?''

"About double if you are near water.''

Boyd smiled. "Well, you've done everything but name the price, Mr. Harris. Could you be a little more specific?''

Jim Harris looked thoughtful. "It's hard to say, Mr. McMasters. I paid ten dollars an acre for this land five years ago. I don't know what it's worth now, probably twenty dollars an acre.''

"Isn't it a generally agreed idea that in open-range country, you own one acre, you graze five on common land? Is that about the right figure?''

Harris nodded. "That's approximately the case, though

some don't always keep to that margin. The kind of operation that I have, which is pure breeding, I don't need to run that many more cows.''

"You own a thousand acres, so you figure that your grazing is around five thousand acres roughly. Would that be about right?''

"Well, actually I graze about ten thousand acres because I have fifteen hundred acres and I've homesteaded two more, about a hundred and sixty acres each. So, I graze a general area of about ten thousand acres, but I'm not cutting anyone off from water, if that was going to be your next question, where they might have a reason to tear down my fences. Like I said, though, I haven't had any fences torn down.''

Boyd said casually, "The one thing I noticed riding here, Mr. Harris, I didn't see much range stock. Nearly everything I saw was either full-blood Angus or Angus cross. Where do you keep your range cattle?''

"Well, I'm low on straight breeding stock right now that I am breeding back to my Angus. This isn't really the time of the year to be bringing in breeding cattle. I'll probably bring them in around August sometime.'' Harris gave Boyd a searching look. "You seem awfully interested in the inner workings of the cattle business, Mr. McMasters. I thought your job was to protect them, not understand them.''

Boyd laughed slightly and stood up. "Curiosity, Mr. Harris. Plain old, out-of-school curiosity. I'd better be getting along now. I need to have a visit with all of my customers.''

Harris said, "Well, I don't envy you going to see Del Cameron. I don't think you will find him a very happy man, and I can't say that I blame him.''

They walked out the back door of the kitchen and around to the front of the ranch house. Boyd was about to step aboard his chestnut mare when he turned and said to Jim Harris, "Say, you don't know a very nice-looking young lady around these parts with dark hair and very green eyes, mid-twenties or so, quite attractive.''

Harris's eyes narrowed. ''Well, you could be talking about my wife Nora, but she is in town. Maybe you saw her there?''

Boyd was on the point of telling about his encounter with the young woman at the creek when some instinct stopped him. Looking at Harris's frozen face and hard eyes, he didn't think it was quite the time to become involved in a domestic dispute. However, he had little doubt that the woman he had seen was Harris's wife Nora, and he doubted that she was or would be going to town for several days. To cover his pause, he said, ''Well, actually, I don't know who it was. She reminded me of someone I knew sometime back—a lady from west Texas. I saw her on the edge of town.''

Harris said, still unsmiling, ''Well, it couldn't have been Nora. She's never been to west Texas. We're from Tennessee ourselves.''

Boyd said, ''I'm much obliged for your time.'' He mounted his horse. ''I'll be back out again as soon as there is something to discuss. I'm happy to have at least one satisfied customer.''

Harris looked up at Boyd and said, ''Good luck with Del Cameron.''

Boyd nodded and spurred his chestnut mare into a slow lope. He gave a backward wave as he passed under the ranch archway, pointing the mare due west toward Cameron's ranch. When he reached the road, Boyd speculated as to why Mr. Harris was being untroubled by the rash of fence breaking and cattle theft. He was also fairly curious as to why Mr. Harris was also homesteading several 160-acre plots, but then when you considered that when you homesteaded a 160 acres it gave you the rights to eight hundred acres of grazing on government land, it made a lot of sense. Those small plots

were worth a lot more than a man gave them credit for. He
settled the mare into a slow lope, a ground-eating gait that
he knew she could hold for several miles. He calculated that
it was ten more miles to Del Cameron's headquarters, and
he hoped that Gates had gotten there and had been able to
find Mr. Cameron so that no time would be wasted in sending for him out in the field.

They were meeting on Del Cameron's side porch. He had a
big, two-story frame house with columns out front that
looked like it would be more at home in Tennessee or Virginia or Louisiana than in western Kansas. Mr. Cameron
looked the same way. He wore drill riding pants with leather
insets, and wore riding boots with flat heels. He looked more
like a plantation owner than a Kansas cattleman. Boyd knew
his age to be forty-eight and that he had a wife named Lucy
and two sons in their twenties by the names of Del, Jr., and
Clay.

   Del Cameron was a medium-sized man with brownish hair
and a lean, slender build. He had brown eyes that now were
almost black with anger. Gates and Boyd were seated in
wicker chairs, a small table in front of them where coffee
and whiskey had been placed. Mr. Cameron had not been
seated after the first few moments. Instead, he paced back
and forth, reviling the marauders who were wrecking his
breeding program, stealing his cattle, and tearing up his
fences. He stopped and whirled on Boyd. ''And when are
you people going to do something about it? This has been
going on now for almost two years, and I have as yet to see
any action from the so-called Cattleman's Protective Association. That idiot Jake Mangus couldn't find a fence breaker
if he was in bed with him. So, you're the one that they sent
down to straighten this mess out. Well, I want to see it
straightened out. Last night we had some more gunplay at

the southern edge of my property. One of my hands could have been killed—he wasn't, but the fact that it is still going on is enough to get me hot under the collar.''

Boyd realized that words weren't going to be of much use in Mr. Cameron's state of mind. He said, ''Mr. Cameron, if you will sit down and take the time to give me a better view of the situation, I can be more effective. I know it's been bad, that's why they have sent me. We have not done our job, I'll be the first to admit it, but I'm going to bend every energy to make something happen.''

Cameron glared at him. ''So you do admit that y'all are not the most efficient operation in the world.''

''I admit that this situation here has gone on for far too long and that we have failed in our efforts to stop your troubles. I'd have to be a blind man not to admit that, but we're not going to get anywhere with just getting angry about the situation. What I need, Mr. Cameron, is information. Before I can do anything, I have to figure out who is doing it.''

Cameron's face got red. ''Doing it? Hell, a blind man knows that damned Asa Hale is doing it, him and that bunch of bastard trash sons of his. Anybody can see that.''

''I don't know that, not enough to take it to the law.''

''Go and look at his herd; go look at my cattle with his brand on them. He hasn't got a pure-blood Angus on the place, yet half of his calf crop are part Angus. If that isn't proof, I don't know what is.''

Boyd said patiently, ''Mr. Cameron, this is open-range country. His argument is going to be that you did not keep your cattle fenced up and they wandered on his range, and that your cows were serviced by his bulls or your bulls serviced his cows, and the calf followed the mamma and then he had a calf. There's no way to argue with that; it's his word against yours. We've got to catch him tearing down fences. We've got to catch him deliberately mixing his cattle with yours, and in order to do that, I am going to need some specific details such as dates and times. Maybe if you will settle down, we could get something done.''

Cameron glared at him for a long moment. He grudgingly pulled out a wicker chair from the table and slumped in it. ''You talk a good game, but that doesn't prove a damn thing. All it proves is that you can talk better than Jake Mangus. I don't know if there will be any more action. As I understand it, you're the brother of Warren McMasters. Is that correct?''

Boyd nodded. ''He happens to be my brother, Mr. Cameron, but that has nothing to do with my job down here. He's my brother when I'm not working. He's not my brother now, he's my boss.''

Cameron waved his hand. ''All right, all right. So there's no nepotism involved. You're a highly qualified lawman. I understand that you used to be a sheriff.''

Boyd nodded.

''Have you ever run into any situation like this before?''

Boyd shook his head. ''No, and I hope to hell I don't ever again either. This is a mess.''

Cameron smiled wanly. ''You're telling me? For all the money that I am paying you people, I ought to be getting more action than this.''

Boyd said evenly, ''Mr. Cameron, all of our Association members pay the same. You are no different than the little man. We don't treat him any different than we treat you. All Association members are just that, Association members.''

''I pay for four brands. I pay a fee for each brand, so don't tell me that I'm not paying more than everybody else.''

''This is not the first time I have heard about that. Would you mind telling me, Mr. Cameron, why you operate under four brands?''

''Initially I was branding my range cattle with one brand, my purebred with another. I had another brand that I was using on the straight cross, and now I have a fourth brand when I am breeding the crossed back to the straight Angus. In other words, I am trying to populate this prairie with as close to a purebred Angus as I can get without spending more money. Do you follow my line of reasoning?''

"Yes, sir. You're using upgrading through breeding.''

"Well, I am glad that you understand that, at least. Your Mr. Mangus couldn't quite get his head around it.''

"Yes, it's an easy concept to understand, and yes, you do pay a fee for each brand, but you're still just another Association member and if you were paying for one brand, I would work just as hard for you.''

"I bet.''

Boyd said, "All that aside, I've got a few questions for you. When you take delivery of cattle, be they range cattle that you are having shipped up from Texas or wherever, or purebred Angus, what railhead do you use to take delivery of those cattle? Where is your shipping and receiving point?''

"Holly, Colorado. It's about ten miles west of my ranch headquarters here. It's the nearest point for me. Cap Wiley uses it also.''

"What about Jim Harris and Asa Hale?''

Cameron made a grimace at the mention of the last name. He said, "Harris uses Ulysses in Grant County, which is south of Lakin about fifteen miles. It's on the railroad that runs from Colorado Springs and Denver through to Holly, then on to Ulysses and then on to Liberal. It would be the closest place to Harris or that damned thief Asa Hale.''

"Those are the only two railheads that anyone in this area would use to either ship or receive cattle?''

Cameron nodded. "Unless you want to drive cattle a long way. The next stop would be Santana, which is a good twenty miles on further. Those are the only places that the railroad stops.''

''There's no sidings that you know of?''

''You mean for the convenience of one rancher?''

''Yes.''

''No. If anyone would have one, I would, since I am the biggest operation around here. The railroad wants too damned much money from the rancher or a guarantee of so much business before they'll throw a siding in just for him.''

''But if you and Asa Hale were of a like mind, combined, could the two of you get a siding put in?''

Cameron thought for a moment and shook his head. ''I don't know because I've never been able to get the slightest idea of how many cattle Asa Hale has. Neither has anyone else, for that matter. I don't think he ships cattle. I think the sonofabitch is so busy building up one hell of a herd, stealing from me and everyone else, that he hasn't had time to ship them.''

''You don't think he is receiving Texas steers?''

''I'll tell you, Mr. McMasters. If you are bringing in feeder cattle, they will already be branded. I have never seen any of his cattle that didn't have his brand on them. It's a lazy A, a cockeyed, slanted, leaning lazy A. I have never seen another brand on any of his cattle. If he is bringing in feeder cattle from Texas or New Mexico, they would have to have a road brand if nothing else, and I have never seen any of his cattle with any other brand on them but his.''

Boyd shook his head and then looked back at Gates. He said, ''Did you know any of this?''

''No, sir, I didn't. I never paid it no mind, never thought to pay it no mind.''

Boyd asked, ''You don't think it's important?''

Gates said, ''Well, I don't see how it ties in.''

Cameron was looking at Boyd, and he said, ''So, your

idea is if Asa Hale's herd keeps growing and he is not importing any cattle, then where the hell are they coming from?''

"Yes."

"I can tell you where they are coming from. My cattle. My herd."

"Now all I have to do is prove it," Boyd said.

"Take a look at them. Hell, Mr. McMasters, he's got some calves over there from this year's calf crop that I would swear are three-quarters Angus. That means, he stole a heifer from me this last spring a year ago and has bred it back to one of my pure-blood bulls. That's the only way that you're going to get a three-quarters Angus. That's exactly what some of his looks like. He comes back for second helpings. Do you see why I am getting so frustrated and angry? I can see the evidence. When I ride down to my southern line, I can see what is happening to my herd. I don't know how many hundreds of thousands of dollars the man has stolen from me."

Gates looked awed. "Mr. Cameron, ain't you stretching that a bit?"

Boyd said quickly, "Gates, you don't know the numbers involved on those purebred cattle. I can easily believe that Mr. Cameron has lost that kind of money without stretching it at all."

Cameron looked at him. "Well, I am glad to see that someone around here is starting to show some semblance of sense. I said that same figure to Jake Mangus and he looked at me like I was crazy. At least you can add and subtract. Now, my main interest is can you subtract the Hales from my backside?"

Boyd stood up. "Mr. Cameron, we are going to stay in Syracuse tonight. I am going to headquarter up there so I can try to keep an eye on what is going on around here.

Now, I am going to ask you to do something and I am going to give you some time to think about it. That river, the Arkansas River, runs between you and Asa Hale, correct?''

Cameron nodded. ''Yes, so what?''

Boyd said, ''I want you to consider putting up a drift fence on the south side of that river, which is still your property. I have drawn maps where you each have deeded property and where you both have common grazing. You have deeded property on that side of the river.''

''Yes, but that has nothing to do with it. You can't fence a man off from water, even if it's on deeded property.''

Boyd continued. ''And further, where there are gaps that you don't own in deed, I want you to go to the county courthouse in Syracuse and file on that land, homestead it. Homestead it in your wife's name, your kids' names, your cousin's name, anybody's name. Invent names if you have to. I want you to put about ten miles of two-stranded barbed-wire fence on the south side of that river.''

Gates said, ''Why, Captain McMasters? You can't do that. You can't fence Mr. Hale off from that water.''

Cameron looked at Boyd. ''McMasters, have you lost your mind? That would be one fence that Asa Hale could legally tear down.''

''No, he can't legally tear it down as long as you have homestead plots along there. The law says you are allowed to make improvements on a homesteaded plot, and an improvement is defined as fencing or a dwelling of any kind. He cannot tear down that fence where you are homesteading. I can tie him up in courts a long time with that.''

Cameron said, ''I don't see what good it will do. So I build a ten-mile fence. His cattle are going to drift to the east or the west and go around it.''

''That much easier to drive them back.''

Cameron said, cocking his head to one side, ''You're deliberately trying to provoke Asa Hale, aren't you?''

"Yes, that's about the size of it.''

"Well, I can't tell you right off right now. I'll have to give it some thought.''

Boyd said, ''You understand that I am not talking about a substantial fence, just something we can call a fence with two strands of barbed wire, fence posts not even sunk very deep in the ground. I would imagine that you have plenty of fencing material on hand.''

Cameron made a wry face. ''I've got a lot of torn-up fencing material on hand.''

Boyd said, ''We'll be going now, but we'll be close. Is there a decent hotel in Syracuse?''

Cameron nodded. ''Yes, the Syracuse House. It's as decent a place as any, but you realize that you're not talking about Kansas City or even Omaha.''

Boyd said, ''You may see me from time to time, and I'll drop in on you from time to time.''

Cameron walked the men around to the front where their horses were tied. He said to Boyd just as he mounted, ''Well, Mr. McMasters, I hope that all of this is not just talk. I'm hoping to see some results. I am almost sick enough of this whole mess to sell up and leave.''

Boyd said, ''By the way, that brings up a question in my mind. What's land near water worth around here?''

Cameron thought a moment. ''Well, I paid an average of fifteen dollars an acre for what I've got, but to tell you the truth, Mr. McMasters, the way things are going around here, I would expect less, maybe a whole lot less. I'm tired of this whole incident that has been dragging on and dragging on. I have had men who worked for me killed, I've had them hurt. There hasn't been a night that has gone by that I have had peace. Frankly, it's not worth it.''

Boyd said, ''One more thing. You mentioned that down

at the southern boundary of your property next to Asa
Hale's you saw some cattle that showed Angus crossbreed-
ing. Is that correct?''

''Yes, hell, yes.''

''Many?''

Cameron thought for a moment, wrinkling his brow. ''I
don't know what you call many. How many horses does a
horse thief have to steal before he's a horse thief? I saw a
few.''

''But they were at the extreme northern end of Asa Hale's
property. If you had that kind of cattle, wouldn't you keep
them back away from you?''

Cameron gave Boyd a look. ''I think you need to meet
Asa Hale, Mr. McMasters. That man is as crazy as hell. He's
dangerous.''

''Have you ever been on his property?''

''A short way onto his property. He ain't exactly what
you call neighborly. If you want a rifle bullet over your head,
you can get one on his property right quick. I didn't get into
the cattle business to get shot. I am a businessman, not a
gunman. That brings up another point. You are talking about
agitating Asa Hale. I assume that you and your men are
going to bear the brunt of whatever fight you are trying to
start because my men work cattle. I don't pay them to carry
guns and risk their lives. I pay them to work cattle. Are we
clear on that?''

''Very clear, Mr. Cameron. I would have been surprised
if you said anything else.''

''By the way, are you planning on seeing Mr. Asa Hale?''

Boyd nodded. ''Those are my intentions.''

Cameron said dryly, ''Well, I hope for your sake that the-
y're Asa Hale's intentions also. I'd be careful were I you.''

Boyd touched the brim of his hat. ''We'll be going now.''

He put the spurs to his chestnut and, along with Gates, rode out of the ranch yard into the green prairie.

As they rode, Boyd asked Gates, "Have you seen a lot of cattle at Asa Hale's place showing a lot of Angus blood?"

Gates said, "Captain McMasters, I am going to tell you straight out. I never spent no whole lot of time on that place. When Mr. Cameron told you that those folks were unfriendly, he was stating a fact."

Boyd said, "Well, we'll soon find out."

As they rode, Boyd's mind was playing with several factors, but there were still several missing links. He wondered what ten miles of fencing would do to Asa Hale.

As if he was reading Boyd's thoughts, Gates asked, "Captain McMasters, you were joshing about that fence, weren't you?"

Boyd shook his head. He looked over at Gates and said, "No. What would make you think that?"

Gates grimaced slowly. "Well, then we might as well get ready for a war, because that is what it would be, a war. If Mr. Cameron goes to stringing fence, Mr. Hale is going to go to stringing bullets."

Boyd almost smiled at him. "Nothing could be more to my liking."

Ten

They got nowhere near Asa Hale's ranch headquarters. Not long after they entered his pasturelands, riders suddenly popped up on their flanks, pacing them at a distance of a quarter to half a mile. It had made Gates nervous, but Boyd pressed on to where he expected the ranch house to be. From a distance, they topped a rise and saw several buildings along with some corrals. Over another rise, a party of men were riding hard toward them. Boyd pulled up his horse and waited as a man Boyd took to be Asa Hale and four other men came skidding to a stop in front of them.

No introductions were made but from the resemblance, Boyd could only conclude that two or three of the other men were Asa Hale's sons. In the hateful face of the weathered old man and the other men with him, Boyd got a strong feeling that he was once again facing the Winslows. He had to squeeze his eyes shut to gain control of himself. For a moment, he almost began to tremble. Then he took a deep breath and was able to talk.

Hale had just one question and that was what was their business on his property. Boyd explained it to him. Asa Hale told them in no uncertain terms to get off his property. He said, "I ain't no member of no sonofabitchin' Cattleman's damn Protective damn Association, and you bastards better get your asses out of here, that is, unless, y'all want to carry them horses. Do you think I have made myself clear, Mr. High-and-Mighty Cattleman's Protective Association?"

Boyd tried to make it understood that he wasn't there to accuse Mr. Hale of anything, but was merely seeking to find out if there wasn't a simple way to resolve the problems of the area. Mr. Hale suggested that if Boyd and Cameron and every other sonofabitch on that part of the prairie would go straight to Hell, it would be the best solution that he could think of.

The conversation ended with one of them pointing a double-barrel shotgun at Boyd's midriff and cocking both hammers. Mr. Hale said, "Now git, and I don't mean any time later, I mean git now."

Left with no alternative, Boyd wheeled his horse and put him in a slow lope with Gates falling in beside him. Neither one of the men looked back. Boyd kept his horse at a good fast pace until they had topped several rises and had come at least a mile. Finally, he pulled the chestnut down to a trot and then on down to a walk. He turned in a generally north-western direction, headed toward Syracuse.

As they rode, Boyd got out a cigarillo and lit it. Beside him, Gates said, "Whoa, Captain McMasters. That man ain't friendly at all."

Boyd was busy looking around. He said, "Gates, we rode at least two miles onto the property, isn't that right?"

"Yes, sir, and I can tell you in no uncertain terms, Captain McMasters, that that is two miles further than I want to ever ride onto that property again."

"Yes, but the point is that we saw a lot of cattle. How many did you see with any Angus blood in them?"

Gates thought for a moment, and then took another moment to look around at the cattle grazing about them. "Well, I wasn't studying about it that much, but now that you brought it to my mind, I don't reckon that I saw all that many. What are you getting at, Captain McMasters?"

Boyd blew out a puff of smoke. "Nothing. I just seen a lot of range cattle, that's what I'm getting at. Where are those crossbred Angus cattle?"

Gates said, "Well, didn't Mr. Cameron say that he didn't see all that many? Don't you reckon that Mr. Hale, like you reckoned before, would have the biggest balance of them south of here, the furtherest that he could get them from where Mr. Cameron could see them?"

Boyd said, "You'd think so. Are we off of Hale land yet?"

Gates nodded his head. "Yonder is the river, so we are off the deeded land. Of course, he grazes right up to the edge of that river, right where you are talking about putting a fence, by the way. I don't see how you are going to get by with that, Captain McMasters."

Boyd pulled his horse up and reached back and got a bottle of whiskey out of his saddlebags. He loosened the cork and had a strong pull, wiped his mouth with his sleeve, and then handed the bottle to Gates. "You want a snort?" he asked.

Gates said, "After that little meeting, I could do with one." He put the bottle to his mouth, and Boyd watched his Adam's apple go up and down three times before he pulled the bottle away. "Boy, that was good," Gates said. "It hit the spot."

Boyd asked, "Gates, have you ever seen Jim Harris's wife?"

Gates looked around at him. He whistled and said, "Oh, my, yes. Ain't she something? Did you see her?"

"Yeah, I saw her. Black hair, real shiny, with real green eyes?"

Gates said, "That's her and all the rest of it that goes along with her. I'm waiting for the day when them titties of hers get loose so I can just get a look at them. I swear, they seem to stand right up there at attention. Yes, sir. She is a mighty wholesome-looking woman."

Boyd said, "Ever seen any bruises on her face?"

Gates blinked. "Now, that's right funny that you should mention that. How come you to bring something like that up?"

"When was it?"

"Oh, six months ago. I had some business that took me out there. She was out in the backyard and I happened to come upon her by accident. She had a swollen nose and what appeared to be a cut lip. I'd taken her by surprise, Captain McMasters, and she put her hands up real quick, and she mumbled something about falling down the stairs and then ran back inside. How do you fall down the stairs of a one-story house?"

Boyd said, "Never mind. Don't make mention of it. Which way is Syracuse?"

Gates pointed his hand through the air in a southwesterly direction. "Right over yonder past that little rise. There's a small creek the other side."

"I got some bad news for you," Boyd said. "I want you to go back to Lakin tonight."

Gates's face fell. "Back to Lakin now? That's fifteen, maybe eighteen miles, and it's going on four in the afternoon, Captain McMasters."

"I know, but I want you to go back and fetch Jake Mangus with you tomorrow."

Gates sighed. "Well, orders are orders. It won't be the first time I've made a night ride."

Boyd said, "It won't be the last either."

Gates nodded hard. "Yes, sir. I was right the first time. You do be an iron ass."

Boyd laughed. "Gates, I wish I had a half of a dozen like you. I'd never get down in the mouth."

Gates looked at him wide-eyed. "Whatever do you mean, Captain?"

"Nothing. You better head on out for Lakin and bring Mangus."

"What about them other two?"

"Nothing about them. I'll be at the Syracuse Hotel."

Gates was about to put the spurs to his horse when he stopped and looked back at Boyd. "Captain McMasters, you know, you talked about that fence. Are we in the right about that?"

Boyd said, "Well, Gates, Cameron is going to string a fence five or ten miles long, whatever I can talk him into, and he is going to file homestead plots at the courthouse in Syracuse. Now, you can't tear down a fence that is on a homestead, so when Asa Hale goes to tearing down the fence, he had better be damned certain he is not tearing down a fence that is proving up a homestead. Now do you get my meaning?"

Realization slowly dawned on Gates's face. "That's pretty slick, Captain. That's mighty slick, as a matter of fact. Yes, sir. You could cause the man to commit an unlawful wrong. I wonder if he is smart enough to know."

"I'm counting on him to not be smart at all. Does he look it?"

Gates shook his head and smiled. "I better get to kicking. I've got a way to go."

Boyd watched him ride off, and then took another drink of whiskey. He had several things on his mind and he was looking for a place to think about them. He wanted that place to be where he could keep an eye on the things he was thinking about. He found it after riding about half an hour. It was a small wooded knoll, almost a mile south of the river between Asa Hale's ranch to the south and Del Cameron's to the north. Off to the west was the town of Syracuse. Boyd led his horse into the wooded area and satisfied himself that the animal couldn't be spotted in the clump of sycamores and cottonwoods. He unbuckled the flap of one of his saddlebags and took out the telescopic sight of his big rifle. He never carried it attached to the rifle until he was ready to use it because it had to be adjusted just right and then screwed into place. The jostling it might receive in the saddle boot would take it out of true, and it wasn't but a moment's work to reattach it.

He took the telescope, went to the edge of the area, and lay down to sight on the places of interest. It was a 20-power scope, and he could dimly see the ranch house and headquarters of Del Cameron. He could not quite see the same on Asa Hale's ranch, but with no trouble he could pick out riders and cattle, even calves. He could see the river very clearly, and even the vague outline of the town four or five miles in the distance. He lay studying the cattle on Asa Hale's ranch, switching it back and forth from there to Del Cameron's. The difference was obvious. Asa Hale's pasturelands were full of ordinary range cattle. On the other hand, most of the cattle on Del Cameron's grass showed distinct signs of the Black Angus breed.

After a few moments, he got up, repacked the telescope carefully in his saddlebags, and then mounted up and started to town. He had several errands that needed his immediate attention once he got to Syracuse.

He hadn't gone very far when he pulled up his horse and stared in the direction of Hale's ranch. With both hands, he gripped the saddlehorn until his knuckles turned white. The appearance of the old man with his wild graying hair and grizzled whiskers and the mean, hateful look in his eyes was so akin to that of Rip Winslow that he couldn't get the picture out of his mind. Then there had been the sons, sitting there on their horses so stiffly beside him, their faces also full of meanness and hate.

Boyd gripped the saddlehorn harder. When he had come face-to-face with them and seen Hale and his brood up close, the desire to draw his revolver had been almost more than he could bear. He had not left just because the old man leveled the shotgun. He had left because he was one flinch from blowing all four of them into kingdom come.

He sat there for a long moment, struggling to regain control of emotions that he hadn't felt for several months. Finally, he took a deep, shuddering breath and forced himself to relax. Asa Hale and his sons were not the Winslows. They had not killed his wife and baby; they had not burned his house. He had to remember that. He had to remember that he was there to do a job and that one had nothing to do with the other. He couldn't allow himself another one of those moments that had come so close to reckless abandonment, where he didn't give a damn what the future held. All he'd wanted was to jerk his revolver out and start shooting. But there had been Gates beside him, and there had been men in front of him who might not have deserved shooting.

Boyd shuddered again, and shook his head and urged his horse forward. It had been a hard test for him, a severe test, but somehow, he felt as if he had passed.

He rode into the little town of Syracuse and hunted up the telegraph office, which turned out to be in the mercantile store. The clerk had to finish wrapping a lady's purchase before he could come and take the wire. Boyd already had it written out and he handed it to the young man, who, after studying it for a moment, sat down, put his hand to the key, and began clacking out the message.

The wire was to Warren. It asked him to go to the railroads and find out what livestock had been shipped to Asa Hale, Del Cameron, and Jim Harris any time in the last eighteen months. He wanted numbers, he wanted points of origin, he wanted dates, and he wanted the information as fast as possible. He had ended it by saying, "Necessary that you put as many men as possible on this. Urgent."

He paid the clerk and asked directions to the sheriff's office. He went outside, mounted up, rode down the street a few blocks, and then tied his mount in front of the sheriff's office.

The sheriff was a comfortably set man in his forties by the name of Howard Duffy. He gave Boyd a warm welcome, bade him take a seat, and then carefully looked over his credentials. When he had finished, he tossed them back to Boyd, saying, "Mr. McMasters, I'm glad to have you here. It appears that we have a little trouble going on. You aren't bringing me more, are you?"

Boyd smiled. He thought he could get along with the man. He said, "Sheriff Duffy, according to my instructions, I'm supposed to stop the trouble."

Sheriff Duffy smiled thinly. He had a big walrus-like mustache on his upper lip. "Yes, Mr. McMasters, but the question is, will it interfere with my job? Are you going to stop the trouble in such a way that it causes trouble for me?"

Boyd said, "Well, I hope not, Sheriff. It could be that I will need the law to act on the side of justice on one or two matters. I don't know that I can arrange it so that you can be there when certain resolutions come about, but I will make every effort to see that the law is represented."

Sheriff Duffy said, "Well, it happens that I appreciate the Cattleman's Association. You boys take a lot of work off the lawmen in this part of the country. I'll back you on anything that doesn't cross too far over the line. You understand me?''

"I understand you, Sheriff. I don't plan to cross any line as far as the law is concerned, but I am concerned about certain parties that take it into their own heads to tear down fences that are on lands that are being homesteaded.''

The sheriff narrowed his eyes. "Now, just who is coming under your interest that is homesteading land?''

Boyd smiled. "Del Cameron.''

The sheriff put his head back and laughed. "Del Cameron proving up a homestead claim?''

"I didn't say he was going to prove it up. I said he was going to file it. Am I correct that if you tear down a fence on a homestead claim, then you have run afoul of the law?''

Sheriff Duffy nodded. "That's true. Am I to understand that Del Cameron, the richest man in these parts, is going to file a homestead claim?''

"More than one, Sheriff, more than one.''

The sheriff laughed again. "That I've got to see. He'll take a lot of horrahing when he goes to register at the courthouse. That I've got to see.''

Boyd stood up. "I'm betting on it, Sheriff.'' He started toward the door, stopped, and then turned around. "I'll be staying in Syracuse for the next week or so. If you need to contact me, I'll be at the hotel. You can find me anytime.''

Sheriff Duffy said, "I hope I don't need to find you, Mr. McMasters. You have the look of a man I don't want to find.''

Boyd gave him a smile and went out the door. He went to the hotel to see to the needs of his horse as well as his own needs.

After a supper in the hotel dining room, he sat in his room, smoking and drinking and thinking. He was fairly certain that he knew who was doing what and who was gaining by it. The biggest problem was going to be to lay hands on the right folks at the right time. He had to make something happen. He thought he could do that, but all of the players were going to have to carry out the roles that he had assigned them.

For a moment, Boyd let his mind wander to Mrs. Jim Harris. Nora, that was her name. He was almost certain that she was the woman he had seen at the creek. His mind wondered what kind of man it took to hit a woman like that. Well, that just might fit in with the scheme he had in mind. It wasn't part of his duties, but he thought he just might make it a part of his duties.

He was tired. It had been a long day and he had missed lunch, and the supper in the dining room hadn't really made up for it. He considered that the time had been well spent. Nothing was going to happen very quickly, and he needed Warren to find out about those cattle shipments. He was also going to have to convince Del Cameron about putting up that fence.

All in all, it had been a good day's work. After a while, he stood up, slowly undressed, and then pulled the covers back. He sat down while he had one more drink and another smoke. His room fronted on the main street of Syracuse, but it was after ten o'clock and other than the faint tinkle of a piano in some saloon down the street, there wasn't much commotion to keep him awake. He finished the last of his drink, turned the lamp down, and went to bed. His last thought before going to sleep was of Martha. He wondered how she was getting along and what she was thinking about. He hoped she was well and as happy as she could be.

The next day, Gates Hood arrived back in town with Jake Mangus. Boyd had lunch with both of them in the dining room of the hotel. He ran a critical eye over Jake, and decided that the agent had been doing more work in the saloon than on the range. It was an appearance he recognized only too well, having seen it in the mirror too many times. Gates was his usual awake, bright-eyed self. He was anxious to know what Captain McMasters was going to do about the trouble. Boyd told him that he didn't know.

"Captain, what's this I hear about Del Cameron stringing drift fence south of the Arkansas River?" Jake asked.

Boyd glanced at Gates. Gates said, "It wasn't supposed to be a secret, was it? We all work for the same company."

Boyd said, "No, of course not. I would have told Jake anyway." He looked at the older man. "You heard right. Any day now Del Cameron is going to start stringing about ten miles of drift fence south of the river."

"He can't do that, Mr. McMasters. He can't fence folks off from common water."

Boyd said, "First of all, he's not keeping anyone out of anywhere. He's building a drift fence, not a closed fence. There will be an end. If anyone wants to go around the fence, all he has to do is ride about five or ten miles to the end of the fence."

Jake said, "I'll tell you who isn't going to like that one bit and that's Asa Hale. He isn't going to like that one damn bit, having a fence between him and the water his cattle use. Mr. McMasters, he'll have that fence snatched up faster than they can put it down."

Boyd said, "He better not. He'll be going to jail if he does, because Del Cameron is going to be filing squatter's claims all up and down the edge of his property. Now, I don't think Mr. Hale is going to know which is squatter's fence and which is Mr. Cameron's deeded property. When Asa Hale goes to tear down any fences, he had better make damn sure that he doesn't tear down any fences used to

prove up a land claim. That's against the law. That will get
the sheriff down on him."

Jake's brow clouded up. "That rich bastard! What put a
bug like that in his ear? That isn't fair, Mr. McMasters, a
rich man fencing a poor one off like that."

Boyd gave a laugh. "Who are you calling poor? Mr. Cameron?"

"Old Asa Hale. He ain't got a pot to piss in or a window
to throw it out of."

"Don't make me laugh, Jake. Anyway, it doesn't make
any difference. It's what Mr. Cameron is going to do."

Jake glanced at Gates and then back at Boyd. "It was
kind of my understandin' that this whole matter was your
idea. Isn't that the fact of it?"

Boyd smiled, but there was no humor in it. He was looking directly at Jake Mangus. He said, "Oh, I don't know.
Where did you hear that? Mr. Cameron doesn't take his orders from me. I might have mentioned something to that
effect, but after all, it's his business. We're here only to help
him, just as we are the rest of the Association's members.
Understood?"

Jake said, "I reckon."

Gates said, "Captain McMasters, when are you planning
on taking a run out to Cap Wiley's?"

Boyd shook his head. "I don't plan on it, Gates. Cap
Wiley doesn't have anything to do with the problem."

Jake's head came up. "You came to that conclusion in all
of two days here getting your feet wet?"

Boyd said, "That's right, Jake. You got an argument with
that?"

Jake stared at him sullenly for a moment, then said, "No,
I reckon not, but if you have it all figured out, why don't
you let the rest of us in on it?"

"I didn't say I have it all figured out, Jake. There's still a few stones I haven't looked under. Maybe you can help me with that."

"Well, I'm hired help. That's what I am here to do."

But in the end, Boyd gave them both no specific orders other than to stay on patrol and keep their eyes open. He said, "Do it separately. I don't want you to be covering the same ground."

Jake said, "Well, them's wise words, Captain McMasters. Two men covering the same ground, they just gettin' half what two men going separate ways can do. That's a fact."

Boyd looked at him for a moment. "I bet you did real good in arithmetic at school, Jake."

For the next several days, Boyd busied himself with visits to Del Cameron and long vigils in his wooded knoll that gave him a good view of the area that he was interested in. Along with that, he had several conversations with the recording clerk at the courthouse. He was also waiting for the return telegram from his brother concerning the cattle shipped to the parties that he had named. On the third day, it came and it confirmed exactly what he had thought. He saddled the roan, giving the chestnut mare the day off, and started for the Jim Harris ranch.

It was a good twelve-mile trip, but he didn't mind. He wondered, however, about Mrs. Harris's condition and if he would get a chance to see her again.

He arrived there a little before lunch. He tied his horse in the front and walked up on the porch of the medium-sized, one-story frame house. It was bright and sparkling, as were most of the outbuildings and the corrals. He had to hand it to Jim Harris. He did keep a neat operation.

Boyd knocked on the door, not really surprised at the number of hired hands he wasn't seeing. He reckoned that they were out on the range, somewhere back north and east of ranch headquarters.

It was Mrs. Harris herself who answered the door. She said, "Yes?" Then she gave a little start of recognition and stepped back in surprise.

Boyd took off his hat. He said, "Howdy. I take it you are Mrs. Harris?"

She put her hand to her breast. "Yes, that's correct."

Boyd gave her his name and repeated what he had told her before, that he was a member of the Cattleman's Association. He said, "I'd like to see your husband on some business, Mrs. Harris."

He studied Nora Harris's face. There were slight traces of the bruise on the one side and her nose still looked slightly swollen, but she had skillfully rouged her cheeks and if you didn't have an eye for such things, you wouldn't notice the swelling around her nose.

She said, almost stammering, "I'm . . . I'm sorry, Mr. McMasters, but my husband is out."

"Isn't he coming home for lunch?"

"I really don't know."

Boyd said, pushing it, "Well, would you mind if I waited? I've ridden quite a way to see him."

She said, "He could be quite a while, Mr. McMasters."

Boyd said, "Well, if you could spare a cup of coffee, I could wait for a while at least."

Nora Harris said, "Well, I am quite embarrassed. When Jim is not at home I don't fix lunch, so I don't have much to offer you. I could, perhaps, fix a little something."

He said, "I had a late breakfast, Mrs. Harris. A cup of coffee would be fine, and perhaps a little of your company."

She blushed immediately. "Well, Mr. McMasters, I don't know if it is seemly, my husband not being at home."

He smiled at her. "Mrs. Harris, I'm an agent of the Cattleman's Protective Association. If you will remember, my job is to protect a rancher's property. I reckon that includes his wife as well as his cattle."

It brought a small smile to her face. She said, "Well, yes, do come in and wait if you wish." She opened the door wider and Boyd stepped into the dim, cool interior of the house.

She led him into the kitchen through the front room and a dining room. The house seemed much bigger from the inside than from the outside. He didn't know about such things, but the furniture appeared to him to be of high quality and Mrs. Harris appeared to be an excellent housekeeper.

She sat him down at the kitchen table and then went to the stove to pour a cup of coffee, asking him if he took it with milk.

He said, "Please, and a little sugar if you don't mind." He watched her, admiring her slim but voluptuous figure under the light blue frock she was wearing. The color went very well with her dark shining hair and her deep green eyes.

She set the cup in front of him and then stood there.

Boyd motioned with his spoon. "You're not going to leave a man just sitting here, are you, Mrs. Harris? Won't you sit down and join me?"

Nora said, "Oh, I have some sewing I really should do."

"Well, Mrs. Harris, I wouldn't want to interfere with your work, but I really thought that you and I could have a little chat."

"Whatever would we talk about? I know nothing whatsoever about my husband's business."

To Boyd's eye, she seemed nervous as she answered him. He said, "Well, let's try anyway. Maybe you could tell me where you are from and how you met Mr. Harris and what brought you to this country."

She sat down, putting both hands primly on the table, but she still would not look him directly in the eyes. He could tell she was nervous, and he assumed that it was from fear that he would mention the incident at the creek the week before.

Boyd said, "I assume you must have come from horse country because the other day when I saw you, you were wearing riding clothes, so I assumed that you get around using a horse instead of a buggy."

She said nervously, "Yes, I ride quite often. It's a pleasure." She made a fluttering motion with her hands. "There's not really much to do around here."

"I don't suppose there's many close women friends."

At that, Nora did glance up into his eyes, finding them sympathetic. She said, "That's true. We seem very isolated here."

"Don't you go into town?"

"It's quite a ways and James doesn't like me to go too often. I have to stay overnight when I go."

"Do you go to Lakin or to Syracuse?"

She was playing nervously with the tablecloth. She said, "Oh, it depends. I have acquaintances in both places and the towns are both about equal for shopping."

"Do you stay in a hotel when you go?"

"I stay in a boardinghouse in Lakin. We have an arrangement with the proprietor, and I don't go to Syracuse unless I go with my husband, and then we stay at a hotel. I do have a friend, a widow lady, that I have stayed with before." Nora suddenly challenged him with her eyes. "Aren't these questions a little personal, Mr. McMasters?"

Boyd looked at her for a long moment. He reached in his pocket for a cigarillo and then lit it. He said, "Personal? I guess you could call my questions personal, Mrs. Harris. I think it's about time that somebody got personal with you. You don't have to take what you've been taking, you know. Ain't no man has a right to hit you like that. The man that does it is a coward."

Nora sucked in her breath and put her hand to her mouth. She stared at him. She said, "Oh, no. Please don't say that, Mr. McMasters, please."

Boyd shrugged. "If you like getting knocked around, ma'am, then that's your business, but there ain't no man worth that. You don't have to take it. In fact, any man that hits a woman ought not to call himself a man."

She said, "I . . . I ran into a tree branch."

"Yeah, just like you fell down the stairs from what you told my agent, the one with the freckles. Mrs. Harris, if you had run into a tree branch, your face would have been scratched. There were no scratches on your face, just a big bruise, swelling, and a bloody nose. That comes from only one thing and that's a fist."

Nora's eyes suddenly brimmed full. For a second, he thought she was going to begin sobbing, but then she swallowed hard several times and then turned her head away. She said in a quivering voice, "You don't understand, Mr. McMasters; you just don't understand."

"What's there to understand? You love him so you let him hit you. How many times is he going to hit you before you don't love him anymore? I was married, Mrs. Harris, and there was nothing that my wife could have done that would have ever caused me to hit her. Nothing."

Nora's head came around and her eyes met his. A tear had overflowed from her swollen eyes and was running slowly down her cheek. She said, "Mr. McMasters, there are some things that you don't want anyone to know. You'd rather bear the pain than the shame."

"I understand, Mrs. Harris. You don't want a neighbor or a friend, certainly not a stranger like me, to know that your husband knocks you around, but the shame is not yours. The shame is his."

She burst out, "But I married him."

"Yes, but making one mistake doesn't mean you have to keep on making it."

Then Nora did cry, sobbing quietly as she sat there with her elbows on the table, her face covered by her hands. Her shoulders shook and he could hear little racking sighs. Boyd got up, went to the back door, and opened it and stood there, staring out the screen door. He waited for at least five minutes. When he turned back into the room, she was gone.

He walked out of the kitchen and looked in the dining room and then in the front room. There was no sign of her. He looked at the head of the long hall that he supposed went back to the bedrooms. In a loud voice he said, "Mrs. Harris, I am staying at the hotel in Syracuse. Whenever you get tired of being hurt, come to me and I will see that the matter gets straightened out. If I am not there, leave a message and I will find you. Mrs. Harris, believe me, I am trying to be your friend. Your husband is heading for trouble and you don't want to be around when it happens."

He was about to turn and leave when a door suddenly opened and she appeared at the far end of the hall. She said hesitantly, "Do you mean that?"

"What? That I'd help you?"

"Yes. Could you help me get away from him? Could you help me get back to my folks?"

"You just say the word. I'll give you all the help you need. I'll protect you all the way."

She nodded her head quickly and then disappeared back into a room, and Boyd heard the sound of the door softly closing. He put on his hat, walked out of the house, and mounted his horse and rode away.

That evening, Boyd had a quiet talk with Sheriff Howard Duffy. At first, the easygoing sheriff was disbelieving, but the more Boyd talked and the more he showed him exactly how the plan was working, the more the sheriff began to see the logic of Boyd's conclusion. And when he showed the sheriff the telegram from Warren about the cattle shipments, the sheriff was convinced in spite of himself. He said, "I'd have never believed it, though. Right up underneath everybody's noses! That's a pretty slick way of doing business, to my mind."

Boyd said, "You can get pretty slick when there's that much money involved."

The sheriff asked, "But are you sure you ain't about to start a range war with that fence?"

"It will never come to that. I'm here because I want to make sure that the law is aware of what's happening. I don't know just how bad it can get, but I don't think it's going to be any picnic. You don't pry a person loose from that kind of money without them doing a little kicking and screaming, so I thought it was best for you and your deputy to know. Although for right now, I'd just as soon you not tell your deputy."

"Are you looking to us for any firepower?"

Boyd shook his head. "No, I've got two other men in Lakin that I'm fixing to bring in. I don't think it is going to come to all that much shooting. I want to keep it legal and above board."

The sheriff nodded. "Well, I'm obliged to you for that."

Boyd said, "How about you and me going down to the saloon and I'll buy you enough drinks to get you in trouble with your wife when you go home for supper?"

The sheriff laughed. "You're taking on a chore of work, young man, a real chore of work. I hope you've got plenty of jingling money in your pockets."

Boyd said, "Try me."

Before they could leave the office, the sheriff stopped and turned to Boyd. He said, "You know, Mr. McMasters, now that I've thought on it, you've given me enough evidence to make an arrest. What reason is there for me not to get on about my business as the sheriff right now?''

''Because you wouldn't get all the quail in the covey. If you let me play my hand out, we could get to the bottom of this whole mess. Right now, you'd just be taking half measures.''

The sheriff studied him for a moment. Then he said, ''Well, Boyd. I hope to hell that you know what you're doing. You'd better not get me in trouble.''

Boyd said, ''Rest your mind, Sheriff. Everything is under control.''

The sheriff fixed him with an eye for a moment, giving Boyd a good looking over. ''Mr. McMasters, I wish you didn't have the look of a wild man so much about you. I can't put my finger on it, but there is something hovering in your face that gives me the impression that you could go in any direction like a tornado at any time. No offense intended, you understand.''

Boyd smiled. ''None taken, Sheriff. That's a right nice compliment.''

The sheriff shook his head. ''See, there you go!''

Boyd laughed again, and they went out the door.

Eleven

The next afternoon, Boyd saw what he was expecting and what he had been watching for. He had ridden out from Syracuse early that morning to have a talk with Del Cameron, who was having serious misgivings, not only about going through the motions of filing the claims, but mainly about building the fence. Cameron said, "Mr. McMasters, I have done what you asked on the claims. I have filed three claims in the names of members of my family. I must tell you that it was the most embarrassing experience. Here I am, a man with considerable property, yet here I am filing squatter's claims."

Boyd reassured him. "Mr. Cameron, the point is not that you really plan to prove up this land. The point is to protect the fence and give us a legal right to defend it, because without a survey, they can't tell what part of that fence is your land and what part is that which you are trying to prove up. That's the whole point."

Cameron pushed his hat back and said, "That's all well and good, Mr. McMasters, but I can tell you right now that Asa Hale is going to react violently to this. We've been putting fencing materials out, and already I can tell that there is increased activities along his northern border. I have seen twice as many riders coming to the river to watch our affairs. I repeat again, Mr. McMasters, my men are cowhands. I don't hire gunmen. I didn't get into this business to get into a war.''

Boyd said, ''You won't be making the fight, Mr. Cameron, not you, nor your sons, nor any of your hired hands. That's my job, the job of me and my men. That's what you pay us for, and I'd be the first one to admit that for the past two years you haven't been getting your money's worth.''

Cameron said, ''That's putting it mildly. Your Mr. Jake Mangus has been as much as a stranger to me as my brother in Philadelphia, and I haven't seen *him* in five years.''

Boyd laughed.

Cameron said, ''I don't like telling tales out of school, but as far as I'm concerned, Mr. Mangus has spent most of his time protecting my cattle in the various saloons in Syracuse and Lakin. I confronted him about it one time, braced him up, and he gave me the understanding that he had a hired hand to do his range riding and patrolling and that he was the boss. I cannot say that I have a complaint about Mr. Gates Hood. He has been trying to do a good job, but I can tell you for certain that if this plan had been put to me by Mr. Jake Mangus, I'd have had no part of it. As it is, I am teetering on the brink of getting out of this business. I'm not a poor man and I don't have to take this sort of trouble. I came here with the intention of leading a peaceful life, raising cattle, and following the example of Jim Harris, but I'll be damned if I am going to keep going through the troubles that I have now. I shouldn't say following the example of James Harris, since I owned land here first, but he is having a great deal more success at it than I am. I suppose that's because he is not as near and doesn't share a mutual border with our good friend Mr. Asa Hale and his brood of vipers.''

Cameron kindly invited Boyd to stay over for lunch. It was a pleasure to sit down with such a genteel family. Only one of his boys was at the table, young Del, Jr., who was twenty-one. Cameron's wife, Lucy, was a wonderful hostess. She was a handsome, red-haired woman whom Boyd took to be in her early thirties. Their cook made a fine lunch of breaded veal cutlets and gravy, fried potatoes, sliced tomatoes, and early peas. Mrs. Cameron offered the thought that nowhere where they had lived had a kitchen garden produced so abundantly.

Cameron said with a sour smile on his face, "Yes, and the cattle would do the same if I could just get somebody to leave them alone and let them breed naturally and produce as the Good Lord intended."

Boyd gave him a wink and said, "Well, the faster we get that fence up, the faster that can happen."

Cameron gave Boyd a worried look. "On your advice, I have directed my foreman to build the fence in a line directly between Asa Hale's headquarters and mine. They are to fence in both directions until they run out of fencing or posts or men. I better not run out of men, Mr. McMasters. I better not even get one of them hurt."

"Your men should have instructions to get on their horses and get the hell out of there at the first sight of trouble."

Mrs. Cameron said, "Del, I certainly hope that you and Mr. McMasters know what you are doing. This scares me."

Cameron looked over at his wife. "Lucy, do I look like I'm easy in my mind about it?"

That afternoon at about two o'clock, Boyd got to the watch point atop the small wooded rise. He rode his horse in, tied him well back into the trees so that he wasn't visible, and took the telescope out of his saddlebags. He went to the western end of the tree line that faced Asa Hale's ranch. He lay down on his belly, propping himself against a tree, and trained the 20-power scope onto the headquarters and outbuildings that were dim in the distance through the magnified glass.

For half an hour he swept the area, searching it as far out as the glass would reach. A little after three, his efforts were rewarded. By chance, he had the glass trained on Asa Hale's ranch house when two figures came out. They appeared to stand talking for a moment, and then one mounted up and turned in the direction that would take him toward the town of Syracuse. Boyd kept the telescope trained on the lone rider, who was moving his horse over the rolling land at a steady lope. He saw the man raise his hand in greeting as he passed other riders and hired hands going about their business of tending to Asa Hale's cattle. About the time he began to approach the river, heading more easterly, Boyd became fairly certain who the man was, and within five minutes he knew for sure. It was Jake Mangus.

Boyd watched until he was certain that the man was headed for town. He wanted Jake to have plenty of head start so there wouldn't be an encounter until he was ready.

He got up, replaced the telescope in his saddlebags, mounted his horse, and then took a slow route back to town and to his hotel. He turned his horse into the livery stable, but before going to his room, he went down to the mercantile store where the telegraph office was located and got off a wire to Warren.

After that, he strolled slowly back to the hotel, got his key, went to his room, opened a bottle of whiskey, and sat down on his bed to have a drink and a smoke and a thoughtful assessment of how best to carry out what he had in mind.

Gates Hood knocked on the door and came in about six o'clock. Boyd gave him a drink and the young-looking agent took a chair, leaning it back against the wall while he sipped his whiskey. He said, "Ain't much stirring out there, Captain McMasters. I drifted up toward Cap Wiley's place, even though you said he ain't no part of this. I still don't know what you mean by that, but I reckon that's the way of it with bosses."

Boyd said, "I'm not saying that he's not affected, Gates, but right now I'm trying to get to the core of the problem and it doesn't seem to be heading up in that direction. Where has Jake been today?"

Gates shrugged. "Beats the hell out of me, sir. I ain't laid eyes on him for two days now. He's come and gone and I've come and gone. I caught sight of him having a beer yesterday evening, but we didn't have a chance to speak."

"I've left word for him to stop by. I don't want you to be too over-surprised by what happens."

The words were barely out of his mouth when there was a slight knock, followed immediately by the opening of the door. Jake Mangus came swaggering through. Even at a glance, Boyd could tell there was something different about him, some newfound confidence to go with his barely repressed bullying attitude. Jake said, "Well, hello there, Boyd. Have you decided to come up to the surface?"

Boyd was watching Jake steadily. He had loosened his gun in his holster and had turned on the bed so that he could keep Jake in full view. Boyd said, "Something like that, Jake."

Without an invitation, Jake went over, upended a glass, and helped himself to a healthy drink of whiskey. He walked over and sat himself on a chair opposite Boyd.

Boyd said, "Have a good day, Jake?"

Jake said, looking narrowly at Boyd, "Middlin'. Just middlin', I'd say. How about yourself, Boyd?"

"I'd rate it better than average, though it looks like I'm going to lose a good man."

Jake looked interested. "Is that so?"

Boyd said, "Yeah. You're fired."

The only one who reacted was Gates. He brought his chair to the floor with a thump. Jake Mangus stopped with the glass of whiskey halfway to his mouth. He stared at Boyd over the top of it and said, "Say what, Boyd?"

Boyd said, "I said you were fired. That means you are no longer in the pay of the Cattleman's Protective Association. That means you are free to go visit anybody you want to, at any time. You savvy?"

Jake blinked and lowered the glass. His face began to get pink, and then slowly rose to a full flush. "What the hell are you talking about, boy? You ain't got no right to fire me. You ain't my boss. You ain't your brother."

"Well, you're fired. You can go on working, but you ain't going to get paid. If you get in my way, I'll shoot you, understand me? And by the way, I didn't say you could have a drink and I didn't say you could call me Boyd. Understand? Only people that I respect are allowed to call me by my first name."

He shifted slightly on the bed, sitting up straighter. Jake rose to his feet. In a quick move, he drained the last of his whiskey and then let the glass fall to the floor. It was a heavy glass that didn't break, but it made a loud thump when it hit the wood floor.

With his voice shaking with rage Jake Mangus said, "Listen, goddamn you, you sonofabitch. You better think this over. You might be asking for a little more trouble than you can handle."

Boyd looked at him calmly. "Would you like to try and give me that trouble right now, Jake? We're both carrying weapons. Would that be your style?"

The man was so angry that he was shaking visibly. He said, "By God, we'll just see about this firing business. I'll fire off a telegram to the head office and we'll see who gets fired, you sonofabitch.''

Boyd, still calm, said, ''You call me that one more time, Jake, and I'm going to blow your damn head off, you understand?''

Jake abruptly turned, flung open the door, and left, leaving the door standing open.

It was quiet in the room for a moment, and then Boyd got up, crossed the room, and closed the door. As he turned back, he yawned.

Gates said, ''What in hell was that all about?''

Boyd said, ''Well, you were here. I fired him. Haven't you ever seen anybody fired before?''

Gates said, ''Yeah, but how come? What did he do?''

''Well, that's not something I want to talk about right now, Gates. Just make sure you don't do it.''

Gates's eyes got big. ''Make sure I don't . . . Captain McMasters, how can I not do something when I don't know what it is that I ain't supposed to do?''

Boyd laughed and sat down on the bed. He took a moment to add some whiskey to his glass and then sipped. Then he said, ''Just to be on the safe side, don't do anything that Jake Mangus ever did. That ought to be clear enough.''

''Golly, Captain McMasters. Them's pretty tall orders.'' He suddenly got a worried frown on his face. He hesitated before saying, ''Captain McMasters, I don't want to be accused of speaking out of turn here, but you ain't known that man as long as I have, and I think there are a few things you might need to know about him.''

Boyd got out a cigarillo and blew out a cloud of smoke. ''Oh, yeah? And what should those be?''

Gates hesitated even more, but finally he said, ''Well, I hate to say something bad about other folks, but I've got to tell you that Jake has got himself a temper and he ain't the nicest fellow that you would want to get mad at you. I ain't saying that he's a backshooter, you understand.''

Boyd looked at him directly. ''Oh, yes, you are, Gates, and you didn't have to tell me that. I'll say it for you. Jake Mangus is a bully, a coward, a traitor, and it wouldn't be any trouble at all for him to be a bushwhacker or a backshooter. That would be his style. I'd be surprised if he tried it any other way. I offered him a chance at me face-to-face. I noticed he didn't take it.''

''Well, I just wanted you to be in the know, if you take my meaning.''

Boyd suppressed a smile. ''Yes, I take your meaning, Gates, and I appreciate the warning, but I've got a line on Mr. Jake Mangus. I had one about fifteen minutes after I met him, but thank you anyway. Now, why don't you and I go down to the dining room and get some supper. Maybe Mr. Mangus will be there and we can throw silverware at him.''

Gates stared at him, goggle-eyed. He said, ''Captain McMasters, you are about the coolest hand I've ever met. First time I took a look at you, I thought you might be about halfway mean or kind of wild.''

Boyd laughed. ''I'm starting to hear that often these days, Gates. There must be something to it. Finish up your drink and let's go eat.''

Walking down the hall, Gates put his hand to his chin and scratched it. He said, ''You know, Captain, it strikes me funny that ol' Jake never pressed you on how come you was firing him. I don't think he asked you out and out. Why do you reckon that was?''

Boyd said dryly, ''Maybe he figured he had it coming.''

''Yeah, but what did he do? I never heard you tell him.''

''Maybe it just came to him that he couldn't work for two bosses at the same time.''

Gates swiveled his head around toward Boyd. ''Huh?

What's that supposed to mean?''

Boyd said, "Ain't you hungry, Gates? Don't you know that the more you talk, the less you can eat? You better quit talking so much and let's go in the dining room and get some vittles.''

"Yes, sir, Captain. Whatever you say.''

There really was nothing to do but wait. His traps, such as they were, were baited and set into place. All Boyd could do was hope his quarry would take a snatch at what looked like an easy prize. Jake Mangus had not left town, but then Boyd had not expected him to leave right away. He'd seen him several times, but their paths hadn't really crossed. There had been one time in the saloon when Jake had been drinking at the bar when Boyd came in for a drink. Mangus had melted back into the tables, joining a card game. Then there had been the time Boyd had seen Mangus coming out of the courthouse and the recording clerk had been kind enough to inform Boyd of Mangus's inquiries. Of course long before, Boyd had insured the recording clerk's loyalty with the aid of a twenty-dollar gold piece. Once, Boyd had seen Mangus riding out of town, headed north. He'd had a fair idea where the man was going and he wished him success. Mangus had checked out of the hotel. Where he was staying, Boyd didn't know and didn't make an effort to find out.

Boyd had received the reply to the telegram to his brother, informing Warren that he was going to fire Jake Mangus. He had given no reasons in the wire, since he figured it would be all over town within the hour. Warren's answer had simply said, "You're the one on the spot. Do what you think best.''

Which was what Boyd was doing. The day after he had fired Jake, Boyd had sent Gates to bring in the other two

men still at Lakin, Earl White and Bob Sweeney. He was of
the mind that White was cut of the same cloth as Jake Mangus, but until he had proof, he'd consider the man just another Association employee.

They had returned, and Boyd had given all three piddling
duties in the east, north, and south of Jim Harris's ranch.
They had asked what they were supposed to be looking for,
but it was only to Gates that Boyd had revealed what he
expected to find in Harris's eastern and southern pastures.
He had not been surprised when the young agent had confirmed his suspicions almost immediately.

He was disappointed at the rate at which Del Cameron
was building fence. After three days, only about a mile had
been finished. Boyd called it to Del Cameron's attention and
said, "I know your heart is not in this, but somehow you've
got to make it look like it. A mile of that kind of fencing
should have been done in a half a day. You should have
three or four miles up by now."

Cameron promised to do better. He admitted that he didn't
much care for Boyd's plan. He was too afraid of the trouble
it might cause and as a result, he claimed that he had very
few cowhands who weren't busy at other chores to put on
the fence. Finally, it began to grow, but still too slowly.
Boyd knew that the fence was one trap that wouldn't be
sprung until there was enough fence to make it worthwhile
to the raiders who would come by dark of night or early
light of dawn to tear it down. What would be the point of
tearing down a short piece of fence that really wasn't in
anyone's way?

On the morning of the fourth day after he fired Jake Mangus, he saw his plan begin to unfold in another direction. He
was riding out to Del Cameron's place to see how the work
was coming along. It was a beautiful summer morning, and
as he cleared the town and set out across the prairie, he could

almost hear the cicadas buzzing and hear the slight breeze as it rustled through the grass.

He was perhaps a mile out of town when he became aware of the man behind him. He had been almost certain that two men had left town at the same time he did, and now as he looked back, he saw another one cutting due west and riding hard. Boyd smiled to himself. He felt certain of the events that were about to begin laying the foundation of the drama he had planned.

Boyd slowed the gait of his horse. He was riding the roan that day and glad of it, because he felt certain he would need a steady mount under him. While the chestnut was an excellent animal for covering ground, she still wasn't as experienced as the roan. He and the roan had been through many a time together, and the horse had good sense and good manners and the judgment to remain calm.

About three miles out of town, Boyd suddenly cut west as a test of the first man's intentions. The man didn't immediately follow him, just continued for a stretch. Boyd let him go on like that for about a mile before he cut back north again. Glancing back, he saw the rider drifting back onto his path. Boyd didn't know the man, but he looked rough enough the one time he had been close enough for Boyd to get a good view of him. As Boyd rode, he kept taking quick, covert looks behind him. He could see the man closing the distance. To him, that was a sure sign that something was about to happen soon.

Boyd calculated that he was within three or four miles of the river. He kept on at steady pace, a slow lope that the roan could hold all day. He peered intently ahead. Suddenly, coming off his left quarter, he saw two horsemen in the distance, bearing down in his direction. He had no doubts as to who one of them was, but he needed them to come in a little bit closer. He took a quick glance backward. His pursuer had closed the distance to about four hundred yards. Boyd looked forward at the men riding hard toward him. He waited, calculating, trying to find exactly the right second to do what he planned.

Suddenly, with no warning, he whipped the roan around in a quick turn and rode straight at the man behind him. It took the man so by surprise that he came on another fifty yards before he tried to pull his horse to a stop, but by then it was too late. Boyd was not carrying his big gun, but he had his saddle carbine in the boot and he pulled it out with his horse at a dead run. As he dropped the reins and stood up in the stirrups, he had a clear shot at the man, who was sawing back on the reins of his own horse trying to bring him to a stop.

At a distance of about a hundred yards, Boyd fired. He saw the man sway, and he levered another shell into the chamber and fired again; this time, the man was knocked out of the saddle. Boyd had already begun turning before the man disappeared into the grass.

Now the two men coming at him from the north were no farther than three hundred yards away. Boyd spurred the roan hard for fifty yards, and then jerked him to a stop and leaped out of the saddle, leaving the horse still moving. He knelt in the grass, sighting on the lead rider's horse. He fired. He must have hit the horse either in the heart or the brain, because the animal immediately collapsed as though his legs had been chopped out from under him. Boyd could see that the rider had had no time to fling himself away from the falling horse and that the horse had him pinned. He could see the rider trying to rear up, thrashing about, but there was no time to look. He sighted on the second rider and fired. The bullet took the horse in the neck and the animal stumbled on for fifteen or twenty yards and began to fall. As he did, the rider leaped out of the saddle. He landed on his hands and knees, and was starting to rise when Boyd ran forward another twenty yards and shot him square in the chest. It knocked the man backward, but he didn't fall. Boyd levered in another shell and then fired. This time, the shot knocked the man over onto his back.

Twelve

It suddenly became very quiet after the explosions of the six shots. Boyd took a moment to reload his carbine out of the spare cartridges he carried in his shirt pocket. When his rifle was full, he caught up the roan, which had run off a few yards. Then he mounted, holding the rifle at the ready, a shell in the chamber, and rode slowly to where the two men had gone down. He didn't pause at the first man, though he was somewhat curious as to why the first shot hadn't knocked him down. Perhaps the brass tack had fallen out. At that moment, he was a great deal more interested in Jake Mangus, who was pinned under his dead horse. He stopped forty yards away. Mangus was staring at him. Boyd called out, ''Get your hands up where I can see them right now, Jake. If you even look like you've got a gun, I'm gonna put one in your ear. You savvy?''

Jake Mangus yelled, ''For God's sake, my leg is killing me! It's broke! Help me, please, help me. I ain't got no gun.''

Boyd urged the roan forward until he was about ten yards away, and he could see that Mangus was unarmed. He slowly dismounted, keeping the rifle at the ready on Mangus.

He walked slowly forward until he was standing over his fallen enemy. Mangus's face was twisted with pain. Boyd could see his rifle was still in the boot, unreachable. His revolver holster was empty. Disregarding Mangus's pleas for help, Boyd searched the area where Mangus's horse had gone down until he had retrieved the man's weapon and stuck it in his belt, only then going up and standing over Mangus.

He said, "Well, Jake, looks like you're in a hell of a mess. Don't you know anything about riding? You're supposed to be on the horse, not the horse on you."

Mangus was writhing around putting his hands to his face. He said in little gasps, "For God's sake, Boyd, help me, help me."

"Ain't I warned you before about getting familiar with me, Jake? I don't care for folks like you calling me by my given name."

Mangus almost shouted. "Captain McMasters, please get this horse off of me! I'm dying, my leg's broke, and I'm hurting like hell!"

Boyd looked the situation over. There was no way he could pull a thousand-pound animal off Jake Mangus's leg. It was Mangus's left leg that was pinned under the horse. Pinned to the hip almost. He flailed his right leg around in agony, stamping at his saddle and leaving dents and gouges from his spur. It was clear to Boyd that the man was in some pain, the way he writhed around with his upper body and his arms. Boyd stood over him and said, "You know, Jake, this is another thing that I got against you. You caused me to kill two good horses. Animals that had done me no harm. I couldn't tell which one was you at that distance, so I had to knock you both down so I could take you alive. Even though you are beat up a little bit, for the time being you are still alive."

Mangus said through clenched teeth, "Captain, have you got any whiskey, could you give me some whiskey, please?"

Boyd said, "We'll get around to that in a minute." He shifted his rifle to his left hand and pulled out his revolver. Very carefully he opened the gate, flipped out the chamber, and removed one of the cartridges. He took the brass carpet tack out of the nose and put it in his pocket. Then he put the cartridge back in the cylinder of the revolver and closed it. He said, "Jake, can you write?"

Mangus stopped his writhing for a moment and stared at Boyd. He said, "Write? What are you talking about, Captain, what do you mean?"

"Can you write? Can you write a fair hand?"

"Hell, yes, I can write. You mean with pen and pencil and paper? Yes, I write a pretty fair hand. I can read, hell, yes. Don't you know that you can't get into the Association if you can't?"

Boyd said, "Well, that's very lucky for you, Jake."

"What has me being able to write got to do with anything?"

Boyd cocked his revolver. "If you couldn't write, Jake, you wouldn't be of any use to me and I'd plug you right here. You may not have figured it out, Jake, but I don't like you very much. In fact, I'm not fond of you at all."

Lying on the ground, Mangus stared up at him. "For God's sake, Captain, what kind of man are you?"

Boyd said, "I'm the kind of man who is asking you if you are going to talk to the sheriff. If you are going to tell him the truth about everything."

Mangus said, pain evident in his voice, "Captain, I don't know nothing. I don't know what you're talking about. We didn't mean you no harm."

"Bullshit," Boyd said calmly. "If you're going to lie, I'm going to give you some of this." With deliberate aim he pointed the revolver at Mangus's left ear and fired, blowing away the better part of it.

Mangus gave a loud high-pitched scream and looked at Boyd with wide staring eyes. He clapped his hand to the side of his head and stared at the blood dripping on his palm. He said in almost a whisper, "You're crazy, you're crazy."

Boyd shifted his aim to Mangus's other ear. He said, "I'm going to ask you one more time. I will warn you that this particular bullet will do a hell of a lot more damage than the other one. It won't just take off part of your ear; it will probably take off the side of your head. You savvy?"

Mangus said, holding up his hand, "For God's sake don't shoot. For God's sake yes, I'll talk. I'll tell the sheriff anything that you say. Whatever you say. Please don't shoot me again."

Boyd slowly uncocked the revolver. He put it in his holster and said, "Get it straight into your mind, Mangus, that when the sheriff gets here you won't decide to change your mind. You're going to tell the sheriff everything you know, and I know everything that you know. You're also going to do a little letter writing for me. You got that straight?"

Mangus had his teeth clenched and his eyes shut hard. He said, "The whiskey, Captain. For God's sake, please give me just a little whiskey."

Boyd said, "Do you understand me, Mangus? Do you understand what will happen if you don't cooperate?"

"Yes, yes, yes. A drink, please, a drink. I'm hurting like hell."

Boyd went to his saddlebags, opened one flap, took out a bottle of whiskey, uncorked it, took a long hard drink for himself, and then walked it over to Mangus and handed it to his frantic reaching grasp. As the man on the ground sucked greedily at the bottle, Boyd said, "You'd better make that last. It's going to take me a while to get into town and get the sheriff and get that horse off of you. Was I you, I wouldn't do no jerking around. All you're going to do is hurt your leg more. If some of your compadres come along to help, I wouldn't let them if I was you. I can promise you, Jake Mangus, that you are never going to get away from me. There ain't no place on this earth that you can go so that I won't find you.''

With that he turned on his heel, mounted up, and rode toward town.

It was over two hours later that Boyd was able to get started back with the sheriff, his deputy, and the blacksmith, who was driving a buckboard. In the buckboard was a long metal pipe with a pulley on top that they intended to use to lift the dead horse off Mangus's leg. It was not that uncommon an occurrence in cattle country, and the blacksmith was the man you went to in just such circumstances.

The sheriff said, ''It strikes me that you were uncommonly lucky to be able to recognize the situation for what it turned out to be.''

Boyd smiled thinly. ''Sheriff, it wasn't hard at all to recognize it. I could have recognized it after only knowing Jake Mangus for an hour and a half. I knew what he would do. He wasn't going to stay fired. It got personal between him and me, and that's where he made his mistake.''

''You don't know who the two men are that were with him?''

''I've got an idea, but I think that you'll be able to judge better, you or your deputy or maybe Mr. Kelterhorn, the blacksmith.''

They came upon the scene within another half mile. The sheriff came upon the first body, the man who had been trailing Boyd out of town. The man was lying on his face in the grass. The sheriff whistled at the size of the hole in his back where the bullet had exited. He said, ''My word of honor, Boyd. What the hell did you shoot him with? A field cannon?''

''No, just this carbine.''

''You must have hit a bone because it sure made a hole in him.''

''Sometimes a soft-nosed lead slug will do that, you know.''

The sheriff said, ''There's no use feeling his pulse. He's about as dead as he can get. We'll load him in the wagon on the way back.''

Boyd asked, ''Do you recognize him?''

''I don't know for sure, but I think he's one of Asa Hale's hired hands. I can't be sure. How about you, Tommy?'' He turned to his deputy. ''Do you recognize this man?''

The young man said, ''No, sir, but then, I never had much truck with that bunch from Hale's place.''

It was another quarter of a mile to where Jake Mangus was frantically waving his arms for them to hurry to his side. But first they stopped at the body of the man who had been slightly in advance of Jake and whose horse had stumbled on. Boyd had been curious as to why the first bullet hadn't killed the man. He was lying on his back two neat holes in his chest.

The sheriff said, ''Now I can identify this one. He is Neil somebody or other. He's one of that bunch from Hale's place. I think he might be a cousin. Hell, he might be kin. A long way removed.'' They turned the body over. There were two large exit wounds.

Boyd said almost to himself, ''I guess his body just kept working after he was dead.''

''What?''

''Nothing. I guess we had better get over here to Jake Mangus. He's about ready to have a fit. A little old broken leg. Just because he's got a thousand-pound horse laying on it he thinks he's hurting.''

The sheriff turned to the blacksmith. ''Mr. Kelterhorn, will you take your buckboard over there and rig your pole so we can get some ropes on that horse and see if we can't pull it off that fellow?''

The stolid-faced blacksmith nodded and drove to where Jake Mangus was lying. Boyd and the sheriff walked up. Mangus began wildly and angrily shaking his finger at Boyd. He said, ''Sheriff, this lunatic tried to kill me. He's a crazy man, I tell you, he's a crazy man.''

The sheriff ignored him. He looked at Mangus's head and said, ''What happened to his ear?''

Boyd shook his head. ''Critter got it, I guess.''

Mangus shouted, ''The sonofabitch shot my ear off, Sheriff! He stood over me and shot my ear off!''

The sheriff looked down and said mildly, ''Just the one?''

Boyd said, ''Mangus, I want you to shut your mouth right now and keep it shut until we get back to the jail. If you don't, we're going to drag that horse off of you instead of lifting it off.''

Mangus gave him a sullen look, and then finally nodded his head.

They put two ropes on the saddlehorn of Mangus's horse, ran them over the wheel on top of the eight-foot-long pipe, and then tied the ends of the rope to the buggy.

With the sheriff on one side of the blacksmith's team and the deputy on the other, they whipped their horses up and threw a strain on the rope. The saddle creaked while the pole slowly straightened, and little by little the carcass of the horse began to rise. Boyd had gone around behind Mangus, and as the horse cleared the few inches that were necessary, he quickly pulled the injured man out.

Boyd shouted, ''I got him! You can let the horse down.''

Mangus was cussing in a slow steady monotone. He still had the whiskey bottle cradled in his arms. It was almost empty. Barely a drink remained.

They picked up the two dead bodies and got them loaded into the wagon. The deputy started off after the horse of the man who had been trailing Boyd.

Finally, they loaded Mangus in the back of the wagon with the gin-pole rig and the two dead bodies. Mangus groaned with their every movement. When he was settled into the wagon, Boyd could hear him talking to the sheriff. Mangus said, "Sheriff, that sonofabitch is a lunatic. He stood over me and just shot my ear off. Worse than that, he asked me if I could write, if I knew my letters. He said if I couldn't, he was going to plug me. What do you reckon 'bout that? The man was gonna shoot me if I didn't know my alphabet!"

The sheriff walked over to where Boyd was standing and studying the two horses. "It appears that I'm not alone in my belief that there is some kind of wild streak in you. How come you to shoot his ear off anyway?"

Boyd looked around at him. "I didn't like the looks of it."

The sheriff nodded. "Sounds reasonable to me."

Afterwards, they had a discussion about how soon the riders might be missed or how soon the dead horses would be found. It was the sheriff's opinion that they were far enough off the beaten track that it would be some little while before any one of the local ranchers was likely to come that way, since it wasn't on the way to town. Judging from the emptiness of the plains around them, no one was grazing cattle on that particular land. The two dead horses had fallen on their left sides, so their brands were obscured. Nevertheless, with some effort, the men jerked the saddles off both horses and loaded them in the wagon.

Boyd said, "I don't want word getting around about this any sooner than it has to."

Sheriff Duffy said, "We can keep it quiet. Of course, I have to take these two bodies into the undertaker."

"Well, whoever you take them to, make sure you tell them to keep their mouths shut. They might not know they are off of Asa Hale's ranch."

"I'll do the best I can."

"What about Jake Mangus? I don't want it advertised that you have him in jail."

Duffy said, "We'll take him to the jail down through the alley and in through the back door so nobody sees. I've just about got an empty jail now anyway. How long are you going to try and sit on this?"

Boyd said, "I need at least a couple days."

Sheriff Duffy said, "I'll do what I can, Boyd. Of course, Mangus is going to have to have a doctor with that leg being good and broken."

"Well, ask the doc to keep it quiet."

"You're not coming back into town with us?"

"No, I was heading out to talk to Mr. Cameron about his fence. I might as well go on, but I'll see you in your office this afternoon."

Boyd actually did not go far enough to see Del Cameron. He just went far enough to see that work was continuing on the fence. He calculated that they had close to two and a half miles up, and with another day it should be three, and in another day perhaps four. That should make a tempting target for the people involved, Boyd thought.

He turned his horse and headed back toward town. As he rode, he reached into his saddlebag and brought out a greasy paper sack. It was full of biscuits stuffed with ham made up by the hotel dining room to carry along with him. The biscuits with the ham made him think of Martha and he wondered how she was doing. He missed her a great deal, much more than he had expected, but there was still nothing he could do about it.

As he rode, his mind turned to Nora Harris. He had been a little surprised at his sudden remarks to her the day he visited her house. He had not intended to make mention of her bruises or the fact that her husband was beating her. It was an uncommon display of minding someone else's business, very unusual for him. It had popped out of him because of Hannah and the fact that she had been mistreated by men—if you called burning her to death mistreating. He couldn't think of any other reason that he would have felt inclined to intrude into Nora's privacy, but he was glad that he had. It had seemed to make an impression on her. She had come out of the bedroom to hear him say that she could come to him in Syracuse and that he would help her. There had been a lot of things he would have liked to tell her that day that would have eased her torment, but he couldn't very well have done that, not with the circumstances being what they were.

It surprised him that he could think of Hannah without the deep gouging fingers of pain spreading all through his chest. It still hurt when he put his mind on her, but now, completely sober, he could call her name to mind, call her face up before him, and think of their past life together without feeling an inability to withstand the deep hurt that had flung him into the whiskey—so deep that he had wanted to drown himself.

He didn't much think that Nora would leave James Harris and run to him in Syracuse. She was too young, too afraid of her husband, too afraid of what people might think. But she was more trapped than she knew if she couldn't get away and had no way to reach her folks or anyone that could help her. For the time being, he had some very important fish to fry and he was anxious to get on with the job. He intended, as soon as he got back to town, to promote Gates Hood to the rank of sergeant, the same rank that Jake had held. That at least would put him in a position of authority over the other two agents.

That evening after taking supper alone at a downtown cafe, Boyd went to the sheriff's house and had a quiet visit with him over a bottle of whiskey in the living room. His wife was a nice, motherly sort who brought them coffee with the observation that it would keep them from looking like a couple of drunkards and then left them to their conversation. They talked about an hour. Boyd explained the details of his plan to the sheriff. When he was through, Sheriff Duffy shook his head.

He said, "Boyd, looks like to me that you are fixing to stir up a hornet's nest. I think that me and my deputy should be there."

Boyd shook his head. "No, Sheriff, I want you on the scene when it's all over with. If you come on the scene before then, it won't be the Association doing its job, it will be the law doing its job, and there might be some questions over whether there were any laws broken. I'd rather not have you there."

The sheriff looked at Boyd hard for a moment. "You know, Mr. McMasters, you have come in and in a few days, you have got me to where I am looking the other way about the spirit of the law."

Boyd said, "Sheriff, I'm talking about the spirit of justice, and the spirit of the law hasn't been able to do anything about the situation that has existed here for almost two years because no real laws that you could see were ever broken in your presence, and they won't be this time either. You've got to let me play this hand out the way I see it."

The sheriff shrugged. "Well, what the hell choice do I have? You are, after all, a private citizen. You are in the employ of certain people in this area and you are acting in that position and that in itself is not against the law. If what happens is what I think is going to happen, there are going to be some laws broken, but if I ain't there to see it, then all I can do is go by the evidence on the ground."

Boyd said, "I can assure you that the evidence on the ground is going to point to the right people."

The sheriff raised his glass. "We better drink to that."

Boyd said "Luck," and knocked his drink back as befits the toast. The sheriff did likewise. "Well, tomorrow morning being Saturday," Boyd explained, "I figure to be at the jail and we'll get that message written by our good friend Jake Mangus and get it sent out to the proper people."

The sheriff shook his head. "Sunday morning. Somehow that don't seem right."

Boyd said, "The business ought to be over in plenty of time for you to teach your Sunday School class, Sheriff."

The sheriff looked toward the kitchen where he could hear his wife rattling the dishes. He said, "Oh, yes. I'd have to be back by then or I'd be in big trouble."

Boyd stood up to go. "Your prisoner in adequate pain, I trust?"

The sheriff said, "Well, the doc has him splintered up. He gave him a little laudanum, but I think he's still hurting enough to suit you." He shook his head. "You ain't exactly overburdened with sympathy, are you, Boyd?"

Boyd said flatly, "Not for the likes of him. If I didn't need the sonofabitch, I'd have killed him out on that prairie."

"You still planning on charging him?"

"Hell, yes. Attempted murder."

"Well, then the state prison is going to get a cripple because the doc doesn't think that leg is going to knit straight.''

"Well, that's fitting. A crooked man ought to have a crooked leg.''

At first Jake Mangus balked at writing the message Boyd had laid out for him, but under threat of having the laudanum taken away from him, and after Boyd's very real threat to take him out on the prairie and dump him, he finally complied. He tried to bargain for whiskey and better food, but it did no good.

The sheriff and his deputy then left Boyd with Mangus in the back cell. As the sheriff left he said, "You do whatever you want to back there. I'd just as soon not know.''

Those words convinced Jake Mangus more than ever that his best bet of remaining even as he was to cooperate with Boyd.

Boyd had brought back a small table and a piece of paper and a pencil. Now he said, "Write exactly what I tell you.''

Mangus took up the pencil with a sour look.

Boyd said, "Write, 'Important you rip up Cameron's drift fence early Sunday morning before dawn. That man I've told you about has been taken care of. I am going to stay in town until Sunday.' "

Mangus said when he was through, "Is that all?''

Boyd said, "Sign it J. The initial J. Sign it like you'd make a capital J.''

When he was through, Boyd took the message, folded it, put it into an envelope the sheriff had given him, and had Jake scrawl the name of Asa Hale across the front. He had to tell him how to spell it.

"That's a hell of a thing, Jake. You're going to prison because of a man you've worked with, and cheated with, and stole with, and you can't even spell his name.''

Jake Mangus looked away. He said, "That's all right,

mister. I'm in here with my leg in a splint and you're having it your way right now, but someday you'll get yours."

Boyd gave him a smile with no humor in it. "Jake, I've already had mine. There ain't nothing that you or anybody else can do to me that will ever hurt me more than I've already been hurt, but that wouldn't be of any interest to you." Boyd turned, walked out of the cell, and slammed the iron door behind him. He could hear Jake throwing curses, but that didn't bother him.

In the office, he waved the envelope at Sheriff Duffy. He said, "Now all I have to do is see that this gets delivered."

The sheriff came around the desk and looked at the envelope. "That's going to work?"

Boyd said, "Don't see why not."

"How did you leave our prisoner?"

Boyd shrugged. "I didn't inquire. I do know one thing. The sonofabitch can't spell worth a lick."

The sheriff laughed and shook his head. "I can't figure you, Mr. McMasters. You look like you ought to be singing in the choir, but then you open that mouth of yours and out of it comes cold steel. Someday I'd like to know your full background."

Boyd fixed him with an eye. "Would you, Sheriff?"

The sheriff faltered and looked at the floor. "Maybe not. Maybe you're right; maybe ignorance is bliss. I just wish, as my wife said after you left the other night, that you could be more at peace with yourself. She said she had never seen a man that was struggling inside as hard as you are."

Boyd said, "Thank your missus very much for her concern about me. I'm all right. I'm a whole hell of a lot better off than I was. I like the work I do, it's good work, and I have an appetite for it."

The sheriff said, "Well, we'll do our part when the time comes. I hope everything works out as you hope."

To Boyd, the best way to get the message delivered was the easiest. He went around to the livery stable, found a youngster of fourteen or fifteen years of age, and asked him if he would like to make five dollars. Of course such a sum instantly got the young man's attention. He was not as enthused, however, when he found where the message was to go.

Boyd said, "You're not afraid of Asa Hale, are you?"

The youngster said, "Well, it ain't so much being afraid of Mr. Hale, sir, but it's the whole general bunch out there that's got a bad habit of shooting at folks that ain't supposed to be on their land."

"Well, tie a strip of white cloth to your saddlehorn. That ought to keep them curious enough to not shoot you on sight. Do you want to earn that five dollars or not?"

"Yes, sir. Who shall I say it come from?"

"Just say Jake. That'll tell them enough."

"Yes, sir. I'm willing to do it. Do you need it done right now?"

"Right now. It's a good two hours' ride out there. I want to find you back here in five hours."

"Yes, sir. I'm on my way."

With that, Boyd went back to his hotel room. It was closing in on noon. He had a couple of drinks of whiskey and then went down to the hotel dining room. He found Gates Hood there, but the other two agents were not in evidence. Gates was still shocked about being promoted to sergeant. It meant a raise in pay to seventy-five dollars a month and a raise in per diem to four dollars a day. It was a sizeable increase to the young man. He still couldn't get over it.

Gates had said, "But Captain McMasters, I'm so damn young. Those other two are older than me."

Boyd had said, "I ain't going by age, Gates. Take the job if you want it. If not, tell me."

Gates had said, "Oh, I'll take it. I'll take it."

Now he looked up gladly as Boyd walked in and sat down at the same table. The waiter came over, and Boyd ordered a steak with a potato and some vegetables.

While they were eating, Boyd told Gates that he wanted all three of the men in his room by four o'clock that afternoon. He said, "You can find them, can't you?"

Gates said, "I can nearly lay my hands on them right now. They're in that cheap cafe a few doors down."

Boyd said, "You just be sure that they are in my room at four o'clock. That's your job, Sergeant."

Gates glowed under the title. "We got doings fixing to happen?"

"I'll tell you about it then."

Boyd looked at Gates's innocent face and wondered what he would think if he knew that his old boss, Jake Mangus, was lying down in the jail cell with his leg broken in three places and an ear shot off. It almost made him want to laugh out loud at the expression he knew it would bring to Gates's face, but unfortunately, the fewer people that knew, the better it was. There were very few people at that moment that he trusted.

He spent the early part of the afternoon resting and taking catnaps. It was going to be a long night and maybe even a longer day on Sunday. He wanted to build up as much stamina as he could. He was even sleeping when the knock came at four o'clock. He sat up on the bed, yawning and rubbing his eyes. His gunbelt was lying on the bed beside him. He pulled it closer before swinging around to put his feet on the floor. He called out, "Come in!"

Gates came in first, followed by Bob Sweeney and then Earl White.

Earl White started to take a chair but Boyd stopped him. He said, "There's no need for you gentlemen to get comfortable. I just have one quick message to pass on to you. I want you to get to your rooms, get to your beds, and get what sleep you can. We are riding out of here tonight at midnight, so make sure your mounts are ready. Take along enough ammunition for your rifles and your side arms.''

Earl White said, ''What in hell are you talking about?''

Boyd said patiently, ''Earl, you have it wrong. It's what in hell are you talking about, Captain McMasters.''

White gave him a sullen look. He said sarcastically, ''All right, Mr. Captain McMasters. What in hell are you talking about?''

''I'm talking about you following orders. That's all you need to know.''

White said, ''Well, I damn well need to know if I'm going to be in a gunfight.''

''I don't know that there's any place in your contract that says you are to be notified a certain amount of time in advance before a gunfight. Why? Are you afraid?''

''Hell, no, I'm not afraid, but I do like to know what I am getting into.''

''How come you're the only one asking that question?''

''So it will be a gunfight.''

Boyd said, ''I didn't say it would be a gunfight. I said to go get some rest and see to your mounts and your weapons and your ammunition. We are riding out of here at midnight. Be at the hotel livery stable at midnight or you're fired. Now, is that clear enough for you, Mr. White?''

Earl White gave him a sullen look. ''Yeah, I reckon, though I would like to know a little more about it.''

''All you need to know is that you are going to be in the company of Sergeant Gates Hood from this moment until we leave. Do you understand that? Did you understand that, Gates? I want you and Mr. White and Mr. Sweeney to be in each other's company until you get to the livery stables at midnight. Is that clear?''

Gates said, ''Yes, sir.''

''And I don't want you talking to anyone. Is that clear?''

''Yes, sir.''

''Do the other two of you understand?''

Bob Sweeney said, ''Yeah, I reckon, Captain. If them's the orders, them's the orders.''

Boyd's eyes swung to Earl White, waiting.

Finally, Earl White said grudgingly, ''Whatever you say, Captain.''

''Then get on out of here and let me get some rest. We're going to be up all night. We're going to be guarding a fence, Mr. White, if that satisfies your mind any.''

Earl White's eyes swiveled quickly to Boyd's. ''That new fence Del Cameron's stringing?''

Boyd shook his head. ''No. Haven't you noticed those new fences that Jim Harris is stringing up on the southeastern side of his property?''

Earl White looked uncertain. ''What are we going to be guarding them for?''

''Because I say so. Now get out of here.''

They finally left, with Gates in his new role of command virtually pushing the other two out the door in front of him. He turned and gave Boyd a semi-salute. He said, ''We'll be there, Captain McMasters, on time and they won't get out of my sight and they won't talk to nobody.''

''Fine, Sergeant Hood. You're doing good work.'' Boyd was thinking about getting up and going to supper. The time was five o'clock, and it was still good light outside. He had pulled on his boots and was about to strap on his gunbelt when there came a light knock on the door.

He yelled, ''Come in!'' The door opened partly to reveal one of the young boys that helped around the hotel toting bathwater, carrying luggage, or running errands. Boyd said, "Yeah, what do you want?"

The boy said, "Mr. McMasters. I've got a message for you, sir, here on this piece of paper."

Boyd said, "Well, bring it to me."

While the boy crossed the room, Boyd dug in his pocket for a quarter and then handed it to the young man. He took the message and noticed that it was stuck together at one end with wax.

Before the boy could leave Boyd asked, "Where did you get this?"

"A young lady gave it to me, sir."

"A young lady?"

"Yes, sir. Well, she really wasn't a young lady, just a little older than I am, but I would reckon that she would want me to call her that."

"Fine, now run on."

After the door was shut, he broke the wax seal of the folded piece of paper and read the message. It surprised him to a degree, but at the same time, it really didn't surprise him. The message said simply, "I have taken your advice and left the ranch. I am at Mrs. Oates' boardinghouse for ladies. My room is the first one at the top of the stairs. If you can come, I would appreciate your arrival as soon after dark as possible. I feel terribly alone and I am afraid of what James may do." It was signed, "Mrs. Nora Harris."

He slowly folded the note and slowly put it in his pocket. He said out loud, "Well, I'll be a sonofabitch. I didn't think she had it in her."

He left the hotel and went to the livery to check on the boy who'd taken the note out to Asa Hale. It had been delivered without incident to one of Hale's sons.

Then Boyd went thoughtfully to dinner, and his mind was so on the upcoming meeting with Nora Harris, and on top of that on the business that would take place in the early morning hours, that he was barely conscious of what he ate. He was pretty sure it was chicken and dumplings, and he was pretty sure that he declined the tapioca pudding dessert, but other than that, he wasn't much aware of the meal. When he finished, he went into the hotel saloon and had a drink of brandy, something he didn't ordinarily do. Somehow it seemed fitting under the circumstances.

He went back to his room, felt his whiskers, and decided he could use a shave. He took off his shirt and gave himself a sponge bath on his upper body, and brushed his teeth with salt and baking soda. He didn't pay much attention to his hair. It just fell where it did once he took his hat off, and he never had much idea what condition his hair would be lying in. After deliberation, he changed into one of the new linen shirts that Warren had bought him in Oklahoma City. He had no idea why, as a woman would say, he was primping for his visit. She was an extremely attractive woman.

She was also, he reminded himself, a woman who had been beaten by her husband and a woman who was coming to him for help. To take advantage of that would be the act of a man Boyd would despise, and he didn't want that man to be himself. At the same time, he couldn't help but look forward to seeing her. He had always liked the sight of a pretty woman. He didn't expect that he would ever get over that.

It was the custom in the Western states to treat boarding-houses just as you did a hotel. You didn't knock before you went into a hotel, and you didn't knock before you went into a boardinghouse. Some had strict rules about visitors and some didn't. He assumed from Nora's note that her board-inghouse allowed visitors and residents to come and go as they pleased. Nevertheless, this was one of the reasons Boyd never stayed in a boardinghouse. Once he had been locked out of one at the early hour of ten o'clock, and once he had been locked in one when he was trying to get out early at four a.m., and in both cases he'd had to wake up an irate landlady who'd made him wish he had left her in peace.

He saw no one as he opened the front door of Mrs. Oates's boardinghouse for young ladies, so he stepped into the front hall. There was a parlor off to the left and some closed double doors to the right. The staircase was ahead of him, and he climbed it and found as soon as he got to the landing that there was no question which door was hers.

He gave the door a light tap, and it was opened almost immediately. She stood there in a light blue, lightweight, off-the-shoulder frock, looking prettier than she had before. She said breathlessly, "Oh, my God. Thank heavens you've come."

He stepped across the threshold and looked around. It was a nice enough room for a boardinghouse, with a bed, a chest of drawers, and a nightstand and a galvanized tub in the corner. He said, "Have you run away, Nora?"

She answered, "Yes. He was getting drunk this morning, cursing. He always starts that way. He cusses everything that has caused him a setback, then he hits the door or something else that can't feel it, and then he starts on me. This time, I knew I couldn't take it anymore, and I remembered your kind words and how brave and how observant you were to see what I had been going through."

He put his hands on her shoulders and looked down into her upturned face. He said gently, "I'm glad you did, Nora. You don't have to be afraid of someone who is so much bigger and stronger than you hurting you all the time. That's not the way it is supposed to be."

She said, "These past three years have been awful. I don't know how many times he has hit me." Her voice almost broke, but she recovered herself. "Most of the time, he is good and hits me only in the body, so that I can cover my shame with clothes, but lately he's started hitting me in the face."

"How did you get away?"

She said despairingly, "I just fled. I was wearing my riding clothes, and I threw some frocks and some other garments and a pair of shoes into a small valise. My horse was already saddled, so I just ran. But Mr. McMasters . . ."

"Boyd," he said. "My name is Boyd to you."

Her big luminous eyes stared up at him. "I brought nothing with me. I have no money, I just have the few things I brought, and I don't know what to do. When I got to town, I thought of you. I hope you meant what you said about helping me."

He said, "Nora, you don't have to worry about anything at all. I'll help you."

Without a word, he reached into his pocket and peeled off five twenty-dollar bills. He laid them on the dresser and said, "Here, this is all I have for now. It's Saturday, and I need to get to the bank. By Monday, we'll be able to send you home. What you must not do is go out. You must stay here."

She said, biting her lip, "He'll find me. I know he'll find me, I know he will."

Boyd stepped back to her side and took her shoulders again and shook her slightly. He said, "No, Nora. He's not going to find you tonight or tomorrow or the next day. He's going to be busy. He won't come looking for you tonight and by tomorrow afternoon, I'll be back here to take care of you. Understand?"

She leaned her head against his chest. "Boyd, I don't even know you and this feels so strange. I've never done anything like this before in my life."

With her cheek pressing against his chest, he unconsciously put his arms around her. He said, into the top of her hair, so glossy and black, "Nora, unusual times call for unusual measures. Having a man who is supposed to love you beating you is an unusual time."

"But you're a stranger." She looked up at him, her eyes pleading with him to say something that would make what she was doing seem right.

"And you are a stranger to me, and yet I don't feel at all awkward holding you like this or helping you. Some people are just meant to meet. Whether it is the first time or the hundredth time, it's always the same. I feel right now like I have known you for years."

She blinked, her big eyes filled with wonder. "That's the strangest thing. I feel the same and I can't describe it. I even felt it that day at the creek when I was trying to bathe the tears out of my eyes, but I felt it for sure when you called to me that day from the hallway after I had gone back to the bedroom. It made me feel stronger, knowing I had someone here I could turn to. I'm so afraid here, Boyd. I can't tell you. We've been here four years. I married James when we came here. The first year was all right, he didn't hit me. He's not a kind man, but I knew that when I met him. My father said he was a man who would accomplish things, who would make money, and that was important to my father, so I married him. My mother said love didn't last, but money did and ambition did. Is that true?"

Boyd shook his head slowly. "It may be true for your mother and your father and maybe for James Harris, but it's not true for you and it's not true for me."

She stood there, looking up to him, her lips slightly parted. Without thinking, he bent his mouth down to hers and all of a sudden, her arms were around his neck and they were kissing passionately. He could feel her tongue exploring his. He could feel the inside of her mouth with his own tongue.

Her whole body was pressed tightly against his.

Before he knew quite how it was happening and what he was doing, he had taken his arms from around her and was unbuttoning the line of buttons that secured her dress in the front. She put her hands to her side and stepped back to give him more room to work. He could feel her eyes on his face. When he got the line of buttons undone down to her waist, she shrugged her shoulders and the dress fell to the floor in a heap. Under that, she was wearing a long camisole that followed the long contours of her body until it blossomed out to accommodate her breasts. He took it by the top and pulled it down. It was silk and it slid down her body as if he was peeling off a second skin. The sight of her breasts almost made him gasp. They were rounded and full and stood directly forward, the nipples pink with a deep rouge color. He knelt so that he could take each in his mouth one at a time. She put her arms around his neck, pulling his face to her breasts, moaning softly.

He stood up and put his mouth to hers and began walking her backward toward the bed. As they got there, her knees bent and she fell back across the bedspread. As she fell, she drew her legs up, spreading her knees.

Boyd could see the thick mound of soft black hairs that grew where her legs joined. Without pause, he buried his face in the silken area, searching for the warm wetness. The scent of her was almost overpowering. As he caressed her with his tongue, she began to pant and to heave her hips, sighing and moaning. It was a strange sensation for Boyd. Only with Hannah had he done this. It somehow made him feel guilty about Martha, which was an unusual juxtaposition of feelings.

There was no time to think of that. She had reached down and grabbed his hands and was tugging him up on the bed.

Thirteen

When he came up beside her on the bed, she stayed him with a hand on his chest. She said, her eyes big and innocent, "Please, show me what to do and help me. I haven't been with a man in a long time. I don't want to disappoint you."

He stared at her in wonder. He could not imagine that her lout of a husband could choose to beat instead of making love to her. Looking down at her, fully stretched out on the bed, he thought she was the most perfectly proportioned woman that he had ever seen. The overwhelming, almost insatiable, hunger overcame him to be inside her, to be a part of her, and it was almost more than he could stand. He knew that he would have to go slowly and gently with her. He didn't want to frighten her.

For a long time, he lay next to her after they had turned lengthwise on the bed. He kissed her on the mouth, on the ears, on the neck, on her breasts, down her stomach, on the inside of her thighs. With each kiss, her breathing rose in intensity. With each caress, she trembled and her hips moved almost involuntarily. With no coaching from him, she reached for his member with both hands and pulled so that he knew she wanted him to bring it up to her. When he slid inside her mouth, it was almost more than he could bear. For a few strokes he was able to control himself. Then he had to say, "You've got to stop, Nora. I can't take it."

Then he was over her, and gently he lowered himself onto her. She guided his member into her, and he fastened his mouth to hers and she brought her legs up to lock them around his hips.

After that, it was like a warm, hazy, slippery dream that just kept getting out of his grasp. He knew that at some point she shuddered, screamed, and bucked against him. Almost immediately, he exploded inside her, and it seemed as if they were going down a mountainside clinging to each other, bouncing and rocking and twirling through the air with great speed. Then, finally, it seemed that they rolled to rest in a very green valley. With a sigh, he slipped off her and lay on his side, barely conscious, barely able to realize what had happened.

After a moment, he raised up on his elbow. She was lying quietly, breathing through her mouth, her eyes closed, her body in repose. He leaned his head down and gave her a gentle kiss on the lips. She smiled without opening her eyes.

Boyd noticed that his jeans and one boot were still on his left leg. So frantic had the first moments been that he had never completely gotten undressed. So, rather than undressing and then dressing again, he put his right leg back into his jeans and then pulled them up and buttoned them. He sat on the side of the bed and saw his shirt on the floor. He fumbled with it until he found a cigarillo and a match. He struck the match with his thumbnail, lit the cigarillo and drew hard, and blew out a cloud of smoke.

He said, "Wow! Could I do with a drink right now. I feel like I've been run over by a herd of cattle."

She smiled and put her hand on his bare back. She said,

"Yes, but such wonderful cattle. I had forgotten how good that could feel."

He turned to look at her. "Nora, I find it hard to believe that your husband could resist you."

She pulled a face and said, "You'd have to know James. At first he made me think he was interested, but I don't think James is really interested in that sort of thing at all."

Boyd said, making a joke, "He doesn't like men, does he?"

"I certainly hope not." She shook her head. "I just think James enjoys being cruel and making money more than anything else. I don't think he understands about love or tender feelings." She looked at Boyd. "It would be very difficult for me to explain James to a man such as yourself because you are so unalike."

Boyd said, "Yes, we're a great deal different. If I had you around the house, I'd never get anything done."

She smiled. "That's the sweetest thing that anyone's said to me for a long time."

After a while, he got up and finished dressing. He sat in the chair, smoking. Now that the passion had passed, Nora had become self-conscious about her nakedness. She'd pulled the bedspread over until she was almost covered. Only one full exquisite breast was exposed. Boyd repeated what he had said earlier about her figure.

It did not bring a pleased look to her face. She said, "That's all well and good for now, Boyd, but what am I to do? I have left James and if I go back, I can expect punishment double what I've gotten before. Now that I've had time to think, I don't know what I will say to my father and mother if I go back to them." She stopped, letting the next thought go unsaid.

Boyd said, "But Nora, they're your parents. If you tell them what's happened, they'll understand."

Nora shook her head sadly. "No, they won't. My mother's favorite expression is you've made your bed, now lie in it. They won't understand why I couldn't be a good wife to James. They will think he hit me because I wasn't a good wife to him, but Boyd, I did everything in my power to please the man, but he didn't care about that. The only thing he was interested in was making money with those wretched cattle of his. He was always up to some scheme, some plan, and if I interrupted him when he was brooding and thinking, he would just backhand me across the face as if I were a piece of furniture in his way."

Boyd said, "I think maybe his scheming days are over with. I think Mr. Jim Harris and I are going to have to have a talk."

She gave him a frightened look. "Oh, please don't, Boyd. I tell you, the man will kill you, he's such a brute."

Boyd got up and crossed the room to the side of the bed. He took her hand and patted it. "Nora, I don't want you to worry. All you have to do is be patient for a few hours and then we'll figure something out. If you don't want to go home to your parents, then you don't have to go home to them."

She said, "If I don't, then how will I make my way? I have no money. I have nothing I can do."

He said, "You don't have any skills like sewing or doing office work that I've seen girls do?"

She shook her head slowly. "No, nothing."

He patted her hand again. "Don't you worry about it. I have a feeling that you are going to find yourself pretty well fixed when this is all over. Have you eaten supper, by the way?"

She said, "We had supper at the regular time downstairs at six. I still haven't explained to Mrs. Oates what I am doing here and I still haven't paid her."

Boyd nodded at the money on top of the bureau. "You can pay her now."

She seemed to shrink. "I hate for you to leave that money. It makes me feel, well, funny. You know?"

He laughed. "You mean because of what happened? What we did?"

"Yes."

"I put the money there first, with no thought other than helping a friend out. Aren't we friends?"

She laughed in embarrassment. "Right now, you're the dearest and only friend I've got."

Boyd said, "Then it's just money between friends, nothing else."

She pulled his hand to her mouth and kissed it, then said, "You are the sweetest man."

"Maybe it just seems that way because you've been with Mr. James Harris too long. I'm really not, you know."

"I don't believe it."

"Well, never mind that. For the time being, you're fixed. When I get this business tended to tonight, we'll see about the long-term future. But don't worry, you won't have to go back to James Harris and you don't have to go back to your parents if you don't want to. My brother runs a company in Oklahoma City that I work for."

"Yes," she said. "The Cattleman's Association. It's strange. James is a member, yet he hates you. The day you came, he cursed you all night long. I don't understand why. He said you were a busybody."

Boyd laughed. "I would imagine that he would say that."

He stayed on with her until almost eleven o'clock, talking about this and that. He was amused when she asked him, shyly, to turn his head so that she could get up and get dressed. He thought it especially funny since he still had the taste of her in his mouth, but he did as she asked.

When he parted from her at eleven, he kissed her several times tenderly, and once again urged her not to worry. "It will all come right. Trust me."

"For some reason, I do." She laughed. "Isn't that strange? I've only actually seen you twice before and now I'm trusting you with my life."

"Other folks have done that on far less acquaintance."

She gave him a look. "You say the strangest things."

"So I've been told."

He kissed her once again, and then left for his hotel room to get ready for the night's work.

When Gates Hood knocked at his door it was ten minutes until midnight. Boyd took a last moment to make sure all his pockets were loaded with as many carbine and pistol cartridges as they could carry. He slung his saddlebags, now loaded only with cartridges for his big rifle and a bottle of whiskey, over his shoulders. He had his six-inch-barrel revolver in the holster and the nine-inch-barrel stuck in his belt. He went toward the door, carrying his carbine in his left hand and his big rifle in his right.

He said to Gates on the other side of the door, "Open it up, my hands are full."

Gates swung the door open and said, "Everybody's ready down at the stables, Captain. Boy, you look loaded for bear."

Boyd said with a wink, "That's because I *am* loaded for bear. I'll tell you a secret about life. Don't ever starve with a bear because the bear starves last, if you take my meaning?"

Gates grinned shyly. "Well, yes, sir. I don't know what it means, but it sounds mighty pert."

As they walked out of the hotel Boyd asked, "Sergeant, is Earl White still bitching?"

"Yes, sir, he is. He's terribly eat up to know what we'll be doing."

Boyd said, "I assume you told him that we would be guarding fence?"

"Yes, sir, just like you did."

"Gates, have Sweeney and White asked many questions about Jake Mangus?"

"Well, surprisingly enough, it was Bob Sweeney who did most of the asking. White just said casually that he heard that Jake got fired and didn't say anything more about it. Took me by surprise. I figured that being the way he was, he would have to know every small detail of the business."

Boyd said, "Yeah, but it doesn't surprise me. It's just about what I figured."

Boyd had considered filling Gates in on the situation, but a natural suspicion had kept him from doing so. Gates didn't even know about the attack that had been made on him by Jake and the other two riders. He also didn't know, unless he had somehow found out and hadn't mentioned it, that Jake was lying wounded in the jail. But there really hadn't been any reason to tell Gates. It was his opinion that if a man didn't need to know about something, and could do his work just as well without knowing, then there was no use burdening him with that extra information.

They went to the livery stables behind the hotel. Earl White stepped forward out of the shadows into the light cast by the lantern of the stable keeper. He said, "Mr. Mc-Masters, I hope to hell there's a damn good reason for this."

Boyd was busy ramming his big gun home in its special boot and tying on his saddlebags. He said, "What do you care, White? The pay's the same, isn't it?"

"I just would like to know what I'm getting into."

"You're getting into your saddle if you want to keep

working for the Association. If you don't, then uncinch your horse.''

White said, "Ain't no need for you to take it like that. I swear, you're one of the touchiest men that I reckon I ever met.''

"And I'm also your boss. Now shut your damned mouth, White. I'm getting sick of you.''

White went off to see about his horse.

Boyd asked Gates, "Are we ready?''

"Yes, sir.''

Boyd swung into his saddle. He was taking his roan because he figured there would be fireworks before the night was out.

"All right, everybody mount up and let's go.'' He rode out through the stable door into the main street and then turned north. Gates rode up on his left, the other two falling in behind.

Boyd said, "Did anybody think to bring any grub?''

Gates said, "I brought some cheese and some ham and some of them saltine crackers. I got a pretty good mess of them.''

Boyd said, "You'll do well, young man. That kind of thinking will endear you to your commander again and again. We better start picking up the pace; we've got a pretty good way to go.''

One by one, the group nudged their horses into a slow lope as they left the outskirts of Syracuse behind.

Fourteen

Boyd headed his group north for longer than would have been necessary had he been taking a direct route to his destination. He wanted to stay as far to the east of Asa Hale's place as possible. Only when the line of trees that designated the river came into view did he begin to bear toward the west. He led them across the river to the north, and then turned due west down the course of the Arkansas River. They were walking their horses now, and he had given orders as they neared the river that there was to be no more talking, no more smoking, and no more noises of any kind. That had caused some murmured comments, which he'd quieted with a sharp "Shut up!"

It was a clear, moonlit night. They rode west. After half an hour, Boyd could feel that they were coming opposite the Hale grazing range. They were protected from view on that side by the rows of trees lining the river. They continued on until, leaning down and peering between trunks, Boyd was able to see the end of the fence that Del Cameron's crew had been building. There were piles of fence posts and coils of wire left where they had knocked off on Saturday afternoon. They went on for another mile, and he stopped them and drew them close.

Boyd said, "We're going to hunt a crossing where we can wade across, and then we're going to tie our horses on this side and walk over. Take all your ammunition and your guns with you. We're going to take positions just inside the tree line on the south side of the river."

Earl White started to open his mouth. He said, "Now, just a—"

Surprisingly, it was Gates who said sharply, "Damnit, Earl. You heard the captain. Shut your mouth and do like you're told."

With the good light of the full moon, it only took a few moments to find an easy crossing in the shallow river, which in some places was no more than ten yards across. In the dry season, it resembled more of a creek than a river, but during the rains of the fall, it could become a fearsome factor.

They tied their horses and then splashed through the water, which came no higher than their knees. They made their way to the far side of the riverbank. The trees were five and six and seven deep. Boyd fanned them out at five-yard intervals, using the southernmost trees as protection. The horses would be safe on the north side of the river from any flying lead if such was to be the case.

Boyd had placed himself at the eastern end of the line with Earl White next, then after him Bob Sweeney, and with Gates Hood anchoring the western end. He had given them strict instructions that if there was to be any shooting, he would be the one to fire the first shot.

He said, looking straight at Earl White, "If anybody makes any noise or makes any effort to interfere with this plan that I have gone through considerable effort to arrange, then they will have to answer to me and it won't just be a matter of their job.''

They were in position and there was nothing to do but wait. Looking up at the low point in the sky that the moon now held, Boyd judged it to be going on near four o'clock in the morning. He got out his watch, but it was impossible to see in the dark under the trees. It didn't make any difference what time it was. If they came, they would come when they came and not before.

Of course, now was the time for doubt, and now was the time for things unforeseen and undone and left undone. Now was the time for uncertainty. Now was the time for anxiety and for worry. Boyd was not particularly good at such matters. He preferred a situation ready at hand, something that could be got at and could be handled with swiftness, with decisiveness, and with power. He was not good at waiting. He was not good at matters that he could not take by the throat. He recognized that weakness in himself, and did what he could to compensate for it by examining and reexamining his every motivation and mood and movement and thought.

Boyd felt sure that he had a clean picture of what had caused the troubles and why and where they had begun. He knew he could end them if he could lure his enemy into a trap. The question was, had he baited the trap sufficiently? Had he done everything possible to put the plan in motion? Well, he thought, in two hours he would know for certain. There was nothing to do now but wait.

He felt beside him as he lay behind the tree. His saddle-bags were unbuckled, both flaps open, the cartridges ready to hand. His carbine was loaded and ready to hand, and so were both of his revolvers. Naturally, since he couldn't smoke, he wanted a smoke more than anything he had ever wanted in his life. As partial satisfaction, he got out the bottle of whiskey and took a pull. It did not satisfy as a smoke would have, which seemed strange considering it hadn't been much over three weeks when nothing but a drink of whiskey would satisfy. It was odd how one's life changed.

He thought of Martha and he thought of Nora, comparing them. There really was no comparison, and he hoped to be able to tell Martha that someday, just how special she was. But there was the night's work to be done before he told anyone anything.

He glanced impatiently south in the direction of the Hale ranch. He wished they would come on and get it over with. He didn't even know what kind of odds he would be facing. They could come with forty men or four, he had no idea. They clearly weren't afraid of Del Cameron's hands, but he knew one thing. When they came, the old man would be along. He'd gotten that much from Jake Mangus. Asa Hale hated Del Cameron and everything that he was that Hale wasn't. The drift fence, as Boyd had expected, had been an insult that Hale had taken personally because it was directed to fence him, and him alone, off.

In talking with Jake Mangus, Boyd had learned that Hale had wanted to tear the fence down almost as soon as the construction had began. He had wanted to go out by himself and rip it up with his bare hands. Hale's hate was so deep, Jake had told him, that it was all he, Mangus, could do to keep the old man from killing Cameron or from having Cameron killed. It was only the prospect of the profits in the future that had stayed his hand.

So there was a good chance that they would come in force, perhaps as many as ten of them. It had been Boyd's experience that people who perpetrated their dark deeds by night felt safer in numbers. The bigger the sin, the more welcome the crowd.

He laid his big gun out in front of him and sighted through the telescopic sight. It didn't work quite as well at night, although it worked better than firing over iron sights, but in the false dawn he was able to distinguish the contours of the prairie. If they were coming, it should be soon.

The thought had no more than crossed his mind when it seemed that he could see a cluster of figures and half-figures bobbing up and down over the prairie some few miles distant. They appeared to be coming at a lope. Boyd watched, waiting, as they crossed one shallow rise after another. Within five or six minutes, they were close enough that he could definitely tell that it was a body of horsemen, and not just cattle suddenly spooked by something and all running in the same direction. Five minutes later, they were within a mile and individual figures were beginning to stand out. He tried to get a count, but the best he could guess was that there were between eighteen and twenty.

As they closed the distance toward the fence, they began to gallop their horses. It was clear they planned to make a fast job of it and get out. Throw a rope on one end of the fence, drag it, and keep on roping it and dragging it, stripping it all the way back to the first post. At least, that's what Boyd figured they had planned.

He lifted the big rifle, propping the barrel up on his left elbow, and sighted on a figure in the middle, a big burly figure that he took to be one of the sons that he had met. He was going to make a good target.

Just then, to his immediate right, he heard Earl White saying in a strange whisper, "My God, McMasters, look at 'em. There's a hell of a bunch of 'em. We've gotta get out of here."

Boyd said harshly in a low voice, "Shut up, White. Get ready. I'm going to fire."

Boyd calculated that they were about a half mile off when he squeezed off the first shot. The booming echo had barely begun to reverberate when the burly man in the center of the pack went flipping out of the saddle, rising higher than the head of his horse with the impact of the bullet. In an instant, Boyd had thrown back the breech and rammed in another shell. He was sighting in on another figure to the left of the man he'd just shot when he suddenly heard Earl White say, "To hell with him, I'm getting out of here. Come on, Bob, let's run for it. There's too many of them. McMasters is going to get us all killed."

Boyd already had his second target dead in his sights. He pulled the trigger, squeezing the rifle lovingly as he did. As the gun thundered in his hands, he saw his target suddenly go out of his saddle as if plucked by a giant hand, but he had no time to savor the kill. He could hear splashing in the water behind him. In one swift motion he wheeled, drawing his revolver as he did, caught Earl White a third of the way across the river, and fired, intentionally hitting him in the leg. White screamed, threw up his hands, and fell into the water.

Boyd said, "Sweeney! Go out and disarm White and drag him back to the bank and watch him. He's under arrest. Knock him out if you have to."

He didn't wait to see if his order had been obeyed. Instead, he turned quickly back to his long rifle, catching the marauders in the telescopic sight. He could see that they were in a state of confusion. They had slowed to almost a walk. First one group would dart forward, and then another group would dart to the side.

Boyd could see a man in the middle—although it was too far for Boyd to be able to distinguish who it was—raise his arm. For a moment, they stopped. Down at the end of the line, Gates was firing his carbine. It was a futile gesture, but Boyd could see that the band of men were calculating that only one gun was firing at them and that it was ineffective. In an instant, the man with the raised arm was shouting something, the words drifting barely and unrecognizably to Boyd's ears. Then the band started forward, trotting at first and then in a full gallop.

Boyd instantly slid back the breech and slapped a fresh cartridge in. He aimed at the men on his left flank. He fired and, without waiting to see the evidence of his shot, threw open the breech and slapped in another cartridge and slid it home, firing almost as soon as he could bring his sight to rest on the line of men. He fired four shots like that, mechanically, deadly, rapidly. Each time the big rifle exploded, either a man came out of the saddle or a horse and rider went down. Now they appeared uncertain. They could see that two guns were shooting at them. Bob Sweeney was still busy with Earl White. He hadn't joined the fight.

Boyd fired the big gun three more times as rapidly as he could. Some confusion was still appearing among the diminished gang of marauders, but at about four hundred yards, they picked their pace up again and began charging toward the river.

Now Boyd could hear both Gates and Bob Sweeney firing.

At about three hundred yards, he fired the last shot from the big rifle, dropped it, jerked up his carbine, and fired off six shots as quickly as he could squeeze the trigger. It appeared to him that the Hale gang was down to less than ten men, but he couldn't be sure. Boyd dug in his pocket for cartridges for his carbine. As rapidly as he could, he loaded six into the breech. He jumped up from where he was kneeling and raced forward the fifty or sixty yards to the fence line. It brought him that much closer to the charging horsemen. Behind the dubious cover of a small fence post, he lay on his belly and carefully fired, picking off targets one by one as the bandits approached. At one hundred yards, his carbine was empty and five men were still coming on.

Boyd was desperately trying to reload his small rifle when

he became aware that Gates had come down to the fence line and was firing into the bunch. He saw Gates drop a man, and then a horse went down. The rest were within fifty yards. Boyd dropped his rifle, went under the lower strand of fencing, and charged the men on foot with a revolver in each hand. He stopped with some little distance between them and knelt down, firing both of his big revolvers alternately.

In the next instant, there were no mounted men left. The only sight before him was a few horses running loose and the cries of wounded men hidden by the high grass. Realizing his danger from men who might be playing possum in the high grass, Boyd turned and yelled for Gates and Sweeney to retreat, although Sweeney had only come out about ten yards from the tree line. Running back to the fence line, Boyd felt a bullet singing over his head. He ducked under the fence, grabbed his carbine, and ran a few more yards before throwing himself to the ground.

The terrain sloped down toward the river, so there was some cover in the contour of the land and he lay there, slowly loading his carbine, waiting for the men in the grass to show themselves. In the east, he could see a few wispy pink clouds as the sun began to nudge against the horizon. He watched the grass carefully, seeing it move here and there as he reloaded both of his revolvers.

Boyd had no intention of charging the concealed men when all he had to do was to wait them out. The ground definitely was in his favor, since he was on the crest of the slope toward the river and the other men were fifty or sixty yards away on flat ground. They might be hidden in the weeds, but pretty soon, the sun would get up and they would have to do something. He knew also from the cries for help that they had wounded. He didn't know if the rest would care or not, but he had no intention of exposing himself or his men to any harm.

Boyd sighted down his carbine, watching the grass. He saw a suspicious movement to his left and he fired, aiming about six inches off the ground. On the heels of the shot, there was a loud cry and a man suddenly rose out of the grass, his hand on his shoulder, and fell backward.

Boyd yelled to Gates, who was in a situation similar to his. "They're in the grass! If you see grass moving, fire into it!"

Gates yelled back. "I got you, Captain!"

A moment later, there came a high-pitched yell. A man's voice said, "Who the hell are you? What do you mean, shooting us up like this? Who are you?"

Boyd motioned for Sweeney and Gates to be quiet, and he himself gave no answer.

Another ten minutes passed. He saw a horse wandering closer to the group on his left. Then he saw the grass waving as a man crawled through it toward the horse. Boyd fired twice in rapid succession, firing at the movement. He heard a muffled groan and then silence. The grass didn't move again.

Again came a call. "Who are you? Who are you sonsof-bitches? Why are you shooting us up?"

The sun was up and it was clear daylight. He could see the littered field of battle. He could clearly see, even in the high grass, because there was a rise behind where the men now were that sloped up some sixty or seventy yards, that there were bodies lying on that patch of ground. He counted eight, maybe nine, for certain. He doubted there were over four or five of the original gang of marauders left.

Boyd decided that it was time to act. He said, "Asa Hale. Asa Hale."

There was no answer.

He raised his voice louder. "Asa Hale. I know you're there, Hale. This is Boyd McMasters of the Cattleman's Protection Association. You're under arrest. You'd better give yourselves up.''

Someone said distinctly, "Go to hell, you bastard."

Boyd immediately fired at the voice. He heard a high shriek.

Someone yelled, "Damn you, you bastard. You're supposed to be dead, McMasters. How come you ain't dead?"

Boyd yelled back, "If anyone is dead, it's your friend Jake Mangus. You better give up, Hale. The sheriff will be here within the hour. You've got wounded and unless you want them to die, you better give yourselves up."

"You say the sheriff is coming?"

"That's correct."

"Then he'll hang you for murder."

"If anybody gets hung, Hale, it'll be you. I know everything about you, so you might as well give up now. You can hang just as quick for cattle theft as you can for murder, and you may hang for both if you don't give up. If you help me now, it might go easier on you."

"Don't tell him nothing, Pa."

Boyd yelled back, "Tell that snot-nosed kid of yours to shut his mouth because the next time he says anything, I'm going to put a bullet in him." .

There was silence on the other side of the fence. Listening hard, Boyd could hear whispered conversations going on among several men.

Hale shouted back. "Hey, you, McMasters."

"What?"

"What'll you take to get on out of here and forget all about this? I'm hurt bad enough as it is and you've killed damned near half of my crew."

"You offering me money, Hale?"

"I asked what it would take to get you on out of here and leave us alone."

"Hale, I wouldn't turn my back on you if I was standing behind a barn."

"You have my word. We won't trouble you no more. How about letting us get on back home and letting us take care of our own."

"I'm content to wait until the sheriff gets here and we'll let him sort it out. If you don't want to do that, then you can stand up, those that can, and walk toward us with your hands in the air."

The same young voice as before yelled out, "You go to hell!"

The "hell" was barely out of his mouth before Boyd fired in the direction of the word. He was rewarded with a loud yell and then a string of curses.

Boyd told Bob Sweeney to go back to the river and bring their canteens forward. He was content to wait for the sun and the prospect of the sheriff to do his work. Another half hour passed, and suddenly he heard Gates's rifle fire and saw a man half lift out of the grass. Then a plaintive voice cried, "Hell, I was already hit once. There wasn't no call for that."

It seemed to be the call for a general babble of voices. Somewhere a voice yelled, "Asa, I've got to have some water. I'm down to licking the dew off the grass."

Another voice said, "Pa, I'm hit. I can't lay here, I'm bleeding."

A voice called, "Anybody got a canteen? For God's sake, my tongue is sticking to the top of my mouth."

Boyd knew that a gunfight was hard work. He didn't know why that was, but it just seemed to drain the juices from a man, and then to lie there, perhaps wounded and without water, had to be torture.

Boyd yelled out, "Hale, we've got water over here and we've got food and we also have the sheriff coming. We've got you pinned down. If you stick so much as a little finger above that grass we'll take it off. You're out of options, Hale. There ain't no choices left. I'm arresting you and when the sheriff gets here, it'll be official. You might as well surrender now and maybe some of your wounded can be saved. If you go on like this, the doctor's going to be cutting off arms and legs because those shells of mine tear a body plumb up.''

A voice said, ''He ain't kidding about that.''

Boyd said, ''Now, I've heard all the talk I intend to listen to. We'll start firing again if you don't come out of there in the next ten minutes and I am opening my watch right now.''

Asa Hale said, ''Hold on there, McMasters. I want to talk to Jake. Where is he?''

Boyd lied. ''Jake's dead. But he signed a statement before he died. There's plenty of testimony against you, Hale.''

''It's lies, all lies. Jake Mangus never told the truth in his life.''

''You got seven minutes left. We know where you are and we have enough ammunition to cover the area.''

It was about eight o'clock, and while he listened to the groans and the moans of the wounded men some seventy or eighty yards away, Boyd sipped at his canteen and looked again at his watch. He was about to announce two more minutes when he saw, back toward town off to his left, some small figures in the distance. One of them appeared to be driving a buckboard or a wagon. It was time for the sheriff to arrive, but he wanted a moment or two alone with Asa Hale, if possible, before Sheriff Duffy arrived and officially took charge. He could handle matters in a manner that the sheriff might not approve of.

He called out, ''You've got two minutes before we start shooting.''

He heard a whispered consultation and then Asa Hale yelled, ''All right, damnit, we're coming out! But you sonofabitches better not shoot. You ain't law, I don't trust you, you work for the rich man.''

"Then how come you haven't joined the Association, Asa? You're rich as hell. You've stolen enough of the other man's cattle, you ought to be rich. If you ain't, it's your own fault.''

"Never mind your sermonizing, Mr. High-and-Mighty McMasters. Now, we're coming out and you keep them guns quiet.''

"If I see a weapon, we'll shoot. Come out with your hands up and come straight ahead.''

"What about the wounded? There's some in here that can't walk.''

Boyd said, "The sheriff will be along pretty soon with the buckboard and he can load them up.''

"Maybe we should just wait for the sheriff.''

Another voice cried out, "For God's sake, Pa. I've got to have some water and I'm still bleeding.''

"All right, damnit, we's a comin'.''

Boyd called out, "Get up now.''

One by one, they stood up and started slowly toward him. Two of them were limping badly, but there were five able to walk all told.

Boyd got up slowly, motioning for Bob Sweeney and Gates to do the same. He ducked under the fence line and moved forward to meet the men as they came. He was holding just his carbine in his hand as they came.

He said to Asa Hale as he came close, "Walk straight toward that fence. Get over there and each one of you get a hold of a fence post and don't let go.''

Hale said, "Go to hell.''

Boyd could see that Asa Hale was not a very big man now that he was viewing him on foot. He barely come up to Boyd's chin, but he was wiry and wild-eyed, with a wild beard and snarly hair growing out from underneath his hat.

Boyd stepped aside to let them walk past him toward the fence. He said to Bob Sweeney, "Sweeney, you guard these men. Gates and I are going to have a look over that field to see who's playing possum out there."

He motioned for Gates to go down farther, and he himself backed off thirty or forty yards and then slowly approached the field where most of the men had gone to the ground. He could see bodies. He called, "If we see a weapon, you're a dead man. One of you might get a sneak shot at one of us, but the other will kill you. Think on that. If any of you are still able, raise a hand."

As he watched, he saw first one, then two, then three, and then four hands go up. Boyd said, "All right, lay still and we'll get some water to you. If you have a weapon near you and you're able, you better shove it as far away as you can."

The dots had changed into full-blown men on horseback and on a buckboard. He doubted the sheriff had brought enough of a buckboard to carry back all the men that were injured, but then the sheriff hadn't known what Boyd had known—how many hired guns Asa Hale really had.

Boyd said, "Gates, you keep an eye on these men. I'm going to talk with Asa Hale."

He walked back to the fence where the prisoners were eagerly passing the canteen back and forth from one set of grasping hands to another. Greedy mouths sucked at it until it was dry, and then went on to the next canteen that Bob Sweeney handed them.

Boyd said, "Bob, you get off to the other side and guard the others with Gates. I want to talk to Asa Hale." Boyd ducked under the fence and then walked up to Hale saying, "Duck under that fence, Hale. You and I are going to walk down to the river and have a talk."

Hale looked around. He said, "I see the sheriff coming.

I'll wait and do my talking until then.''

Boyd leaned down and got his face close to the man's cruel eyes. He said, "Hale, I'd hate for my rifle to accidentally go off and gut-shoot you right now."

"You wouldn't dare."

Boyd pulled the hammer back. It went *clitch-clatch*. He said, "You want to bet your belly on it?"

Asa Hale suddenly changed his mind and bent down under the fence. He walked on ahead of Boyd as they headed down the incline and into the trees.

Boyd stopped him before he had gone too far. "Turn around, old man. You and I are going to reach an understanding."

Asa Hale turned slowly, his face expressing the hatred that went clear to his soul. He said, "I ain't reaching no understandin' with you, you sonofabitch, ya hear me? I don't know what went wrong, but you're supposed to be dead on your ass right now." He started to reach out a bony finger to tap Boyd on the chest to emphasize his words, but he never got within a foot of Boyd's chest. Boyd grabbed the finger in midair, bent it backward, and broke the bone. Asa Hale let out a piercing scream and fell to his knees. He was almost sobbing as he looked down at his hand.

He said, "My God, you broke my finger. Are you crazy?" He looked up at Boyd. "Jake said you was a madman. He said you was most likely to do anything. You've hurt me awful."

Boyd put the rifle under the old man's chin and pushed it against his scrawny neck. He said, "Listen here, Asa Hale, when that sheriff gets here, you're going to tell him the whole story, straight and right. You're going to do that for two reasons. One, if you do, you're going to get off lighter than you would otherwise. The second reason is the most important. If you don't I'm going to kill you, you sonofabitch. Get that straight in your mind, I'll kill you in cold blood. You look like someone I've already killed, someone that I hated beyond reason. I feel that you remind me enough of him that if you gave me a chance to kill that sonofabitch the second time, that would be like a dream come true.''

Asa Hale's mouth was open. He remained there on his knees staring up at Boyd. He swallowed, his Adam's apple bobbing. He said, ''I need a drink of water. I need something to eat. I'm sick to my stomach and my finger is paining me something fierce.''

Boyd stepped back. He said, ''Get up and get back with the others. When that sheriff talks to you, you better talk straight, not that it matters since we already have the whole story from your partner, Jake Mangus. We know that you're not the top gun; you ain't smart enough to be. It's him that we're after. You don't amount to a hill of beans to me other than the idea and pleasure of separating your soul from your body. That's why you're going to talk, old man.''

Boyd marched Asa back to the other prisoners while they waited for Sheriff Duffy and his party, who were no more than a mile off now. Boyd could dimly hear some faint moaning from the grass, but there wasn't anything he could do for the wounded.

Gates Hood chose that moment to come over. He asked, ''How're you doing, Captain?''

Boyd looked around. ''I think we made a pretty good haul.''

''Boy, you really had them set up, you and that big rifle of yours. That was a sight to see. It looked like you were mowing hay with that thing.''

''I want to compliment you on what you did, Gates, on keeping up fire when I had stopped shooting.''

The young agent got a pleased look on his face. He said, ''I might have known that you'd figure that out. I seen when you first hit them that they didn't know where the shooting was coming from, they were so far from anything. Even though they were way out of my range, I thought I would give them some muzzle flashes and make them think the attack was from one man on the end, way down there.''

Boyd said, ''And you caused them to charge, which is exactly what I wanted them to do. You're going to make a good agent, Gates. You already are, but that was good thinking.''

''I'm just proud that you took notice, Captain.''

''Hell, I had to notice. They were undecided. If I had fired that big rifle again, they might have flushed like a covey of quail, but when you went to letting off with that little pop-gun, they saw something they thought they could overcome, so here they came.''

Gates got a troubled look on his face. ''Captain, I don't blame you for shooting Earl White when he turned tail and ran away. Maybe he didn't have as much steel as a man in this business ought to, but is that going to finish him? With the Association, I mean?''

Boyd laughed shortly and without humor. ''Finish him with the Association? Earl White is going to join his compadre, Jake Mangus, in the jail at Syracuse, along with several other people. Earl White's not guilty of cowardice; he's guilty of cattle theft. He wasn't running away from that bunch because he was afraid they would shoot him. He ran because he was part of the deal.''

Gates stared at him open-mouthed. He stammered, ''He was what? Earl was . . . what? And Jake Mangus is where?''

Boyd said, ''I'll tell you about it later. Right now, here comes the sheriff and I've got to go meet him and get this thing sorted out. You go and bring Earl up here with the rest of them. Take Bob along if you need to. Earl ought to be able to walk, though. I think I just hit him in the fleshy part of the leg. I don't think I broke the bone."

He walked off, leaving the young agent staring at him trying to sort through things. It would be a long time before anyone would ever understand the confused affairs that had occurred in Hamilton County.

Boyd met the sheriff as he came riding up. He could see that the sheriff had brought the doctor who had worked on Jake and that another man drove the buckboard.

The sheriff pulled up his horse and sat there, surveying the scene, the prisoners lined up along the fence, the pasture full of dead and wounded. Finally, the sheriff looked down at Boyd and said, "Well, McMasters, I'll give you credit for one thing. You said that I wouldn't want to be here to see this, and you were damn well right about that. Exactly what are you going to charge these men with? The ones that you haven't killed, that is."

Boyd said, "Well, I reckon we'll start with cattle theft, add to that attempted murder, add to that wanton destruction of property, and then add to that illegal trespass."

The sheriff let out a short snort. "Don't you think that illegal trespass is a mite hard, Boyd?"

Boyd kept his face straight. "I believe in the letter and the spirit of the law, Sheriff."

Sheriff Duffy shook his head. "Like hell you do." He dismounted. "Well, I reckon we'd better get this mess cleaned up. What's the first thing we need to do?"

Boyd thought for a moment. "Well, I guess we ought to get the doctor started on the wounded. You'll probably want to load them into the buckboard and head into town. There's some that are going to have to lay out here until you get a bigger wagon, but they're not going to mind. Then we've got these gentlemen up here at the fence. The main one is Asa Hale, and he has quite a few things he wants to tell you."

Sheriff Duffy nodded. "I see you've got my work nicely cut out for me. I appreciate that."

Boyd smiled. "Anything to lighten the load on a brother officer, especially an elected one."

"Especially one with a badge, don't you mean?"

Boyd said, "I've also got an Association agent by the name of Earl White, as you well know, who suffered a wound to the leg. I've half a mind to implicate him, but he was a fairly small part of it. I'll leave the charges on him up to you. As far as I'm concerned, he hasn't worked for the Association since he got shot."

The sheriff said, "Let's get on over here and see what Asa has to say."

"Let's make it quick, Sheriff. You and me still have one more stop to make."

Sheriff Duffy stopped and looked at Boyd. He asked, "You still intend on going through with it the way you told me?"

"Exactly."

The sheriff nodded. "Well, I won't argue with you. This has been your show and you've cleaned up a mess in my front yard that has been going on now for two years, including murders, and I never was able to get a thing done until you came along."

"All I want is the last shot."

The sheriff said, "You'll have it. Now, let's go and let old Asa scream and cry for a while before he tells us the truth."

Together, they walked toward the prisoners at the fence.

Fifteen

It was about a ten-mile ride from the location of the fight to the Harris ranch. The sheriff and Boyd arrived there shortly before one o'clock. As they passed through the gate and into the ranch yard, the sheriff said, "Well, it's your boat to row. Do what you think is best. You begun it. I'll just stand back and watch while you finish."

Boyd said, "What about the legality? Ain't I supposed to raise my hand or something?"

The sheriff said, "You already did. You're deputized. I now designate you as a sheriff's deputy of Hamilton County in hot pursuit of a prime suspect. Does that suit your legal sensibility?"

"Just as long as it does yours."

They slowed their horses down to a walk as they approached the house. The sheriff said, "I hope he's home and not gone off, looking for his wife. You know, that was mighty distressing for me to hear about him hitting that pretty young thing. A man that would do that could spoil milk just by looking at it."

"He may look like a choirboy but there's a lot of the devil in him. But what he did, he didn't do out of meanness. He mainly did it out of just pure plain old greed and the lust of the old greenback dollar. He had about as pretty a wife as a man could want, and you know, Sheriff Duffy, he never paid that woman no attention, he was so busy chasing the almighty dollar.''

Sheriff Duffy hung his head. "I should have seen it," he said. "I just should have seen it."

Boyd said, "Don't be so hard on yourself, Howard. There was no way you could see it. We had a man here on the spot who had the resources and could have supplied you with the information. He was on to it but, unfortunately, he was bought off. You never had a chance after that."

Sheriff Duffy shook his head. "I don't blame Del Cameron for not thinking much of me, I wouldn't either if I was him. He kept telling me that something was bad wrong, and I kept telling him that Asa Hale wasn't mixing his cattle and getting off with the calves because he didn't have any of the Anguses. I bet I rode that Asa Hale's range ten times and I never saw many calves that had any sign of Angus blood in them. Of course, Cameron couldn't go on the range because Hale would have shot him."

Boyd said, "Howard, just as I said, there was no way for you to be in the know, the damn plan was too clever. The cleverest part was that the one man that could have turned it up, Jake Mangus, was in on it, and then when my brother sent the other man up, Earl White, they let him in on a piece of it. Well, do you want to knock or do you want me to?''

The sheriff heaved a sigh. "I still think you ought to take the credit for this."

Boyd gave him a grim look. "My credit is fixing to come right now. That's all the credit I'm looking for." He knocked loudly on the door.

The house seemed quiet. Boyd knocked again and then glanced at Sheriff Duffy. He said, "I don't care if I catch him here or where I catch him, but I will catch him. Are you sure there's no chance he could have gotten word, Sheriff?''

Howard Duffy shook his head. ''Not from my end of the table.''

Boyd was about to speak when the door was suddenly jerked open. Jim Harris stood there, a day's growth of beard on his face, his hair uncombed. He looked and smelled like he'd had more than his share of whiskey.

Then he recognized his guests and tried to pull himself together. He said, ''Sheriff, you haven't come about my wife, have you? About Nora?''

Sheriff Duffy looked innocent. ''Your wife? I don't know anything about your wife, Mr. Harris. Is something the matter with your wife?''

Harris's anxious face smoothed slightly. He said, ''No, not really. She's just a day late from shopping. I suppose she just stayed over, you know how women are.''

Boyd asked, ''Aren't you going to invite us in, Mr. Harris?''

For the first time, James Harris seemed to take notice of Boyd. He stepped back slightly. ''Of course. Come on in the kitchen, I've got some coffee on.''

Boyd said, ''Oh, I don't reckon that our business will take long enough to drink a cup of coffee, Mr. Harris. I just upset the sheriff here. He said that you told him that you had about fifteen hundred acres under deed. I bet him ten dollars an acre that you haven't got any more than five hundred acres. Who wins?''

Harris looked rapidly back and forth between the sheriff and Boyd. He said, ''I don't know what you're talking about, Mr. McMasters, but if there's some sort of implication in there, I'm not certain that I quite get it.''

''Well, it has to do with the common practice of grazing

five acres for every acre that you own outright or have home-steaded. You're grazing about nine thousand acres, and I don't think you should be grazing but about twenty-five hundred. What do you say to that, Mr. Harris?''

James Harris stiffened. They were still standing very near the front door. Harris said, ''I resent your tone of voice, sir. My business is my business and none of yours or the Association that you work for.''

''Of which you happen to be a member of, in good standing, having paid your dues. Also, another member in good standing is Mr. Del Cameron, who happens to have a great many more acres than you, but for some reason not quite as many purebred cattle.''

Jim Harris took a step backwards toward the kitchen. He said, ''Sheriff, I resent this man's tone, this man's implications. You're certainly welcome here, but not him.''

Boyd said, ''Are you asking me to leave, Jim?''

''I am asking you to get off this property and to stay off this property and I will expect a letter of apology from your superior.''

''Well, as I told my brother, I ain't got no superiors and damn few equals. But I do have something for you. Would you glance up there at the ceiling for a second?'' With his left hand, he pointed up toward the ceiling.

Instinctively, James Harris shifted his eyes upward. As he did, Boyd stepped forward with his left foot and hit James Harris as hard as he could flush on the jaw. The blow sent the larger man backwards, stumbling, falling. He caught himself from going down by grabbing the sill of the door that led into the dining room. Boyd took two quick steps forward and kicked him under the chin as Harris struggled to get to his feet.

Harris fell through the door into the dining room, shaking his head, trying to scramble to his feet. As he was halfway up, Boyd reached up and grabbed him by the shirt, and then hit him with his right fist again. This time, Harris staggered backwards and fell, hitting his head on the hardwood floor.

The sheriff was leaning against the wall, looking at something off in the distance, trying to act as if the fight were happening to someone else at some other place on the map.

Boyd stood over Harris, his chest heaving. Harris began to struggle to his feet. Boyd leaned down and took him by the shirt front and helped him get up. This time, he hit Harris with his left fist, driving full from the shoulder as hard as he could into the man's face, which was beginning to pulp up. Harris fell through the doorway and landed in the middle of the kitchen. Then Boyd was over him, straddling him. He slapped Harris in the face until the man was gazing up at him.

Leaning down, Boyd said, "That was from Nora, your wife, you low-down, wife-beating sonofabitch." He began rhythmically hitting Harris in the face, first with his left fist and then with his right. The blows caused Harris's head to whip first to the right and then to the left. Just before the sheriff pulled him off, Boyd had the satisfying sensation of feeling Harris's jaw break under one of the thunderous left-handed punches he had just delivered.

The sheriff had Boyd under the arm, pulling him back. He said, "My God, Boyd. Stop now. You've beat the living stuffings out of him, he's half dead. You're going to kill him. You go on outside and cool off while I tend to him. We've got to have him in shape to hang."

Boyd jerked loose. He said, "Not yet, dammit." He went in and shook Harris until the groggy man's eyes opened. He shouted down in his face, "One more thing, you're under arrest for murder, attempted murder, cattle theft, and anything else I can think of before it's all through."

As Boyd walked toward the front of the house passing the

sheriff, the sheriff shook his head and said, "Boyd, when you set out to make a point, you make it. Are you satisfied now?"

Boyd said, with all of his feelings contained in one word, "Yes."

He passed out of the front door and into the clean air outside.

There was really nothing to keep him there. It was all over with. Jake Mangus, Jim Harris, and Asa Hale were all in jail under various charges. Earl White was disgraced and dismissed from the Cattleman's Protective Association. In the end, Boyd had decided not to press charges against White. The sheriff had been willing to let him go, and Boyd had done so with the advice to Earl White that if he ever laid eyes on him again, he'd kill him where he stood.

He'd said, "You better find out what part of the country I am in. You'd better make that your business for life and then stay out of that part."

Boyd had gone out, along with the sheriff, and visited with Del Cameron and received his thanks. Then lastly, he had talked to Nora, explaining to her what her options were. She had chosen the one he recommended, and he thought she would be happy. He'd advised her to turn to Gates Hood for advice and protection, saying that he was a good man and could be depended on. She had parted from him reluctantly.

He'd left Gates in charge of the station with Bob Sweeney to help. Gates had wanted to ride to the train station in Garden City with him, but Boyd had said no, he'd never been one for drawn-out good-byes. He'd told Gates that he was going to recommend to his brother that he be given another promotion and maybe a new station with more men under his command.

Boyd had said, "You're a good man, Gates Hood." Then,

barely suppressing a laugh, he'd said, "Even if you do look fifteen years old."

After that, it was simply a matter of riding back to Garden City, staying overnight in the hotel, and then making the two-day train trip back to Oklahoma City, where his brother waited, as well as Martha.

He spent most of the trip thinking, not about what had happened in Kansas, but about the future. He thought about the job, but mostly, he thought about Martha. By the time the train pulled into the outskirts of Oklahoma City, he was still not certain which way the wind was going to blow him.

Boyd sat in his brother's office, finishing up his report. He'd gotten in late the night before, and had simply gone straight to a hotel and spent the night. That morning, after breakfast, he'd come directly to see Warren.

Warren said, "Well, it sounds so damn simple when you lay it out like that. I'm surprised nobody in the area could see it."

Boyd said, "There was one man who knew what was going on who wasn't part of the crooked business, not at first. That was Jake Mangus, though I don't think he knew how it really worked, but they bought him off quick. In fact, the business couldn't have worked for very long without Jake's cooperation. It would've become obvious, even to Del Cameron."

Warren said, "I have to admit that you had me confused with all those telegrams that you kept sending. I now understand why you sent the one about who was receiving range stock. Now it makes sense, but when you first sent it, I thought, what in hell is going on in his mind."

"That was the key to the whole thing, Warren. Asa Hale and Del Cameron were receiving range-grade breeder stock, but James Harris wasn't taking any shipments, and yet he

was continuing to build up a crossbreed herd. He had the
Anguses, but what was he breeding them to? He had no
range cattle, and yet all of a sudden he's got a herd almost
as big as Del Cameron's. That's what put me on the right
track. That, and a natural suspicion of Jake Mangus. The day
I saw him coming from the Hale ranch—a ranch, by the
way, that I couldn't get a mile inside of without being challenged, yet he seemed to have free run of the place . . . As
soon as I saw him coming from the ranch headquarters, I
knew he was part of it.''

"So Del Cameron was just sitting there, getting robbed
blind.''

"That's about the size of it. They were tearing up his
fences and mixing Asa Hale's cattle with his, producing
good crossbred Angus calves.''

Warren said, "But the sheriff never could find any crossbred Anguses on Hale's place. Not in any quantity.''

"That's right. A couple of times, Cameron did see some
freshly branded crossbreeds there and knew they had Angus
blood in them. By the time he could get the sheriff out there,
those cattle were gone, both mother and calf. Momma cow
and get were gone over to Jim Harris's place.''

"So they were hiding them in plain sight? On Jim Harris's
place.''

"Of course. Del Cameron kept screaming that he was seeing cattle with Angus breed in them with a lazy A. Well,
you know how easy it would be to turn a lazy A into a
rocking J, which was Harris's brand. Plus, I would imagine
all they were doing was hair-branding those calves, and
when it grew out Harris would brand them with his iron.''

Warren said, "Then Harris never had as big a spread as
he reported to us that he had.''

Boyd nodded. "He never even had five hundred acres.
The man had a good idea. He had known Del Cameron from

back in Tennessee and after he got started up, it wasn't growing as fast as he wanted, so he talked Del Cameron into coming out there and starting up a breeding operation to match him, actually to be his supplier. He'd filed a bunch of squatter's claims, most of them in his wife's name. That's why his fences were never torn down. That's why Cap Wiley's fences were never torn down; there was no need. Del Cameron had all the breeding material they needed.''

· "So they were sitting there literally robbing Del Cameron of hundreds of thousands of dollars?''

"I guess you could put that big a price on it. I didn't know just how small an operation Harris had until his wife came to me and, in the course of one night, I learned an awful lot about what Harris had. I had to break Asa Hale's operation. He was the one that was dangerous. The murders, I think, were what started their downfall. He was hiring gunmen to protect his interests. Once you start hiring gunmen, you can expect that sooner or later they are going to shoot somebody. Cameron lost three men. Of course the murderers will never be found. They were probably some of the men I shot.''

Warren asked, "What about Jim Harris? He reported that two of his riders were killed.''

"Never happened. His wife told me that at no time did he ever have a man shot. She said that the day the sheriff came out to have a look around, she put it up to Harris and that was the day she got the worst beating of her life. No, that was just to look like he was also being victimized, but he wasn't. He was claiming the acreage so he could have greater grazing land. He didn't even know the price of the land. I mean, I know Del Cameron owned what he owned— I checked the records—but I couldn't see that big of a difference for the price in what Harris owned and what Cameron owned.''

Watten sighed and looked out the window. "Well, Boyd, you did a hell of a job, but then, I didn't expect anything less. Oh, by the way," He swung around toward Boyd. "We got a money order in yesterday from Del Cameron for a thousand dollars. He specified that it was to go to you for the work you did up there. Boyd, you're getting rich in this world."

Boyd said, "Just put it in the bank. I'm really not interested."

Warren said, "What about Harris's wife? What's become of her?"

"Actually, she is in pretty good shape if she will take ahold of herself and start being a woman instead of a little girl. She's got a fine cattle operation going there. Naturally, we thinned it out pretty good when we appropriated some of the cattle back to Del Cameron, which was only fair. We also cut Asa Hale's herd and pretty well made restitution to Cameron for his losses."

"Yes, but what is going to become of her?"

"She's got a nice operation there, a good foreman, three or four good men, and she's got a good breeding setup. Then, Gates will be there to help her along. She can't go back to her parents, and her husband will probably be hung. I don't know what the disposition of that is going to be. Do you approve of me letting Earl White go?"

Warren shrugged. "It was your job, you were the boss on the spot. I don't see where it could have been done any better."

"Well, all this talking has made me thirsty. Let's go over to the saloon and have a drink of whiskey."

Warren said, "Before we go, Boyd, I'd like to know how you feel about the job."

"It's all right. It keeps a man busy. It fulfills some parts of me."

"Are you willing to keep on with it?"

Boyd nodded slowly. "For the time being until I tell you otherwise."

Warren said, "We've got a spot of trouble down near the border around Del Rio. Would you be interested in going down there?"

Boyd shook his head. "No. If you remember, you promised me I could drift from one station to another. You asked me to go on this one specific job just to get my feet wet. Now, I think I'll drift for a while. If I happen to drift toward Del Rio, fine, then I'll give them a hand. Otherwise, I couldn't say right now where I am going."

"I take it that you haven't seen Martha yet."

Boyd looked down. "No."

"What are you going to do about her, Boyd?"

Boyd looked at his brother. "I don't know. I still don't have any answers for her yet."

Warren asked, "You are going to go see her, aren't you?"

"I don't know if I should or not, Warren. I don't know if I should let it go any further than it already has. I'm not ready for it to go any further yet."

"At least give her the chance to understand that, Boyd. She's a very understanding woman, you know."

Boyd said, "Yes, but she's got the right to expect something in return. She can't go on giving and me taking. I've got to have something to give back and right now, I'm not sure that I do."

"Don't you think that she has the right to hear that from you?"

Boyd stood up. "Come to think of it, I think you're right. I guess it would be only fitting for me to have that first drink back here with her. Do you reckon she still has some of that brandy you took her?"

Warren smiled. "I would imagine."

Boyd put on his hat. "Then I guess I'll take a run by and say hello to her and see how she's doing." He turned and started for the door.

A word from his brother stopped him.

Boyd said, "What?"

Warren carefully put his hands on the desk top. He said, "Tell me, Boyd, why did you draw Asa Hale and all of his men into that trap? Just to make sure they couldn't vote in the next election? God knows you killed enough of them."

Boyd said uncomfortably, "They were going to rip up that fence."

Warren looked at him keenly. "Don't bullshit me, Boyd. I know you. They weren't within a quarter of a mile of that fence. Who were you killing, Boyd?"

Boyd looked at his brother for a moment as his mind went back to what Martha had said, that he could kill a thousand men and sleep with a thousand women but he'd never find his past. He said, "You figure it out, Warren."

Then he turned on his heel and walked out of his brother's office, out of the building, mounted the roan, and started toward Martha's house, uncertain what he would find either in her or in himself.

Turn the page for an exciting preview of the
next installment of

McMASTERS:

Silver Creek Showdown

Boyd McMasters's next assignment is to
investigate a case of cattle rustling in the
little town of Silver Creek, Texas. But what
looks like a simple case of finding four head
turns into a big deal when those four head
are prize bulls worth twenty thousand
dollars—and worth killing for....

Look for this adventure coming from Jove
in August 1995!

The settlement of Silver Creek looked just like a hundred other cowtowns Boyd McMasters had seen in the West— right down to the man who came flying backwards through the batwing doors of a saloon to land with a puff of dust in the street in front of Boyd's horse.

The grulla shied nervously away from the man, but Boyd brought the horse under control with an expert hand. A second later there was a huge crash of glass as another man came sailing through the saloon's big front window. Boyd heard men yelling and women screaming and the thud of fists against flesh and bone and the sharp splintering of wood as tables and chairs were overturned and shattered into kindling.

There was trouble in Silver Creek, all right, Boyd thought. This fight might not have anything to do with the problems that had brought him here, but it was going to wreak some havoc anyway.

And there was always the chance that it *might* be involved in the job, too.

So far he hadn't heard any guns going off, which was good. As long as the men inside the saloon were just brawling with their fists, there was a better than even chance nobody would be killed. It was when the guns came out that men died.

Boyd heeled the grulla forward, reining the horse toward the hitch rail in front of the hardware store next to the saloon. He swung down from the saddle, looped the reins around the rail and jerked them tight, then strode back down the street to where the first man who had been knocked out of the saloon had pushed himself onto hands and knees. The man knelt there, shaking his head slowly. Beads of blood welled from a cut on his cheek and rolled down his face to drip off his chin, going first one way then the other as he shook his head.

Boyd reached down and grasped the man's arm. ''Let me give you a hand, mister,'' he said as he hauled the man to his feet. There was more strength in Boyd's rangy frame than most people would have thought from looking at him. ''What's going on in there?''

The man's lips were swollen from a punch and his voice was thick as he replied, ''We're tryin' to teach those bastards from the Rocking T a lesson they won't forget any time soon!''

It was like Boyd had thought was probable, the battle was between cowhands from a couple of rival ranches. He said, ''Who do you ride for, amigo?''

The man backhanded some of the blood from his face. ''The JF Connected, of course. Thanks for your help, mister, but lemme go. I gotta get back in there and help my pards!''

With that, he pulled away from Boyd's grasp and launched into a stumbling run that carried him to the entrance of the saloon. He slapped the batwings aside and plunged back into the melee.

Boyd glanced at the other victim of the fight, the one who had come crashing through the window of the saloon. The man was still lying on the ground with broken glass scattered all around him. He wasn't moving, but Boyd could tell he was still breathing. Boyd walked over to the man, the shards of glass crunching under his boots, and hooked a toe under the man's shoulder to roll him over onto his back. Boyd hunkered beside him and slapped his face lightly a couple of times, backhand and forehand. The man's eyelids started to flutter.

"Who do you ride for?" Boyd asked when the man's eyes finally opened.

"Hunh . . . what the hell . . ."

"Who do you ride for?" Boyd repeated.

"R-Rockin' T . . ."

Boyd stood up and let the man lapse back into semi-consciousness. There was a faint smile on Boyd's lips as he turned and strode toward the entrance of the saloon.

He wondered fleetingly where the local law was. There was so much noise coming from the saloon that somebody packing a badge should have showed up by now. Even if the marshal didn't hear the ruckus, someone should have fetched him. A good two dozen citizens, maybe more, stood around in the street near the saloon, craning their necks to get a glimpse of the chaos inside through the busted-out window. Surely one of the townies had run down to the marshal's office by now to let him know what was going on.

Several men stood aside when Boyd walked up. That wasn't surprising since he carried himself with an air of authority that came naturally to him, having once been a lawman himself. And he looked tough enough to back up just about anything he wanted to do, too. He was a medium-sized, sandy-haired man, not an overpowering specimen physically, but his toughness was in his eyes and the tanned, weathered features of his face. He wore a fairly new light brown Stetson, a hickory-colored work shirt with the sleeves rolled up a couple of turns against the Texas heat, denim pants, and well-broken-in boots. Holstered on his right hip was a revolver he had modified himself with his gunsmithing skills, a .40 caliber on a sturdy .42 frame. He had the look of a man who could use a gun, as well as work on one.

He pushed through the batwings after a second's pause to make sure no one would crash into him as soon as he stepped inside the saloon. The fracas was still going on, but it seemed to be concentrated on the far side of the room now. The saloon was one of the biggest buildings in Silver Creek, since it had two stories instead of just one, and the girls who worked here in spangled dresses and tights had retreated up the stairs to the balcony, where they now stood shouting encouragement down to the battlers below. Boyd saw a couple of bartenders venturing an occasional glance over the hardwood bar that ran along the right-hand wall. To the left was a piano, and the fellow who normally played it, a gent with pomaded hair and sleeve garters, had turned over his bench and retreated behind it. A few men were sprawled senseless amidst the wreckage of several tables.

Boyd spotted the man he had helped up in the street outside. The JF Connected cowboy was now clubbing another man on top of the head with a mallet-like fist. The Rocking T puncher went down, but before the man from the JF Connected could find another adversary, somebody brought a chair crashing down on his head from behind. Boyd winced.

Somebody plucked at his sleeve, and he looked over to see a pasty-faced man in a cutaway coat. The man had a goatee and a thin mustache and was a gambler from the look of him. He said, "I'd steer clear of that donnybrook over there if I was you, my friend."

"How do you know I intend to take a hand?" Boyd asked.

"You have the look of a man who searches for trouble,

assuming it doesn't find you first.''

Boyd smiled a little, but the expression didn't reach his eyes. The gambler had him pegged, all right. Trouble had found him plenty of times in the past, and now his job was to look for it. Usually, it wasn't very hard to find.

Inclining his head toward the battling men, Boyd asked the gambler, ''What started this?''

The nattily dressed man shrugged. ''*Quien sabe*? They don't really need a reason other than the fact that some of them ride for Jonas Fletcher and the others for Mike Torrance. That's plenty of motivation.''

Boyd nodded and turned his attention back to the fracas in time to see one of the men reaching for a holstered gun.

The saloon was big but not *that* big. If guns started going off, there was a good chance that innocent people would be struck by at least some of the flying bullets. Boyd's hand shot out and closed around the neck of a whiskey bottle that stood on a table within arm's reach of him. The waddy trying to fumble his gun from its holster was only about fifteen feet away from him. Boyd's arm flashed back and then forward, and the half-full bottle thumped heavily against the back of the cowboy's head. He forgot all about pulling his gun as he stumbled forward a couple of steps, went to his knees, then pitched onto his face, out cold.

''Good throw,'' the gambler said dryly over the shouts and screams. ''I'm Anthony Hagen.''

''Boyd McMasters.''

''When that fellow wakes up, he's not going to feel very friendly toward you, Mr. McMasters.''

Boyd's casual shrug told eloquently just how concerned he was about that possibility.

One of the struggling men suddenly broke free of the brawl and lunged toward the stairs that led to the balcony and the second floor. He had made it up only three of the steps when another man caught him from behind and jerked him around. The man's hat had been knocked off, revealing thick, curly brown hair. His face was lean, his mouth wide and expressive. As he opened his mouth to yell his dismay, Boyd saw that there was a wide gap between his front teeth. The man who had caught him had broad, massive shoulders, and he seemed to have no trouble picking up the first man by an arm and a leg and slinging him back into the middle of the pile. Several men went down under the onslaught, sprawling every which way.

The curly-haired man who had served as a makeshift battering ram landed heavily and rolled over several times, then came up on his hands and knees and struggled to his feet. This time, instead of trying to escape up the stairs, he made a break for the entrance. Boyd had to step aside hurriedly to avoid being run down. The fleeing man knocked the bat-wings back and ran into the street.

The gambler, Hagen, laughed. "Chuck doesn't have much stomach for fighting," he commented.

"Chuck?" Boyd asked.

"Chuck Fletcher. Jonas's little brother."

Boyd nodded and, since Hagen seemed willing to answer questions, asked another. "How come the marshal hasn't put in an appearance yet?"

"He'll show up as soon as he realizes what's going on."

"You mean nobody's gone to fetch him by now?"

Hagen gave him a look that indicated disbelief. "What, and interfere with a fight between the Rocking T and the JF Connected? This town depends on those two spreads for its livelihood, Mr. McMasters. Nobody wants to risk offending either Jonas Fletcher or Mike Torrance. Their men do pretty much as they please in Silver Creek."

"So instead of running for the law, the owner of this place lets those boys wreck it? That's hard to believe."

"Believe it," Hagen said. "I own this saloon. And I know that Jonas and Mike will stand good for any damages."

Boyd nodded slowly. If that was the way Hagen wanted to do business, that was his affair.

At that moment, the batwings were slapped open again and a lanky, middle-aged man with graying hair and a sweeping mustache hurried in with a shotgun in his hands. There was a tin star pinned to his shirt. He bellowed, "What in blazes—"

"Please, Marshal!" Hagen said. "Don't fire that scatter-gun into the ceiling again. We like to never got the holes patched from last time."

The star packer blinked and said, "Yeah, but—"

That was as far as he got before Boyd saw one of the combatants turn toward the door with a gun in his hand.

Boyd palmed out his own revolver, not with the blindingly fast speed of a shootist but rather with the quick, sure efficiency of a man long accustomed to handling guns. The cowboy was lifting his pistol and almost had it lined up on the marshal when Boyd's gun roared.

There hadn't been time for any fancy shooting. A shot directed toward the man's head or torso could have gone past him and hit somebody else if Boyd had missed. So he shot toward the man's feet instead, intending the bullet as a distraction more than anything else, even though it went against the grain for him to pull trigger without having someone's death as his goal. If he missed, the slug likely wouldn't hit anything except the planks of the floor.

He didn't miss. The gun-wielding cowboy let out a howl of pain and jumped several inches in the air. He went over backwards, landing on his rump, and the impact was so jarring that he dropped his Colt. It thudded to the floor beside him, unfired. He had come down with his right leg stretched out in front of him, and he stared disbelievingly at the smoking hole in the toe of his boot. Then he swayed and his body fell backward. His head thumped against the floor.

A shocked silence had fallen over the saloon after the explosion of the gunshot. Everybody stared at Boyd, including the marshal and Anthony Hagen. Boyd replaced the round he had fired with a cartridge from one of the loops on his belt, then slid the gun back into leather. He nodded toward the man he had shot and said, "Somebody better pull that fella's boot off and take a look at his foot. I might've blown a toe off."

"Who the hell are you?" demanded the marshal.

"Name's Boyd McMasters."

"What'd you shoot that fella for?"

Boyd frowned a little in surprise. "Looked to me like he was about to shoot you, Marshal. I didn't figure you'd like that."

"Mike Torrance ain't goin' to like it, neither, when he finds out you've maybe crippled one of his best hands!" The lawman gestured curtly at the injured man. "Somebody yank his boot off!"

One of the men who had been fighting only a few moments earlier leaned over and pulled the man's boot off. The sock underneath was bloody. The man who had taken the boot off looked up and reported solemnly, "Looks like his middle toe's plumb gone."

"Shit!" the marshal said, his displeasure obviously heartfelt. He turned to Boyd and went on, "You're a stranger here, mister. What the hell brings you to Silver Creek, anyway?"

"My job," Boyd replied grimly. "And right about now, I'm beginning to wish I'd never heard of this sorry little place!"

If you enjoyed this book, subscribe now and get...

TWO FREE

A $7.00 VALUE—

If you would like to read more of the very best, most exciting, adventurous, action-packed Westerns being published today, you'll want to subscribe to True Value's Western Home Subscription Service.

Each month the editors of True Value will select the 6 very best Westerns from America's leading publishers for special readers like you. You'll be able to preview these new titles as soon as they are published, *FREE* for ten days with no obligation!

TWO FREE BOOKS

When you subscribe, we'll send you your first month's shipment of the newest and best 6 Westerns for you to preview. With your first shipment, two of these books will be yours as our introductory gift to you absolutely *FREE* (a $7.00 value), regardless of what you decide to do. If you like them, as much as we think you will, keep all six books but pay for just 4 at the low subscriber rate of just $2.75 each. If you decide to return them, keep 2 of the titles as our gift. No obligation.

Special Subscriber Savings

When you become a True Value subscriber you'll save money several ways. First, all regular monthly selections will be billed at the low subscriber price of just $2.75 each. That's at least a savings of $4.50 each month below the publishers price. Second, there is never any shipping, handling or other hidden charges—*Free home delivery*. What's more there is no minimum number of books you must buy, you may return any selection for full credit and you can cancel your subscription at any time. A TRUE VALUE!